Praise for

"Simone balanc... exquisitely rendered characters."
—*Entertainment Weekly*

"Passion, heat and deep emotion—Naima Simone is a gem!"
—*New York Times* bestselling author Maisey Yates

"Simone never falters in mining the complexity of two people who grow and heal and eventually love together."
—*New York Times* bestselling author Sarah MacLean

"Small-town charm, a colorful cast, and a hero to root for give this romance its legs as it moves toward a hard-earned happily ever after. [This] slow-burning romance is well worth the wait."
—*Publishers Weekly* on *The Road to Rose Bend*

"Simone masterfully balances heart and heat...building a convincing slow-burning romance."
—*Publishers Weekly* on *Christmas in Rose Bend*

"I am a huge Naima Simone fan. With her stories, she has the ability to transport you to places you can only dream of, with characters who have a realness to them."
—*Read Your Writes*

"[Naima Simone] excels at creating drama and emotional scenes as well as strong heroines who are resilient survivors."
—*Harlequin Junkie*

Also by Naima Simone

The Road to Rose Bend
Christmas in Rose Bend
With Love from Rose Bend

Look for Naima Simone's next Rose Bend novel
available soon from HQN

For additional books by Naima Simone,
visit her website, www.naimasimone.com.

NAIMA SIMONE

Mr. Right
Next Door

HQN

ISBN-13: 978-1-335-44801-9

Mr. Right Next Door
Copyright © 2023 by Naima Simone

Trouble for Hire
Copyright © 2023 by Naima Simone

PLEASE RECYCLE

THIS PRODUCT IS RECYCLABLE

Recycling programs
for this product may
not exist in your area

For questions and comments about the quality of this book,
please contact us at CustomerService@Harlequin.com.

HQN
22 Adelaide St. West, 41st Floor
Toronto, Ontario M5H 4E3, Canada
www.Harlequin.com

Printed in U.S.A.

CONTENTS

MR. RIGHT NEXT DOOR

To Gary. 143.

To Connie Marie Butts.
I'll miss you forever and love you longer than that.

CHAPTER ONE

WHAT IN THE actual *hell*?

Cursing is for those with small vocabularies and even smaller minds, Jenna Elizabeth Landon.

Jenna threw back the bedcovers, cringing as her mother's cultured voice floated through her head at—she glanced at the digital clock on her bedside dresser—seven-twelve in the morning.

Jesus probably hadn't even risen from the grave on Easter morning by seven-twelve. Because it was such an ungodly hour!

Horrible music—and she used the term loosely—currently blared through her windows at top volume.

Stalking across her bedroom, she snatched her silk robe, shoved her arms into the sleeves, slid her feet into her slippers, and headed down the hall. She crossed the living room and charged outside.

Damn. A hard shiver rippled through her as the cold wind copped a feel under her robe. September early mornings in the southern Berkshires didn't play around. It'd warm to the low sixties later in the day, but for now? Jack Frost was getting friendly with places only Dream Jason Momoa had touched lately.

The strings of guitars and fiddles, the bass of drums and the twang of a male voice complaining about not having to be lonely tonight were even louder as she

marched down the front steps. She didn't bother with
the walkway but cut across her pristine lawn, and once
more her mother's voice snapped out a reprimand in
her head.

*Ladies glide, Jenna. You're not marching off to war,
for goodness' sake.*

*That's what you know, Mother. I'm definitely headed
to battle.*

Awesome. Now she was arguing with her mother's
imaginary voice in her mind.

Arms crossed in front of her waist, she stepped over
the stone path that separated her driveway from the one
that belonged to the empty house next door.

Correction. The *formerly* empty house next door.

Apparently she had a new neighbor.

And though she hadn't met him yet, she already
knew three things about him.

One. He was a *he*. And it wasn't just the wide shoulders or the back muscles flexing under a red-and-blue
flannel shirt in a dirty dance that clued her in. Or the
tight ass and powerful, thick thighs in faded blue jeans.
Nope, it was the combination of…*everything*. Even with
the top half of his body stuck under the hood of his
truck, he was most obviously a *he*.

Two. Her new neighbor's taste in vehicles left much
to be desired. The dark blue monstrosity with a wide
camel-colored stripe down the side panel landed somewhere between monster truck and *I hear banjos in them
there hills*. Huh. Someone was overcompensating.

And three. His choice in music was terrible. Oh the
guy's singing voice might be okay, but all that *whining*. For
the love of all that was holy she wanted to make. It. Stop.

"Excuse me," she called out. When he didn't budge,
she tried again, louder. "Excuse me."

Nothing. Not even a twitch of those broad shoulders.

Irritation spiked inside her. She hated being ignored. It was an effective weapon in her father's arsenal, one he'd wielded during her childhood and even now as an adult. Nothing belittled a person more than making them feel beneath acknowledgment.

She tightened her arms over her stomach.

And glared at her neighbor's wide back.

Gritting her teeth, she marched forward and none too gently poked him in a shoulder that had absolutely no give. She might as well have jabbed a rock.

"Shit!" Her neighbor jolted, and a baseball-hat-covered head smacked the hood with a resounding *thwack*.

Ouch. That had to hurt.

"Son of a *bitch*." He straightened. And straightened. And straightened.

And she tipped her head back and looked up. And up. And up.

A fourth thing she now knew about her neighbor. He towered way over six feet.

And owned a voice that probably rivaled the power and rumble of the engine in that heap of junk masquerading as a truck.

Okay, technically, that was five things.

"Excuse me," she tried again, stepping closer but still leaving space between them. Yes, it was seven in the morning, but she hadn't lost all her senses. She was a single woman with crime shows on her TV, after all.

He whipped around, his heavily muscled arm lifted as he rubbed the back of his head. Thick eyebrows arrowed down over indigo eyes that must be a trick of light. Short tufts of black hair stuck out from under the cap, grazing bold cheekbones and drawing attention to his mouth. Equally dark scruff covered his jaw and chin, yet Jenna could still glimpse a faint cleft.

"Yeah?" her neighbor muttered, still massaging the back of his head. "And why the hell were you sneaking up on me like that? You damn near gave me a heart attack."

She gaped at him. Was he for real?

"Sneaking up on you?" she repeated. "Excuse you, but I don't *sneak*. And if you hadn't had that noise blasting, then you'd know I've tried to get your attention several times and you didn't hear me."

"So your next option was giving me a concussion?"

She sniffed, hiking up her chin. "So now I'm responsible for your dramatics and lack of coordination?"

"Dramatics and…" His scowl deepened and his eyes darkened from indigo to a dark denim. "What do you want besides busting my ass and giving the neighborhood a peep show first thing in the morning?"

Irritation gave way to outrage. Narrowing her eyes on him, she fisted the lapels of her robe and yanked them tight around her neck—even though they were already closed. *Peep show*? His rude manners and *wah-wah-wah* music were the only reasons she stood out here in her pajamas in the first place.

She offered him one of her patented sharp-as-a-blade smiles. And the words to match.

"What I want is for you to show common courtesy to your new neighbors and not blast your music first thing in the morning while other people are trying to sleep. Or do they not teach manners along with how to boil peanuts, hunt critters and brew moonshine wherever it is you just trucked in from?"

His wide shoulders drew back. His thin nostrils flared and those lips pulled tight at the corners.

One second guitars wailed and in the next, silence boomed.

Then a wide grin spread over his face, rivaling the steadily rising sun.

She blinked.

Wow.

No "wow," she scolded herself. *You will not be awed by him. Get yourself in check.*

"Well, I profusely apologize, lil' darlin'," he drawled, cocking his head. And that drawl dripped like sun-warmed honey. "When the real estate agent sold me the house, she told me the one to the left was vacant and a hard-of-hearing granny lived on my right. Which, in hindsight, still isn't that good of an excuse. Because I didn't think about anyone other than my immediate neighbors, right? Doh!" He smacked his hand against his forehead. "So sorry again, lil' darlin'."

Hard-of-hearing granny. Jenna ground her teeth as annoyance flashed through her. Gwendolyn Dansen had been the agent for his house. And true, no one lived in the house on his left. And Mrs. George's hearing had been failing when Jenna had bought the house on the right, with its white shutters and wide porch. But that had been two years ago. And Gwendolyn damn well knew it. Just wait until she saw the wench...

You're weaning off of terrorizing Rose Bend's citizens with bitchiness, remember?

Sorry. Old habits die hard.

And yes. She was standing in her pajamas, in front of her new neighbor having a full-fledged conversation with herself.

Well, she might be trying to tilt a new leaf—turning it completely over was a little late at this point—but she'd make an exception for this guy.

"Was that really necessary?"

"The apology? Yes." His grin widened, and though this one was more authentic, it also carried an edge. "And the rest of it? Oh most definitely. If you're going to make assumptions about me, Malibu, then I'm going to do my damnedest to live up to them."

"Malibu?" she snapped.

Yes. Because that was the most important detail in what he'd just said.

"Yeah." The corner of his mouth quirked up in a smirk that shouldn't be sexy considering it clearly mocked her. He flicked a hand in her direction, waving it up and down, from her long red hair to her shell-pink toes. "As in Malibu Barbie. You might wanna go back to your dream house before you catch a cold."

Her lips popped open.

Son of a—

Then music blared again.

"Are you serious right now?" she yelled, jamming her fists on her hips. "Didn't we just have this discussion?"

He turned back to the open hood of his truck but glanced at her over his shoulder, arching a dark eyebrow. "Yeah. Turn off my music because people are asleep. But you're up now, Malibu."

Then he gave Jenna his broad back, dismissing her.

Well, wasn't that… Damn.

Glaring one last hole in his back, she spun on her heel and marched across her lawn. She refused to look back as she charged up the steps of her porch.

The house that had been a balm for her soul from the first moment she'd pulled up to the curb.

A sanctuary threatened by Mr. Monster Truck.

Here was her haven, with its fairy lights, porch swing

and backyard brook. A place where no one rolled their eyes at her or cringed when they saw her approaching. A place where her last name didn't inspire as much resentment as it did respect.

A place where she could close the door, lower the mask and simply...be.

Fear shimmered inside her. Only the iron decorum Helene Landon had drilled into her daughter from the time Jenna had been old enough to haul herself out of her toddler bed kept her shoulders from slumping and her head from bowing.

One never committed the ultimate sin of revealing weakness. Especially not in public.

Most especially if your last name was Landon.

Some habits really did die hard.

And some haunted a person. God. Usually, she left everything related to Jasper and Helene Landon at the curb; they didn't even follow her onto her porch. But now, they encroached like skulking shadows.

This time, she did look over her shoulder to the man blasting his music again, and an irrational spurt of anger flared in her chest.

He had caused this disturbance.

He, with his ugly truck, loud noise, big presence and condescending grin.

Maybe they just needed distance. That's what made great neighbors. He might live next door but that didn't mean they needed to talk. This initial interaction could be their last.

If she was good at anything, it was alienating people. Shutting them out and walling herself in.

She was an old pro.

Ignoring Mr. Right Next Door wouldn't be a problem at all.

CHAPTER TWO

Isaac Hunter drove down one of the familiar streets in the village of Mount Holly, Massachusetts, one town over from Rose Bend.

Huge sugar maples lined the sidewalks. Older, well-kept, single-family homes with flags waving from their porches crowded next to one another. And though the September air had turned cool, people hung out on porches and steps or postage-stamp-sized front yards.

Mount Holly was a quaint village so small they had to travel twenty minutes to Rose Bend to get McDonald's. They had a QuikMart, twenty-four-hour LaRue's Diner and an old-fashioned pharmacy with a malt fountain. But no place to get a Big Mac.

It was a tragedy.

Yet, his hometown had been the perfect place to grow up. Where a half-wild boy could roam free with confidence, knowing that not only his older sister and mother looked out for him but also a whole neighborhood. It'd truly taken a village to raise him. Especially since his deadbeat father had been out of the picture before Isaac could form sentences.

Even as his mother met another man and his biological family grew with another sister and brother—and another man left—their neighborhood family remained steadfast, loyal and *there*.

And as Isaac pulled up in front of the yellow single-family home in need of a coat of paint, something pulled tight inside him loosened.

Until this moment he hadn't grasped how much he needed to be here. Needed to be…home.

He pushed open the door to his beloved 1989 Ford F-150. Just as he stepped out, the front door to his family's home flew open and his nine-year-old nephew, Jacob, burst onto the porch.

Arms stretched wide, he yelled, "He's here! Uncle Isaac's here!"

Then like a heat-seeking missile, he charged down the steps and across the front lawn. Isaac swept the kid up and over his shoulder.

"Isaac," Lena called from the top step, exasperation and affection filling her voice. His older sister shook her head, crossing her arms. "You're going to drop him."

Isaac snorted. "How dare you, woman? I've pile-driven two-hundred-pound men into mats for a living. You think I can't handle one squirmy, stinky, scrawny—oops!" He dipped his shoulder, allowing Jake to plunge down his chest, grinning at his nephew's delighted scream, catching him before he hit the sidewalk. "My bad."

Tossing Jake back over his shoulder, he continued up the walkway.

His nephew belatedly yelled, "Hey, I'm not scrawny!"

By the time Isaac climbed the steps and set Jake next to his mother, his oldest nephew, twelve-year-old Edward, and his niece, five-year-old Bella, spilled out the front door. It never ceased to amaze him that his sister—reserved, serious, responsible Lena—had named her children after the ménage in *Twilight*.

"Uncle Isaac! Uncle Isaac!" Adorable Bella, Belle for short, jumped up and down arms outstretched, and he obliged by picking her up and settling her on his hip.

She grinned wide, her freckled cheeks plumping, and he poked a finger through the gap where her two front teeth should be. Giggling, she wrapped her arms around his neck and smacked a loud, wet kiss on his cheek.

"Hey, Uncle Isaac," Ed greeted with a hike of his chin, already too cool for a hug.

Amusement and a pang of regret echoed in his chest. Living in a different state and being on the road had meant missing much of his nephews' and niece's milestones.

Those were the moments he'd never get back. ·

And the last year had shown him nothing was guaranteed. Dreams could shatter with one negligent blow.

So he'd be more careful, more intentional. And that began with his family.

"What's up, Ed?" Isaac bumped his nephew's fist.

"It's about time you made your way here," Lena gently scolded. "Mom's been cooking the fatted calf for the last few hours and has smacked our fingers if we dare to come close. We're all starving so get your a—" she shot a glance at her kids "—butt on in here."

"Yes, ma'am." He saluted, and they both smiled as the kids' laughter surrounded them. "It's good to see you, too, sis."

Looping an arm through his, she guided him inside. As soon as he crossed the threshold, delicious aromas met him. Roasted chicken. Potatoes. Gravy. Green beans. He closed his eyes and inhaled. All his favorites. Yet, underneath those scents hovered others—lemon Pledge, the cinnamon candles his mother bought from the QuikMart, the faint fragrance of the lavender powder she used instead of perfume.

They were the scents of home.

And they welcomed him.

"Mom, the prodigal son has returned," Lena called out, shutting the door behind her.

Alice Hunter appeared in the entrance to the kitchen wearing a green turtleneck and black pants under an apron. More than a few strands of gray twined through her dark hair. Her makeup didn't try to conceal the crow's-feet fanning from the corners of her blue eyes or the thinner lines along her nose and mouth.

Until this moment, he'd held it together.

The flight from Tampa into Boston. The drive into Rose Bend. The inauspicious meeting with his new, uh, fiery, beautiful neighbor. The return to Mount Holly.

Yeah, he'd held it together.

But one look at his mother, at his rock… She'd always been his safe place to land and had never made him feel like a burden for falling.

And God knew, right now, he was falling.

"Well? Are you going to stare me to death or are you going to come over here and give me a hug?" his mother demanded in that deep smoker's voice, although she'd quit nearly twenty years ago.

"I'm thinking," he said, his voice also hoarse, but from the fear of cracking and burying his head against his mother's belly like he used to do as a boy. There, he'd felt safest. "Did you get shorter since I last saw you?"

She drew herself up to her full five feet eight inches.

"Boy, it's been a year since you saw me. A year too long. You better get over here and hug me before I remember I'm pissed about that and start swinging."

Laughing, he set Belle on the floor, then strode down the hall to his mother and wrapped her tight in his arms. And when hers came around him, surrounding him in love and lavender, he closed his eyes, inhaled and locked his knees to keep from sinking to the floor.

In gratitude. In pain. In joy.

He was finally home.

"So YOU READY to start this new job on Monday?" Lena arched an eyebrow at Isaac as she slid a fork and plate of lemon pound cake in Belle's direction.

Shaking his head, Isaac took a long pull from his Sam Adams before answering.

Yes, he was ready.

Yes, he was glad to be back home.

Yes, he wanted normalcy after fourteen years of the nomadic, chaotic lifestyle of his chosen profession. *Former* profession.

And all that was true. He *was* ready; he *was* glad. But then, he…wasn't. Because the reality couldn't be summed up into something so simple. Life didn't work that way.

If it did, he'd still have a marriage.

He'd have a wife who looked at herself in the mirror and didn't see a failure.

He'd have a wife who hadn't cheated on him with a man he'd respected.

He'd have a child cradled in his arms, their cries and laughter filling his ears and heart.

He'd have a glittering future filled with a beautiful family, a career he loved and limitless possibilities.

Instead he was back where he started.

But he couldn't tell his family that. He didn't want to hurt them, and it was one thing to think it, but to say it?

So instead he said, "Ready as I'll ever be."

"My friends are so psyched that Mr. Right will be coaching our wrestling team," his sixteen-year-old brother, Colin, crowed from across the table. He shoveled food into his mouth as if he hadn't just gorged on two plates of chicken, potatoes, gravy and green beans. "We're never going to lose another match now."

"I wouldn't go that far," Isaac murmured.

"I would." A mutinous expression passed over Colin's face as he forked up more cake. "You're the best. Hell, you retired a Wrestling Federation Conference world champion—no one could beat you. And no one can."

"First, watch your language," Isaac admonished.

"Sorry," Colin muttered.

"Second, you're a bit biased." Colin's lips parted in what would no doubt be an argument, but Isaac held up a hand. "I love you, too, though." He grinned. "I'm going to do my best to help. But I'm assistant coach, not head coach. Even your sister couldn't pull enough strings to conjure up an education degree. And besides, Rose Bend High School already has a coach." Again, Isaac held up a hand to cut off his brother. "Who has graciously agreed to let me assist."

When Lena, a math teacher at Rose Bend High, had mentioned to Brian Camden that Isaac intended to move back home, the social studies teacher and head wrestling coach had begged her to ask Isaac if he would consider coaching. Before Isaac had given an answer, the man had come back with an offer from the school board. Not that Isaac needed the money; he'd invested wisely over the years. But he hadn't been raised to be idle.

And he loved kids.

And he loved wrestling.

So he took the position and donated the salary back to the program.

"Are you going to miss it?" his mother quietly asked.

"Define *it*," he replied with a soft chuckle only lightly edged with bitterness. "Professional wrestling? My old life? Marriage?"

Myself? Who I used to be?

"Yes."

He shrugged. "I would be lying if I said no. It's all I've known for so long. It's going to take some getting used to." Like losing a limb. "But this is home."

"But you've been Mr. Right for twelve years. It's not going to be easy getting to know Isaac Hunter again. Or redefining who he is after all this time."

A hole yawned inside his chest. His ex-wife had guided his career. As the CEO and part owner of one of the world's largest and most popular wrestling promotions, she'd been the perfect person to school him. There were those who gossiped that he'd fucked his way to a championship. But those who mattered knew he'd worked his ass off from day one.

And as hard as he trained, he loved even harder.

Until the day Diana had betrayed that love with an unfortunate butt dial so cliché it would've been comical if it hadn't been his marriage and career going down in flames.

His mother was right. For the last twelve years, he'd lived in a world where others wrote the script. But he was no hypocrite. He'd loved it. Every second in the ring. Every bruise and pain. Every roar of his name.

He'd loved it. Craved it.

And now, he stared into the abyss of figuring out who he would be without it.

"Wrestling coach seems like a good place to start," he murmured.

She reached across the table and squeezed his hand. "Sounds good to me, too." Giving him one last pat, she picked up her coffee and eyed him over the rim of her cup. "Now, how's the house coming along? I still can't believe you wouldn't let your sisters and me come help you move in." She snorted. "You'd think you'd be grateful for more hands. Instead, it's like you're afraid of us seeing the place."

"More like afraid of us helping him decorate," Lena added with smirk.

"You're not wrong." He held up the hand not wrapped around his beer, warding off his mother's glare. "But yeah, not sorry. I've lived in a professionally decorated house and had little choice in furniture or what went on the walls. This is my first home that's all my own. I know it sounds overboard, but I want to choose each lamp and then pick a place for it. Same with art, couches, tables, all that."

"I get it," Alice grumbled but her eyes sparkled.

With pride, he liked to think.

"Tell us about it, then, if we can't see it," Lena said. "I've only seen the pictures you sent us. Do you still like it as much in person as you did over your computer?"

He nodded. Visualizing the simple rustic home, he could honestly say, "Yeah, I do. Three bedrooms, two baths, fireplace in the living room and master bedroom, a sun- and mudroom. I have a huge backyard with a privacy fence for when the kids come over, and I'm having a new playground set delivered next week."

"With a swing and slide?" Belle piped up, blue eyes wide and mouth covered in lemon icing.

"Of course," Isaac said, rearing back as if offended she'd even ask. "What kind of playground doesn't have swings and a slide?"

Isaac chuckled as Belle grinned and resumed eating cake.

"Big ears," Lena muttered, earning side eye from her daughter. "Well, I'm glad you love the place and it's everything you wanted it to be. Nothing worse than expecting one thing and it turns out to be something else."

He stilled, listening for a hint of resentment in his sister's voice. Only when he didn't detect any did the tension melt from his body. If anyone had cause to be cynical, it'd be Lena. Ed and Jake's father had sold her on a golden dream that had turned out to be tarnished brass.

Thank God for Kenneth Epps. Not for saving his sister. Lena Hunter didn't need anyone to rescue her. No, the quiet, dependable handyman would always have Isaac's gratitude for showing Lena that not all men would disappoint her. And of course for being a wonderful stepfather to Ed and Jake and father to Belle.

Sipping his beer, Isaac squinted then tipped the bottle in his sister's direction. "Hey, where's your better, hairier half? I have a few things I want done to the place and would like him to take a look at them."

"So wait, let me get this straight." Lena tilted her head, the light of battle entering her eyes. "Kenny gets to see the house before I do?"

The corner of his mouth quirked up. "Since it's in a professional capacity, yes."

"Are you shi—" Lena glanced down at Belle, who stared up at her. Clearing her throat, she smiled, sliding a hand down one of her daughter's pigtails. "Kenny's down at Ms. Reese's repairing her back stairs. Her son, daughter-in-law and grandkids moved in, and God love 'em, but they've already started tearing up the house."

"I remember Kyle," Isaac said, nodding. "I also find it poetic justice that his kids are hellions considering what he was like back in the day. I just hate that Ms. Reese's house is paying the price. Again." He winced. "But yeah, tell Kenny to give me a call when he has a moment."

Unbidden, an image of his neighbor, with eyes the color of a cloudless summer sky and hair like autumn leaves, flashed through his mind. And his mouth twitched with the smirk he couldn't control.

"What's that about?" his mother asked, twirling a finger in the direction of his face. "Something's going on, so don't tell me nothing."

He swallowed the reflexive *nothing* and shook his head. "I was just thinking about my new neighbor. We kind of got off on the wrong foot." He snorted at the understatement. "And I'm envisioning how the construction noise is going to go over." A grin slowly curved his mouth. "Not well, I imagine."

Lena rolled her eyes. "Seriously? Leave it to you to be in town five minutes and already meeting a woman."

"He's Mr. Right." Colin reached across Belle and held out his fist for a bump.

He didn't leave his little brother hanging, but inside his head, *hypocrite* blared like a tornado siren.

"He met her," his mom said, eying him with a *look*. "But something tells me that legendary charm of yours didn't win her over. Spill, boy. What happened? What'd you do?"

"Me? Why do you assume I did something?" At her bland look and Lena's snicker, he dropped the innocent act. "Okay, fine. I *might have* played my music a little too loud while working on my truck."

"What's wrong with that?" Colin asked in true teenage fashion.

"It c*ould've* been a little after seven...this morning." His mother stared at him, blinking. "In my defense," he rushed to explain, "my real estate agent told me my neighbor was an elderly woman who spent the fall and winter in Florida with her son, not a prickly redhead who really, *really* hates country music."

Silence fell over the table. Lena and his mother shared a look, and he frowned.

"What?" he demanded. "Now, what was that—" he waved a finger back and forth between his mother and sister "—about? And don't try to tell me 'nothing.'" He arched an eyebrow, tossing his mother's words back at her.

"This redhead," Lena hedged. "Tall? Blue eyes? Personality of a blade saw?"

"Really, Lena." His mother tsked, admonishing her. "A blade saw? That's unnecessary." She paused. "And inaccurate. There's nothing loud or obvious about Jenna Landon. She's not her father. No, she's more like a stiletto. Sharp, deadly and pretty. That one will slice you to pieces with her tongue and leave you bleeding out on the floor."

His sister's description plus his mother's? That sounded 'bout right. Especially since he'd been the recipient of said sharp tongue.

"Jenna Landon?" He leaned back in his chair, crossing his arms over his chest. "The name doesn't sound familiar."

"It wouldn't," Lena said with a shrug. "She and her family have lived in Rose Bend all their lives, and her father was the mayor there after you left for Florida. Not like we all ran in the same circles." His sister snorted, rolling her eyes. "And believe me, they have no problem letting you know it."

"The mayor's daughter?" His chin jerked up at that bit of news, and his knee started jumping, an involuntary nervous tic he'd never tamped down. "Huh."

Images from that morning popped in his head like camera B roll.

Whipping around to find himself face-to-face with a goddess embodying two of the most powerful elements in the world—fire and water. Hair of flame. Eyes of ocean.

Maybe he'd slammed his head on the hood of the truck harder than he'd believed.

Had to.

Because no flesh-and-blood woman could possibly be that fucking beautiful. Especially so early with no makeup, bedhead and pajamas that hid much more than they revealed. But that golden skin only added luminescence to those mysterious eyes. And drew attention to a ripe, sensual mouth that looked permanently stained pink, as if it'd just been kissed. Just as that long, thick hair appeared as if fingers had recently been tangled in the strands.

Even the boring robe and baggy pajamas couldn't hide the tight sweetness of the body beneath. When she'd propped her fists on her hips, the motion had pressed the layers of material against her slender form, accentuating firm breasts and a lovely curve of hip. When she'd turned and marched away from him, the robe had pulled tight across a gorgeous ass and molded to long, toned thighs.

He shouldn't have let his neighbor's questionable

taste and stunning beauty blind him to what had been right in front of him. That pampered skin. The perfectly layered hair. The manicured, pale pink nails. Wealth bore a certain glow, carried a particular scent. And if he hadn't allowed their meeting—and that pretty poison mouth—to distract him, he would've noticed.

After all, he'd lived with wealth for more than ten years. He was well acquainted with how it caused rot from the inside out.

"My house, it's not in a bad area at all, but it's not an affluent one either. Why would the mayor's daughter live in such a modest home? Is she estranged from her family? Or is she slumming it?" he asked.

Lena rolled her eyes. "Oh believe me, Jenna Landon is a chip off her father's block. And that would be the one marked rich, arrogant, rude, snobbish and mean. Why she's living next door to you, I can't say. Jasper Landon built a McMansion a few years back. God knows there's enough room for him, his wife, Jenna and half the town." She scoffed, shaking her head. "I remember when that thing went up. I don't even live in Rose Bend, just work there and the gossip ran rampant about it. Objectively, it's a grand, stately place. But it's also an eyesore."

"And you live right next door to her?" Alice murmured, huffing out a laugh. "I'm assuming from your brief description that your first meeting was pretty, uh, memorable."

"Yeah." He lifted the bottle again, took another sip. And yes, he was stalling. "She insulted my music, my manners and called me a redneck all in one breath."

"Wow." His mother blinked.

"See what I mean?" Lena flipped her hands up.

"It's the truck, isn't it?" Colin asked with a wince.

Isaac whipped toward his little brother. "What about my truck?" he demanded.

"Nothing." Colin leaned back in his chair, a grin spreading over his face. "Nothing. I'm just saying… Is that what you plan on driving to school on Monday? Or do you have another car? One without so many, y'know…colors. And wheels."

"There are four wheels, man."

"Yeah, but they're so *big*. So they look like eight."

"Respect the truck." Isaac jabbed a finger in Colin's direction, adding a glare for good measure, before turning to his mother. "Right. Wow. She made a snap judgment about me. And I kind of…"

His mother arched an eyebrow. "You kind of…"

"Called her Malibu Barbie and told her to go back to her dream house."

Lena's sharp crack of laughter echoed in the kitchen, and guilt worked its way underneath his ribs. His mother had raised him to be a gentleman. And as raw as his new neighbor rubbed him, he could've controlled his mouth. That had been his job for years. Follow the script. And he'd never had a problem doing just that. He'd been Mr. Right in the ring and out. Perfect manners. Perfect lines.

Yet one icy woman with hair of fire had him losing control of his tongue.

That…unnerved him.

And he'd returned to Rose Bend, and Mount Holly, to find peace, a new version of home, a new version of himself. Not to be…unnerved.

"Oh I bet she just loved that." Lena released another chuckle. "I'm surprised you still have your balls. That one's known for snatching 'em off."

Belle halted in the middle of scraping icing from her plate and looked at Isaac. "You have balls in your truck, Uncle Isaac? Are they the pretty ones with glitter?"

His niece's obvious misinterpretation had laughter gathering in his throat. Only by sheer force of will did he swallow it down, in fear he'd hurt Belle's feelings.

And that he'd have to explain what balls her mother had been referring to.

Yeah, no way in hell was he broaching that topic.

Looks like he would be returning here tomorrow with a back seat full of glittery balls. And *holy shit*, he'd heard it as soon as he'd thought it.

"Sorry, Belle, I forgot them back at the house. But I'll bring them tomorrow, okay? Promise."

Appearing a little mollified, she shrugged a tiny shoulder. "Okay." Then she scrunched up her freckled nose. "I like Ms. Jenna. A lot," Belle informed everyone at the table.

Both of Isaac's eyebrows winged up and he struggled to hold back a grin at his niece's very adult-sounding announcement. It seemed they'd all forgotten about the big ears at the table.

"That's, uh, nice, Belle." Lena tugged her daughter's pigtail. "But are you sure we're talking about the same lady? How did you meet her?"

Belle rolled her eyes. "Ariel. She's Ariel."

It took Isaac a minute—he'd lived in Florida, but his Disney-speak was rusty—but he quickly caught up. *Right.* The redhead mermaid.

"She got me an ice cream cone when you had to yell at parents and Colin took me for a walk."

Isaac glanced at Colin for a translation.

"Lena had a parent-teacher conference, so I took

Belle and Jake to get a cone at Six Ways to Sundae. I got there and didn't have enough money and Ms. Landon paid for all of us," Colin explained.

From the blush staining his face, he appeared to remember the occasion as, uh, fondly as Belle.

"'Us pretty girls got to stick together.' That's what she told me." Belle beamed. "I like Ms. Jenna."

Hell. Isaac took another sip of his beer, but it did nothing to wash away the regret coating his tongue. Did Lena feel as shitty as he did about speaking ill of someone in front of a child? No matter how true their words might be.

But that was just it… Coming from a world where the story line and the truth blended into an alternate reality, he questioned what his eyes saw, what his ears heard.

Lena and his mother saw Jenna Landon and her family as—paraphrasing—condescending, mean, rich assholes.

Yet…

Why couldn't he forget the flash of sympathy in her blue eyes when he smacked his head on the hood of his truck?

Why couldn't he eject from his mind glancing over his shoulder and catching sight of her slumped shoulders as she stood on her porch, staring at the front door?

His grip tightened on the bottle before he slowly set it down. The *whys* didn't matter. As harsh as it sounded, Jenna Landon didn't matter. She was his neighbor; that was it. A quirk of fate and geography.

He'd returned home to figure out his next steps.

Not to figure out Jenna Landon.

CHAPTER THREE

JENNA SLID HER car into a parking space on Main Street and switched off the engine. On a Sunday afternoon, pedestrian and street traffic were light, which meant two things.

One, quickly picking up a dessert for dinner with her parents at Six Ways to Sundae and still arriving on time shouldn't be a problem.

And two, *dammit*, quickly picking up a dessert for dinner with her parents at Six Ways to Sundae and still arriving on time shouldn't be a problem.

Surely, a hangry mob wanting ice cream would be the perfect excuse for showing up late or even avoiding the dinner altogether.

Then again...this was Jasper and Helene Landon. He'd want to know why Jenna hadn't thought ahead and avoided the crowd. And Helene would demand to know why she was at a pedestrian shop like Six Ways to Sundae in the first place, picking up—gasp!—a store-bought cake.

Either way, Jenna would gravely disappoint her parents. Again.

Jasper and Helene subscribed to the Dr. David Bruce Banner school of thought when it came to disappointment. As in, you wouldn't like them when they were disappointed. So Jenna tried to avoid it. And them, if she were brutally honest with herself.

Sighing, she pushed open the car door and stepped into the September afternoon sunshine. The breeze wrapped around her and tickled the pink, white and yellow awning above the ice cream shop. It flapped lightly, as if inviting passersby inside. And maybe she was stalling.

To everyone else in this town, Jenna Landon was the dutiful mayor's daughter, an adoring daddy's girl.

They didn't know shit.

Didn't know her. Which was why she couldn't wait to shake the dust of Rose Bend, Massachusetts, from her Jimmy Choos.

But another moment of standing on the sidewalk in the middle of Main Street and people would start to gossip. And it didn't take much for people to gossip in this town. Especially if your last name was Landon.

It was almost physical, the slip of her mask into place. And after fourteen years, second nature. The tilt of her chin. The lock of her jaw and curl of her mouth. The narrowing of her eyes. Squaring of shoulders, ruler-straight back. Unhurried stride. People moved out of her way, not the other way around. The effect? Haughty. Confident. Powerful.

A Landon.

The ping of her cell pulled her back. Her parents, no doubt. Her stomach twisted, but she gritted her teeth and glanced down at the screen anyway.

Are we meeting tonight? I got an idea to talk over with you.

Not her parents. The name above the message notification sent relief spiraling through her. One of the few people she could call friends. How sad that he didn't know it. She tapped out a reply.

Yes. I'm out now but will be home about eight and ready to work.

Cool. Hit me up then.

Tucking her phone away, she pulled the entrance door open and a cool whip of air greeted her as she stepped through, feeling lighter than she had moments earlier. If Willy Wonka owned a storefront, he'd probably hit up Cecille Lapuz for interior design. Pinks, light blues and yellows swallowed the space. Round tables and dainty chairs claimed the floor. A glassed-in freezer stretched across one side of the store while a tall, refrigerated dessert case packed with gorgeous cakes occupied one wall. A freestanding counter with bins of toppings stood in another corner. It was a child's fantasy.

What would Cecille say if she found out a version of her shop was featured in a certain young adult paranormal series?

The business owner would probably love it…until she discovered the identity of the author. Cecille didn't have much use for Jenna.

Jenna's smirk deepened, as did the ache buried deep. Deliberately she shoveled on mounds of *I don't give a damn* over the inconvenient throbbing as she approached the counter.

A young man rang up the customer in front of her, and Jenna waited, perusing the dessert case. Just as she settled on a peach pie with caramel drizzle, her cell phone vibrated.

Her stomach tightened again. This time, she knew who it had to be.

What if I don't answer?

The question flashed through her mind for a self-destructive moment. But as quick as it did, she banished it. Why waste time on a mutiny that would be squashed?

Inhaling a breath, she slipped the cell free and glanced down at the screen, frowning: 3:27 p.m. Dinner didn't start until four. She had more than enough time to arrive at her parents. Then she read the text.

Just a reminder. Dinner starts at 4 p.m. sharp. Don't be late.

Only her mother could make a reminder sound like a threat.

Her jaw clenched, her fingers curling around the cell before she could remember her very public location. Deliberately relaxing her grip and her body, she tucked the phone in her purse, turned back to the case and removed the pie.

One good thing about bearing the title of town mean girl. No one dared approach to ask if you were all right. Either they were too scared or didn't care. Both suited her just fine.

Liar.

She banished that snide voice in her head, and out of the blue, a memory assailed her.

Her, at six, curled up next to her dad on the living room couch in the childhood home she'd loved, watching one of the older detective shows he'd favored while he'd eaten a big bowl of rocky road ice cream. Sometimes it was hard to believe that softer, more affectionate man had existed. The man who had called her princess, enjoyed spending time with her and shared his favorite ice cream.

She put the pie back, halted in front of the freezer and stared down into it.

"Hi, Jenna. Can I help you?"

Jenna lifted her gaze to meet the light brown eyes in the pretty, unsmiling face of Florence Dennison. The young woman, whose family owned a bed and breakfast in town, worked here regularly. She also happened to be the sister-in-law of her nemesis. Jenna's lips stretched into a cool smile even as her heart thumped. Funny, that occurred whenever she came into contact with anyone wearing the last name Dennison.

Was it guilt? Shame? Anger?

Envy?

"Yes," she said, nodding toward the buckets of ice cream. "I'll take a quart of rocky road."

"Got it." The young woman turned with fluid grace to get a container and begin scooping the dessert into it.

"How's your family, Flo?" What was she doing? *Just get the ice cream and go.* "I heard your sister and Owen are settling well in New York."

"Leo's good." Flo didn't pause in her scooping.

"And Nessa and Wolf? Olivia's still acclimating back to small-town life, I can only assume Nessa is experiencing the same, moving here from Boston after living there all her life. It's a little ironic, isn't it?" She cocked her head, her hair falling over her shoulder. "Both of them moving from the same city for the same man. They have so much in common."

A muscle ticked in Flo's jaw, and she paused in her steady scooping. Guilt and shame deepened in the pit of Jenna's stomach. But she couldn't stop the words. Even knowing bringing up Olivia Allen—her best friend and Flo's brother, Wolf's, ex—would rub the other girl the wrong way, Jenna couldn't stop reverting back to old habits that, though toxic, were comfortable…safe.

With a couple more flicks of her wrist, Flo finished filling the container, fit the lid on top, then set it on the glass counter with a smile as cold as the ice cream.

"Everyone's fine, thank you for asking. Terry will ring you up."

Without waiting for Jenna's reply, she moved on to the next customer, gifting them with a warmer, more genuine smile. The sight of it shouldn't have had a twinge echoing behind Jenna's rib cage—but it did. Even though she deserved Flo's dismissal. Hell, she'd begged for it.

Because that's what Jenna did. She offended, alienated and intimidated. And when people drew away a… relief released inside her like a valve twisted for steam to escape.

She was safe for a little longer.

Yes, it was twisted, dysfunctional. Meant she was… broken.

But it worked. Until it didn't.

"Damn, Malibu. So it isn't just me. You seem to have the same effect on everyone."

That voice.

Jenna stiffened, a current of pure electricity jolting through her as if she'd been hot-wired. Heat licked at her belly, flaring lower and spreading into a sudden, delicious ache that stole her breath. Only years of practice kept her from betraying the unexpected flash of pleasure before it climbed in her chest, causing her breasts to swell, her nipples to tighten. Mortification poured into her, fueling the fire like gasoline until she damn near burned with it.

What. The. *Hell?*

She didn't do *heat*. It was about more than a lack of control—something she also didn't *do*. And if she'd learned anything, it was that attraction was nothing more than an excuse to be out of control.

No, it went deeper than that.

She just didn't...*feel* heat.

A lukewarm tickle. Yes. Even appreciation for a beautiful person. Sure. But a Pompeii, watch-it-all-burn conflagration? No. That wasn't her. She wasn't capable of it, and she'd come to accept that about herself. Had even come to be grateful for it.

But now...

Her fingertips pressed against the frosty quart of rocky road. The bite of it forced her to be present, grounded instead of sinking further into the thick, hot waves crashing through her body.

Fixing her patented smile, she turned and faced her neighbor.

"Well, if it isn't Mr. Monster Truck," she said, sliding a gaze up and down his big frame, taking in the plain white dress shirt stretched over broad shoulders, the thin leather belt that accentuated his flat stomach, and the dark, slim-fitting pants that clung to powerful thighs. Dragging her gaze up, she met his unique indigo eyes and her breath... No, her breath did *not* evaporate from her lungs. "I didn't hear you drive up.

Must've been the lack of sirens pulling you over for noise pollution."

"And I didn't know you were in here. I missed your Corvette convertible parked outside." The corner of his sensual mouth quirked, and a corresponding tug yanked hard beneath her navel. He jerked his chin in Flo's direction. "What'd you do to piss her off? It takes a certain gift to have a person look at you like they want to take a dump in your rocky road. I mean, Malibu, c'mon. Ice cream is the happiest shit on earth. And somehow you've ruined it. So what did you say?"

Damn him for standing so close she had no choice but to inhale his woodsy scent of leather, cedar and a hint of spice.

Damn her for wondering if that scent originated from a cologne or from his skin like a pheromone.

She smothered a groan. *God, woman. He low-key insults you, calls you by that awful nickname and still you're ready to sniff his neck. Get it together.*

"About her personally?" Jenna arched an eyebrow. "Nothing. But one of her relatives might be my nemesis."

"Oh that all? You only have one?" He scoffed, waving a hand. "I've had four nemeses. One is amateur territory."

She blinked. Who actually admitted to having four archenemies? But then again, based solely on her own interactions with the irritating man, she understood.

"I have no idea how to respond to that." She paused, tilted her head and narrowed her eyes. "Well, yes, I do. But it's Sunday, and I went to church earlier so I'll refrain."

Those violet eyes glinted. With humor or malice, she couldn't decipher. But both had her breath hitching, and if that didn't concern her, then she should hightail it back to church and beg Pastor Noel for intercessory prayer.

"Does it make me a sad sack that I kind of don't want you to refrain?" he murmured. "That I want to hear what that wicked mouth of yours will flay me alive with next?"

Sounded like she needed to drag him with her to altar call.

"Excuse me?" The young man at the register interrupted with a little cough. "Can I help you?"

Warmth crawled up Jenna's throat. At what point had she become so wrapped up in her conversation with her neighbor—wrapped up *in her neighbor*—that she'd forgotten that she stood in line?

That would be when she'd first heard that silk-and-gravel voice in her ear.

Turning around, she stepped up to the counter, setting down the container.

"Will that be all for you, ma'am?" he stuttered, his attention shifting over her shoulder and landing on Mr. Monster Truck. The young man's eyes widened.

Huh. Jenna stared at him, bemused. "Yes, that's all I have." Jenna paid for her purchase and shifted out of the line, not daring to glance behind her. Her wayward gaze—and libido—couldn't be trusted to look anywhere but toward the exit.

Pushing out of the store, she inhaled the crisp air desperately. It contained the faint hint of rain that clung to the clouds, the aroma of gravy and ground beef from Sunnyside Grille across the street. She dragged in more of those scents, attempting to drown out the other, headier one still clinging to her senses.

"Malibu, hold up."

Her footsteps faltered but she forced herself to keep going. After all, he could be talking to someone else. Even though she was the only person out on the sidewalk.

"Jenna."

She jerked to a stop.

He knew her name.

Which meant he also most likely knew about her. Or he'd heard about her. No one—not the townsfolk, not even her best friend, Olivia, and definitely not her parents—*knew* her.

But, even with their ignominious first meeting, she'd hoped their neighborly…*connection* would remain untainted by her reputation, her past. By *her*. She'd clung to that. Now, she grasped at nothing, like fog slipping through her fingers.

Humiliation churned in her stomach, but she turned, pride tilting her chin.

"Isaac," her neighbor said, moving in a graceful stride that should have been incongruous with the towering height and width of the man. "Isaac Hunter. Seems only fair you have my name since I know yours."

"Great." She offered him a small smile. "Now I can stop calling you Monster Truck… Or not."

"That's fair." He frowned. "Monster Truck? Seriously?"

She shrugged. "What do you want?"

She scanned him from the top of his dark, loose curls to the tips of his shiny black Bruno Magli dress shoes. Sue her. She knew shoes. And apparently, so did Isaac Hunter. How did a man who'd worn plaid like he'd walked out of casting for the next *Dukes of Hazard* remake afford a pair of Bruno Magli shoes?

Not her business.

He stepped closer. "I've been meaning to catch you, but either I got home too late or your car wasn't in your driveway." Tunneling a hand through his hair, he dragged the loose curls out of his face, and a small huff of laughter escaped him. "And it could be I've been a bit of a bitch."

She tilted her head. "Now you have my attention, Monster."

Another hard chuckle. "Contrary to my—" he paused and a self-deprecating smile ghosted across his lips "—*performance*, I'm not an asshole. And I don't make a habit of being disrespectful to women. Which I was to you the other morning. I'm not making any excuses. I own my behavior, and I'm sorry for it."

Jenna stared at him.

A unicorn. A thing of myth and magic. That's what Isaac Hunter had become right before her eyes.

A man who apologized.

Not her father, who'd rejected her for daring to be less than perfect. And threatened to punish her if she dared to repeat that unpardonable transgression.

Not Chris Rappaport, her father's campaign manager, who'd claimed to love her, then abandoned her after her father's loss to Coltrane Dennison, Rose Bend's new mayor.

No, not one man in her experience had offered an *I'm sorry* for any hurt, small or heart shattering.

But this man—this stranger—doled one out casually, almost negligently.

Damn him.

Damn. Him.

She stood there, struggling to maintain the cool,

composed facade that had become as much a part of her as her red hair. Struggling to process this change in her worldview—that men could not only have remorse but that they were also capable of humbling themselves to admit it.

Maybe she should be thankful for this revelation. At twenty-nine she'd learned something new about people—something…nice. Which was shocking, because most times, people tended to disappoint.

But she *wasn't* grateful. She didn't *want* his apology. Didn't *want* this newfound revelation.

What she desperately *needed* was for everything to remain status quo. For the people in Rose Bend to continue viewing her as arrogant, mean and rude. For her father to successfully kick-start his reelection campaign and go back to ignoring her. To get the ball rolling on her exodus out of her hometown.

She needed Isaac Hunter to be like all the other men in her experience.

She *didn't* need her neighbor to be anything other than the man who indulged in too much plaid and too much country music and happened to live next door to her. Anything else would make him different.

Different was dangerous.

So, no, she didn't want his apology. And screw him that for one bright moment she did…and was damn near brought to her knees by it.

"Fine," she ground out, forcing her lips to maintain her smile even though it felt brittle and fake. "If that's all, I'm late to a dinner. Have a good evening, Mr. Hunter."

He frowned, his eyes narrowing, and she caught the confusion in his gaze. "Jenna—"

His arm lifted toward her, and fear speared her chest.
God, no. He can't touch me.

It might crack her fragile facade.

She sharply pivoted. Away from his attempt at reaching out to her. Away from the contradiction and…temptation of him.

And if it struck her a bit too much as if she were running away, well, she didn't want to be late for dinner.

That's all.

Jenna Landon didn't run from anyone.

And maybe if she said it enough times, she would convince herself.

CHAPTER FOUR

"THIS CAMPAIGN WILL surpass my past efforts. Especially the last one."

Jasper Landon momentarily glowered, picking up his tumbler of eighteen-year-old Scotch that no one else at the table was allowed to imbibe. He stared down in the amber depths before sipping, his dark eyebrows arrowed in a brooding V. "I refuse to have a repeat of the last one."

"That's why we're starting early, Jasper," Helene Landon said, voice calm, soothing as she cut into her perfectly prepared filet mignon. "Beginning now allows us plenty of time to raise funds and support. You'll win this time, honey. The people of this town will see the error of their ways and vote for who they should've last year."

Jenna sank her teeth into the inside of her lip, trapping the words that piled up in the back of her throat.

After serving two terms as mayor of Rose Bend, her father had been bested by Coltrane "Cole" Dennison, a local attorney and a member of one of the town's most respected families. The loss had enraged Jasper. Honestly, Jenna didn't know what embittered him more. The fact that he'd lost at all or that he'd lost to a younger Puerto Rican man he deemed to be beneath him.

For months, he'd stomped around muttering about

"diversity for diversity's sake." And as a member of the town council, he'd delighted in creating stumbling blocks for Cole at every opportunity. Like the bully he was.

Yet part of her still craved that bully's approval, his attention, even if most of the time it came with soul-stripping criticism. She craved that bully's love.

It was the same part of her that had bought his favorite ice cream even knowing the odds leaned in favor of him either ignoring the gesture or berating her for it.

It was the same part of her that had ceased being the perfect daddy's girl at fifteen when she'd messed up so badly her parents had never forgiven her.

For the last fourteen years, she been striving for a full pardon from the intolerable sin of not being perfect.

That's why she showed up to every "family" dinner when beckoned. Acquiesced to every demand without argument. Played the role even when it eroded her soul.

"I'm counting on it," her father muttered, forking green beans into his mouth and chewing them as if the vegetables had personally offended him. "The people here let me down once. How they haven't seen through Cole Dennison's fluff and expensive gestures just boggles my mind. He's going to bankrupt Rose Bend with his useless pet projects before I return to office. And everyone seems just fine with it." He jabbed the air with his fork. "I have to run again to *save* this town from Cole's ineptitude *and* from their own ignorance."

Now they'd arrived at the Great White Savior section of the evening. She kept her gaze pinned to the grilled tomato on her plate so neither of her parents would catch the eye roll she couldn't contain.

Because Cole's "useless pet projects" included an

elder and children's care center, a more inclusive motorcycle rally, and increased promotion and attendance at the annual town festivals, which had meant more revenue for Rose Bend businesses. Cole had made a positive impact on the town in the months he'd been mayor. But of course, her father couldn't see that. Or rather, he'd never admit it.

"Jenna?"

She lifted her head, meeting her mother's gaze. From the impatience glittering there and the sharp tone, it must not have been the first time she'd called Jenna's name. Anxiety pulled tight in her belly, and she carefully set down her fork and knife on either side of her plate, giving Helene her full attention.

"Yes, Mother?"

"Where were you just now? Because you're definitely not here, giving this conversation the focus it deserves." Her silken tone was familiar, and that particular note heralded polite but cutting censure. Jenna braced herself. "Maybe we're boring you. Or maybe we should send you back to the children's table where such rude, disrespectful behavior is tolerated. We can arrange that if you believe keeping up with our conversation is beyond your capabilities." Her mother arched a perfectly sculpted auburn eyebrow, her ice-blue eyes as razor-sharp as her words.

Shame poured through Jenna, scalding and thick. It crawled up her neck, creeping into her face, but she fought it back, deliberately picturing icy tundra and huge snowy floats, then peaceful fields with gently blowing grass. The tactic was a survival technique she'd adopted years ago. If her mother scented emotional blood in the water, she attacked. Even if that victim was her daughter. Hell, for fourteen years, since Jenna had shown how fallible she was, she'd become Helene's favorite target.

Jenna dipped her chin, gifting her mother with a small nod.

"That won't be necessary, Mother," she said. "I'm able to follow along perfectly well." She offered a civil smile, devoid of warmth. Those were the only smiles traded in this house. "I've always said the last mayoral election was a fluke. People can have their heads turned by the new and shiny but they'll become jaded—" God, how did she not choke on the words right now? "—by 'new' soon enough. And then they'll return to what, or rather who, has always been steady and consistent. They'll look for that in the next election, Dad."

He lifted his glass for another sip, his gaze narrowed. Only when he leaned back in his chair and nodded did the band around her chest loosen and she released a low, imperceptible breath. But she didn't relax. No, she didn't dare relax. Not at this table. Not in this house.

Not with her parents.

"You're right." Jasper set his tumbler back down. "You're absolutely right. And I need to start reminding the people of Rose Bend why I'm the right face and choice for this community."

Jenna bowed her head, bile sliding in her stomach. Her father was too politically savvy to be an outright bigot, but that "right face" comment... No one with two working brain cells could miss what it meant. She reached for her fork, fisted the silverware. This was the paint she'd allowed herself to wear.

No. She wasn't a victim. At some point, she'd become a volunteer. Out of fear, out of pathetic need. Out of desperation. Whatever. But she'd rolled in the same colors as her father and her mother. And now it would require a jackhammer and a prayer to scrape them off.

Her secret fear—the one that had her waking up in the middle of the night, sitting on her porch swing in the dark—was that she'd never be able to get it off.

"But if I'm going to be successful, everyone's going to have to pull their weight. That includes you, Jenna. We can't afford anything that will shame the Landon name. Do you understand? No mistakes that will bring embarrassment."

She didn't reply, hurt crowding her throat. The fault had to be some deficit in her. She didn't try hard enough. Wasn't...enough.

"Before it gets busy in the next couple of weeks, I'm going to need your help at the store in the mornings. One of my employees left on maternity leave and I need you to train her temporary replacement on the book-keeping system. Shouldn't be more than two weeks," her mother said.

Helene owned the Bath Boutique, a shop that sold soap, lotions and fragrances. Contrary to her cold manner with Jenna, she was an excellent, successful businesswoman. The turnover in her store had been low through the fifteen years she'd owned it. Between the competitive wages she paid, health insurance and flexible hours she offered, people rarely left her employ. A pity Helene treated her employees with more respect than she did her own daughter.

But then her mother didn't believe her employees were spoiled and useless.

That's what her parents thought of her. A burden.

She could easily disabuse them of that notion. But their reaction to her truth wouldn't be worth it.

She'd rather continue living the lie.

"Of course," she murmured.

"I'm also going to need you to make yourself available," her father added. "None of those excuses you seem to be giving more and more lately are going to fly. And," he cleared his throat, "I've been meaning to tell you. I've invited Chris Rappaport to return as my campaign manager. He should be arriving in a couple of weeks. I expect you to behave like the young woman we raised and treat him with respect and dignity."

"Excuse me?"

Shock barreled through her. She couldn't have heard right. Couldn't have heard *that*. Because it would mean her father had rehired her ex, regardless of how he'd mistreated his daughter. The ex who'd claimed to love her but had disappeared without a word as soon as his employment with her father ended, as if his relationship with her had been a part of the job description.

Thank God she was sitting.

Because her muscles had locked, and she couldn't move. She couldn't speak. Could only stare in confusion as knowledge sank past the astonishment.

Her father demanded complete loyalty from those around him, but especially from his family. Yet, he had none for her.

And oh God, did that hurt.

This was just one of many cuts he'd inflicted over the years, and she should've bled out by now. But no. Her stubborn heart continued to pump, despite the aching.

Helene sighed, reaching for her glass of Merlot. "Don't be dramatic, Jenna. We simply don't have the patience for it. This isn't about you. Chris Rappaport is the best and your father deserves the best." She eyed Jenna over the rim of the glass, gently swirling the wine. "Maybe this is a blessing in disguise. You can find closure about why he broke up with you so…suddenly."

Translation: *What did you do to make him leave you?*

Some people might've allowed the words to break them. But not her. The words refined her, honed her. Built an unbreakable glass cage around her where she could look out and others could peer in while careful, vital distance was maintained.

And yet…

A fine crack zigzagged across that glass.

"Closure isn't necessary," Jenna said, voice even, almost pleasant thanks to years of practice. "My relationship with Chris is in the past, and you're correct. This is about Dad. And Dad—" she looked at him "—if you believe Chris is who you need to win the election, then you should hire him again."

Bullshit. He abandoned and humiliated your daughter. You should be placing me over your political aspirations. You should love me.

Choose me.

The scream burned on her tongue, but she smiled and mimicked her mother, lifting the wineglass and sipping her Merlot. Swallowing the bitter alcohol she hated along with the equally bitter diatribe she'd never vocalize.

"Good. That's the attitude I need to win this. When he arrives, I don't want there to be any awkwardness."

A burgeoning anger swelled inside her. Ruthlessly, she tamped it down, refusing to give her parents any more ammunition to turn against her. But the echo of that rage pulsed against her throat, and no amount of wine could stop it.

"Now." Jasper clapped his hands once, then picked up his fork and knife and resumed eating his dinner. "About the carnival. I've planned it to be the kickoff of my campaign. Henry Kingston, as well as other businessmen here in town, have already donated. Of course, we'll need to raise more funds, but this is the perfect start. Get the backing of the businesses, their owners, the professionals and the church leaders in this town. They will tell the people how to vote.

"That's something Cole Dennison doesn't understand. Last time he ran on that sentimental family-and-community platform, pulling on people's heartstrings. Didn't hurt that he'd just lost his wife and baby either," he muttered, as if affronted that Tonia Dennison had the nerve to die in childbirth, ruining Jasper's mayoral run.

"I'm certain Cole didn't consider the loss of his family a political windfall when he ran for the position," she murmured.

"Don't be naive," Jasper sneered. "It's unbecoming. Everyone has an agenda. No one's above it. Not even Cole Dennison." He cut into his steak harder than the meat required, and his lip curled. "Even Saint Cole couldn't object to an autumn carnival. All I had to do was trot out phrases like 'good for the community' and 'town morale,' and he and the rest of the council were all on board. Chris was right."

"Chris?"

"Yes." A smirk rode his mouth. "He was aware of my...contentious relationship with Cole. But he advised me to approach the board differently. Once more, Chris proved why he's the perfect person for the position of campaign manager and adviser. It nearly killed me to kowtow to the council, but we got it done. Now..."

Jenna picked up her fork and robotically lifted another piece of tomato to her mouth, chewing without tasting. As her parents conversed, she listened with half an ear, responding when needed and doling out appropriate answers. By the time she stepped out on the wide wraparound porch with its tall, gleaming columns, tension pulled her so tight, her muscles screamed in agony.

Deliberately, she inhaled a deep breath and rolled her shoulders back, closing her eyes. Though every instinct told her to escape, she didn't move. It felt too much like running away. And given everything that had occurred behind her in that house, she couldn't concede this one small thing. It was a tiny victory, considering. But it was something. To her, anyway.

Slowly, the stiffness eased from her body, and she shifted closer to the top step. Tipping her head back, she stared at the vast star-dusted sky.

When she'd been a little girl, she'd imagined each twinkling speck had been a gift from her father. When she'd grown into a jaded teen, she'd stopping seeing the sky as a special gift from father to daughter, and instead saw its possibilities. Viewed the horizon as a great place of potential that stretched far beyond Rose Bend, beyond its suffocating perceptions and expectations...beyond her parents.

She hadn't tested that potential yet.

But she would.

In two months.

That's how long before she could climb in her car with a U-Haul behind her and drive past those town limits without looking back.

Get her house sold, her father's reelection campaign kicked off so he wouldn't be suspicious about her plans and then she would be out of Rose Bend and on to her new life.

It wouldn't be a problem. After all, she was a master at keeping secrets.

Inhaling another deep breath, she descended the steps and headed to her car.

It was only a little after seven. Plenty of hours left in the evening to get some work done.

For the first time that day, a semblance of peace stole through her. Because also for the first time that day, she was headed home to the only thing in her life that hadn't let her down.

There lay her safety, her refuge.

She walked away and didn't look back.

CHAPTER FIVE

ISAAC HAD LIVED in one of the most exciting cities in the United States. He'd traveled all over the world and visited more than his fair share of restaurants and coffee shops in all those places. There'd been that kitschy, hole-in-the-wall shop in Las Vegas that served one hell of an espresso. And that gorgeous, quaint café in Brussels with the most fragrant, strong Americano he'd ever tasted.

Still, in a picturesque town tucked in the southern Berkshires, he'd somehow discovered the Shangri-La of cafes.

And he hadn't even tasted one drop of coffee yet.

He dragged in a lungful of the aroma of roasted nuts, caramel and vanilla. And something else so sinfully sweet his back teeth ached. It would take a much stronger person than him to resist the lure of the sparkling case of doughnuts, muffins and scones that ran across the front of the store. The source of the "sinfully sweet." His stomach growled, and when the older man in front of him grinned at him over his shoulder, Isaac returned it. No shame in his game. He'd walked in hungry, and the scents filling the space had only increased the pangs.

At six feet five inches tall and weighing in at 265 pounds, for years, he'd maintained a strict protein-and-calorie-heavy diet plan, as well as a grueling and disci-

plined workout regimen. It'd been mandatory to remain
in peak athletic condition to perform at the level required for his career.

Of course, he still enjoyed cheat days or a great cup
of coffee. Especially the coffee. Which explained why
he stood in this shop now, nose-hustling like a fiend.

And for facing his first day of work at the high
school, he needed the biggest cup of caffeine this place
had to offer. Matter of fact, if they had keg size, that
would be even better. He could just roll it in the back
of his truck—

"'Scuse me, Mr. Right?"

Isaac tensed at the tremulous, hopeful whisper behind him. No, he didn't recognize the voice, but the
excited tone? Oh that, he identified easily. Curving his
mouth into a broad smile, he turned around and greeted
two girls, who appeared to be between fourteen and
sixteen, one with pink braces.

"Since I'm going to be a familiar face around here
from now on, how about just calling me Mr. Hunter?"
he gently asked. "And you two are?"

They didn't seem offended at all by the correction of
his name. Instead, the girls glanced at one another and
then looked back at him, beaming harder.

"Cool. Mr. Hunter," the one with the braces said.
"I'm Tyra Miles."

"I'm Jessica Barrett," her friend piped up. "We were
wondering if…" She didn't finish the sentence but held
up her cell phone.

And he wasn't so out of touch that he didn't interpret that correctly.

Nodding, he held out his hand. "Here, let me take it.
My arms are longer."

The girls giggled, and he grinned again, and this time it was more genuine. Regardless of his...complicated feelings toward his career and retirement, he'd always loved interacting with his fans. The muck of his marriage, his eventual disillusionment with the WFC and the uncertainty of his future couldn't touch the purity of the connection he'd had with them.

Holding the cell at an angle, he snapped selfies with both teens. Then waited while the girls switched phones and took a couple more. By the time they finished, other customers had their own phones out, covertly taking pictures or outright staring. Isaac glimpsed recognition on some of those faces and curiosity on others. Both had his skin prickling and nerves jangling down his spine.

"Thank you so much," Jessica gushed, tucking her cell into her backpack. "Is it true you're coaching at the high school?"

Isaac nodded. "It is. You two don't go there?"

Tyra shook her head. "Next year. We're still eighth graders. But my brother does. When he told me you were going to start coaching the wrestling team, I didn't believe him. Now I'm not going to hear the end of it." She pulled a face, and Isaac held back a snort, sympathizing with her. Damn right she wouldn't. *I told you so* among siblings was a currency that never earned out. In the next instant, though, her face brightened and she held up her phone. "Is it okay if we post these on social media?"

No.

The word reverberated against his skull. And only by sheer will did he contain the shout. A good thing since he would've scared the teens and everyone in the café. Including himself. He'd come to Rose Bend to distance

himself from the WFC, from Mr. Right, to forge a new
path that comprised… Yeah, he had no idea what yet.

For now, he was the new wrestling coach. But he
was also still Mr. Right, a three-time WFC world champion. He couldn't change who he was. And truthfully,
he didn't want to. It was a part of him, and in spite of
the hell he'd gone through, he was proud of it.

"Yeah, no problem." He smiled, covering the pain.
Performing even without a camera around. "Now if
you two don't hurry, you're going to be late for school."

"Shoot, you're right." Jessica scrunched up her
nose, smacking her palm to her forehead. "We saw
you through the window and kinda forgot about being
late." She tugged on Tyra's arm, waving to him. "See
you later, Mr. Hunter!"

"Make sure you get a glazed doughnut," Tyra called,
following her friend toward the exit. "Ms. Autumn
won't tell but she *most def* puts something illegal in
those things. They're *that good*!" Giving him a full arm
wave, she and Jessica ducked out the exit.

"Should I apply for the position of president of your
fan club or is it too late?"

That pearls-and-sex voice dripped sarcasm and just
a hint of disdain. And yet his dick still stirred and hardened. Huh. Who knew his kink was snobby?

Turning, he met the long-lashed, summer-blue eyes
of his neighbor.

"Why, good morning, Malibu." The corner of her
eye twitched at his nickname, and he smiled. Fuck if it
didn't feel good. Real good. But this was Jenna Landon,
and he'd give it two minutes before she opened her
mouth and ruined it. "Don't you look pretty as sunshine

today. No wonder it's overcast out this morning. The sun wouldn't dare show its face with you out and about."

She stared at him, unblinking. Not even a tremor of her lips indicated humor, and damn if that didn't cause lust to bolt through him faster, hotter.

"I thought we established that the southern-fried Dixie routine wasn't necessary," Jenna said, crossing her arms, and God help him, drawing his gaze to the lush rise of flesh pushing against a green-and-white-striped V-neck sweater.

He jerked his attention back up, but this woman wasn't an idiot. Far from it, and the narrowing of her eyes proved it. Part of him expected her to call him on his shit, but she didn't. Because Jenna Landon didn't do anything as mundane as *expected*. Not from the moment she'd charged out of her house in her pajamas and confronted him. Still...

The flash in her eyes, which he would've called desire on any other woman *but* her, grabbed him by surprise. And shook him. Hard.

"Not the way I remember it." He cocked his head. "Do you have freckles?"

She blinked. Finally. "What?"

"Freckles? Do you have them? I was too distracted by...other things the morning we met to notice. And something tells me you would consider them a flaw and would cover them with makeup. Personally, I find them adorable and hot. Especially on redheads. And I think you, Malibu, could rock the hell out of some freckles."

Her lips parted, and for a second no sound emerged. Then, she gave her head one shake, her arms falling to her sides. Inside he clapped with glee, like a kid winning a toy in one of those rigged carnival games.

"Do you hear how inappropriate you are?" she asked, anger adding an edge to her voice.

He grinned. "Oh yeah."

She glared at him. He grinned wider.

Several seconds passed before the lack of noise penetrated, and he broke their visual warfare. Glancing around, he met several gazes aimed in their direction. More like the gazes of the whole café.

Shit.

Back in Tampa, their conversation would've been ignored. Hell, people would've moved around them to place their orders, grab condiments and go about their business. But they weren't in Tampa. They were in Smalltown, USA. Where everyone was in everyone else's business and loved to be there.

He shifted his attention away from the fascinated gazes and returned it to the stunning redhead. Saw the moment she realized they'd become the morning's entertainment.

If he expected Jenna to wilt under the concentrated focus, he underestimated her. She met each pair of eyes with a steady, damn near haughty stare, silently daring each of them to look their fill. And after a moment, they all glanced away.

Holy fuck.

"Damn, that's a talent. I don't know whether to be impressed. Or scared."

Pink stained her cheekbones, so sharp they could draw blood from the poor soul simple enough to try and touch. Was he that poor soul? The hot charge in his veins and dull pounding in his cock mournfully assured him that yeah, sorry, but he was. Maybe no one else noticed the fine tension that pulled her shoulders *just* a little higher and tugged her back *just* a little straighter, but he did.

Fuck him, but he feared there might not be much he missed about Jenna Landon.

Including that cool, bold fragrance of gardenias mixed with an earthier scent that called to the side of him that wasn't the gentleman his mother had raised him to be. That side craved to discover if her golden skin bruised because he wanted to mark her. To see her throat bear the brunt of his lips, his teeth. Watch the delicate skin high on her inner thighs darken from his less than careful touch.

Yeah, he wouldn't be careful with her.

He suspected too many people were too intimidated by her. If there was one thing he couldn't stand, it was being..."people." Not with her. That he felt the need to be culled from the herd with a woman he barely knew should've terrified him.

Who was he kidding? It did. It scared the hell out of him.

Another woman of her ilk had shredded him, then watched him walk away. Not that he had the slightest intention of getting involved in another relationship. But even fucking Jenna Landon had COMPLICATION written in full caps all over it in neon, blinking red. As red as that long hair pulled back in a sexy high ponytail.

Jenna had issues and layers. Anyone with eyes willing to look could see that. And he had his own. He'd come back home to unpack his own baggage, and he couldn't give what he didn't have. More importantly, he didn't want to.

He'd done that with Diana. Given and given and given more even when there'd been nothing left. Now, he stood here, empty and alone. Not his choice, but one he'd had no option but to accept.

But now? This was his choice and he wasn't going through that hell again. Ever.

Stepping back, he nodded toward the counter, choosing to ignore their audience. Wasn't the first one he had.

"Will my treating you to a cup of coffee make up for my bad manners? And I hear the doughnuts here are really good."

"Sorry, Mr. Hunter. But they don't serve enough coffee or doughnuts in here to make up for your lack of manners," she said, ice coating every syllable.

Mr. Hunter.

Ouch.

The return of the cold, the hardness. But for whose benefit? His...or the customers surrounding them?

"This is my first day of work at the high school. How about you call a cease-fire on the hundred years of winter?"

Surprise flared in her eyes and irritation flickered inside him.

She arched an eyebrow. "Nice. I'm impressed."

"Don't be. I saw the movie."

Yes, he had seen *The Lion, the Witch and the Wardrobe*. But he'd also read the book. Multiple times. And had the entire seven-book collection of the *Chronicles of Narnia* in a box back at his house, waiting to be unpacked.

Why he didn't just say that to her, he couldn't explain. Maybe it had something to do with that surprise he'd glimpsed in her gaze.

Maybe, hell. Definitely.

It pricked at a sore that had never fully healed. Aside

from the close friends he'd made while in the WFC, most people assumed Diana had been the brains in their relationship. That Isaac had been the younger, prettier "trophy wife" without a thought in his head. But that hadn't been true. All those hours and miles on the road, he'd spent a lot of them in books. Fantasy. YA. Autobiographies. Thrillers. Sci-fi. Didn't matter.

Yes, Diana had introduced him to his wealth management team, but he didn't sit idly by allowing them to handle his earnings without his active input. He'd been raised by an independent, brilliant single mother who could do with ten dollars what Jesus did with five loaves of bread and two fish. He'd learned from her and supervised his money, invested it, bought real estate.

He wasn't dumb. He wasn't just arm candy.

And yes, goddammit, he was projecting.

Anger at her, at him, at a whole slew of people in Tampa that he couldn't—wouldn't—rail against, spun through him. Turning away from Jenna, he shifted forward in line, avoiding that still-arched eyebrow and bright gaze. Unfortunately, that meant meeting the curious stares that continued to be directed their way.

He smothered a sigh.

Great. They would be on the tongues of every gossip by midmorning.

If this was a slow day.

"Your first day at the high school? A little dressed up for crossing guard, aren't you?" Jenna drawled, but the tone had lost its barb, its frost.

"Y'know, you're right. I don't need a hit of caffeine when I have this punch of Malibu heat first thing in the morning." She rolled her eyes and he grinned. "And since you asked, I'm one of the new wrestling coaches."

"Wrestling?" she asked, and that gaze of hers touched his shoulders, chest, abdomen and thighs. *Shit.* Now the town gossips would be whispering about him sporting wood in middle of Mimi's Café. "So, what does that entail? You having those poor boys flipping the tires on that truck of yours as part of their training?"

He snorted. "Funny, Malibu. One day you're going to respect my Baby."

"That figures you'd infantilize a vehicle."

"No, Baby. That's her name. As in Frances Houseman. 'Nobody puts Baby in the corner.' That's where I found her. The far back corner of a car lot in Mount Holly when I was seventeen. Paid fifteen hundred dollars for her and seventeen years later, we're still together. Longest relationship I've ever had." And the most loyal, but that was neither here nor there.

"And you two look very happy together." She paused. Squinted at him. "Baby? From *Dirty Dancing*? Seriously?"

He nodded gravely, settling a hand on the small of her back and ushering her forward to the counter. "Very."

"Good morning," a woman with beautiful dark shoulder-length curls and light brown skin greeted them with a wide smile. "Hello, Jenna, and nice to meet you, Mr. Hunter. How can I help you today?"

Jenna flicked a glance in his direction and stiffened beneath his palm, but that was the only indication of her curiosity about why the woman behind the counter addressed him by name.

"Good morning, Autumn. I'll have two regular coffees. Both black. And I'll take care of whatever Mr. Hunter is having."

Isaac frowned. "No. I offer—"

But Jenna waved away his objection. "It's your first day at a new job, Monster. And likely my one and only good deed of the week. Don't deprive me."

Despite the disconcerting warmth that hit his chest at the return of "Monster" instead of "Mr. Hunter," an instinctive protest still sat heavy on his tongue. It might be chauvinist as hell, but it went against the grain having a woman pay for him. Even if it was a cup of coffee. Especially given that he'd been viewed as a kept man for twelve years. One might say he had a complicated relationship with receiving gifts.

But Jenna wasn't his ex-wife, and he was here to start over.

He could start here.

With a cup of coffee.

"I'll take a caramel cappuccino with a shot of espresso. And whipped cream."

Autumn, as Jenna had called her, smiled. "You got it."

As she turned away, he glanced at Jenna, who again stared at him. He shrugged. "What? If I wanted a bland, boring cup of black coffee, I could do that at home. I'm here at a badass café, I'm getting a badass drink. Oh wait. That reminds me. Hey, Autumn!" he called out. The other woman turned around, holding a to-go cardboard cup with the pink-and-brown Mimi's Café logo scrawled on the side. "Can you add a couple of glazed doughnuts to that order? I heard they're amazing."

"Of course," she said, her smile widening at the compliment.

"And…thank you," he murmured to Jenna. When she stared at him, he jerked his chin toward the small crew preparing orders. "For the coffee and doughnuts."

"Oh." A moment of silence and a slow blink. "You're… welcome."

He started to frown at that weird reaction to a thank-you when she moved ahead of him, walking to the end of the counter. Her ruler-straight bearing and silence didn't invite conversation, and though the questions beat at him, he quietly waited on their order. Moments later, a young guy brought a light pink bag and handed it to Isaac. Without hesitation, he dug into his bag and pulled out the first doughnut. He bit into it and groaned as the sugary fried dough hit his tongue.

"Holy shit," he mumbled around the sweet snack. "Tyra wasn't lying. What the hell is in this doughnut? Let me tell you, I've lived in Tampa the last fourteen years, and I'm about ninety-five percent sure it must be something imported off the coast of Florida."

Jenna snorted. "First, as the newest wrestling coach, you probably want to clean up that language before you head into the high school. Second, you could be—"

"Sydney!"

Jenna's low, honeyed voice cut off as the server called out a customer's name, and Isaac watched as Jenna's expression closed like a door banging shut. Her eyes, bright with sharp wit only seconds ago, went dark, and the tiny smirk that had tilted the corner of her red-painted mouth disappeared, leaving her face as smooth as glass.

What just happened?

"Excuse me."

He turned, moving to the side. A lovely, petite woman stood behind him holding the hand of an adorable toddler. Pain gut punched him. The doughnut, which had been so fucking good in his mouth only seconds ago, tasted like dust and lodged in his throat.

It caught him by surprise, this soul-deep ache. Stupid of him to believe he'd gotten over the worst of it. Or maybe it'd just been a while since he'd been in contact with young children so he'd convinced himself...

The baby he and Diana lost would've been this child's age now.

A little over a year ago, it had been impossible to look at a child and not see the one who would've been theirs. To think about when he would've been holding his head up. When they would have gotten a play mat for learning to roll over. Would his first words have been Dada or Mama?

He jerked his gaze away from the tiny beauty with the dark curls and wide brown eyes like her mother.

It hadn't been the same with the failed rounds of IVF. Those heartbreaks had shredded him, and God, he'd underestimated how they'd wounded Diana. But they'd lost those little lives before they'd been fully developed. Before decorating a room for them. Before holding them. Inhaling their scent.

No, the loss of their baby had been different. And irreparable.

And now, he couldn't look at a young child without seeing the one he could never cradle against his chest again.

"Isaac?" Jenna murmured.

He had to go. Get out of here. Panic clawed at his throat. He was...suffocating. Drowning. Right here on dry land in the middle of a café. Air. That's what he needed. Air that wasn't shared by a baby that reminded him of the one that could've saved a dying marriage.

"I have to go," he rasped. Dropping his bag on the counter, with the lone doughnut he couldn't stomach any longer, he backed away. "Thank you for the coffee. I need to get to…work."

"Isaac…" Jenna said again.

But he'd already turned toward the exit. Pushing through the door, he burst out onto the sidewalk as if expelled from a cannon. And he didn't stop.

He didn't stop walking until he reached his truck, yanked open the door and hauled himself into the driver's seat.

And he still didn't stop.

Not when he pulled into morning traffic, rolled down the window and let the air rush over him, cooling his overheated skin.

And he still didn't stop.

Not until he pulled into the high school lot and parked in the back corner. He pulled his cell phone out of the console, pulled up his favorites list and his thumb hovered over the contact he'd never got around to erasing.

Diana.

The only other person who would understand this hollow pain.

Closing his eyes, he clutched the cell. But in the next instant, he tossed the phone away as if it stung his palm.

"Fuck." He scrubbed his hands over his face. A harsh roar built in his chest and rumbled into his throat. In the end though, a barely there whisper filled the cab of his truck. "Just…fuck."

He'd come to Rose Bend to start over.

But in the end, he couldn't escape the past.

CHAPTER SIX

"WELL, THAT WAS...INTERESTING," Sydney Dennison drawled, accepting her drink from the Mimi's Café server and throwing Jenna a sidelong glance. "Still have the same effect on people, I see."

Jenna tried hard not to look in the direction Isaac disappeared.

Tried...and failed.

There had been something bleak in his eyes before he'd cleared a path out of the café. Her heart pounded with the memory, and only Sydney's shrewd, narrowed gaze prevented her from pressing a fist to the place where pain pulsed. But that would mean betraying weakness in front of the person who was one of her weaknesses. The person she'd once called a best friend but who'd become an enemy. And Jenna only had herself to blame for that.

The fifteen-year-old Jenna had cut Sydney from her life, calling it triage. But adult Jenna had ensured those bonds remained exorcised out of habit and cowardice.

And now, staring into the derisive brown gaze of the woman who'd once been her best friend, Jenna wouldn't know how to begin to bridge that yawning divide even if she had the courage to try. Which, for the record, she didn't. Some dogs were better left sleeping.

"Well, we can't all have the disposition of—well, I

better not say in the vicinity of tender ears." Jenna's lips curled but not into what even the most Pollyanna of personalities could interpret as a smile.

She peeked down at Sydney's daughter, Patience, and pure golden sunshine swept through her. It was impossible to look at that beautiful little girl, have her smile up at you and not feel…good. Clean. Accepted.

Even Jenna.

"Sometimes I believe it must be so miserable being you. But who am I kidding?" Sydney shook her head. "You enjoy being a—" she thinned her lips, throwing a glance down at her little girl who tipped her head back and beamed up at her "—meanie. You thrive on it."

"Meanie?" Jenna snorted even as a voice in her head screamed, *You don't know me. You don't see me.* "This is the real world, Sydney, not some Disney sitcom. But kudos for getting creative for little Patience there."

She dismissed Sydney just as one of the café employees called Jenna's name and appeared at the counter with her two coffees and Isaac's caramel cappuccino.

"I don't get it," Sydney murmured behind her, almost so low Jenna didn't catch it. Almost. "Leo said you're not that bad. She's been through everything I have with you. More, since I left this town for eight years. I just don't get it when she's usually so discerning when it comes to people. What does she see that no one else does?"

That sucker punched Jenna, driving the breath from her lungs. She was thankful, in that moment, that her back was to Sydney. Because Jenna wasn't certain she'd been quick enough to school her expression.

Her pain.

Her secret.

Her shame.

In a crazy, spontaneous shared moment of vulnerability, Jenna had made the mistake of allowing Leontyne Dennison to see all three. It didn't matter that Leo had once been the third member to round out their best-friend trio in childhood and as teens. Jenna had cut off Leo, too, same as Sydney. Had resented—had hated—Leo...same as Sydney.

And now, Jenna had never felt more exposed. As if her skin had been turned inside out for the whole world to gawk at.

Anger sparked inside her like pieces of sharpened flint struck together.

Some of us can't live our heartbreak, our joy, our grief, our love out loud like you, Sydney, and know that on the other side we will be accepted instead of slapped down. Some of us can't just rebel and know that when we go back home there will be exasperation but also an open door and love. You have that assurance—I don't. I didn't fourteen years ago and I don't now. So don't fucking stand there and judge me. Not with your husband, daughter and happy family around you.

The barrage of words scalded her throat, but she didn't release the torrent.

Because Jenna Landon didn't do weakness. At least not in front of others.

"I'm guessing that question is rhetorical and one for your bestie, isn't it? Besides—" she accepted the carrier with the to-go drinks—including Isaac's forgotten cappuccino—and bestowed her coldest *you're the shit on the bottom of my shoe* look, ignoring the self-loathing in her gut "—this appears to be your issue, not mine. Better drink up that coffee first if you intend to do all that philosophizing this morning, Buttercup. But count me out. I really don't give a damn what you see when you look at me. Unless it's how amazing these shoes are."

Giving Sydney a smirk, Jenna circled around her and headed for the café door. But not before she glanced down at Patience one last time. Because yes, Jenna did have a weakness.

And she prayed Sydney didn't notice.

It was a minor miracle Leo hadn't shared Jenna's secret with Sydney—Jenna had half expected her to as the two women were thicker than thieves, even more so since Sydney had married Leo's brother Cole.

But Leo hadn't.

Her parents hadn't told anyone about Jenna's miscarriage to protect their image. But Leo had no other motive other than to protect Jenna's privacy. And for a woman who viewed vulnerability as a weapon to be abused by others, she valued that. And she feared it.

So she prayed Sydney didn't notice the effect her little girl had on Jenna.

Moving on automatic, Jenna strode the brisk five-minute walk down the block to the Bath Boutique. At seven thirty, the store wasn't open yet, but her mother's manager would've arrived by now. Jenna knocked on the pristine glass door with the store's elegant logo and waited. Moments later, Kathy Monroe appeared and unlocked the front door.

"Hey, kiddo!" she greeted with a warm smile stretching across her face and lightening her gray eyes. "Your mom told me Friday that you would be joining us for the next couple of weeks. That news made my day. Come on in."

The other woman's obvious happiness at seeing

Jenna stole some of the sting out of her mother telling the staff Jenna would be at the store a full two days before even "asking" her. Some, but not all. Especially since two weeks here in the boutique meant shifting her entire work schedule around to accommodate her mother. It was inconvenient at best, and at worst? Well, it very well might put her behind on her current project.

Still, telling her mother no hadn't been an option. And she considered spending time with Kathy a perk. The other woman had worked with Helene at the boutique from the moment she'd opened the doors. And Jenna had come to love the woman like an aunt. Unlike her own mother, Kathy was never selfish or stingy with her affection, and like a dry sponge left out in the heat, Jenna soaked it up. Even knowing she would be derided for it later.

Jenna stepped into the store, and as Kathy locked up behind her, she set the coffees on the glass counter containing the more expensive perfumes, colognes and several exclusive pieces of jewelry inspired by the fragrances.

"Thanks, Kathy." She picked up one of the cardboard to-go cups and turned, extending it to the manager. "I come bearing coffee. Black since I know Mother keeps creamer and sugar for you guys in the break room."

"Thank you, sweetie." Kathy accepted the brew and sniffed it, groaning. "Mimi's. I take it back. You're not a sweetie. You're a goddess. I usually don't have time to stop by in the mornings since I have to drop my grandkids at school now. I miss Autumn's coffee. This is such a treat. Thank you," she said again, lifting the lid and taking a sip.

"That's right. Mother mentioned your daughter

moved in with you. She and the kids are lucky to have you," Jenna murmured.

More like Helene had snarked that Kathy's daughter's worthless husband couldn't hold down a job so now her daughter was mooching off her mother. And inconveniencing Helene because Kathy had to switch up her hours to pick up her grandkids from school.

But Jenna would never tell Kathy that. Not when it would hurt the other woman's feelings. Who did it hurt for Kathy to believe Helene was a benevolent employer?

Kathy waved a hand, dismissing Jenna's praise. "It's what family does. Take care of each other. I'm sure your parents would do the same for you."

No, they wouldn't. And she could say that with a certainty.

Family didn't guarantee a safe place to land.

And only those who'd always had a safe place believed that.

"Mother said I'm supposed to be training an employee on the accounting software. I'm assuming you're still using the same point-of-sales and bookkeeping systems?"

"Yes, it's still the same. Thank goodness you learned it when we first implemented the software a few years ago. It's like having a permanent trainer on retainer," she said with a smile and another sip of coffee. "And if no one else says it—" she paused, covered Jenna's hand and squeezed "—thank you. For sacrificing your time to help out here. You don't have to, but thank you for agreeing to do it."

Jenna blinked at the unexpected sting in her eyes. Well, damn. She turned, on the pretense of grabbing the second black coffee, avoiding Kathy's gaze. When was the last time anyone thanked her? For...anything?

Isaac.

Without her mind's permission, she traced the rim of the extra cup.

Isaac had thanked her just this morning for the cappuccino and doughnuts. And she'd been so unused to that small show of appreciation that she'd been overwhelmed. Even more overwhelmed than she had been as he stood in that café, his dark beauty and immense height and width vacuuming all the oxygen out of the place.

Where was he now? Where did he go after he'd fled the coffee shop? Because that's what he'd done. Fled. With that haunted look in his indigo eyes, harsh lines carved into his fallen-angel face. Demons might as well have been snarling at his heels.

And if anyone recognized demons, she did.

"Jenna?" Another gentle squeeze to her hand. "You okay, sweetie?"

Startled from her thoughts, Jenna managed to control the jerk of her body. Inhaling a deliberate breath, she schooled her features into the polite, inscrutable mask she'd perfected over the years.

"I'm fine. Sorry. Just running the accounting program through my head." Lifting the coffee from the tray, she turned to Kathy. "What time is— Who am I training again?"

"Lynn Wakefield. She's a new hire since you've last been in here. But I think she'll catch on quick. You might not even need the whole two weeks. I told her to get here at eight—oh wait. There she is now."

Jenna glanced down at the thin gold watch circling

her wrist. Seven forty-six. Not bad. She liked this Lynn already.

Her opinion of the woman only improved as the hours sped by.

Lynn was lovely with her sheet of straight dark hair and smooth chestnut skin. She shared that she used to own a small custom blanket store with her fiancé before he died a couple of years earlier. They'd used a similar accounting system, which explained why she caught on so quickly. Sympathy swelled, though Jenna did her best to hide it. She wouldn't know how to comfort Lynn or say the right words—Jenna owned that—but she sensed the other woman wouldn't have appreciated an unsolicited show of consolation. In that, Lynn reminded Jenna of herself.

Her sympathy for the woman deepened.

Jenna couldn't imagine anyone voluntarily wanting to be like her.

By the time five thirty rolled around, Jenna closed out the program, tired but satisfied with the day's progress.

"You did great today. I don't think you need to come in so early tomorrow since you've grasped most of it. In the morning, we'll start on payroll and then Wednesday we can integrate the POS system." Jenna opened the bottom desk drawer and removed her purse.

"Sounds good. And thank you for your patience. I know I asked a lot of questions," Lynn said with a wry smile.

"It's not a problem. That's how you learn, and I didn't mind," Jenna assured her.

"I could tell, and I appreciate that. You are nothing like I've heard from—" Lynn broke off, slashes of scarlet streaking across her cheekbones. "I'm sorry. I didn't mean... God, that was so rude..."

Hurt shimmered under her skin. Yet, she couldn't say, *No worries, it's fine.* It wasn't fine. Nothing about being known as the town bitch was *fine*.

"Jenna, I'm—"

"Excuse me, Lynn." Helene appeared in the doorway of the office, her blue gaze fixed on Jenna. "I need to have a word with my daughter, please."

"Of course." Lynn nodded. Jenna handed the other woman the small leather backpack she'd tucked in the drawer with her purse. Accepting it, Lynn stood. "Again, Jenna, thanks for everything today, and I'll see you tomorrow."

"You're welcome. Have a good evening," Jenna murmured.

Moments later, the door closed behind the employee, and as soon as the lock caught with a soft *snick*, an invisible lever dropped in her stomach, cranking a cord so tight it threatened to snap. Most daughters felt joy, peace—safety—in their mother's presence.

Jenna felt the need to scan the room for the largest piece of furniture to take cover behind.

"Is there something wrong, Mother?" Jenna asked.

Because one, there was always something wrong. And two, regardless of how she wanted to make herself a smaller target for her mother's jabs, she refused to cower. Besides, when her mother scented proverbial blood in the water, she attacked.

Jenna refused to be a willing victim.

"Is there something wrong?" Helene repeated, moving into the office, smoothing away nonexistent wrinkles on the elegant light blue sheath dress that skimmed her slender form. "You tell me, Jenna," she said, crossing her arms over her chest. "Tell me if Marilyn Olsen, chairwoman of the board I'm sitting on for the Rose Bend Beautification Committee, approaching me at the end of the meeting to ask about my daughter's public flirtation with a stranger in the town coffee shop, followed by an argument with Sydney Dennison can be labeled 'something wrong'?"

Bitter dread flooded her mouth. *Dammit*.

She should've foreseen this. From the moment she'd met those curious gazes focused on her and Isaac, she should've been on guard for this confrontation. Shame on her for not shoring up her defenses. She'd pay for it now in emotional wounds she'd need to lick later.

"I see the gossip network is in full working order," Jenna drawled, mimicking her mother's pose. But while Helene's exuded irritation, Jenna's was self-protection. "They really should work on accuracy. I didn't indulge in a *public flirtation* with a stranger. Although, I did have a normal conversation with my neighbor who happens to be the new wrestling coach at the high school while we waited in line for coffee. This version sounds much less salacious, but it also happens to be true."

Her mother didn't speak, studying her with unwavering scrutiny. Jenna battled back the urge to fidget.

"Your neighbor? Since when?"

"A few days ago."

"You didn't mention him at dinner Sunday evening."

"I also haven't mentioned the newlywed couple two houses down or the single mom who moved in down the street last month. And I failed to bring them up for the same reason I didn't bring up my newest neighbor. They're nonfactors in my life."

Something loud and defiant roared in her head. *No*, she argued with that nearly primal sensation. *He's my neighbor. Nothing more, nothing less. Not even a friend. He's...no—*

Her mind shut down on that thought.

She couldn't allow herself to call Isaac Hunter *nothing*.

Silence stretched between her and Helene.

"From the way it was described to me, you two seemed to be having a pretty...intimate discussion. Are you sure he's just a neighbor, Jenna? And I want the truth."

"I'm not sure how one has an intimate discussion in the middle of a café, but yes, Mother, he's just a neighbor."

And if he isn't? Why is that your business?

But she trapped those inquiries and they burned her throat.

"Good." Helene nodded, unfolding her arms, but her expression didn't soften and neither did her gaze. "Keep it that way. A wrestling coach, for goodness' sake, Jenna." Her lips twisted in a distasteful moue. "Really. You're supposed to avoid the appearance of impropriety. We can't have people believing you're associated with a high school *wrestling coach*. You must be more careful in the future."

Jenna clenched her jaw.

"Now," her mother said, then paused, eyes narrowing, "explain away the confrontation with Sydney Dennison as easily as you did the new neighbor." Helene tilted her head. "Explain why you engaged in a heated discussion with Cole Dennison's wife in a café full of people."

Helene couldn't bring herself to call Sydney "the mayor's" wife. The resentment ran that deep.

"Again," Jenna said, struggling to hold on to her patience. God, the busybodies here were just another reason she couldn't wait to leave. "An exaggeration. Yes, we had words, but it wasn't an argument, nor was it prolonged enough to be 'heated.'"

"You shouldn't be talking to her *at all*," Helene snapped. "What did your father and I just say at dinner? Don't do anything that will embarrass him or set tongues wagging. You don't think petty back-and-forths with Cole's wife fall under that? Consider the optics, Jenna. It could appear as if you're antagonizing her. Especially with her daughter there. She looks like the sympathetic figure, while you, the white, unwed, privileged, wealthy, childless daughter of her husband's opponent are cast in the role of the bully. Or in this social climate, the 'Karen.'" She sneered, curling her fingers in air quotes. "Neither one of them are worth the backlash it could bring to your father. *Think*, Jenna. Use the brain we spent a fortune on for that Ivy League college education."

She breathed through fire, inhaling carefully as if a blowtorch had been taken to her lungs. It required every bit of strength, of self-control to not buckle under the agony rolling through her.

Anyone listening to the tirade could take their pick of the harsh criticisms to unpack. But only one of them struck a blow…as Helene had intended.

Childless.

It echoed in her head.

Gaining volume until it rang clear as a bell.

Her mother had twisted that knife deeply, intentionally because it would humiliate the most, bleed the worst. Sometimes, Jenna thought Helene hated her for what had happened.

Because Helene blamed Jenna for a mistake she'd made as a naive fifteen-year-old. Because of that mistake, Helene believed she'd never be a grandmother. And she would never forgive Jenna for it. Never let her forget it.

As if Jenna's sole worth culminated in who she permitted between her legs and what emerged as a result.

She was more, dammit.

She *was*.

And God. Why did it sound like she was trying to convince herself?

"In a town this size, it will be impossible to avoid Sydney. And the gossips are going to have something to whisper about it. But I'll do my best to not appear intimidating."

She damn near choked on the last word. It diminished the strength Sydney possessed. That woman had never backed down from Jenna. Not even when she'd first returned to Rose Bend and Jenna had been at her most hateful.

No, she had to be honest, even if it was just with herself.

When she'd been at her most jealous.

"Just remember this isn't about you. Every word, every action, every mistake reflects on your father, on me. We can't afford any missteps. *I'm sorry* doesn't fix problems. So don't create problems, Jenna."

Be perfect.

Her mother didn't utter the command, but the weight of it pressed down on Jenna's shoulders. She'd been bearing this burden since she was a girl and yet it hadn't become lighter or easier to carry in all these years.

It still threatened to bury her.

"Understood." Jenna picked up her purse off the desktop where she'd laid it and slid the strap over her shoulder. "If that's all, I'll see you tomorrow."

"It is. I hope you will keep our talk in mind."

Jenna nodded. Helene needed to have the last word and Jenna just needed to…escape.

Crossing the office floor, she grasped the doorknob and stopped herself from wrenching the door open. With a reserve that belied the nerves screaming inside her, she stepped through, quietly closing the door behind her.

Moments later, she emerged into the evening air. Dusk had come and gone, and she fell in with pedestrian traffic, striding toward the parking lot. She reached her car, unlocked it and slid inside. Instead of starting the engine, she sat there, fingers curled around the steering wheel, staring out the windshield.

Two women, one older and one younger, passed by. Huddled close to one another against the cool night air, arms linked, their heads bowed close, Jenna guessed they were mother and daughter. And not just because of the gray that streaked the older woman's hair and the similar smile they shared. It was the way the younger woman playfully leaned her head on her mother's shoulder. And how the older woman patted her daughter's hand then stroked her hair. The easy affection spoke of a bond, of a relationship, no fear of rejection.

Something Jenna didn't have with her mother.

Something she'd craved for so long the ache had become ancient, hollow, a whisper of what it used to be.

But it took only a kind word, a compliment, a glimpse of a mother and daughter in an unguarded moment to refresh the ache.

Slowly, she started the car and pulled out of the parking lot.

Two months.

She had to hold on for two more months. So what if it tasted like running away? For too many years, she'd stood caged in her parents' shadows. She deserved to break free. To live free.

And this time, she refused to ask for anyone's permission.

Just...two more months.

Then she could breathe.

CHAPTER SEVEN

ISAAC TURNED BABY down his street and guided her toward home. Yeah, it'd only been a few days since he'd moved into his new house, moved to Rose Bend. And again, yes, he had to acclimate... Still, neither were *home*.

Hell, he'd lived in Tampa for fourteen years, twelve of those in a palatial oceanfront mansion that had never truly felt like his, although Diana had insisted differently. Still, it'd contained every creature comfort and state-of-the-art technology known to mankind. And yet...

Home had been, and he suspected always would be, the crowded, single-family home in Mount Holly.

He released a sigh. That's where he should've directed his car after his first day on a new job. Toward Mount Holly, where his mom and family were probably getting ready to sit down to a noisy dinner with delicious food weighing down the table. They would've made room for one more. And they would've been excited to hear about his first day with the team.

That's how his family was—each person's news and was everyone's news. One person's win belonged to everyone. So yes, he should be at that table.

But instead, he headed to the empty, lonely house he was determined to make a home.

Old-fashioned streetlamps illuminated the road and guided him to his driveway. He'd had the foresight to leave a lamp on in one of the living room windows, and the welcoming golden glow alleviated some of the heaviness from his chest.

He tried not to compare this homecoming to one he would've received back in Tampa, and failed. Returning from a show on the road, the house, with its floor-to-ceiling windows and walls of glass had always been lit up. Even if Diana had been the only person inside, which had been rare. Not that Isaac could blame her. He'd seldom arrived without two or three people in tow.

Now, in hindsight, it almost seemed as if neither of them wanted to be in the house alone…together. Because then they might have to talk to one another about subjects deeper than schedules, camera angles and doctor visits. Subjects like why they were so desperate for a child. Why she'd chosen him to be her husband when she'd only turned from him in the end.

Pulling Baby to a stop in his driveway, he cut off the engine. He jerked on his tie with one hand, removed his keys with the other and shoved out of the truck. He strode to the walkway leading to his porch, but at the last moment halted.

And glanced over at the dark house next door.

What the fuck? Keep moving.

His mind snapped the order yet his feet didn't get the message because they pivoted and headed away from the warm, golden light in his window.

"Shit," he muttered. "What the hell am I doing?"

But he still didn't stop walking across Jenna Landon's front yard or climbing her porch steps. An inexplicable *something* urged him toward the door. That *something* felt perilously close to the feeling that had propelled him twelve hundred miles from home to Flor-

ida with no goal other than to be a famous wrestler with
the Wrestling Federation Conference. It was an almost
visceral, instinctual need to *move*, to *do*.

Why should he feel that now, on his neighbor's dark
porch? Yeah, he wasn't about to analyze that.

"You're at the wrong house, aren't you, Mr. Hunter?"

The smooth pearls-and-sex voice came from his left.
He froze, his fist raised to knock on the door. That low
timbre stroking through him in a sensual caress. Slowly
lowering his arm, he turned.

Holy. Shit.

Jenna railing at him like an enraged Valkyrie in ugly
pajamas had set his blood on fire. A cool, aloof Jenna in
a café with her stiletto-sharp cheekbones, red-painted
mouth and shadow-darkened blue eyes had wrapped
around his cock.

But a relaxed, casual Jenna curled up on a porch
swing in an oversize, light brown cardigan with black
leggings molded to her slender, long legs damn near
had him coming right there.

Just one. Goddamn. Look.

The growl that rumbled in his chest grappled for his
throat, and he locked it down.

Jenna Landon looked like she'd just climbed from a
warm, sheet-tangled bed, grabbing the closest clothes
to throw on before emerging outside. Her dark fire hair
tumbled over her shoulder and a pale shaft of moonlight
caught the high tint of color on her cheekbones. Likely
from the bottle of wine on the floor and the almost full
glass she cradled between her slim fingers.

"I was thinking the wrong house but now that I've
spotted that—" he dipped his chin toward the bottle
"—I'm reconsidering. You sharing, Malibu?"

She studied him for several silent moments, shadows shrouding half her face. He could *feel* those bright eyes. And though he could enumerate many circumstances under which he'd like to have that gaze on him, now did not make the list. Because he suspected that incisive inspection perceived too much, wine or no wine.

Like why he stood here, hovering on her porch.

Finally, she nodded and shifted, unfurling those long, gorgeous legs. Good God, he could watch that sight on repeat for the next twelve hours.

"I don't mind sharing just this once since it looks like you're having a hard day."

"I'm not the only one. And don't bother." He waved a hand, managing to unglue his feet and stride forward. Bowing down, he swept up the bottle—and got a lungful of gardenia and *her* scent. He couldn't explain how he knew; he just did. Earthy, warm, sensual. Fire. *Her.* "I'm not going to make you get up to fetch a glass when you look all comfortable. I'll just take this." He held up the bottle, swinging it lightly.

Without breaking their visual connection, he removed the cork and took a long sip.

The dry Cabernet Sauvignon flowed over his tongue, and as he lowered the bottle, he returned her stare... and waited.

And decided not to question the racing of his pulse.

"Was that little demonstration supposed to prove something to me?" she finally asked. "Well, other than verifying your day was shittier than mine."

Busted.

"Wow, Malibu. I think that's the first time I've heard you curse," he teased, but then his lips twisted into a rueful smirk. "Truthfully?" He gingerly sank down on one of the wicker armchairs across from her. Once certain it could take his weight, he sprawled his legs out in front of him, balancing the wine on his stomach.

"That'd be novel."

"Here's one thing I can promise you, Malibu. I might wake you up in the morning with quality country music." He held up a hand when she arched an eyebrow. "It's damn fine music and we can argue that another time. An argument you will lose, by the way. And I might detest your taste in coffee and ice cream. I mean, c'mon, black and rocky road?" He gave a full-body shudder. Yuck. "Still, there's one thing I won't do. And that's lie to you.

"Will I avoid the hell out of you before hurting your feelings? Sometimes. Because I have a mother and two sisters, and I know what can happen when I'm asked if jeans make an ass look too big. Which, can I just point out, there's nothing wrong with a big ass? But apparently, that's not the right answer. So when pressed, I'll give a truthful answer."

"So what you're promising me is you'll tell me the truth? Unless I'm asking about my fashion sense or my…assets. Then you'll avoid me like my last name is Ripper and you're a Whitechapel soiled dove. I have that right?"

"Exactly."

She stared at him. Then snorted.

"Is it sad that yours is the best offer I've had in a long time?"

He scoffed. "No." He lifted the bottle for another sip and squinted at her. "Well. Maybe." He cocked his head. "What're you doing out here, Malibu? I don't have anything against drinking alone, but everything good?"

"You first, Monster," she said, voice as cool as ever, but she cradled that glass just a bit closer. He fought back his frown. "After all, you came over here and confiscated my wine. And start with why you're embracing my alcohol like you're in a committed relationship."

He glanced down, and hell, his hands were clasped around the thing as if he was afraid it would make a break for it.

"Right. My reason behind the 'little demonstration.'" He sighed, tipping his head back against the wall of the house. Admitting this would be easier if he wasn't looking her in the eyes, and yes, he got how that sounded. "I guess, part of me wanted you to kick me off your porch. At least then I could walk back to my house with my dignity."

"Because you don't want to be here."

"No," he murmured, rolling his head to the side, and meeting her gaze. "Because I do."

Silence throbbed between them, and his words reverberated in the dim corner of the porch, pounded against his skull. Dammit, he would regret this in the morning. No, five minutes from now. But right now, he—*shit*.

He didn't want to be in that empty house with the still-unpacked boxes containing memories—good and bad.

Didn't want to be in the silence.

Maybe the bigger question should be, why did he hate the quiet so much? Why was he afraid of it? Why was he afraid to let himself sit in it?

What did he think he'd discover about himself?

"Tell me about your day," she said, almost…gently. He hadn't heard gentle on Jenna before, so he couldn't quite be sure. But yeah, it sounded like it. And that warmed him more than the wine.

"I arrived at the school and met with Brian Camden. Do you know him?"

She sipped her wine. "In passing. A teacher at the high school. I think his girlfriend works at the library."

"God, small towns." Isaac huffed out a laugh and downed another swallow of Cabernet. "I'd forgotten, and if I'm honest, I missed knowing the connections of that person to this person. That just doesn't happen in cities like Tampa. But yes, he's the social studies teacher and the wrestling coach. He pretty much told me that while the title of head coach is his, he's letting me have free rein and turning the team over to me. No pressure or anything."

She tilted her head, a wrinkle forming between her brows.

"That's, uh, either really flattering or really lazy. And granted, I don't know Brian Camden well, but he's never struck me as lazy."

Isaac chuckled, and he knew it sounded as dry as the wine.

"No, there's nothing lazy about him. I sat in on a couple of his classes. I'm telling you right now, teachers are not paid enough. That shit is like herding cats. But he's abdicating the responsibilities of head coach to me, except for the title, because one, he's a teacher at the high school and I'm not. Two, I've wrestled since I was in middle school. And three, I've been a professional wrestler for the past fourteen years."

She straightened, and her hair fell over her shoulders and breasts like liquid fire. He swallowed. Hard. And glanced away, lifting the bottle again.

"Wait a minute." She held out the hand not wrapped around the glass, shaking her head. "A professional wrestler? Like I'm-going-to-the-Olympics professional wrestler or John-Cena-you-can't-see-me professional wrestler?"

"You can't see me?" He rolled his eyes. "John Cena is a sixteen-time world champion and that's what you think of?"

"And he's a film star."

"Hello? This is my story," he pointed out.

"Sorry." She fluttered her fingers. "Please continue."

"Thank you." He dipped his head. "And yes. John-Cena-you-can't-see-me professional wrestler. I was with the Wrestling Federation Conference, the WFC, as Mr. Right for twelve years. Three-time world champion before I retired a couple of months ago."

"You're kidding me."

He took in her wide eyes, parted lips and stunned expression. And tried not to be *too* offended.

"No." He spread his arms wide, still clasping the neck of the bottle between his fingers. "I'm not kidding."

"So, thousands of screaming fans, stadiums, rings and body slams. *That* professional wrestler?"

He arched his eyebrows. "Are you going to be able to wrap your head around this? Or should I give you a minute?"

She tucked a thick strand of hair behind her ear. "You drop on me that you are a world-famous athlete and then don't give me a moment to digest this news?"

"Digest? Yes. Shock and amazement? A little less of that, if you don't mind," he drawled. "And besides, apparently, I'm not too famous. You didn't recognize me."

She shrugged. "Don't take it personally, Monster. I don't follow sports. And, honestly, I'm impressed. I thought you were a country bumpkin with a big-wheel fetish. Now I know you're a big-shot, famous country bumpkin with a big-wheel fetish."

Laughter rumbled in his chest, but he stifled his grin, giving her a bland glance. "Thank you for that."

"You're welcome." She shrugged. "But go on with your story. You arrive at the school. Meet Brian and he basically turns over the team to you because you're Mr.... What was it? White?"

"Right," Isaac corrected. "Mr. Right. As in the man of your dreams."

"Wow." She blinked. "This keeps getting better and better."

"Do you want to hear this or not?" he growled, amusement replacing the painful hollowness that had driven him across her lawn.

"Please do."

"So I spent the day with Brian, and he introduced me to the principal, the administration, other teachers, and finally, during fifth period, I met the team in the weight room."

He set the wine bottle down next to the chair and laced his fingers over his abdomen. The warmth from the humor she'd stirred in him started to ebb as he remembered standing in that large, well-equipped weight room with boys of varying ages and sizes, all staring at him.

"When I retired from wrestling, I honestly didn't have any plans other than returning home. Starting over and doing something different from what I'd done the last decade. When my sister proposed this position, I didn't think, I took it. Why not? I love kids, and wrestling… It's been a part of my life for so long, it's what I love, I enjoy. And I'm damn good at it."

He fell silent.

"Isaac?"

He started, jerking his gaze from his lap to Jenna. Until that moment, he hadn't realized he'd glanced away from her. Until this moment, he hadn't realized this was the first time she'd said his name.

It tore through him like the fiercest storm. Then rippled over him in the gentlest breeze.

His name in that ice-and-fire voice was both condemnation and revelation.

"Yes?" he rasped, because revelations were hell on the voice.

"Can I share something with you?"

"Of course."

She took another sip from her wine and studied him over the rim. "One of the features that sold me on this house was the porch. I loved it—especially the swing. It begs for someone to relax here with a good cup of coffee or glass of wine." She slightly tipped hers up. "And I enjoy doing just that. But only at night. I can curl up, and no one's able to see me. Daylight is too harsh, too… intrusive. But nighttime…that's different. It softens, it protects. Under its cover you feel safer." She took another sip and loosed a soft hum, her lashes lowering before she met his eyes again. "What I'm trying to say, Isaac, is whatever you share here stays in the dark. The sun will burn away my memory. So pick up your wine, Monster, and talk."

Safe? He hadn't felt safe in a long, long time. And why he did feel safe with a woman his sister described as having the "personality of a blade saw" he couldn't begin to explain. He didn't know Jenna Landon. He could easily state his dick liked her more than he did. And yet…

He shifted, propping his forearms on his thighs and staring at his loosely clasped hands.

And talked.

"Even showing up in Tampa with only thirty-two hundred dollars in my pocket and no job, no permanent address beyond an extended-stay hotel, I didn't have doubts about succeeding. About getting into FTR, about—"

"FTR?"

"It stands for Future. It's the developmental program of WFC, where wrestlers are trained and mentored. In FTR, we're all looking to be 'called up' and be the next breakout star. That's the hell of it, Malibu, I never doubted I would be called up. Arrogance? Or just stupidity? Whatever it was, it got me to the top of my profession. Got me my dreams. But standing in the high school weight room in front of those boys, the confidence that has always been a part of me was nowhere in evidence. I felt like a fraud. Like I didn't belong there. What if I…?" He trailed off. Swallowed hard but forced the confession past the constriction that damn near strangled him. "What if I disappoint them? What if I'm not who they need me to be?"

What if I'm not enough?

That, he couldn't voice.

The whisper barely floated through his head before he eclipsed it.

But he didn't shut it down in time. Not before it triggered thoughts of the other times he hadn't been enough.

To be a father.

To be a husband.

He was well acquainted with the bitter flavor of disappointment and the thought of tasting it again... His stomach cramped.

"You're underestimating them and yourself," she said in that cool tone of hers. And it sluiced over him like a wave of refreshing water. "Between your experience, your knowledge and your love of the sport, who better to teach those kids? And you already have a connection with them. Most, if not all of them, will feel they know you through your professional persona. The foundation has already been laid. It's up to you to build on it. And you sitting here on my porch worried about that connection—that says you'll be careful with them. That you'll build something strong and long-lasting."

She paused, and he lifted his head to look at her, expecting to find that direct stare on him. Instead, it was aimed at her glass of wine, as if it had transformed into a scything bowl and she sought answers in its depths.

"You'd be surprised how many kids are happy when you show up. There are some who don't have adults willing to do that. You can't go wrong by starting there."

Who hadn't shown up for her?

But almost immediately he shook that question free. If gossip was to be believed, she was the ex-mayor's spoiled, much-loved daughter. She'd grown up in a big home, with wealthy, adoring parents. Attention—or lack of it—wouldn't have been an issue for Jenna Landon.

And yet...

And yet, he couldn't stop the urge to shift over to that porch swing, cup her chin, tilt her head back so he could stare into her eyes and see the truth for himself.

What had she said? In the dark, she felt safer? Maybe in the shadows, those summer-sky eyes would reveal more than they would in the bright light of day.

"You said my day was shittier than yours, implying you had a shitty day," he said, straightening and grabbing the bottle of wine again. "Your turn. You know us Southerners are darn good at dispensing good ol' common sense wisdom."

She lifted her head, her eyebrow arching high. "Monster, you're as Southern as my Magnolia Bloom matte lipstick."

"Details, Malibu. Details. Now spill. On a scale of one to ten, one being singing birds and mice cleaning your house and ten being waking up bare-assed in a zombie-infested Atlanta hospital, how was your day?"

"On that scale?" She flip-flopped her hand. "I'd say about a five."

"A five, huh?" He smirked, but he noted the careful, tight grip on her glass. The curl of her toes into the swing cushion. The slight, almost imperceptible pull of her shoulders toward her ears. All signs of someone bracing themselves...protecting themselves. From what?

"What happened, Jenna?" he softly asked, the biting urgency in him belying the quietness of his tone. "Someone say something to hurt you?"

"Hurt me?" She tilted her head and a corner of her mouth lifted in a nearly-there sneer. "Me?" she repeated. "Isaac, you knew my name before we could properly introduce ourselves. That means someone probably regaled you with a full description of who I am. Do I sound like the kind of person who can be hurt? Especially by something someone *says*? News flash, Isaac. I am that *someone*."

"Oh my sister warned me about you."

What had he expected to flash across her face at his announcement? Anger? Irritation? Surprise? Anything but the awful resignation that flickered in her eyes. As if she'd readied herself for his, what? Rejection? Scorn?

Oh believe me, Jenna Landon is a chip off her father's block. And that would be the one marked rich, arrogant, rude, snobbish and mean.

Lena's words echoed in his head, but they just didn't jibe with the elegant woman who sat across from him, unaware how her pose—those beautiful, fantasy-inducing legs curled up under her hips, her arms almost crossed in front of her, clasping that tall glass of dark red wine—revealed a whisper of vulnerability she would deny.

A vulnerability she would resent him noticing.

"While my sister said you had the temperament of a blade saw, my mom compared you to a stiletto. I'm still not sure if she meant the blade or the shoe. Both are sharp and definitely pretty. She said that tongue of yours can cut a person to ribbons. I'm a witness." He held up a hand, palm out, smirking. But a moment later, he lowered it, and he let his smirk ease into a smile. "My niece, on the other hand, she likes you. Calls you Ariel from *The Little Mermaid*. The Disney version, mind you. She also remembers you buying her, her brother and uncle ice cream."

"I should've made the connection," she said, tapping a fingernail against the bowl of her glass. "You're Lena Hunter's brother."

"Yes." If possible, her expression became more

guarded, and he silently cursed. That hadn't been his intention. Especially when she'd been the most relaxed he'd ever seen her. "Which one are you, Jenna Landon?" he asked, his frustration leaking into his abrupt question. "The cold, reserved woman with a lethal tongue? Or the kind, generous woman who buys children ice cream when they don't have enough money?"

She silently stared at him, and he could've sworn sadness flashed in her eyes. But if it had, that emotion disappeared an instant before the corner of her mouth curled into a humorless half smile.

"Take my advice, Isaac. Don't make the mistake of reading more into me than what you see. Then you'll really know disappointment."

She unfolded her legs and rose from the swing. Wordlessly, he handed her the bottle, but she shook her head, and her smile warmed just a bit. The hit to his gut could be defined as more than *just a bit*.

"You keep that," she said. "Consider it a gift."

He arched an eyebrow. "A gift for what?"

"For the upcoming winning wrestling season, of course." She shook her head, heading for her front door. "You're really going to have to work on that confidence, Monster."

"Jenna?" he called out just as her hand curved around the knob.

"Yes?"

"I don't want the sun to burn away this night. Remember it."

She didn't move, didn't look at him. And when she finally entered her house, softly closing the door behind her, she didn't answer him either.

Or maybe, her silence was answer enough.

CHAPTER EIGHT

JENNA CLICKED ON the images tab and picture after picture filled the screen. Though she sat in the public library, using their Wi-Fi, she scrolled through each one.

She couldn't help herself.

Isaac Hunter, also known as Mr. Right, three-time Wrestling Federation Conference champion and two-time world tag team champion. One of the WFC's biggest and most popular brands in the promotion, he was its franchise player and its public face for almost a decade.

When she'd left the Bath Boutique for lunch, she'd come to the library with every intention of getting work done on her project. She'd found a small table in the corner near a window. After opening her laptop and her current project, she typed several sentences into her document. But then she'd ended up in the search engine, entering Isaac's name and conducting a deep dive as if he were the subject of a research thesis.

And now she skimmed through the images—skimmed. Hah. She examined, studied, analyzed.

Isaac, in a perfectly tailored pinstripe gray suit entering an arena. The dark waves of his hair skimmed his chin, the faint dip in his strong, stubborn chin more evident without scruff dusting his face.

Isaac, in the ring, standing on the ropes, sweat dampening his hair and dotting his chest. Black tights and boots molded to his slim waist and long, powerful legs.

Good Lord… She couldn't tear her gaze away from the magnificent…animal in the image. That beautiful, strong body that commanded her to look, admire. Lust. And she couldn't deny that order. He stole her breath.

Shaking her head, she gripped her wireless mouse harder and scrolled down. Only to halt on another picture. Try as she might, she couldn't move further.

Isaac, walking down a sidewalk, cameras flashing, with a gorgeous Black woman on his arm. She clicked on the image, finding a small gossip article about a restaurant opening and Diana Martin, CEO of the WFC, attending, escorted by her husband, professional wrestler Isaac Hunter.

Husband.

Jenna's heart thudded against her sternum, the beat echoing in her head, her ears. Isaac had a wife. A stunning, successful, wealthy wife. She was a CEO, for God's sake. Jenna flattened a palm to the area just below her breasts, where a knot of apprehension pulled.

No, not apprehension. Something darker, more twisted.

Like envy.

And…betrayal.

But that was absurd. They weren't friends. Nor confidants. He didn't owe her any explanations.

A memory of the night before drifted into her thoughts. Of Isaac sprawled in a chair on her porch, talking about his first day, confessing his insecurities regarding his new job. He'd shared some details about his past career, about his life in Tampa, but not about his marriage, his wife. Why?

With firmer movements than necessary, she closed the picture, leaving the others filling the screen. Wishing she could stop herself, but unable to, she clicked on another link. And then another. More pictures appeared on the screen. Isaac in the ring and with other wrestlers. Again with his wife. But it wasn't the photos that set her pulse thundering. It was the actual article.

It relayed the details of Isaac's divorce from Diana Martin after twelve years together and ten years of marriage, and his subsequent and curiously timed retirement from wrestling. Checking the date of the article, she noted it would've been only months later that he arrived in Rose Bend.

Is that why he'd moved here, bought a cute but small single-family home and accepted a low-paying job as a wrestling coach? Was he licking his wounds? Was he…hiding?

"Yes and amen. Now there's perfect evidence of how much God loves us, am I right?"

Jenna stiffened, straightening away from her laptop before slowly turning around and facing the woman behind her. Leontyne Dennison, Leo to her family and friends, stood there, grinning down at her, blue-gray eyes shining. The lovely brunette owned and ran Kinsale Inn along with her family, though for the past few months she'd done so part-time from New York, where her fiancé lived and played quarterback for the Jersey Knights.

"What're you doing here?" Jenna asked.

Instead of being offended at her rude question, Leo laughed.

"Oh how I've missed your sunny disposition. So much so that when I stepped in here and saw you sitting in this corner, I had to come over and bask in your effervescent glow." Leo waved a hand, apparently encompassing Jenna's...glow. Then she tilted her head, eyes squinting. "Or...that could be the result of the souls you've eaten for lunch. I'm just not sure."

Jenna snorted. Okay, so that was pretty funny.

"Don't you have a mattress to flip or an engaged couple to swindle out of their hard-earned money?" Kinsale Inn had also become a premiere wedding venue under Leo's guidance.

"When I could be here with you? Not a chance." Gripping the back of Jenna's chair, Leo leaned forward, narrowing her gaze on the computer screen. "So what're we looking at? Is that Mr. Right?" She stretched an arm over Jenna's shoulder and rolled her finger over the mouse, sending the picture skimming up. Her appreciative hum echoed in the air. "Oh yes, it is."

"Objectification, Leontyne?" Jenna curbed the insane urge to snatch the mouse out of Leo's hand and click to another screen. "Seeing as you're married to a man who is the subject of plenty of women's fantasies on a regular basis, I would've thought you'd be above that."

"Like hell. Have you seen the thighs on that man? They're sculptural masterpieces and deserve to be worshipped. And yes, I'm engaged to Owen but I'm not such a hypocrite I'd begrudge the sisterhood their appreciation of that man's superior body." Leo peered at the screen, then at Jenna. She wanted to duck her head to avoid that sharp, speculative gaze. "But why are you over here in a corner, surfing the net and ogling Mr. Right? Why hide it? I bet people would find you tons more relatable if they knew you eye-fucked Mr. Right along with the rest of us peons."

Good. God. "One, could you please keep your voice down? In case you haven't noticed, we are in a public library. Emphasis on the 'public.' And two—" Jenna arched an eyebrow "—what about me says I give a damn if people find me relatable?"

"Oh sweet pea, you don't really want me to answer that, do you? And besides, I don't have the time. I have to meet Owen at Mimi's Café for lunch. And though I begrudgingly like you, you're no match for him." Leo jerked her chin toward the laptop. "I would've never taken you for a professional wrestling fan. Hell, I would've doubted you even knew Mr. Right existed."

"Why do *you*?"

She shrugged. "I have a thirteen-year-old brother and sister. And Wolf."

Rounding the table, Leo pulled out the chair across from Jenna and plopped down. She folded her arms on the tabletop and that blue-gray gaze remained on her face, and Jenna forced herself to meet it. One of the characteristics that made Leo such an amazing businesswoman was her inability to back down from a challenge. Just months ago, she'd entered the town's annual beauty pageant even though getting on a stage terrified her. But she'd pushed through because that's what Leo Dennison did. That brazen courage and boldness had always mystified Jenna...and angered her. Angered her because she lacked what she so admired.

Still did.

She detested that part of herself.

"That still doesn't answer how you know him. Or are you a closet WFC fan? Because if that's the case, we can get a wrestling night going at the inn, ask Moe to bake cookies and settle in for some good ol'-fashioned ring action."

Jenna stared at her. "No, I'm not a fan."

And she didn't even address the offer for a get-together at Kinsale Inn with her family. The very idea was so ridiculous she didn't bother entertaining it.

"So what gives?" Leo tapped the top of the monitor. "Jenna, you may have tried to erase our friendship, but surely you can't forget that I can keep this up all day or you can just tell me what you're not telling me. I'm sure Owen would understand."

Jenna narrowed her eyes, irritation flaring. At Leo's shit-eating grin. And at Leo deliberately bringing up memories of a time when she'd been so innocent.

So different.

So happy.

A sharp retort that she had only one friend, Olivia, and she was currently in New York on business, hovered on her tongue.

But it didn't emerge. Because underneath her irritation, humor flickered. Because yes, she did remember what an absolute pest Leo could be. It was one of her more hilarious and endearing qualities. And Jenna... had missed it.

Not that she could ever admit that to Leo. She had a hard enough time admitting it to herself.

"Fine. If it will make you go away." Leaning back in her chair, Jenna crossed her legs. "He's my new neighbor."

"Neighbor, huh?" Leo peered at her, head tilted. "Nope. Not buying it. You liiiiike him."

"Seriously?" Jenna scoffed, barely managing not to roll her eyes. "What are you, twelve?"

"Oh. You must really liiiiike him." Leo jabbed a finger at her. "You're being a little bitchy."

"Love must've softened that mind of yours even further. I'm always a bitch, Leo."

"Bullshit." A small smile lifted a corner of her mouth. "No one messes with the bitch just like they don't mess with the good girl. Remember those words?"

Of course Jenna did; she'd said them to Leo just a few months ago when they'd been in the beauty pageant together. Back then, she'd meant them as a taunt, though. Leave it to Leo to twist her words around and make them a teachable moment.

"We both use our images to hide behind, to keep people at a distance. Your problem, dear Jenna, is I know you. I knew you when we were girls and I'm becoming reacquainted with you now. There's no going back for me and you."

"Are you threatening me?" Jenna asked, her frantic pulse and the prickling sweat on her palms belied the cool disinterest of her tone.

Because, oh God, fool that she was, she was interested.

She could count on one hand the number of people she could call friend—and still have two fingers and a lone thumb left over. Yes, she had no one to blame but herself.

Yet…slowly suffocating in a town full of people as they stared right at you? It was the loneliest and scariest feeling in the world. She'd cried out for help, to be *seen*. Sydney had rebelled, and Jenna had turned mean.

No one had ever asked why.

Yes, she couldn't wait to get out of Rose Bend because this town had failed her. But here Leo sat, dangling Jenna's most secret desire in front of her.

I see you. I want to get to know you again. I'm not leaving you.

Out of habit, Jenna wanted to lash out. Tell Leo she didn't need her company or her witticisms. Just because they'd shared the tragedy of their miscarriages didn't make them bosom buddies. That ugly, *terrified* part of Jenna longed to destroy this tenuous connection before it could grow into something more.

Something she could depend on.

Something she could love.

Something that would hurt like hell when it was snatched away.

That's what life had taught her, after all. *Love will only disappoint. Because love depends on people.*

Still…knowing all of this, she didn't stand, pack up her laptop and walk away from Leo.

She'd analyze why not later.

"If that's how you'd prefer to take it," Leo answered her question with another wide grin. "I call it a promise. A very firm promise." Her voice dropped into an ominous tone, but her cackle of laughter ruined the effect.

Not many people crowded the library in the middle of the day, but several of them glanced their way. Remi Howard, the librarian, tossed a look in their direction, but instead of a warning stare, her eyes widened and her lips parted. The surprise wasn't that Jenna sat in the library; this place had become her second home for work. No, the surprise etched on the librarian's face probably had more to do with someone willingly sitting across from her—especially Leo Dennison.

Jenna understood Remi's astonishment. She felt it as well.

"So what's the deal?" Leo tapped the top of the monitor again. "He's your new neighbor." She shook her head. "I've only been out of town for three weeks. And a celebrity moves in right under my nose. The grapevine around here is slipping! No one dropped this on me in the twenty-two hours I've been back."

"It's not like celebrities in Rose Bend are an oddity. Your fiancé, for example. A Super Bowl–winning quarterback. Ring a bell?" Jenna drawled.

"Meh." Leo waved a hand. "He's a football player. Mr. Right is an honest-to-God *superstar*. I mean, Sonny doesn't think I know it, but he has the Mr. Right action figure." Leo twirled a finger over the computer. "So you're googling your neighbor? There's this thing the rest of us mortals do and it's called talking. Why not just try that with him?"

Jenna heaved an aggrieved sigh. Outwardly, she sounded put-upon, but inside, panic clawed at her. There was a certain comfort in the familiarity of being alone. She knew it, understood it. This friendliness that Leo extended… Jenna couldn't trust it. Was too scared to trust it. Because a tiny part of her longed for what Leo offered.

"We're not doing this, Leo." Jenna exited out of the browser. "Whatever this—" she waved a hand back and forth between them "—is supposed to be."

"This," Leo said, mimicking her gesture, "is friendship. Or my version of a friendship submission hold. Get it? Submission hold? Wrestling?" When Jenna stared at her without blinking, Leo shook her head. "You have so much to learn if you're going to pin that man down for the count. Pin him down for the count? Get it? Cause's he's a wrestler?"

"Either that pity dick Owen's been giving you has pickled your brain or there is something seriously off with you."

Instead of being offended at Jenna's reference to her tumultuous beginning with her fiancé, Leo laughed again, garnering another round of looks in their direction. The woman was going to get them thrown out of the library. Wouldn't her father just love that bit of gossip?

"Do you really want to talk about my husband's dick? I mean, we can. Like how he keeps me super relaxed when he does this cert—"

"Hard pass."

"That's what I thought." Leo smirked, then pushed back her chair and stood. "Okay, nice diversionary tactic. But I'm here in town for the next couple of weeks. This isn't over. I'll have my answers, and probably over wine, pasta and cheesecake. I picked up a couple of things from Owen's chef." She wiggled her fingers and rounded the table. "And this is Rose Bend, which means you can't avoid— What the hell is *that*?"

Leo leaned all the way over Jenna's shoulder, peering at Jenna's screen, her eyebrows halfway up her forehead.

The granddaddy of all curses flew through Jenna's head. And right on its heels, her mother's voice hissed a scathing reprimand about manners. But Jenna couldn't care. Not with Leo staring at the laptop monitor where Jenna had mistakenly left up the contract she'd been reading before she'd started her internet deep dive on Isaac Hunter.

Fear froze her. Ready excuses crossed her mind but she couldn't grasp one of them.

"What is this, Jenna?" Leo dragged another chair closer and sank down into it. She jabbed a finger at the screen. "Why does that say Publishing Agreement? And please explain, why does it say Jenna Landon writing as Beck Dansing?"

"Could you keep your voice down, please?"

In a life of secrets, this was one of her biggest. Besides her miscarriage, this was the one she guarded the fiercest. No one but her publisher, editor and Olivia knew the truth. If her parents ever discovered her career as the *New York Times* bestselling young adult author Beck Dansing... Jenna shook her head.

God, how could she have been so stupid? So reckless and irresponsible? For five years she'd been so careful. Now the one thing that had been hers, that had been her joy, her safety net, was threatened with exposure. And she had no one to blame but her—

"Jenna." Leo covered Jenna's fist, which sat clenched on her thigh. "Jenna, look at me."

She jerked her gaze away from the laptop monitor and looked at Leo. Noted the concern in Leo's blue-gray eyes. The concern, the lingering shock and...pride.

That couldn't be right.

"You're fucking Beck Dansing? *The* Beck Dansing? The mysterious Beck Dansing that doesn't do signings or public events, that no one has seen?"

Still unable to speak, Jenna nodded. And even that hurt. After guarding this secret for so long, it went against the grain to admit anything easily.

"Jenna," Leo whispered, shaking her head, a smile

slowly curving her mouth. "How…? What…? I don't even know where to begin."

"I don't…" Jenna cleared her throat and fought the reflexive urge to pull her hand from under Leo's. "Can we save that for another day, too?"

Leo's expression softened, and she squeezed Jenna's hand.

"Yeah, we can."

"And, Leo, if you—"

"I won't tell a soul. Your secret stays with me. You can trust me."

Studying her for several long moments, Jenna nodded once more. "Okay."

"Good. But we're having this conversation. And I will hunt you down." Leo stood again. Then chuckled wickedly.

"What?" Jenna asked, wary as she closed out the contract and shut down her computer.

"Oh nothing." Another dark laugh. "I was just thinking… Beck Dansing is one of Sydney's favorite authors. Which makes *you* one of Sydney's favorite authors. Oh this is too delicious."

Okay, that *was* a little funny, considering Sydney detested Jenna.

Jenna arched an eyebrow. "You're finding way too much humor in that."

"Oh I am. I really am." Leo laughed. "Just promise me this." She touched Jenna's shoulder, halting her movements as she slipped her laptop in her bag. When Jenna looked at her, Leo said, "If you ever come clean, please, please let me be the one to tell Sydney."

She couldn't help it. Jenna huffed out a reluctant, soft bark of laughter.

"Deal, Leontyne. If that happens—and it never will—you can reveal the news to your friend so you can witness her heartbreak."

"You're the best, Jenna Landon. C'mon—" Leo tipped her chin up "—we can walk out together if you're leaving."

"No." Jenna met Leo's gaze and didn't waver even though the other woman frowned. "I'm heading to my mother's boutique. And though you think you want the start of this friendship, I doubt you've thought this through enough to be seen with me." Especially on Rose Bend's Main Street.

"Too late. I've already been seen with you." Leo waved a hand around the library.

"You know what I mean." And by that, Leo knew *who* Jenna meant.

Sydney Dennison would not be happy about Leo having a friendship with Jenna. Not after the hurt Jenna had inflicted on both of them, but especially on Sydney after she'd returned last year.

"I know what you mean," Leo agreed, seeing more than Jenna was comfortable with. "But unlike a certain pair of parents who want to dictate who their loved ones associate with, my family doesn't insist on a hive mind." She cocked her head. "They also believe in letting go of the past, and grace." Leo smiled. "Well, most of us."

"Good to know."

"I'll leave you to it then. Remember. Wine and pasta." With that goodbye, which sounded too much like a warning, Leo gave her a cheery little salute and walked away.

What the hell had just happened?

CHAPTER NINE

"ALL RIGHT, GUYS, circle up," Isaac called out, his voice ringing in the gym.

The group of twenty-two teenage boys who'd just returned sweaty from their cardio warm-up of jogging and running up and down the bleachers hustled over to gather around him.

"We're moving on to situations. Get into a high-crotch single leg position. One, two, three. Break."

On his word, the teens disassembled, finding partners. In each pair, one boy hooked the other person's leg on their arm, while his partner extended his arm, grabbing the first boy's thigh.

"On my whistle." Isaac paused, held up his stopwatch, then blew his whistle, the sharp note echoing off the gym walls.

For the next two hours, he and Brian worked on double leg takedowns, top and bottom positions and several other exercises that would create muscle memory, build up endurance and agility. By the time Isaac called the boys together again, sweat poured off their bodies, and they either stood or leaned over in that loose-limbed way that denoted exhaustion.

Perfect.

Isaac grinned.

"Line it up. Ten minutes of hell."

Groans filled the air, and he grinned wider. Passing the watch to Brian, he walked over in front of the team.

"Ready?" He lifted his chin at the head coach. "Push-ups!"

He dropped down and pumped out ten push-ups with the kids.

"Sit-ups!"

Flipping to his ass, he knocked out ten sit-ups.

"Mountain climbers!"

And they cycled through—sprawls, bear crawls, crab walks, duck walks, fireman carries, suicides and sprints. Isaac powered through the brutal marathon of exercises along with the team. Exhilaration that was the result of a good workout raced through his system.

"Great practice, guys, and strong finish. Well, good finish." He snorted. "Before you leave, weigh in." More groans peppered the air. "That's what I want to hear. Let's go."

With some good-natured muttering and complaining, the boys headed toward the weight room.

"They're looking good," Brian said, watching the team as another of the assistant coaches headed to the weight room to start the weigh-in.

After each practice, the boys stepped on the scale to ensure they were in their weight class. Of the twenty-two boys, they had a few wrestlers for the 135-weight class. Some for the 160 and 170, and Dorian, who was in the 200-pound weight class but could actually wrestle as a heavyweight. The rule was an athlete could wrestle up, but not down. Both Isaac and Brian believed Dorian could hold his own as a heavy weight. He was that damn good.

"Yeah, they are. By the time the first match gets

here in November, we'll be in good shape. And they'll only get better, their skills sharper, as the season progresses," Isaac agreed.

He'd only been working with the boys for a week now but damn if he wasn't already invested. For some of them, wrestling was clearly a fun extracurricular activity and another way to hang out with friends. And hey, nothing wrong with that. But for a few of them, like Dorian, this sport embodied more. It represented the difference between struggling to hold down a job while attending community college or receiving a full ride to a college or university of their choice. Those stakes were as big as they got.

And though he might question his purpose, he didn't question why he was in this school, with these teens. He had the knowledge, skill and experience they needed. And maybe, at this transitional moment in his life, he needed them, too.

"I knew they would respond to you." Brian clapped him on the shoulder, smiling. "First, you'd never catch my ass down there doing the ten minutes of hell." He laughed, shaking his head. "They bitch and moan but they love that you're grinding it out with them. You're good with them." He sighed, wincing. "I'm going to owe your sister big, and she's never going to let me forget it."

Isaac chuckled. "Yeah, man, sorry. Lena's never met an *I told you so* she didn't love."

"Damn," Brian muttered, then grinned. "You have dinner plans? I'm meeting Sarah over at Sunnyside Grille. You're more than welcome to join us. She's been dying to meet you anyway. I'm not supposed to tell you this, but she's a WFC superfan."

"I heard nothing."

He laughed. "So what about it? You keep your mouth shut about me telling secrets and come to dinner with us?"

"I'd love to, but I have a date with boxes I *still* haven't unpacked. If I want to keep my mother from invading my new house, I need to get all that squared away. But rain check, okay?"

"Definitely."

Forty-five minutes later, Isaac strode across the dark parking lot, waving goodbye to the last of the wrestlers and their parents. It'd been a good day. He'd started it off by spending the morning with his mother. Living in Tampa, he'd missed just dropping by her home on a whim. All the friends and found family couldn't replace the one he'd been born into—not being with them had been like having a limb amputated.

Now, after practice, as the parking lot emptied out, he couldn't battle back the thought anymore.

Will she be out on her porch tonight?

The question filtered through his mind, unbidden. And with it tagged along an image of a certain leggy redhead curled up on her porch, wineglass in hand, beautiful features relaxed, summer-blue eyes alert.

He'd looked for Jenna every evening, seeking her out in the shadows of her porch. But in the week since he'd joined her for that impromptu talk, the swing had been empty. Matter of fact, he hadn't seen Jenna in the last seven days at all. As if she had been actively avoiding him.

Or it could've been him who'd been doing the avoiding. Because both relief and need had twisted inside him every night he'd pulled into his driveway and spied the empty porch.

Relief, because that night had left him emotionally

stripped. He hadn't come to Rose Bend to form connections—certainly not with his beautiful yet prickly neighbor. His motives in moving here were discovering who and what he would be without the career that had shaped him for over a decade. Without the role of husband that had settled him for nearly as long. He didn't have time or the inclination for...connections.

Need, because of the very thing he said he didn't want. Those damn connections. On that porch, she had erased that ever-present loneliness. And for that moment, he'd felt understood.

It was dangerous, that feeling.

So yeah, best that Jenna hadn't been on her porch. Best that she'd removed temptation. Because he couldn't honestly say that had she been sitting warm and sweet in that swing that he wouldn't have joined her. And released more truths. And shared more of himself.

Yeah, definitely dangerous.

His cell vibrated in the pocket of his black sweatpants, and he paused near the door of Baby, removing the phone. Peering at the screen, he froze. The ringtone continued, pealing in the night air until it eventually stopped. And he still stared at the screen, which now bore the identification of the person who'd phoned him.

Diana Martin.

His ex-wife.

He'd taken many blows to the gut in his career. But none hurt like seeing his ex's name on his phone after months of silence. Like the little girl in the café the week before, he'd believed he'd healed. He'd believed he'd moved on.

How humbling to find out he'd lied to himself.

The phone rang in his hand again.

Shit.

He could *not* answer once more.

Or he could hit Accept, get this over with and find out what Diana wanted.

Gritting his teeth, he pressed his thumb to the screen and lifted the cell to his ear. "Hey, Diana."

"Isaac." His ex-wife's smooth, cultured voice caressed his ear. "Hello. How are you?"

"Good. How're you doing?"

"Fine. I'm doing fine."

Silence settled between them, and Isaac blindly stared at the tan-and-blue side panel of his Ford F-150, one hand still holding the cell and the other gripping the back of his neck. Even though he couldn't see Diana, he could easily imagine her sitting in her favorite royal blue office chair, dressed in one of her signature sexy power suits, gorgeous natural curls brushing her shoulders. Though it was almost six o'clock in the evening, she would appear as fresh as if it were eight o'clock that morning.

Diana never failed to look like exactly who she was—CEO and part owner of the world-famous WFC.

That had never been their issue, though.

Diana wanting to have it all—career, marriage and motherhood—and discovering she couldn't? That had torn them apart.

"What's going on, Diana? Everything okay?" Isaac pressed. Diana didn't do anything without purpose, and he needed her to get on to her reason.

"Yes, I'm sorry for calling out of the blue. Especially since we haven't talked in a while." Since they'd sat across from each other with their divorce attorneys at a conference table. "Paul brought an opportunity to me, and I promised him I would reach out to you."

Paul would be Paul Judd, head of Creative at WFC. He'd led the team of writers for the last ten years, and Isaac respected the man. But what "opportunity" could he possibly have to talk to Isaac about, seeing as how Isaac had retired from the WFC?

Unease curled in his stomach.

"I don't know what this—"

"Just please hear me out before you say no?" Diana asked. Then continued on before he spoke. "You retired as an undefeated champion, even though the title stayed with the organization. Still, you're an incredible fan favorite and many of them would love to see you return, even if it's for one special show. And that's what Paul is proposing. A story line with Daryl Granger that leads up to a one-night main event. The fans would love it, and we would definitely make coming out of retirement— even temporarily—worth it for you." She paused. "Not that you should've retired in the first place."

Isaac swallowed a heavy sigh, weariness seeping into his bones.

"We've been over this, Diana. My retirement is final, and I'm good with it—even if you and Paul might not be. While I appreciate the thought—" and he wasn't naive enough not to believe Paul and Diana had both considered how his return would affect WFC's bottom line "—I'm going to pass."

"Isaac," she said. "I don't want you to be rash. Take a beat, think on it and call me back tomorrow with an answer—"

"Diana, what're you doing?" he quietly asked.

A beat of silence, and then her sigh, full of frustration, filled his ear.

"I'm still looking out for you, that's what I'm doing,"

she snapped. "Our marriage didn't work out. That... happens." Her voice faltered, but almost immediately firmed. "That's life. But it isn't a reason to throw away your hard-earned career when you are at the pinnacle. *What am I doing?*" she repeated on a scoff. "I'm trying to stop you from compounding one misguided mistake with another one. It's not too late to come back to Tampa, Isaac. Come back to the WFC, and it can be as if you never left."

At the very last second, he clamped his teeth together and trapped his bitter bark of laughter.

"You can't be that naive, Diana." The corner of his mouth curled, and it felt hard. "I can return and somehow get spontaneous amnesia, forget about you having an affair with a man I called friend? Just carry on and *pray* that ratings don't dip so Paul doesn't work all that shit into my story line? No. I lived it. I refuse to play it out in front of millions for a buck and *entertainment*."

"That wouldn't hap—"

"Dallas, Rick and Donna."

Silence greeted his pointed reminder. The engaged couple had broken up, and when Donna began dating another wrestler, Paul wrote an angle for it. What had been an amicable breakup turned toxic. No, Diana couldn't make those promises to him. If it would engage the fans, raise ratings and bring in money and sponsors, she wouldn't nix the idea. It didn't make her a bad or greedy person; it made her a smart businesswoman.

Unfortunately, it also meant his feelings didn't mean shit when up against the bottom line. He hated to admit this, even to himself, but he didn't trust his ex-wife.

And fuck if a little piece of his heart didn't crack all over again.

"I wouldn't do that to you," Diana softly insisted. "I wouldn't do that to us."

"And I don't believe you," he replied, just as softly, with no anger. The rage had burned out a year ago, leaving only the ashes of grief. How sad was it that he mourned their friendship more than their marriage? "My answer is no."

"This is your pride talking, Isaac," she murmured. "I'm still going to give you a few days to think it over." She paused and a sigh reverberated down their connection. "There's nothing I regret more in my life than hurting you. I handled the aftermath of the adoption...badly."

The aftermath of the adoption. As if she described debris scattered across their lawn following a Florida storm.

We lost our child. The child who was already ours in our hearts.

The shout rattled against his skull, and it amazed him she couldn't hear it. But as quickly as the anger surged within him, it settled back into his dumping ground for emotions too overwhelming to deal with.

Regardless of her choice of words, Diana had been as devastated as him—if not more. She'd been the one to put her body through the discomfort of IVF treatments only for them to fail. Only to suffer a miscarriage. The adoption had been their latest attempt at a family, not their first. And Diana had been exhausted, grieving and angry as hell.

So out of that dark, whirling vortex of emotion, yes, she'd handled the fallout of the adoption badly. It didn't excuse her turning away from him, from their marriage, but with distance, he understood it.

Didn't mean he wanted to waltz back into the remnants of the world he'd left behind and stare into the faces of the people who'd blown it to pieces either.

"We're past that," Isaac said, reaching for the truck's door handle and yanking it open with more force than necessary.

He climbed in and started the vehicle as if he could drive away from this conversation. Instead, he gripped the steering wheel and stared out the windshield, wanting it to be over but unable to hang up on her. He respected her too much. But she needed to let him go. To let him move on. Because *this*, he thought as his grip tightened on the steering wheel, it was slowly grinding him to dust.

"Are we, Isaac? Are we really past it?" she whispered.

"Yes, we are." At least, he was trying to be. That's what this move to Rose Bend was about. Starting over. Learning to…be. "Diana, is there something else going on that you're not telling me about? With WFC? With you? Are you okay?"

"Would you still care?" She loosed a huff of sharp-edged laughter. "Would that have you leaving your picture-perfect town to ride to my rescue?"

"If there's one person who can damn sure rescue themselves, it's you," he said, but he couldn't abandon someone who'd been such an integral part of shaping who he was today. "But if you need a dented knight as backup, are you asking for one?"

After a long pause, she snorted. "No, Isaac, I'm fine. Just a little…melancholy tonight, I guess."

"Melancholy, huh?" A ghost of a smile whispered across his mouth. "The only time you'd break out the ten-dollar words were when we argued or you'd had too much to drink. We're not at each other's throats, so are you sipping on that Macallan from your office bar?"

"How do you know I'm in my office? And yes," she said, and he caught the warm smile in her voice.

"Because I know you," he murmured.

"You do. You're the only one who does."

He'd believed that to be true at one time. But now, he'd amend that statement. He knew as much of Diana as she would allow anyone to know.

In the end, that hadn't been enough for either of them.

Especially not him. Because if a person closed off parts of themselves, then he could never fully trust them. Because they didn't trust *him*. And what was a relationship without the foundational bricks of faith, of belief in one another?

Easy. There wasn't a relationship. Not a real, healthy one meant to go the distance.

"I'll leave you to your evening, Isaac," Diana said on a sigh. "But I'm not giving up on convincing you to reconsider this business proposition. I'm not accepting no right now. Just...think on it." Exhaling, she went silent for several moments, and Isaac almost thought she'd disconnected the call when she spoke again. "And thank you for answering the phone."

Before he could reply, she did hang up. Slowly, he lowered the cell from his ear, dropping it between his thighs. He'd come to Rose Bend, come home, to escape his past.

But what could he do when it refused to leave him alone?

CHAPTER TEN

JENNA PARKED HER car at the curb in front of her house, switching off the headlights. Not that she needed them. The old-fashioned streetlamps posted at regular intervals along the residential street provided adequate light for the path from the sidewalk to her porch.

And tonight, so did the lamp hanging from the propped-up hood of the truck in the driveway next door.

Déjà vu.

The huge, built man bent over the front of the truck—Baby, she silently snorted—with his head and shoulders inside the guts of it. The only thing missing from the first morning was the ear-splitting blast of bad music.

The chime of her cell dragged her from her inappropriate contemplation of her neighbor. Reaching across her console, she pulled her phone free. Spying the name on the notification, she opened up the message app.

I. M. Kelly: Checking in. Haven't heard from you in the last few days. Let me know if you're writing later.

I. M. Kelly, the number-one *New York Times* bestselling romance author. Also known as Israel Ford, the bartender over at Road's End, the local dive bar, at least he was until several months ago.

Jenna hadn't been the only person shocked to learn

they'd had a famous author living incognito among them for nearly two years—especially since Jenna had known the author for five years. They were published by the same house, met on the online authors group, and had formed a friendship, often brainstorming, critiquing each other's work and doing word challenges together, even though they wrote in different genres. When I.M.—Israel—had gone through a bad divorce and stopped writing for a couple of years, Jenna had missed him. But seeing as they'd only known each other as their pen names, she hadn't been able to reach out to him other than through their message app.

And now… She huffed out a laugh. What were the odds that two bestselling authors hid out here in Rose Bend? Except she hadn't outed herself. And had zero plans on doing so.

Israel had fallen in love, overcome writer's block and started writing again. All Jenna had ever had was this secret passion, this career, and revealing the truth would mean losing it. A Landon writing something as frivolous as YA paranormal books? Her father would see it as a personal affront, and her mother would consider it another of Jenna's shortcomings.

But at least she now had her friend back…even if he had no idea who she was.

And if he were to discover her identity, he might abandon their friendship.

A knot lodged in the base of her throat as she tapped out a reply.

Beck: Doing fine. Life decided to rear its ugly head a little, but everything's good. I'm definitely writing tonight. I'll let you know what time.

I. M. Kelly: Good. See you then.

Just as she was about to turn her phone off another text came through. A smile curved her lips as she pressed the notification and a picture of her best friend Olivia, feet propped up on her hotel bed and holding up a wine bottle filled the screen.

Olivia: Wish you were here, babe!

Jenna blinked back a sudden burn in her eyes. God, she missed her. Olivia had been away on business for a month now, setting up a technology system for a new company. Though Olivia had moved back to Rose Bend, her job still demanded some travel. And Jenna wished she was with her friend, too.

Out of Rose Bend.

Shaking her head, she typed out a quick reply, re-placed her cell, and grabbing her purse, exited the car. Rounding the hood, she glanced in Isaac's direction once more, unable not to. This had become a habit of hers—peeking over at his house when she arrived home, before hurrying into her house. Hurrying lest he catch her spying on him. Especially when she'd been so pro-active in dodging him.

Isaac Hunter was like that brown leather Fendi Sun-shine purse in Copley Place in Boston.

An utter temptation she couldn't afford.

She was horrible at evading temptation.

Exactly why that purse sat on the top shelf of her closet *and* she strode across her lawn toward her neighbor.

And as she neared him, the harsh admonishments in her head didn't stop her feet from moving forward.

Definitely didn't prevent her from admiring the stretch of black cotton over his shoulders and back. Thick muscles flexed and shifted in an erotic dance, mesmerizing her. He ought to charge money for this show. And it should shame her that she ogled the man, objectified him as Leo had accused earlier, but she couldn't help it.

He was beauty in the flesh.

And there was no way she could let him know.

Knowledge like that in his hands would render her vulnerable. And she didn't do vulnerability. Didn't do anything that resembled weakness. People were much too quick to take advantage of that.

She gave her head a hard shake. If she harbored any sense of self-preservation, she should be satisfied with her Fendi purse and walk away before he noticed her. Or go buy the pink Fendi if she needed to indulge.

Because shelling out thirty-one hundred dollars would be a hell of a lot less destructive than approaching this man who threatened her determination to make it through the next two months without causing any waves.

Isaac Hunter was the very definition of *waves*.

And yet, she still approached him.

"If your truck requires this much work, maybe you should consider trading it in for something from this century."

He didn't lift his head—didn't even glance over at her.

Well, damn. She frowned. That was rude.

And after she'd used one of her best lines, too.

Oh wait. She noticed the black bud tucked into his ear. That explained him ignoring her.

She reached up and tapped him on a shoulder.

He jerked, slamming the back of his head against the underside of the hood.

"Son of a bitch!"

She grimaced. Yes, absolutely déjà vu.

Whipping around to the side, he stared at her for a solid, heavy moment. Then, lifting one hand to rub at the back of his head, he removed his earbuds with the other. The twang of guitars and a woman's voice poured out of the little black pods.

"I wasn't blasting my music this time, Malibu. So now what's your excuse for trying to give me a concussion?"

She arched an eyebrow. "Fun?"

His eyes narrowed, but the twitch of his mouth ruined the effect. "I always suspected that beautiful face hid the soul of a sadist."

Beautiful face?

She fought not to betray her reaction to the throwaway compliment. Of course, she'd been called beautiful before—that wasn't arrogance, just fact. But never, not since she'd been a naive teen, had the compliment given her butterflies. It embarrassed her to even think the word, but that fluttery, too warm, twisty sensation just under her navel was definitely...butterflies.

"You could've asked anyone in town, I'm sure they would've gladly informed you."

He cocked his head, studied her in the glow from his lamp. Only years of existing under Helene's "tender" tutelage kept her from glancing away. From revealing how exposed she felt.

"This is the second time you've made a point of mentioning how everyone else in this town sees you. And how I should form my opinion of you based on theirs.

If I didn't know any better, I'd think you were trying to scare me away."

"Scare? No. Offer you a neighborly warning? Maybe."

"Is that why you came over here? To deliver that warning?" He plucked a rag from the pocket of his black sweatpants and wiped his hands, his gaze not wavering from hers. "I get we don't know each other that well, but I'm not the type to substitute people's views for my own." He paused. "It's a Southern thing."

She wasn't going to smile. She was *not* going to smile.

"No, actually, I came over here for purely selfish reasons. To satisfy my curiosity. You choose the oddest times to work on your truck. Right at dawn or in the dark. Why not—I don't know—during the day? Or even put it in the garage where it's not an eyesore."

"One—" he flicked up a finger "—Baby is *not* an eyesore. Two," he continued, adding another finger, "no one touches her but me. And three…" A small frown marred his forehead, and he lowered his hand, tucking the rag back into his sweatpants.

"And three?"

For the first time since crossing her lawn, she looked at him—really looked at him. Noted the dull indigo eyes. Noticed the taut clench of his jaw and the stiff angle of his chin. Caught the almost mechanical movement of his usually graceful body.

"Three," he continued, releasing the rod holding up the hood and gently lowering it. Turning to her, he said, "Working on the truck, no matter the time of day, calms my mind. Lets me think. Or not think. Which, sometimes, is much better. Anyway—" he shrugged a shoulder "—it's cheaper than therapy."

"You're apparently a big-deal star athlete. You can afford therapy."

He stared at her, then snorted. "Fair point. But I can't get grease under my nails sitting on a counselor's couch."

"Why do you need to think—or not think—tonight?" she asked, uncertain why she continued to press him. Hadn't this been the very reason she'd stayed inside the house this past week? So she wouldn't get involved? That night on her porch had been an aberration. Yet here she stood…aberrating.

With this man, she couldn't help herself.

And that sent alarm skittering through her. Because she couldn't explain it. Couldn't resist it. And like on her porch a week ago, she found she didn't want to.

"Have you eaten dinner?" The question popped out before she realized it. But she didn't rescind it.

For the first time in longer than she could remember, nerves tumbled through her belly as she awaited his answer. Excitement.

Yes, that's what rippled along her veins like a crackling current. It'd been so long, it'd taken her a moment to identify it.

"No," Isaac said. "I haven't. You offering?"

"I'm offering," she confirmed.

A smile slowly curved his lips.

"Then I accept. I'm driving." He jerked a thumb over his shoulder.

"Hold up there, Monster. I'm not getting into that relic. *I'm* driving."

"What?" He frowned. "I may not be offended at your attitude toward Baby, but she's not as forgiving. Besides—" he jabbed a finger in the direction of her black BMW M4 "—I'm not fitting in that."

"You're abnormally large, but of course you'll fit. Let's go." She pivoted and started back across his drive-

way. "And don't even think about demanding to get behind the wheel. No one drives my car but me."

"Damn women's lib," he muttered behind her.

"Yes, yes, we're fighting the patriarchy tonight. Now
hurry up. I'm feeling like a bacon cheeseburger."

"Well, shit, Malibu." He jogged to catch up with her.
"You should've led with that."

She didn't stop, didn't turn around or glance over
her shoulder. Which was a good thing. Otherwise, he
might've glimpsed the smile curving her mouth. And
well…no. That couldn't happen. Not when she wasn't
comfortable admitting that smile existed.

"So where are we going?" he asked, pausing next to
the passenger's door.

She pressed the key fob, unlocking the car. "I'm
going to tell you what my parents used to say to me—"

"You're such a pretty little girl and we love you?"

Jenna blinked, her lips popping open in surprise.
Well, no. Her heart clutched. She hadn't heard anything
like that in so long she couldn't even recall the last time.

"No," she said, quickly recovering and opening
her door. "Get in, be quiet and you'll see when we get
there."

Isaac laughed. "Sweet talker."

This time, she suspected he saw her smile.

And she almost didn't mind.

"PROMISE ME YOU won't take offense, okay?"

Jenna glanced at Isaac as she slid a French fry between her lips, eyebrow arched.

"Understanding that I'm taking my life in my hands
when I say this," he said, his own fry clasped between
his fingers. Waving it up and down, he narrowed his

eyes on her. "Nothing about you says, 'I know where to find the best bacon cheeseburger in the vicinity of Rose Bend and Mount Holly.'"

"You're lucky this burger has me particularly mellow or else I would be offended," she said.

He wasn't lying.

Marilyn's Hamburger Haven was a dining spot in Haroldstown, a slightly larger town than Rose Bend, and she'd discovered it on her way to the hospital there. The place wasn't much of a looker, but it served the juiciest, most delicious burgers in New England.

Just another secret she kept to herself.

And not so much the burger joint, although her mother would definitely throw an unladylike fit if she discovered Jenna ate something as plebian and calorie-laden as greasy ground beef and fries. No, what worried Jenna more was her mother and father finding out why she was out in Haroldstown in the first place.

Secrets.

She sat on a throne of them.

He chuckled and nodded to the view in front of them. "How did you find this place?"

Jenna turned her gaze to the water beyond them.

The moon reflected off the surface, and the tiny ripples in the river carried the leaves that had fallen there like little canoes to a faraway destination. *This place* was an isolated, beautiful spot on the other side of Rose Bend. A small dock stretched out over the water, and on the other side of the bank, the lights of the town shone like jewels under the shadows of Monument Mountain and Mount Everett. During the day, the gold, red and orange leaves would provide a brilliant mantle of their own over Rose Bend, like a queen's royal robe, declaring her glory.

And at night? It proclaimed another, different beauty. A quieter, more subtle one, but no less stunning. A person just had to look.

"By accident, actually," she murmured. "I was on my way back home from Haroldstown one day and happened to spot it. You can't really see it from the road because the dock is hidden by that small rise." She waved at the hill behind her. "But I did and had to stop. And I ended up sitting on this dock for hours. That was my first time, but not my last. It's…peaceful out here." She closed her take-out box and set it aside then pulled her coat tighter around her neck. "Since you were searching for a little peace earlier while working on your truck, I figured maybe this place could offer you some."

"Thank you," he said. "For this place. And the burger."

"And the bacon. Bacon makes everything better."

"Facts."

They glanced at each other. Snickered.

In the next moments, their amusement passed on the evening air, quiet replacing it.

"Remember what I said on my porch? The same goes for here. Whatever you say stays between us." She curled her legs under her, turning to face him more fully. "So do you want to tell me what had you under the hood of your truck 'calming your mind'?"

He bent his knees and propped his forearms on top of them, his big hands hanging in front. "That must be your favorite pose. You sat like that on your swing, too."

Shock reverberated through her. No one noticed details like that about her—or if they did, no one had shared them. That he noticed made her feel special…

seen. And how did that reflect on her? That the smallest kindness could leave her so shaken? So humbled?

So hungry?

Better not to dwell on that.

"Are you stalling, Monster? You don't have to talk if you don't want to. We can just sit here or head back. Your choice."

He gazed out over the water for several long moments, and finally his broad back rose and fell on a sigh.

"My ex-wife called earlier."

Those words shuddered through her like an earthquake. Well, she hadn't expected *that*.

"I take it you don't speak to her often."

"No, not since the divorce." His eyes narrowed on her. "You don't seem surprised to hear I was married. I don't remember mentioning it the other night."

"This is a small town." She'd been busted by Leo researching Isaac but damn if she'd admit that to him. "Gossip and God are religions."

"Right," he drawled. "Gossip, God and Google."

"The great triad, I hear."

He snorted, a smile flirting with his full mouth before he sobered.

"She called to offer me a business proposition. Which would include me temporarily coming out of retirement, returning to WFC for a short-term story line and a one-time event."

When he fell silent, Jenna murmured, "And this is a bad thing?"

Yes, it is, a voice whispered across her mind.

Why? He was her neighbor. They didn't have a relationship. All they had was an early-morning dustup and a late-night conversation. She wasn't even sure they liked one another. So what did it matter if he returned to wrestling?

It did.

And it did, because for the first time, she'd met someone who didn't judge her based on her past—a past she'd written but couldn't edit—and it felt good.

Yet dangerous.

She waited for that other shoe to drop. Even now, a tiny part of her expected him to realize he shouldn't be here with her. Not because she was Jenna Landon, ex-mayor's daughter and golden girl of Rose Bend. No, because he would glimpse the imperfections, the secrets, the facade that sat on her like flaked gold. Then he would leave without looking back.

Like Holden Daniels, after the most traumatic period of her life.

Like Chris.

Like her parents. They hadn't left physically, but emotionally? She'd been orphaned fourteen years ago.

"On its face, no, the proposition isn't a bad thing," he said, thankfully snagging her from her thoughts. "But it wouldn't be a retired world champion stepping back into the ring for a special one-night event. For me, it would be returning to a world I walked away from and acting like nothing has changed. Like *I* haven't changed. For twelve years, I lived by a script, pretending to be this character. I chose to do that for my career, I'm not signing up to do that in my personal life. I left for a reason—or reasons. There's no going back, no matter how I might wish things turned out differently."

"By 'reason,' do you mean your divorce?"

"One of the reasons, yes."

Jenna nodded. God, she didn't want to ask the question poking at her, but apparently, Isaac had it wrong. She wasn't a sadist but a masochist. And prying into his business knowing she might not want the information proved that theory.

"Do you still love her? Is that your other reason for not wanting to return?" Jenna went still as she awaited his answer.

"Not how you mean, no." The frown wrinkled his forehead again.

"Please don't say, 'I love her, but I'm not in love with her.' The cliché might compel me to shove you off this dock. And fair warning, that water is freezing this time of year."

He exhaled on a low chuckle. "Since skinny dipping wasn't on my bingo card for this week, I'll pass."

Skinny dipping.

That big, wide-shouldered, deep-chested, powerful-thighed body naked and wet. The image of him emerged in her head, vivid and so damn real, she could feel the droplet of water on her fingertip…on her tongue. Suddenly the cool night air wasn't a problem. Not when she burned from the inside out.

She blinked and shifted her gaze away from him, staring at the ethereal view of Rose Bend under the inky sky and pearlescent moon's glow. It was safer.

"Yes, I love Diana, my ex-wife. When you spend over a decade of your life with someone and go through the worst life has to throw at you, then a signed piece of paper can't eliminate the experiences that bond you. Or the love that brought you together in the first place. But those feelings shift into something different. Because those same experiences irreversibly change you.

And you just can't see each other the same way. Still, the feelings don't disappear."

She understood that.

The echoes of love remained like distant whispers on the wind.

"She cheated."

Jenna didn't have to look at him to feel his weighty, concentrated gaze.

"I never said that."

"Didn't you?"

She finally glanced at him and immediately became ensnared by his dark stare.

Protectiveness emanated from the stiffness in his frame, the hint of warning in his tone, the narrowing of his eyes. Even now, as his body language confirmed her guess, he sought to protect his ex. What must that be like? To have someone cover you, put your welfare ahead of their own? She didn't have that—didn't think she'd ever had that.

A hole creaked just behind her sternum, and she rushed to cover it before a scream could rush out of it. Because if one cry sneaked out, she might not be able to shut down the others that followed. That patch might collapse under the deluge, taking her with it.

And she'd worked so hard not to break.

To ensure no one would ever break her again.

"I won't make you say it," she murmured, her heart thudding against her rib cage. "I wonder if she knows that she still has a fierce protector in you."

"Maybe I'm protecting myself," he said, shifting his body slightly toward her. "Have you thought of that? Did you consider that I might be the one with something to hide? That I inflicted the damage?"

She had considered it. For several seconds.

"Yes. And no, that isn't what's happening. One, I don't think you would defend yourself. You would just be honest and own your shit. And two, you wouldn't try so hard to convince me that you were the offender."

"You've known me five minutes, Jenna."

No heat colored his tone. Just the mildest curiosity and more than a hint of *I'm about to shut this down*. Yet, it was the lack of anger that propelled her to continue speaking.

"And three, you're the former world champion who walked away from the height of his career to hide in Rose Bend. Yes, all of us inflict damage," she agreed. God, she should know. "And maybe you are protecting yourself, or you wouldn't be here. But your idea of protection is wrapping yourself in wool, insulating yourself from whatever it is you left Tampa to escape."

"'A wicked man flees when no one pursues,'" he murmured, tapping his foot. "That used to be one of my mom's favorite scriptures, one she'd throw at me when I was a kid." His heavy sigh punched the air, and he bowed his head, tunneling his hands through his hair. "We...lost our son almost two years ago."

Shock reverberated through her like a sonic blast, and she planted a steadying hand behind her on the dock. It took every scrap of control not to curl in on herself.

Or crawl into his lap and wrap her arms around him. Offer both of them comfort.

"He..." She paused, slicked her tongue over suddenly dry lips. "He died?"

"No."

Relief poured through her, that flood washing away

the grief and pain for him—for her. Then he turned his head and looked at her. And that relief became a rock that sank to the bottom of her stomach. The stark agony in those indigo eyes, it stole her breath. His baby didn't die—thank God—but whatever happened…it'd felt like a death. His eyes didn't lie.

The harsh rasp of her breath echoed in her head. Comfort wasn't her…area of experience. Though she'd seen others offer it, she'd rarely been on the receiving end. And giving it…well, that terrified her. What if her best intentions only made the situation worse? What if he didn't want comfort from her? What if she put herself out there only to have him turn away—

The questions screamed in her head. She dropped her other hand to the outside of her thigh, palm up.

"I don't know what to—" she began, the words tripping over themselves. Embarrassment flashed through her and she stopped. "I want to—" She tried again. And stopped again.

But this time, mortification didn't halt the verbal stream.

The warm, rough palm sliding over hers did.

"We'd gone through a private adoption agency that paired pregnant mothers with adoptive parents for their babies. Her name was Shelly, and out of three possible couples, she chose us. Said we felt the most like family to her. And we treated her like she belonged to us. Either me or Diana went with her to the prenatal appointments. When she graduated from college with her master's, we attended the ceremony. We included her in the decisions when we started decorating the nursery. She became more than the young woman carrying the baby we'd desperately wanted for years. She became…

family. Our son—because even though he wasn't here yet, he was already our son—had made our family complete. And we were…happy. Fuck, we were so naively, stupidly happy."

He tipped his head back, and his throat worked as he swallowed. Her fingers itched to stroke that strong column, to trace the telltale sign of his emotional battle.

"Shelly asked Diana to be in the room with her when she gave birth, and I waited outside. Those were the longest nine hours of my life. But when I got to hold my son…" He released another sigh and it trembled on the night air.

For a moment, his fingers reflexively tightened around hers, and she gripped his harder. Gave him something—someone—to cling to.

"I'd never believed in love at first sight or miracles until the moment I held him in my arms," he continued. "I've fought in rings, wrestled against men twice my size and won. But staring down into that pink, wrinkled face, cradling his negligible weight against my chest—I've never felt so powerful or fragile at the same time. And then, thirty-four hours later, that joy had transformed to the kind of pain that leaves you wondering how in the hell you're still breathing. The adoption counselor called us the morning we were headed to the hospital to pick up Sam—that's what we'd named him. Samuel Liam Hunter. Shelly had changed her mind. She'd decided to keep him."

"Isaac…" Jenna breathed.

His foot tapped harder, quicker.

"We…we were broken after the loss of—Sam." He emitted a harsh laugh that had to rub his throat raw. Because it sounded like it hurt. "Do you know this is the first time I've said his name out loud since then? And twice in a matter of seconds. This must be that healing I've heard so much about."

Jenna briefly closed her eyes, and a memory flickered across her eyelids. Isaac in Mimi's Café. The stricken look on his face when he'd glimpsed Patience, Sydney's daughter. The hurried rush to the exit as if he were chased by ghosts—and in a way, he had been. Ghosts from his past that still howled in his head, his soul.

"This adoption," he continued in that low, worn voice, "was our latest attempt to have children, but nowhere near our first. Throughout our marriage, Diana suffered through failed rounds of IVF, a miscarriage. For years, she wouldn't even consider adoption, but it wasn't until IVF was no longer a viable option that she finally gave in. I convinced her this could be our path to being parents, that we didn't have to give up on our dream. She tried *because of me*. And *that* happened. She was there when he was born, for God's sake. Got to hold him, hear his first cry. Diana wasn't the same, and all because I pushed the adoption idea. We were broken after Sam, but *I* broke *us*."

Jenna glanced down at their clasped hands, studying them. And for a moment, she pressed their palms together harder, needing to imprint the sensation of his toughened skin to hers. Maybe he needed that from her, too.

"I'm sorry about Sam. I—" Out of habit, her throat closed around the next words, trapping them.

The subject skated too close to her own secret, and she'd kept it for so long that her self-preservation instincts kicked in. She couldn't risk it. Though she apparently trusted him enough to sit with him on this out-of-the-way dock in the dark. But trusting him with knowledge that rendered her vulnerable? She couldn't do it.

Life had taught her what happened when she gave pieces of herself to someone. They rarely gave them back. And if they did, those shards were shattered beyond repair.

"Isaac." She released his hand and shifted, turning more fully toward him. "I can only imagine the pain and loss you and Diana suffered." Almost the truth. She could do more than imagine. "That *you both* suffered. Every failed IVF, the miscarriage, every dimming of hope, another inch of a dream slipping away—you can't survive that and not emerge unscarred. And that was before the adoption. An adoption you agreed to do as a couple."

Jenna tilted her head, her gaze running over the grim line of his mouth, the stark jut of his cheekbones. The purple, almost black shadows in his eyes. "You went into it as a couple," she said, "eyes wide open to all the possibilities of what could happen. To suggest that you pressured her actually steals her agency over how she decided to pursue motherhood."

A small frown creased his eyebrows, and she gripped the hand she'd released only moments ago. A surge of heat barreled up her arm and into her chest. Her breasts swelled, growing heavier, nipples beading with that bolt of lust. She almost jerked her hand back, but something needier had her holding on.

Holding on to that heat she hadn't experienced in— God, this didn't have a comparison.

Holding on to the emotional connection she craved just as much as that punch of lust.

"Isaac," she continued in spite of the convoluted and murky emotions swirling inside her, "the adoption falling through wasn't your fault. It wasn't anyone's fault. From what you described, I'm sure Shelly loved you and Diana as family and fully intended to let you adopt her baby. But when she looked at her son, she couldn't give him up. That decision had to be so difficult for her, knowing her greatest joy would cause you two so much pain. There's no way you could have predicted that, Monster," she murmured. "Let the guilt go. It's not yours."

His eyes briefly closed. She didn't speak, granting him time to gather his thoughts. But when she tried to untangle her fingers from his to stand and grant him privacy, his grip tightened, refusing to let her go. A dangerous joy welled inside her. She took a moment to indulge in it before ruthlessly smothering it.

Enjoying it would lead to seeking more. And that would lead to addiction and disaster. For her.

"Let go of the guilt over your ex's actions after the loss of Sam, too," she quietly said. "Grief and pain—they make us lash out, burn bridges, hurt others because we can't contain the overwhelming agony in ourselves. We go scorched earth, and only afterward do we look around and survey the damage. And feel regret for it."

Faces of those she'd left in her path like wreckage swam in front of her eyes, and though she wanted to erase them, she didn't—wouldn't. She had to sit in the knowledge that she'd caused pain and live with it. Some things she couldn't outrun.

"She was your wife, and you were her husband.

Turning away from you and the marriage didn't solve the problems you had. Breaking vows didn't make the pain disappear. You didn't drive her to cheat. That was her choice and hers alone."

"I didn't say I blamed myself for that."

"Didn't you?" Jenna murmured, repeating her words from earlier. "I think you should lay down the burden of guilt and let that man who's running stop and rest for a while. He must be exhausted as hell."

His shuddering sigh was the only response she received. That and the bowing of his head.

Silence fell over them. The soft ripple of the water, the muted sounds of nocturnal insects and the occasional swish of a passing car on the road above them occasionally broke the quiet. The air cooled even more, and the breeze crept beneath the collar of her coat, tickling her neck, yet she didn't move. There'd been a time—several times—when she'd sat, huddled alone in the dark wishing someone would refuse to leave her there by herself. Would just hold her hand.

Another strong breeze swept over them, and she shivered.

"Let's get out of here," he said.

Isaac loosened his fingers from hers, unfolding his big body and shoving to his feet. She flattened her palms to the dock to follow his lead.

"Here, Malibu." He extended his hand toward her, and she stared at that wide palm as if she hadn't been clutching it for the past forty-five minutes.

Unease spiked within her, and God, wasn't that a case of closing the barn door after the horse had bolted. Squelching the ridiculous disquiet stealing through her, she slid her hand over his, and he tugged her to her feet with a strength that had heat unfurling in her stomach. And as quickly as those flames ignited, she worked to extinguish them.

Not the time, not the place.

And you're delusional if you think you have any control over this. She'd learned the cold, harsh way what happened when she allowed her vagina to overrule her reason, her logic. Hell, she still suffered the consequences now. Every glance into her parents' faces reminded her of the repercussions of losing control.

Isaac bent and picked up the remains of their dinner, tossing it into the plastic bag. But when she turned to leave, he didn't follow. Not hearing the heavy fall of his footsteps behind her, she glanced over her shoulder. He remained standing on the dock, his large frame silhouetted by the moon. Pivoting back around, she waited, again not rushing him.

"Thank you," he finally said, his low, worn voice carrying the short distance to her. "I—" He thrust a hand through his hair, fisting the thick dark strands before his arm fell to his side. "Thank you," he repeated.

And those two words contained a wealth of things left unsaid.

"You're welcome," she whispered.

He walked toward her, closing the distance between them.

She should've started toward the car parked on top of the hill. Instead, she remained frozen, watching his long-legged, sensual stride bring him to her. He halted in front of her. And she held her breath as he slowly lifted a hand, cupped her jaw and brushed the pad of his thumb over her cheekbone.

She ached with raw need as he dropped his arm and stepped back, leaving her skin hot, flushed—branded.

"You, Jenna Landon, are a heel."

She blinked, the dense fog enshrouding her brain taking precious seconds to dissolve and lift.

"What?"

The corner of his mouth quirked, but those deep purple eyes roamed her face as if seeking out every one of her secrets. A quiet panic infiltrated her surprise, and she shook her head.

"A heel," he said. "It's a wrestling term. It's the person who pretends to be the bad guy for the story line, for the cameras, but in real life they're not. Since I've stepped foot in Rose Bend my family has warned me about you. Hell, *you've* warned me about you. And I've seen with my own eyes how you interact with people, like in the coffee shop. But it's for show, isn't it? Oh I'm sure it serves your purpose, whatever that is. But it is not who you are."

He leaned forward, his breath ghosting over her lips, and for a moment her heartbeat stuttered. Because in that moment, she imagined what his kiss would taste like. Earthy, spicy and an indefinable, musky flavor of *him*.

"I got your number, Malibu."

He was bluffing.

That all-too-incisive stare studied her for a reaction, and she met his gaze, steadily, without blinking.

But inside?

Inside, she quaked.

He threatened her with the very thing she feared most—and craved most.

To be seen.

No one had taken the time, the effort to really look beneath the hair, the clothes, the attitude. They'd always accepted her at face value and either been intimidated or put off. No one had gone that extra step to ask why, to see more.

To discover if *she* was more.

Yet...

The thought of anyone attempting to dig beneath that surface terrified her. Because what if they only uncovered fool's gold? What if they found out she was far from the perfect daughter, the perfect socialite, even the perfect snob? What if they discovered the only thing perfect about her was how flawlessly flawed she was?

"I'd hate for you to get your hopes up, Monster," she said. "There's no pretense about me. I'm the real deal."

Better if he believed the negative.

That way, if he discovered the truth, the disappointment wouldn't be so great.

Turning, she walked away from him. From temptation.

"Let's go. You have school in the morning."

CHAPTER ELEVEN

ISAAC CLIMBED HIS neighbor's porch steps for the second time in three weeks. And for the second time in three weeks, he followed a whim, acting purely on impulse.

A Saturday morning, he should be relaxing on his couch or taking in a college football game or even restocking his pitifully low refrigerator and cupboards. Anything other than showing up at his neighbor's house with a spur-of-the-moment invitation that she would almost assuredly turn down.

This was Jenna Landon, after all.

The queen of Say No First and Slam the Door in Your Face Second.

He snorted to himself, then still raised his fist and knocked. When several moments passed without an answer, he knocked again. And then again, just 'cause.

Before he could knock a fourth time, the door opened, and he stared at Jenna through her storm door.

Yeah, this had to stop.

His dick got hard for her.

That he could handle. A man didn't stare at a woman with hair like gold and fire, eyes like summer and a face that could easily grace the cover of a magazine and *not* get hard.

But it was more than that.

Excitement and lust sped through his veins like they

were a racetrack. He'd known addicts to all kinds of drugs—steroids, opioids, cocaine, just to name a few. A person didn't swim in the treacherous seas of entertainment as long as he had and not see some shady shit. The one thing all addictive behavior had in common, though, was the addict's craving for the next hit.

That's what Jenna Landon had become for him.

His next hit.

His very fucked-up way of avoiding the murky, unknown future that stretched out before him.

His very fucked-up way of avoiding the painful past that stretched out behind him.

What would Jenna say if he told her, *I'm using you to forget*?

He thought back on the woman who'd held his hand on the dock several days ago. Recalled the firm, soothing hold, the straightforward gaze and the even more no-bullshit conversation. Would she appreciate his honesty? Or would she resent him for taking advantage of the kindness she would deny she possessed?

The answer to that scared him.

"Monster," she greeted in that almost aloof tone that stroked over his skin.

Yeah, if she understood what that voice did to him, she might never speak to him again.

"Malibu." He jerked his chin toward the storm door. "Can I come in?"

For a moment, he sympathized with a vampire, waiting on that coveted invite inside a house. He sensed not many people received it, and damn if he didn't want it. Hunger for it.

Several moments passed before she released the latch on the storm door and she pushed it open, silently issuing that invitation. Fierce satisfaction lit him up like a torch.

Stepping forward and into her home, he didn't even pretend to curb his curiosity.

The small, postage-stamp-size entryway boasted four gorgeous paintings of New England small towns in every season and a brass umbrella stand packed with a rainbow collection of assorted parasols. And mounted on the opposite wall, an oak mantel that contained no personal pictures, just…Christmas village miniatures? His eyebrows jacked high. Okay, that was unexpected.

He waited until she moved out of the foyer toward the spacious, airy living room with its tall, wide windows and beamed ceilings. The area poured into a slightly smaller dining room with even more windows from which he glimpsed a slice of backyard. He returned his rapt attention to the room they stood in, soaking in every detail and trying to ferret out what he could about the beautiful enigma in front of him.

Books.

Damn.

So many books.

They crowded several floor-to-ceiling shelves, perched on the end of a glass-and-wood coffee table, filled the obviously custom-made cubbyholes on the end tables.

Jenna Landon must love to read.

Fascinated, he surveyed the rest of the room, taking in the elegant but comfortable-looking slate blue couch, love seat and a recliner. Yeah, he would not have pictured her relaxing with her feet up in a recliner. Dainty, antique and uncomfortable chairs that didn't invite any-one's ass to dare sit on their cushions, yes. But not a leather piece of furniture with cracks in the arms from overuse, with a dark green blanket tossed across the back as if waiting for its owner to pull it across her lap.

The entire effect loaned the place a coziness he wouldn't have associated with her—or what he knew about her. The books, the recliner, the paintings, the Christmas miniatures...none of it—fit.

Switching his focus back to Jenna, he swept his gaze down her slender form, taking in the side braid that rested over her shoulder, the tip brushing the rise of her firm, small breast. He feasted on the sight of the over-size black sweater that slid off one delicate shoulder. Yes, it hid her curves, but it also had him damn near obsessed over what all that knit concealed. Dark denim molded to her toned thighs and calves, and for a moment, he stared at her bare feet with their toes pained an unexpected and delightful black.

He slowly grinned.

"A heel."

She didn't roll her eyes, but Isaac suspected it was a close call.

"Besides educating me on wrestling lexicon, why are you here?"

"Wrestling lexicon." He snorted. "You have such a— Oh you're working?" He dipped his head in the direction of the dining room table where a laptop sat along with a couple of notebooks, highlighters and pens.

Curiosity stole through him, and he even stepped toward the room before he drew up short. He, more than most people, understood the need for privacy, and he wouldn't violate hers by copping a peek at her papers or screen. But damn if that insatiable hunger to unearth more about Jenna didn't ride him hard.

"What exactly is it that you do, Malibu? You already know I coach but you never did give quid pro quo. What requires you to work on a Saturday morning?"

If he hadn't been scrutinizing her so closely—if he hadn't appointed himself a student in the study of her—he might've missed the flicker of *something* in her eyes. But he didn't miss it. And as a man who'd been left decimated by secrets, he should've been backpedaling out her front door. Instead, he remained standing there, intrigued.

Maybe because he hadn't known her that long.

Maybe because of the instances of her weary, almost war-torn wisdom that contradicted the haughty, beauty-encased-in-ice exterior.

Maybe because of the flashes of vulnerability that knocked the wind out of him harder than his body slamming into the mat.

It could've been one of these or all of them. He didn't know what kept him there when every instinct warned of lies. Secrets. Uncertainty.

Pain.

It seemed his youngest sister, Violet, had been right all along.

Men were idiots.

"I'm a sometimes bookkeeper for my mother. A sometimes secretary for my father. I'm whatever they need me to be. *Daughter* is not only my relationship but my job description."

The even tone gave nothing away. Except that it was *too* even. *Too* smooth.

"And what do you get in return?" he asked.

She arched an eyebrow. "The satisfaction of a job well done."

Not *Thanks*. Not *What're you talking about? We're family*. Not even *Paid*.

Just an answer that smacked of her parents' selfishness and cheap labor.

Something told Isaac that if and when he ever met the elder Landons, he'd find them to be entitled, arrogant assholes.

Just a feeling.

"And which are you working on now?" He hiked his chin toward the dining room. "Bookkeeping or secretarial duties?"

"Neither because I'm talking to you." She crossed her arms over her chest, and his gaze dipped to the firm mounds hidden beneath the sweater. "Now how about you tell me what you're doing here?"

"Nice side step there," he praised. "Seriously, though? Side note. You're going to have to work on this whole Welcome Wagon thing. First you insult my truck and my taste in music while wearing ugly-as-fuck pajamas. And now you invite me inside your house but with manners a little on the—" he waffled a hand back and forth "—shrewish side. Don't kill the messenger. I'm just calling it like I see it." He held up his arms, palms shoved toward her. "How do we grow without constructive criticism?"

"You can grow. On the other side of my door. Or better yet. On the other side of *your* door," she offered pleasantly. Well, if not for the slight clench of her teeth, it would've been pleasant.

"See?" He jabbed a finger at her. "That right there. I've been wracking my brain—"

"Don't hurt yourself."

"Only proving my point, Malibu," he said, and damn

if he wasn't fucking *enjoying* himself. "As I was saying, I've been wracking my brain trying to figure out why we—of all the people in the world—would end up neighbors. I mean, you might live in a cottage but the blood that runs through your veins is so blue I feel the urge to bow. While me, I'm New England blue-collar through and through. Just check the dirt under my nails."

"And here I thought you were a good ol' Southern boy."

He shrugged. "My point, Malibu, is we couldn't be more opposite. You're polite and reserved. I'm loud and more prone to offer my opinion even when it's not asked for. You're gorgeous and untouchable, I'm gorgeous—" she snorted and he grinned "—and have more scars covering my body than skin at this point. But—" he unfolded his arms and took a step in her direction, his smile ebbing "—nothing happens in a vacuum, and we were brought together for a reason."

"That sounds pretty, but unfortunately I don't believe in kismet or fate," she said, voice cool and aloof as always.

Except for that flicker in her eyes. And unlike before, he could identify it.

Uncertainty. Unease.

Oh he had Jenna Landon a little bit nervous.

He smiled.

"Good thing I believe in it enough for both of us, Malibu," he murmured. "Here's the thing. Twice now, you've saved me from getting too deep in my head. Twice, you've pulled me back from the edge when I was close to going over. I get what people see when they look at you. Cold. No heart. But it isn't true."

He paused, his fingers straightening, flexing by his thighs. "After losing Sam and after the divorce" he shoved out, "I couldn't talk to my family because I didn't want to burden them. And fuck if I know how I unloaded on you, but I did. And I thank you for it. You have no idea how grateful I am for your porch, your dock and you. Thank you, Jenna, for not letting me disappear."

If her parents didn't say thank you, as he suspected, he damn sure would.

"I—" Her lips parted, then closed. Her blue eyes clouded for a moment before she glanced away from him on the pretense of heading toward her laptop. "You're welcome," she said, lowering the monitor.

"What makes you uncomfortable with someone saying thank you?"

"Don't be ridiculous." She closed notebooks, then stacked papers on top of them.

"Then why the sudden urge to house clean rather than look at me?"

She froze in the middle of aligning pens next to her computer. No, that wasn't avoidance *at all*.

"There." She lifted her head, her gaze connecting with his, unwavering and determined. "Happy?"

"Immensely." He waited a beat. "No one gives you appreciation often, do they?"

"I'm a bitch, Isaac. Cutting remarks, gossip and being spiteful as hell usually don't warrant much gratitude."

"And maybe if you didn't tell me that with just a little too much desperation in your voice, I'd be more inclined to believe you."

Her eyes widened, and she shook her head, fingers

curling over the back of the dining room table chair. "Take a walk down Main Street, pull over a car and ask the person in it. Or better yet, ask anyone down at the high school. They'll let you know about me. Why are you so determined to believe in something other than the truth? Because of a couple of late-night conversations over wine and burgers? Don't delude yourself."

"You might want to stop warning me away from you," he gently advised. "The more you do, the more I want to find out what you're so scared for me to find out."

"You should go," she said.

There she went, trying to shut down a conversation that veered too close to a sore place for her. And once again, he would let her get away with it.

For now.

But only because he had other plans.

"Oh I'm going, Malibu." He nodded. "But not without you."

She frowned. "What're you talking about now?"

"That's why I'm over here on this Saturday morning. I'm heading out for the day. And I won't be alone. I'm taking you with me."

Her chin jerked back, and she stiffened, surprise flaring in her summer-blue eyes.

"Not going to happen."

"So going to happen."

"No."

"Yes." And before she could rebut, he held up a hand. "I wasn't finished with my theory about why fate brought us together through geography and real estate. You've helped me, and I'm supposed to do the same."

"I don't need—"

"Help. Anything. Anyone," he listed. "Did I cover everything? But it's not true. And you know it even if you're not willing to admit it." He moved forward again, and if possible, she stiffened further. But he didn't allow that to stop him from talking, from pushing her. "Jenna, if I feel too much, you won't feel enough. No—" he shook his head "—that's not the truth. I actually believe you also feel too much. You just won't show it. Won't let anyone see it. The reason for that is a conversation for another time, but I now understand my assignment. You, Jenna Landon, need loosening up. And I've accepted the job."

She stared at him. Her lips moved. Stilled. She stared some more.

"Speechless. Now there's a reaction I hadn't factored in," he mused.

"There's a whole house with your name on the deed. You should go to it."

He winced, but then followed it with a chuckle. "Well, that didn't last long. Damn, Malibu. That mouth is one of the sexiest *and* the deadliest things about you."

"Really?" she drawled, leaning a hip against the table. "And what's the other thing?"

"Easy," he shot back. "Your eyes. Because that color is so pure, so gorgeous, when I look into your eyes, it's every punch, every suplex, every pin I've taken."

"Is that the deadly part?" she asked, and though the question emerged as sarcastic he caught the faint tremble in it. Heard the uncertainty there.

"No," he murmured. "The way my chest squeezes like I'm about to have a fucking heart attack when I look into your eyes and see the pain and anger you deny... that's the deadly part."

She didn't say anything. Hell, he didn't know if she breathed. And goddamn, he'd gone too far, said too much. That'd always been a problem for him. Never knowing when to back off. Hadn't that been what Diana had told him? Leave well enough alone. Everything doesn't need to be picked at. Wasn't that why she'd gone to Sean? Because Isaac hadn't left her in peace?

"What exactly does one wear on a mysterious Saturday morning outing?"

He blinked, her reluctant words hauling him back into the present. Reluctant, but dammit, he'd take it.

"What you're wearing is fine. Jeans, but you'll need a jacket. And boots. And not any of those sexy pairs with the stiletto heels. I'm talking about shit-kicking boots. You have any of those in your closet, Malibu?"

Pushing off the table, she strode across the room, tossing him a superior look.

"I'll see what I can manage."

"Just out of curiosity," he called out as she reached the hallway. "What would you have done if I said your ass?"

She paused, her hand on the doorjamb. After a moment, she glanced at him over her shoulder.

"You would be on my porch and I would be sitting down at my laptop by now."

He nodded. "Truth?"

She inhaled, barely audible, but then said, "Yes."

"Number three on my list are your legs. Gorgeous and lethal as fuck. I'm glad I went with the eyes, though."

She wanted to smile.

He saw it with the nearly imperceptible twitch of her lips, but she turned and disappeared down the hall before she let it loose. That would be his goal for today. See that smile in full force. Jenna Landon uninhibited. That both terrified and excited him. The combination was a high he should walk away from.

She reminded him of his ex in so many ways.

Both wealthy.

Both emotional bomb shelters.

Both secrets and pain wrapped in beauty.

Yeah, he should be running far and fast given the definition of insanity 'n' all that.

Yet…here he stood. Apparently one of those people who needed a side of pain in order to feel even the slightest bit of pleasure.

And just what the hell did that say about him?

Shaking his head, he strode toward one of the massive bookshelves, as if he could just as easily walk away from the questions whirling in his head.

Her interests seemed to run the gamut of genres. Thrillers. Horror. Biographies. Romance. And several shelves dedicated to young adult fiction. Huh. He ran a fingertip along the spine of one hardcover in particular. Interesting.

"I'm ready."

"You're a Beck Dansing fan." He pulled free one of the popular YA author's books, holding it up before opening the cover and thumbing through the pages. "It looks like you have almost every one of his books. My brother, Colin, is a huge fan. I bought him the autographed, hardcover limited edition set of the first series for his birthday a couple of years ago. He's a good kid, but I think he'd take you out if he saw your collection."

"I enjoy his writing." Jenna cleared her throat. "Does your brother have that one?"

Isaac snapped the book closed, glancing down at the cover with a shrug. "I'm not sure. Most likely he has the paperback or the e-book. He buys every one that comes out. But the hardcover? Probably not, considering the price tag and he's sixteen."

"Take it."

"No." He wheeled around, sliding the book back into its place on the shelf. "No, thanks," he said, softening the abrupt refusal. "He's good."

Shrugging into a short, camel-colored leather jacket, she crossed the room, coming to a stop next to him. Her gardenia scent teased him as she reached for the book.

"It's not charity." She held the book out to him. "It's a gift from one reader and fan to another. Here," she said, pressing it against his chest. "This isn't about you, but about your brother. And he'll enjoy it. Regardless that it's from me. Take it."

Isaac met her gaze, and slowly lifted his hands. Their fingertips brushed, settled next to one another. One slight glance against the softest skin and he *wanted*.

Wanted her.

Wanted to please her.

"All right," he murmured, accepting the book. "Thank you."

She nodded. Stepped back.

"Thank *you*."

He didn't ask her to expound; he understood. And he could only return her nod with that *Regardless that it's from me* throbbing in his chest like an irritated scar.

"Let's go." He pivoted, heading toward the door. "I need to get you out of here before you realize what you've agreed to and change your mind."

"That's the problem," she said, palming her keys. "I don't know what I've agreed to."

"Look at you taking risks already. Next thing you know, you're going to be Rose Bend's answer to Evel Knievel."

"Laying it on pretty thick there, Monster. You might want to quit while you're ahead."

"Duly noted." He strode ahead of her and pulled open her front door, grinning wide. Excitement tripped through him. "But let me just add one more thing—you're going to love this."

"THERE'S NO WAY in hell I'm doing this."

Jenna stared at the death machine on two wheels Isaac had just rolled out of the shed behind his family's house.

His family's house.

That bit of information she'd deal with in a minute.

But the fact that he wanted her to get on the motorcycle and actually ride it with him took immediate priority at the moment.

"Nope."

"Malibu."

"No." She shook her head for added emphasis. "If this was your grand idea for 'loosening me up'—" and yes, she threw in the finger curls because his assessment of the proverbial stick up her ass still stung "—I'm afraid you're going to be disappointed. There's no way in hell I'm getting on that thing. Not happening."

"Famous last words."

"I know." She nodded. "And if I ride that thing, they will actually *be* my last words. Because I'll die."

He snorted. "Malibu, c'mon. That's not a wee bit—" he squinted, holding up his finger and thumb "—dramatic?"

"Do I need to drag out statistics?"

"Wait." He cocked his head, a glint entering his indigo gaze. "Do you really have them?"

For the love of… "No." His lips parted, and she pointed a finger at the motorcycle that she swore sat there, glaring at her. "No, I don't have the statistics on me, and *no*, I'm not getting on that bike."

He crossed his arms, eyes narrowing on her, his legs shifting as he widened his stance. Thick thighs strained at the light denim, and she had no problem imagining those powerful legs controlling the dangerous monster parked several feet away. Or how that wide chest would provide resistance to the buffeting wind. Or how his big palms and long fingers would grip the handles with ease and absolute confidence. The sight of that assurance, of those muscles shifting and working would be…foreplay. Orgasmic. Because instinct whispered he would be the same in bed. Powerful. Dominant. At ease. Confident.

And hot as all hell.

Heat simmered low in her belly, flames licking at the underside of her skin.

Just another reason to stay far away from the machine and Isaac on it.

"Correct me if I'm wrong, but hasn't Rose Bend hosted an annual motorcycle rally for years? One the town is pretty well known for? You mean to tell me you've never participated in it? At all?"

"Yes. Yes. No. And again, no." She shrugged. "Sorry, Monster. But you're going to have to rethink this plan. Maybe karaoke. I've heard it works wonders."

According to Israel, it'd helped when he'd been "dating" his now-wife, Korrie.

Isaac choked out a laugh. "Jenna—"

The low rumble of a car engine cut off the rest of his sentence, and they both turned to see the SUV park at the curb in front of his family's home. The side door slid open and a tiny young girl tumbled out, her feet barely hitting the ground before she charged at full speed toward Isaac.

"Uncle Isaac!" she yelled, flying past Jenna, her dark blond pigtails streaming behind her.

"Hey, Belle." He grinned, hunkering down, arms outstretched to catch the little girl.

The sight of him holding the child—knowing his history, knowing his desire for a family—struck her like a hot poker to the chest.

Blinking, she tore her gaze away from them to watch the small parade of people march up the driveway at a slower pace.

Two women walked just behind a boy of about twelve or thirteen and another who looked to be a couple of years younger. Isaac's family. Probably his mother and sister, and his niece and nephews. Jenna recognized the little girl and the youngest boy from the ice cream shop. Of course, when she'd treated the kids and the other teen that had been with them to cones, she hadn't known Isaac. Hadn't known they were related to him.

Would she miss those kinds of connections when she left Rose Bend for a bigger city? Most times she found that sense of *everyone knows everyone's everyone* stifling, suffocating.

And then sometimes it could be…comforting.

No second-guessing. This close to getting out of Rose Bend, she couldn't second-guess her decision.

Giving her head an abrupt mental shake, she refocused on the group approaching her. The younger woman's expression wasn't unwelcoming, but it could definitely be described as careful and *cool*. Curiosity gleamed in his mother's gaze, though she, too, appeared reserved. The children bore none of the adults' distance. Excitement vibrated off of them, even the preteen. Of course, the boys' attention was focused on the motorcycle, not Jenna.

"Holy crap!" The oldest boy crowed, half running toward them. He skidded to a stop in front of the motorcycle, staring down at it like a kid presented with every gift on his wish list on Christmas morning. "You're taking the 'Busa out today, Uncle Isaac?"

"I plan on it." Isaac effortlessly held his niece aloft with one arm and clapped a hand over his nephew's shoulder, squeezing it. "I'm trying to convince Ms. Landon to go with me."

His nephew slid a glance at Jenna, pink staining his high, sharp cheekbones. As quick as he looked at her, he shifted his gaze away, staring at Isaac again.

"If she doesn't want to go, can I ride with you instead?"

Isaac barked out a crack of laughter, and Jenna swallowed a snort. Wow. She appreciated that kind of opportunistic spirit.

"How about give me a little more time to convince her before jumping in her spot, 'kay?" Smiling, Isaac turned to Jenna. "Jenna, this, uh, eager soul is my nephew Edward. The other one thinking I don't see him putting his grubby lil' paws all over my seat is Jacob. And this adorable darling is Bella. We call her Belle."

Edward. Jacob. Bella. No. No way—

"Yep." Isaac snickered. "You heard right. My sister, the no-nonsense one over there with the total stone-face, is an absolute Twihard."

"Bite me, Mr. Right. If I recall, you went and watched every movie with me. And I borrowed *your* books."

Isaac spread his free arm wide. "Lena, damn. We have company. Mom," he whined, waving a hand toward Jenna. "Get your daughter. She's embarrassing me. And here I didn't spill about that whole My Little Pony obsession to Kenny when you first brought him around," he growled.

Lena shrugged but her eyes narrowed on Isaac. "There's nothing wrong with liking My Little Pony."

"There's liking and then there's loving. And until you're twenty-two?"

"You know what?" Lena snapped, jabbing a finger in her brother's direction. "I got—"

"Children, please," their mother interceded, lifting her hands and her voice. Aiming a smile at Jenna, she said, "Please forgive them. I promise you, I raised them, not a she-wolf."

"Tomato, tom-ah-to," Lena grumbled. *"Oof."*

His mother maintained her smile in spite of the elbow she'd just planted in her daughter's stomach.

"See, sweetheart," he cooed to his niece. "Your mother is why your uncle can't have nice friends."

"Daddy said Mommy eats people for lunch," Bella whispered back at the volume of *the people next door can't hear you*, nodding sagely. "She doesn't though. She eats bologna."

"For the love of…" Lena muttered. "Kenny's going to pay for that one."

"Jenna, before you demand I whisk you away from all this craziness—and possible cannibalism—I'd like you to meet my older sister, Lena Hunter, and my mom, Alice Hunter. There's also my brother, Colin, who you already met at Six Ways to Sundae and my youngest sister, Violet, who's a junior at Boston College." No one could miss the pride painting his voice. "The last person missing is Lena's partner, Kenny. He's probably around the neighborhood being a good Samaritan. I think that's his full-time job," he teased.

"He's with me, isn't he?" Lena smiled, and for a moment, her face lost the aloofness, her strong features softening, and the dark purple eyes she shared with Isaac lit with a lovely warmth. But then she shifted that gaze to Jenna. "It's nice to meet you, Jenna."

The even tone could mean anything from *Welcome to our home* to *Fuck you*. Given Lena's shuttered gaze, Jenna figured it leaned more toward the latter.

"Welcome, Jenna." Alice Hunter moved forward, extending her hand toward Jenna. "We've heard so much about you."

At that, Jenna couldn't contain her small snort. Alice's eyes flared in surprise, and the apology scrabbled up Jenna's throat. Contrary to popular—or unpopular—opinion, she'd never made a habit of being rude to her elders. But the apology lodged in her throat. Yes, this was Isaac's family, and for some reason she'd rather not analyze, their disapproval caused a deep ache in her belly. But pretending they didn't would only increase the awkwardness.

And God, she was so damn tired of being fake.

Of being someone else for the sake of other people.

Of never feeling safe or comfortable in her own skin because it offended.

Isaac had said his purpose in moving next door had been to help her take risks. Maybe that started here. With his family, and not that bike.

"I'm afraid to ask," she said, falling back on the tone she'd adopted over the years that was as much a mask as the helmet on the back of Isaac's motorcycle. "You could have heard anything from my sterling reputation in Rose Bend or my memorable first meeting with your son."

Once more surprise flashed in Alice's blue eyes but this time, so did amusement.

"Both."

Jenna arched an eyebrow. "In my defense, the music sounded like cats in heat."

Alice laughed aloud, then slapped a hand over her mouth, sliding a side glance at Isaac.

"It was Blake Shelton. Mom, you like Blake. You, too, right, Ed?" he asked his nephew.

His nephew tipped his head back, scrunching his nose up as if considering. "Depends. If I say yes, can I go for a ride on the 'Busa?"

"Really, dude?" Isaac gave him a fierce scowl. "*Et tu*, Brutus?"

"I don't know this Brutus guy, but I'll like him, too, if I can go for a ride on the—"

"Ed, you're not getting on that motorcycle, so forget it," Lena said, her voice firm.

Her son must've heard the no-nonsense tone because he wheeled around, whining, "Aw, Mom. But Ms. Jenna's not going to do it."

"No, Edward."

"Are you scared, Ms. Jenna?" Bella asked, concern dripping from her high, sweet voice. "I ride with Uncle Isaac. He's good. He won't drop you." She shook her head, pig tails swaying back and forth.

Awesome. Shamed by a little girl no more than seven years old. Even she had ridden a motorcycle.

A hand patted Jenna's hip, and she looked down to meet Jacob's soft brown eyes. "Don't feel bad. It was the Gold Wing, not the 'Busa," he said, as if she would understand the difference between the bikes. The young boy patted her again, offering comfort.

Jenna battled back a smile, not wanting to hurt his feelings.

"Thank you, Jacob."

He nodded, then turned back to the motorcycle, his job apparently done.

"What Jake means is the Honda Gold Wing is a different bike from the Hayabusa. It's built for long-distance rides and touring and I can add a backrest. Perfect for when I want to take the kids on rides. The 'Busa is a different motorcycle. It's a sports bike built for speed. It would be irresponsible of me to take a child Jake or Belle's age on a motorcycle with that much power because they don't have the arm strength to hold on to me. But no matter what motorcycle I'm on, I'm careful. I've been riding for over twenty years, and I'd never place you in danger for pride's sake. Just like I care for my niece and nephews and place their safety first, I'd do the same with you." He reached for her, trailed his fingers over the back of her hand. "Let me show you another view of Rose Bend. Like you shared with me. Trust me."

Her gaze dipped to where he touched her. His hand

dropped away, falling back to his side, but the tingling sensation remained, sizzling over her skin like a sun burn. He tempted her.

Trust me.

Did he have the slightest clue what he asked of her?

He requested what she didn't—couldn't—offer her own parents.

And yet...yet, she wanted to give that to him. To herself. At least, to an extent. She owed it to herself to try. Wasn't the move out of Rose Bend all about being a different person from the one she'd portrayed for so long? Being her true self? Being true *to* herself?

She glanced over her shoulder at the motorcycle.

It seemed funny that the hill she was willing to make her stand on should start with a sports bike.

That ride is so unseemly. No daughter of mine will ever be caught on one of those filthy things.

The motorcycle rallies bring in revenue for the town. But that doesn't mean we have to get dirty for the cause.

Her parents' voices drifted through her head, condemning the rides and riders that gathered from all over the country in their town every year. Subconsciously, had Jenna allowed their snobbery to shape her opinion? Was that what lay behind her objection to trying this new adventure?

That possibility alone nudged her into a decision.

"Okay. I'll do it."

The smile that slowly spread over his face and the light in his cobalt eyes poured pure sunshine through her veins. For that smile, for that pleasure, she had to stop herself from agreeing all over again.

Oh no. Oh *no.*

She was in so much trouble.

And she still wasn't going to walk away.

At least at fifteen, she'd had the excuse of naivete and her age. Now, at twenty-nine, she couldn't claim either.

So when this whole thing blew up in her face—and it would, since history had taught her that happy endings were not in her canon—she would have no one to blame but herself.

"Your funeral, Isaac. You break Rose Bend's princess, and there's going to be hell to pay," Lena drawled.

A frown slammed down on Isaac's face and there was nothing mock or playful about this one. Jenna's belly constricted at the expression that warned his intention to head into battle on her behalf, but she couldn't let him. This was her battle.

Still.

She didn't have to think back on the last time someone had defended her—or attempted to.

Never.

"Seems I'm not the only one with the personality of a blade saw," Jenna said, lifting the corner of her mouth in a half smile.

Lena narrowed her eyes on Isaac. "Really?"

"Don't be upset with him," Jenna interrupted, with a small shrug. "I took it as a compliment."

She snorted. "You would."

"Okay, that's enough out of you." Alice slid a glance toward Lena that a child of any age would obey, and Lena wasn't the exception. "And all of you. Let's leave your uncle Isaac to get on with his ride." She waved her hands in shooing motions. "Ed, Jake, move. Let go of your uncle, Belle, and come on. And it was a pleasure meeting you, Jenna. Isaac will have to bring you back for dinner or lunch."

Of course, the offer was probably just polite but that didn't stop it from feeling any less...nice.

Jenna cleared her throat, dipping her chin. "Thank you. The pleasure's mine."

Amid grumbles from the kids, his family retreated to the house, leaving her and Isaac alone.

"Your family is great," she murmured, the smack of the storm door still echoing in the late-morning air.

"Jenna, I'm sorry about Lena. She's my older sister and a little protective. But she doesn't mean any—"

She jerked her head toward him. "Don't ever apologize because someone who loves you, and who you love in return, defends you. That's a gift, Isaac. You treasure it. But you never, ever apologize for it."

Her vehemence seemed to flutter between them like frantic butterfly wings. He peered at her with an intensity that had her itching to do something foolish just to escape like jump on that motorcycle and drive off.

"It's a shame," he said. "If she got to know you, I think she'd like you. Here." He picked up a black matte helmet from the back of the motorcycle. "Let me show you Mount Holly and Rose Bend like you've never seen them."

His gaze roamed her face as if searching out a puzzle. If that were so, he had no hope of solving hers. There were too many pieces missing. But that didn't stop her from yearning for him to find those pieces, care enough to figure them out and put them back together again.

Yearning to discover who she could be on the other side.

"Okay," she whispered.

"Okay."

He lifted the helmet, fit it over her head and pressed his forehead to it.

Pressed his lips to it.

Her breath evaporated from her lungs.

That full mouth hadn't touched her skin but it might as well have because a fever ignited within her. But no medicine could ease these symptoms. No prescription or days of rest could break its hold. And in this moment, with his breath fogging up the face mask, she didn't want its hold broken. She longed to get tangled up, lost in that hold.

He dropped his hands and stepped back, reaching for the other helmet. Once he settled it over his head, he led her to the motorcycle, straddled it, then guided her on to the bike behind him. She'd seen hundreds of the machines. How could she not with as many rides that had been held in Rose Bend over the years? And yet, this was her first time perched on one of them.

But that wasn't what made this event momentous or special.

Being perched on the motorcycle behind *him* did.

On instinct, she leaned forward, wrapped her arms around his lean waist, pressed her breasts to his broad, strong back, thighs cradling his. Her fingers interlocked against his abdomen, and even through his leather jacket, she could feel the solid muscles underneath. Feel the dance and play of those muscles as he shifted into place and started the powerful machine beneath them.

It roared to life and...*whoa.*

Good God.

Should it be so *sexual*?

The motorcycle hummed beneath her, between her legs, and holy hell, she fought not to fidget. Fought not to grind herself against the sexy-as-sin male whose big body already spread her legs wide. This full-body clinch already beat out the best sex she'd ever had. Nothing and no one had ever transformed her into a living flame before.

Nothing, no one, had ever triggered an ache so hot, so…ravenous that it both scared and fascinated her.

For far too long in her life, she'd let fear dictate her actions. Maybe, for once, it was time to allow other emotions to lead.

"You ready?" Isaac's voice echoed through a microphone in her helmet.

"Ready," she replied. No hesitation.

And no fear.

CHAPTER TWELVE

So THAT's WHAT a pure adrenaline rush felt like.

Wow.

Jenna now understood why people chased it like a hit of drugs.

An unrestrained and unexpected swell of laughter escaped her. The helmet trapped the sound, thankfully. But when she pulled the head covering off, she met a pair of wild indigo eyes, and the gleam in them assured her Isaac had heard.

"I don't need to ask, do I?" he murmured.

"No." She handed him the helmet and shook her head. "No, you don't."

Smiling, he set the helmet on the back of the motorcycle next to his. Excitement pumped through her veins, and her muscles continued to hum as if she were still on the bike and the long stretch of mountain road above Rose Bend and Mount Holly. She briefly closed her eyes, seeing all that autumn glory again.

Even through the visor, the colors hadn't been muted. Maybe because, for the first time, *she* hadn't been muted. Everything had been in perfect, startling, almost painful clarity. Like a person emerging from an underground cavern into the sun for the first time after living for years in the dark. The wind against her body.

The power of the motorcycle vibrating under her. The adrenaline pouring through her.

The heat and thrilling strength of the man in front of her.

It'd been like flying while restrained to her own skin.

On her porch, she'd witnessed his vulnerability.

On the dock, she'd experienced his trust.

Now, she'd tasted his wildness.

The voice in her head that had been an adamant murmur of caution now screamed at her.

You should've kept your distance. You should've listened. Now you're in too deep.

She turned, walked several steps away from Isaac, not really seeing her surroundings, just desperate to place space between them.

Yes, she was in too deep.

And she would pay the consequences for it.

But she still had time to mitigate the damage.

Because she had to stop fooling herself.

Isaac Hunter was a force of nature. And no one walked away from that unscathed.

Her cell vibrated in her jacket pocket and she didn't need to glance at the screen to identify who called. It was the same person who'd called during her drive to Isaac's family's home. Her father. She should answer. Jasper Landon wasn't a person who appreciated being ignored. But at this moment, when she teetered on the edge of euphoria and vulnerability...

No, she wasn't dealing with her father right now. Or letting him ruin her.

"Hey, Malibu." A big, gentle hand settled on the small of her back.

A halo of warmth radiated from his wide palm to her

belly and upward, to her sensitive, heavy breasts and tight nipples. Then south to the swollen, damp flesh between her thighs. What the ride had begun, just a touch from him continued. Transforming her into a tuning fork of desire.

"You okay?" he prodded. "That first ride can be a little intense."

"I'm fine," she lied.

Then, as much to change the subject as in interest, she scanned her surroundings. They stood in a meadow, surrounded by a small forest of trees. The afternoon sun beat down on them, but the branches and leaves provided a natural shelter and the beams filtered through them. She moved forward several steps, and with a gasp, drew up short just as Isaac's fingers closed around her upper arm. The meadow dropped off in a sharp incline to a large lake below.

"That was—unexpected."

"You can imagine as asshole kids we'd sometimes let people walk right over the edge into the water." Jenna whipped her head around and gaped at him. He winced. "Did I mention we were assholes? And I like to think I've matured since then. Look." He glanced down at his hand around her arm. "I stopped you."

"Right. Thanks," she said dryly. As dry as she wanted her clothes to remain. "I take it this was a popular spot when you were younger."

He shrugged and released her. But he shifted closer so he stood beside her, his shoulder brushing hers. Though their jackets and sweaters separated them, a bolt of electricity charged through her from that point of contact. She should move away. Nothing about a voltage *that* powerful could be good for her control or resolve.

She didn't move an inch.

"In the summer, yes," he said. "But my favorite time of year has always been now when it was deserted, quieter."

"Quieter?" She tilted her head, studied his profile with the slight bump to the bridge of his nose, the scar to his jaw. He was imperfect and utterly perfect. "I would've pegged you for having friends around at all times. One of those annoying popular people."

"Takes one to know one?" he teased, a corner of his mouth hitching.

She shrugged. Why bother denying it? She had been popular in high school. But mean people often were.

"I had friends," he said. "Plenty of them. Still do. But sometimes they're just a distraction from everything else going on in life. It works for a while. But there comes a time when there's not enough noise, not enough friends, not enough parties to drown out the thoughts in your head. That's when you just have to sit with yourself. Be with yourself."

"And you like yourself? Is this place where you discovered that?" She wasn't being facetious; she genuinely wanted to know.

What must it feel like to genuinely like the person you were? To have no shame or regrets?

"Most days, yes." He nodded, but the small, rueful smile that ghosted over his full mouth belied those words. "But no, this isn't the place I discovered that. This spot will always hold a special place in my heart because it's where I had my come-to-Jesus moment." When she blinked then just stared at him, he nodded again. "I'm serious. Right here is where I decided I was going to be a wrestler."

Turning more fully toward him, she stuffed her hands in the pockets of her jacket and said, "I can't wait to hear this."

"I was twelve, and after school one day, I hitchhiked all the way out here."

"You didn't."

"I know. I know." Isaac held up his hands as if warding off the lecture that really did hover on her tongue. "But I was twelve, it was Mount Holly and I believed nothing bad could happen to me. And yeah, I was twelve and stupid." He chuckled.

The sound ebbed, and he squinted, staring off over the lake as if even now he could glimpse the impetuous youth he'd once been.

"I sat down underneath that tree right there." He pointed toward a red maple with a thick trunk that sat like a king on its majestic throne closest to the incline. "My right eye was killing me and already swelling shut. By the time I returned home there wouldn't be any hiding that I'd gotten into a fight after school. Plus, that little bastard Chris Merritt's mother would probably have called Mom by then. Because I'd dared to touch her precious boy. Didn't matter that he'd beat my ass. Or that her son had started it by talking shit about my mother. I committed the cardinal sin of putting my hands on her son."

His hands curled into fists, but after a moment, he straightened them. A faint frown whispered over his expression, but a second later, it disappeared and he shook his head.

"Anyway, I hid out here, putting off going home and just thinking over and over about how I got my ass handed to me by one of the biggest bullies in the middle school. And how I failed to protect my mother. At twelve, I felt like a failure. Small and insignificant. The night before, I'd watched 'Stone Cold' Steve Austin wrestle. He was one of my favorites. He didn't give a damn, and we loved him for it. No one would've dared walk up on Stone Cold and talk smack about his mother. No one pushed him around because he was strong, didn't take anyone's shit, and right then, I wanted to be just like him. Sitting under that tree over there—" he dipped his head once more in the direction of the sugar maple "—I made up my mind I *would be* just like him."

He didn't drag his gaze away from the tree. As if it were a talisman holding him bound to a past that had gifted him with a future and now a present.

"But it'd been about more than standing up to bullies. It'd also been about being so rich I could take care of my family. So rich the Merritts of this world would no longer look down on me or my mom. It'd been about people seeing me different. If fans cheered for me, then obviously that meant they didn't care if my mother was pregnant by a man who wasn't my or Lena's father. Or that me and Lena didn't have a father, for that matter. No, shit like that wouldn't matter if people yelled my name and held up signs and foam fingers for me."

She wanted to enfold his hand in hers, lead him over to that tree where his life had changed, guide him to the ground where red-and-orange leaves littered the grass and wrap her arms around him.

Her heart ached for him, and an apology burned on her tongue. No, she'd never physically abused anyone. But her tongue had inflicted a lot of damage. She had been someone else's Chris Merritt, and tears pricked her eyes. All the excuses and justifications—the miscarriage, the pain, the rage, distant parents, the loneliness—couldn't erase the actions staring her in the face now.

She couldn't give him what that little boy owed him all those years ago...what she owed her own victims. But she could give Isaac what he'd selflessly gifted her in almost every interaction they'd had and she'd yet to offer back.

Vulnerability.

Truth.

"I have a favorite spot, too," she murmured.

"The dock?" he asked.

"No." She inhaled a deep breath, held it for a couple of seconds, then slowly exhaled it. As far as secrets went—especially hers—this one was minor, but she'd never admitted it aloud before. And she had to almost physically push it out. "It's Boston Public Library. You'd think given how successful both of my parents are I would've been much more well traveled as a child. But no, they didn't leave Rose Bend often. I think they enjoy being big fish, and once they travel, they're not as known, not as important. As a result, I didn't visit Boston for the first time until I was seventeen years old. My aunt visited from Oregon and my parents allowed her to take me for a weekend trip."

Jenna sucked in another breath and slowly released it. Isaac's gaze brushed over her cheekbone, temple, the corner of her mouth like a lover's caress, and she mentally ordered her hand to remain in her coat pocket.

"Stepping into the Boston Public Library for the first time was a...revelation," she breathed. "Of course, I'd seen pictures of buildings like that with its architecture and art, but to walk into it, to see it with my own eyes..." She shook her head. "It'd been the difference between looking up a recipe for New York cheesecake online and actually tasting it for yourself. The marble vestibule. The immense, Italianate courtyard. The murals. And of course, the books. Oh my God, the books. I hadn't wanted to leave. We'd visited several historical, amazing places that weekend, but I made my aunt bring me back to the library two more times before we headed home."

After she'd lost her baby and alienated herself from her friends, books became her savior. She'd always read, but they'd become her lifeline, tethering her to their worlds when hers had been rocked so catastrophically. She'd felt welcomed by the many characters, felt accepted and like she belonged. It'd been after her visit to Boston that she'd started writing her first book.

So in a sense, as this place had been Mr. Right's origin story, so had Boston Public Library been Beck Dansing's.

"I should've guessed your place had something to do with books," he said with a soft chuckle that had her skin pebbling with pleasure. And not just because the sound was rough and pleasant. But because he knew her. "All anyone has to do is take one look at your house and see where your love lies. I'd even say it's a passion," he murmured.

Passion. The word tumbled out there between them. He'd meant it as an intellectual pursuit. But that's not how her body interpreted it.

Something needy and hard pulled low in her stomach, and it echoed between her legs.

Something, hell. Lust. Desire. Greed. Call it what it was.

"That's my problem," she said, the confession escaping before she had a chance to lock it down. "No one in this town bothers to take a look. And I can't really blame them. Not given my past and present. What have I done to redeem myself in their eyes? But I can't continue to live my life as Jenna Landon, Jasper Landon's daughter. Or Jenna Landon, bitch of Rose Bend. Even if I wanted to change, I won't be allowed to. And I'm tired, Isaac. I'm tired of paying for sins that are mine and that aren't. So I'm leaving. I'm leaving Rose Bend and starting over in a city where my parents don't matter. Where my past doesn't matter. Where Jenna Landon is just a name and where I can be anyone I want. I'll be free."

A heavy silence fell between them, and only the whistle of the gentle breeze and the quiet lap of the water below broke it.

"You're moving? Leaving?"

She nodded, although she couldn't look at him.

"I promised my father I'd help him make it through this autumn carnival he's sponsoring. Stand by his side and put on the facade of the happy family. It's my last dog and pony show for this town. Then, at the beginning of the year, I'm leaving. I haven't decided if I'll rent out my house or sell it. But I'm moving to Boston. The city is big enough, diverse enough, beautiful enough to lose myself in, to discover who I am, who I want to be." It was also the place where a part of her had begun all those years ago. Maybe it could happen once more. "I'll rent an apartment for a while before I buy a place. I don't have all the details figured out, but then again, I don't think I have to. As long as that first step is in place, I'm ready."

And God, she was so ready.

Yet, she still wouldn't look at Isaac.

This time she listened to that small voice that whispered a warning. Isaac Hunter threatened her resolve. Her control. Her knowledge of who and what people were, and how, ultimately, they would fail her and she would disappoint them.

So no, she wouldn't look at Isaac. Because she couldn't have him placing this promise to herself in jeopardy.

"So I'm going to have to get used to a new neighbor?" He emitted a sound that could've been a snort or a tsk. "I don't know, Malibu. After being bum-rushed at the ass crack of dawn and being called a rude-as-fuck country bumpkin, you're going to be a hard act to follow."

Her bark of laughter caught her by surprise and she covered her mouth, even though only the two of them were there to hear it.

He arched an eyebrow at her, his indigo gaze glittering. But after several moments, the humor there ebbed, and a seriousness eased over his expression. He lifted a hand, gently but firmly grasping her chin, tilting her head back. She had no choice but to meet his eyes, and even if his fingers weren't gripping her face, branding her, she wouldn't have been able to glance away. A fierceness swirled in those eyes, flattened that mouth, creased those eyebrows.

No, she couldn't look away if she wanted.

And she didn't want to.

"You said you can't blame people in this town for not taking a look. For not seeing you. Okay, you might not blame them. But I will. I do. I know the cold and prickly persona you give off. And that tongue can slice fast and deep. But I've been in Rose Bend for a matter of weeks. Weeks, Jenna. And I see there's more to you than ice, thorns and sharpness. All I had to do was take the time to look. To want to look. Most people have been here for years. If they've never bothered to see you're worth the effort of just *looking*, then yeah, I blame them."

"You don't know what I've done."

"Maybe not. But going by the number of churches in this town, a lot of people apparently believe in forgiveness—or claim to. So it seems to me, whatever you've done, they should extend some to you."

His thumb brushed the skin under her lip, sweeping once. Twice. Before he dropped his arm, leaving the imprint of his hand behind.

Her tingling skin mocked her.

Jenna stared at him, then slowly shook her head.

"Half of me wants to thank you for that," she said, voice rougher, hoarser than she would've liked.

"And the other half?" he murmured, lifting his fingers to her again. Sweeping his thumb over her chin again.

Sending a wave of heat swamping her again.

She cleared her throat, but it had no effect on her voice. "The other half wants to wrap you up in wool and shield you from yourself. A person with that kind of Pollyanna outlook on life cannot be safe in the world unprotected."

His hand stilled on her face. Surprise flared in his eyes and then…delight that ignited a sensation she shied away from identifying. Lust, she understood, as unwelcomed and inconvenient as it was. But that effervescent *stirring* in her chest? No. She wanted no part of that.

Stepping back from the temptation of him, she said, "Thank you for pushing me outside of my comfort zone today. I wouldn't have missed this for the world."

"You're welcome, Malibu." He didn't move forward

and try to recover the space she'd placed between them. But he didn't need to. Those eyes, with their knowledge and perception and—God, she had to be projecting that emotion—*something*, stole across the distance, crowding into her personal space. Filling it. "Anytime you need to go for a ride, you know where to find me."

No way he'd meant for that to be sexual.

Not that it mattered. Her body interpreted it with a *Kama Sutra* translator.

Oh yes. Time to retreat. Fast. Before she did something incredibly impulsive and destructive.

Like take him up on his imaginary offer.

"THANK YOU AGAIN for today." Jenna stared out the windshield as Isaac guided her car down their street.

A pang of disappointment echoed in her chest, and she sank her teeth into her bottom lip, trapping the impetuous request to turn the vehicle around and go anywhere. To the ice cream shop. To the diner. To The Glen, the field at the end of Main Street. Anywhere but home where this day would end.

"And again, thank *you* for coming out with me," he said. "It's progress that you let me drive your car, but one day you're going to actually ride in my truck."

She softly snorted. "Do cats wear boots and frolic with unicorns in this world where you exist?"

His low, rough chuckle filled the interior of the car, skimming over her skin and increasing the temperature.

"I don't care what people say about you, Jenna. You're a fucking delight."

How that both hurt and touched her. Pained and pleasured her.

"I didn't mean to hurt your feelings," Isaac murmured, and a big hand covered hers.

The *You didn't* lodged in her throat.

But she couldn't utter it because of the debate waging in her head over whether or not to snatch her hand from under his.

It wasn't just the physical act; God knew she wasn't a virgin or a stranger to sex. But that was…sex. Sometimes enjoyable, most times okay.

But never emotional. The one time she'd allowed her heart to become involved, she'd failed herself and been abandoned by the person she'd trusted as well as the parents who were supposed to love and protect her.

And that hand over hers was *emotional*.

Fortunately, he pulled up in front of her house and she didn't have to untangle the sticky web of thoughts in her head. But that relief dried up when Isaac parked behind a slate grey Mercedes and two people opened the doors and stepped out.

All the moisture in her mouth disappeared, and her heart pounded against her chest like fists against a steel cage. A droning sound buzzed in her ears, and in a moment of absolute insanity—or vulnerability—she flipped her hand over and grasped Isaac's. Hard.

"Jenna? What's wrong?"

His voice came to her as if from a long tunnel, not from right beside her. She'd *tried to* answer, but her tongue had thickened, and she couldn't.

"Sweetheart." His fingers tightened on hers, tugging gently. And she submitted to the subtle but firm demand to look at him. Numbly, she tore her gaze from the couple on the sidewalk to stare at him. "What's wrong?"

Sweetheart.

The endearment almost blazed away the cold that seeped under her skin to the bone and marrow beneath. Surely someone had called her by a pet name before— how sad would it be to go through all these years and not have been given one sweet nickname?—but for the life of her, she couldn't recall it. There was only now that tender *sweetheart* in his whiskey-over-gravel voice.

And she couldn't enjoy it.

Not with her parents standing there like vultures ready to pick over the carrion of any happiness that remained from this day.

She'd lied to Isaac earlier. Well, hadn't confessed the whole truth.

They were half the reason why she sought to escape Rose Bend.

Sought to run to a place where she wouldn't have to face the constant disapproval that even now etched their faces.

"It was a good day, Monster," she whispered. "And for the record, I wouldn't mind living in your Pollyanna world. Not at all."

"Jenna…"

She untangled her fingers from his, and not risking another look over her shoulder, she pushed her car door open and stepped out. Resolve straightening her back and shoulders, she headed toward her parents. There would be no avoiding this confrontation as she'd done her father's phone calls. Foolish. Hadn't she said Jasper Landon wouldn't be ignored? This little visit was the consequence.

"Dad. Mother. I wasn't expecting you this evening," Jenna said, voice carefully even. No emotion. Neither of her parents appreciated histrionics.

"You would have if you'd bothered answering my phone calls," her father snapped in greeting.

His gaze flickered over her shoulder, and she didn't have to follow it to see Isaac behind her. She'd heard the driver's door close and *hadn't* seen him walk over to his house. But of course he wouldn't let her face whatever had caused her reaction in the car alone. That wasn't in his DNA.

After meeting Jasper and Helene Landon, he would regret that chivalry.

"I'm sorry," Jenna lied. "I must have had the ringer off and didn't realize it."

"That's just irresponsible." Her father frowned at her, then once more glanced over her shoulder. "Who is this? Are you going to introduce us? Since this is obviously why you were so preoccupied you couldn't answer a call from your parents."

She bristled at the *this*, as if Isaac were an inanimate object instead of a person. Usually her parents drew on their social faces in front of anyone outside the family. That they didn't in front of Isaac betrayed the strength of their annoyance.

Or that they didn't consider him worthy of hiding their true faces.

The second option ignited a flame of anger behind her sternum.

"Mom, Dad, I'd like to introduce you to Isaac Hunter, my new neighbor." She glanced at Isaac over her shoulder, briefly meeting his steady, dark eyes. "Isaac, these are my parents, Jasper and Helene Landon."

"The new neighbor," her mother repeated, undoubtedly recalling Jenna's insistence a couple of weeks ago that he was a "nonfactor" and "just her neighbor." And here they'd caught her getting out of her car with him on a Saturday evening—after avoiding their calls all day. "And the wrestling coach at the high school."

Only her mother could add enough inflection to make *wrestling coach* sound one step away from *drug dealer*. Shame coated her in a grimy filth.

"That's right," Isaac said, his voice a deep rumble. "As the ex-mayor, and given you're both business owners, maybe I can count on you to donate when fundraising time comes around for new team singlets."

Her father's mouth pinched, his eyes narrowing as if he'd sucked on a barrel of lemons.

"Have Brian Camden contact me or my wife. You are the *assistant* wrestling coach, right? We should probably talk to him about any financial matters."

Jesus.

Is this what she did to people? Was this how she deliberately cut them down and hurt them?

Yes, and you know it.

Bile churned in her belly, surging for her throat. It burned, and she desperately swallowed it back down.

Miraculously, a chuckle rolled from behind her, shivering over the nape of her neck. She fought against closing her eyes and leaning back against that wide chest.

"Point taken, Mr. Landon." He laughed again, and if possible, her father's face tightened even more. "I'll let Brian know to reach out."

"If you'll excuse us, Mr. Hunter, we'd like to speak to our daughter alone, please," her mother said, and it wasn't a request.

Again, Isaac didn't seem fazed by their rudeness. He settled a hand on the small of her back, and neither of her parents missed the action. Their gazes dipped to

where he touched her, and she couldn't stop the curl of
dread from twisting inside her.

"Of course." Isaac bowed his head and murmured
in her ear, "You okay?"

She nodded. "Yes, thank you."

He paused, studied her for a long moment. "Okay."
Straightening, he stepped back and smiled at her parents.
"Nice to meet you, Mr. and Mrs. Landon. Good night."

She watched his broad frame stride over to his property, and a longing yawned inside her. For the guts to ask
him not to go—or take him with her. But not just that.

She'd witnessed the love between him and his family today. It was the same love that existed between
Leo and the Dennisons. Even Sydney and her parents,
though they'd experienced pain in their relationship.
All of them had real love and acceptance.

That's what lay behind her longing.

Why had Isaac showed her that today?

It only pounded home, as she faced her mother and
father, what she didn't have.

What her foolish, foolish heart yearned for.

"Well, can we continue this conversation in your
house instead of outside on the sidewalk like tonight's
entertainment?" her father snapped, waving a hand toward her porch.

Smothering a sigh, she led them into her house and
living room. With other families, the parents might have
taken off their shoes and coats and sunk down onto the
couches, curling up and getting comfortable.

They were not that family.

Jenna had removed her jacket, but her parents elected
to keep theirs on.

Come to think of it, this was only the third time her

parents had visited her home and they'd never taken off their coats. Because they'd never eaten a dinner, shared a cup of coffee, spent an evening.

No one had.

The utter *wrongness* of that struck her in the chest like a debilitating blow, but she had to absorb it and keep moving.

She didn't have time to dwell on that right now. "The assistant wrestling coach, Jenna? Really?" her mother demanded, crossing her arms.

"And isn't he some kind of former wrestler?" Jasper scoffed, flinging a hand. "God, Jenna. He's not even a real athlete."

"There are millions of fans who would disagree with you on that point, Dad." Jenna courted disaster by defending Isaac. But damn if she'd allow her father to throw one more barb at Isaac while she remained silent.

"You promised me there was nothing going on between the two of you." Helene studied Jenna through a narrowed gaze. "And yet, my eyes weren't deceiving me just now when I saw you with him. And he *is* the reason we couldn't reach you today, isn't it?"

"Of course, he was," Jasper interrupted. "This is what I was talking about, Jenna." His mouth firmed, and he gave his head that slow, familiar shake—the one that set her stomach twisting with anxiety because she'd somehow let him down. "I told you weeks ago that my reelection campaign would require all of our efforts and full attention. I also warned you that we couldn't make mistakes or do anything that would bring embarrassment on our family name or on me. And that includes gossip over your unsavory behavior with a man who used to make his living rolling around in a ring."

Unsavory behavior?

What century were they in? The 1800s?

"I spent an afternoon with my neighbor who happens to be a respected athlete and high school coach. I'm sure if his reputation and skills weren't exemplary, the school board wouldn't have hired him. Nothing gossipworthy happened. If anyone saw us in the first place."

"Don't be naive, Jenna," her mother ground out. "This is Rose Bend. Expect for everything to be seen. And it doesn't matter if you two were going to church together. It's the fact that you were *together*. The appearance of committing the sin is enough to make it fact. And do you have any idea who you're getting involved with?" Helene shifted closer, her eyebrow arching high. "Let's just put aside that he's what, a wrestler? Actor? Entertainer? Sideshow act? But he's also a nobody from Mount Holly who married the much older owner of the company he worked for to sleep his way into a cushy position instead of working for it. And then, when she'd served her purpose and he'd reached as far as he could in his questionable career, he divorced her. That's who you're choosing to spend your time with? That's who, just by affiliation, will be reflecting on us. I told you, this is about more than you, Jenna. But once again, you're being selfish and inconsiderate."

Each word pummeled her, bruising her, leaving emotional marks behind.

Her mind rejected her mother's summary of Isaac and his character—neither of her parents knew the truth about him and it wasn't her place to divulge what he'd shared. But her heart...her heart soaked in every unspoken word in Helene's criticism.

You've let us down. Again.

Why can't you do anything right?
You're an embarrassment.
You only care about yourself.

Those statements should be tattooed into her skin by now. She'd lived them, become them. And no matter how hard she tried, she couldn't overcome them. For fifteen shining years, she'd been perfect. A daddy's girl. The golden child who could do no wrong...

Were you, though? Was everything as good as you remember?

She blinked. Where had that thought come from? She shook her head, but it was too late. The seed took root in her brain...

"Jenna, are you going to answer me?" Helene waved fingers in front of Jenna's face. "Or do you not have an answer? Because you didn't know about this man who just moved in next door and yet you decided to jump in *your* car with him, am I right? Once again, your decision-making leaves so much to be desired. Is it any wonder your father and I still have to support you? God knows what happens when we aren't there to advise you, to make sure you're doing what you're supposed to."

Jenna's stomach pitched. She didn't need to ask what her mother meant by that. The last time Jenna had kept a secret from them, she'd ended up pregnant, had miscarried and had nearly destroyed the reputation of the family in Rose Bend.

"Your mother's right. If it were up to me, you wouldn't have moved out of the house. I still don't understand why you did. There's more than enough room for the family, and how does it look to people that our single daughter doesn't live under our roof?" He glared, scanning the living room as if it personally offended him.

"It looks like what it is. A grown, independent woman moving out of her parents' house to her own home," Jenna said, suddenly tired. Tired of this conversation. Tired of feeling like the scolded child called on the carpet. Tired of not being enough.

Just…tired.

"Grown? Independent?" Jasper flicked up a finger to correspond with each of her points. "When we still deposit money into accounts to support you? Is that your definition of independence?" He chuckled without humor. "If not for my sister not minding her business, you couldn't even have afforded to buy this house."

And that still stuck in his craw. How her aunt Carrie—the same aunt they'd shipped her off to when Jenna had become pregnant and who'd taken her to Boston the first time—had left Jenna a small inheritance instead of leaving anything to Jasper when she'd died several years ago.

Both of her parents would choke on the knowledge that she hadn't touched their "allowance" for years. Their monthly deposits sat in a separate bank account accruing interest and dust. Since she'd received her first advance, she'd stopped living off their money. Because their "generosity" had strings.

"Other than to remind me—" *not to fuck up more than I have* "—of my responsibilities, was there a reason you needed to get in touch with me today?"

"Yes, Jenna," Jasper said with exasperation in his voice. "Chris arrived in town this morning. We were inviting you to dinner so we could begin planning the carnival in earnest. Chris was looking forward to seeing you again, but you, of course, were nowhere to be found." He slid his hands in the front pockets of his pants, drawing his shoulders back. "Now we know why."

Her stomach bottomed out, but she didn't show the weakness. Others, she might inadvertently reveal, unable to help herself. But this one? No. Because she could see they expected her to crack a little. After all, Chris was another sign of her failure.

"Well, I'm sorry I missed dinner. I'm sure we can reschedule since Chris will be in town until after the carnival."

"That's not the point," her mother said, tugging on the hem of her peplum jacket. "It's about accountability and loyalty. Are we going to be able to count on you, Jenna? Or can we expect more of these disappearing acts?"

"I'll be there."

"Good. I don't want a repeat of this conversation. We all need to do our part." Her father clapped his hands. "Well, your mother and I have to leave. Henry Kingston invited us over to his house for drinks. He's also having several other members of the business community over. My campaign hasn't even officially started and already I have the support of those who really matter in this town." He turned to her mother, waving a hand toward the front door. "Are you ready, Helene?"

"Yes. Jenna, we'll see you tomorrow for Sunday dinner." It wasn't a question or an invitation but a demand, and Jenna treated it as such, nodding. "Good night."

In moments, her parents exited, shutting the door behind them. The only evidence they'd been there were the faint traces of her mother's lilac perfume and the cold in Jenna's chest.

CHAPTER THIRTEEN

"IT'S SO PRETTY, Uncle Isaac!" Belle squealed, waving her pumpkin-spice cupcake toward the arch of autumn-colored leaves, pumpkins and sunflowers that stretched over the middle of Rose Bend's Main Street.

At some point during the week, the brick buildings, with their already colorful storefronts, the old-fashioned gas lamps and benches dotting the sidewalk, had been transformed into some kind of autumn fairyland. And he wasn't even given to flights of fancy. But here they were.

Garlands of leaves and orange lights wrapped around black iron posts. Fat pumpkins nestled in patches of crisp hay sat next to benches. More lights, leaves and plants he couldn't identify adorned buildings and draped above awnings. Rose Bend had officially welcomed October. All he had to do was glance down at his niece's face to confirm it. And his nephews', for that matter. Even Edward, the too-cool-to-show-emotions preteen, looked impressed.

"It is pretty," Isaac agreed, eyeing his niece and making sure she didn't accidentally smack someone with her cupcake. As adorable as she was, orange icing on clothes tended to deduct cute points. "So where do you guys want to go first?"

"The park!" Belle yelled. Because with her, nothing could be spoken with an inside voice.

"The library." Jacob shoved the last of his own cupcake into his mouth and tossed the wrapper and napkin in a nearby trash can.

"The ice cream shop," Edward said.

"Dude." Isaac shot a pointed glance at the cream-filled doughnut his nephew polished off. "You just had two doughnuts."

Edward tossed the dessert wrapping in the trash can. "And I saved plenty of room for my favorite caramel fudge brownie sundae."

Isaac cocked his head, squinting at the boy's stomach. Reaching out, he poked it. "Just how far down does that bottomless pit go? And do cars and small structures fit in there, too?"

Batting his hand away, Edward grumbled, "Cut it out, Unc." But a grin flickered at the corner of Edward's mouth.

"Okay." Isaac straightened, clapped his hands and rubbed them together. "Divide-and-conquer time. Since your dad is out at my house building a fabulous play set—"

"Why didn't he let you help, Uncle Isaac?" Belle asked him, licking icing off her fingers. "I think you could find your ass with a hammer. It's easy! I can do it!"

Oh shit.

"First, honey, when your mommy asks, you heard that word from your daddy, not me, 'kay? And second, I can totally find my a—uh, butt with a hammer. Still, we'll do what your daddy says and stay away from the house while he works. That means we're going to do this in teams." He patted his chest. "Team Park. I'll take Belle over there. Ed, you're Team Library. Take Jake over there and afterward, stop by to get ice cream." He removed his wallet from his back pocket and handed his oldest nephew a twenty-dollar bill. "We'll meet back here in front of Mimi's Café in two hours. Deal?"

The two boys wasted little time racing off down the street, and Isaac turned and watched them, holding Belle's hand, and not moving until they climbed the library's steps and disappeared inside the double doors.

"All right, Belle, let's hit this park and get the fun started."

"Yeah!"

Isaac grinned. Lena was going to need to teach Belle about speaking at a volume somewhere between cracking glass and tornado siren.

With Belle keeping up a steady stream of chatter that only required his occasional reply, they headed down the street toward the pretty town square—also beautifully decked out in autumn glory—where the town park sat on the other side of the street.

"Oh wow! Look at that!" Belle tugged on his hand, stopping him in his tracks and trying to drag him in the opposite direction of the square. "A wheel, Uncle Isaac! A wheel!"

Isaac looked up, glancing in the direction his niece pointed.

Oh.

A Ferris wheel soared to the sky in the distance, its colorful baskets gently swaying in the fall breeze. The iconic ride wasn't one of his favorites, yet delight tickled him, reverting him to a young boy excited over the knowledge that a carnival loomed on the horizon.

"Can we go see? *Please?*" Belle stretched the one syllable to about four, and he hesitated.

"Honey, the carnival isn't open. They're probably just setting up some of the rides. It's going to be boring for you to stand there and watch."

"No, it won't, Uncle Isaac. *Please?*"

He sighed. It would take a much stronger man than him to resist that plea or the big puppy dog eyes that went along with it. He was such a sucker, and Belle no doubt knew it.

"Fine, for a little while, though. Then we head to the park."

"Okay!"

They walked the short distance to the end of Main, where a huge, open field claimed the rest of the street. Several pockets of people gathered along the sidewalk in front of the meadow, and Isaac and Belle joined them. He'd been correct. While the Ferris wheel appeared to be fully erected, it stood alone. Workers milled about and a small tent claimed a spot near the parking lot on the far right, but no other rides had been constructed yet.

"Isaac? Isaac Hunter?"

He turned at the sound of his name, the charming, professional smile he'd perfected over the years already fixed in place. Funny how he slipped into the Mr. Right persona out of habit.

Funny how he hadn't done that with Jenna. As a matter of fact, he'd been the exact opposite of charming.

That should've been his clue right there that she was different. She hadn't allowed him to be overly polite or retreat into a character he'd played for over a decade.

Jenna had demanded he show up as himself. Demanded that he was real.

He forcefully dragged his thoughts away from the beautiful woman with hair like flame and eyes like the most refreshing water. Instead, he focused on the tall, wide-shouldered man approaching him with an outstretched hand. Isaac's smile warmed into a genuine grin as he moved forward, extending his own hand.

"Hey, Owen. Long time, no see."

"Not since that literacy foundation gala. It's good to see you again, man. But what the hell? Rose Bend?" The championship-winning quarterback of the Jersey Knights laughed. "I know the world is small, but this is ridiculous."

"You're telling—" A tug on his hand and Isaac peered down at Belle, who stared up at Owen with her big, pretty eyes. "Yes, honey?"

"He said 'hell.' Mommy said we can't say that word. Even though Daddy says it's okay 'cause it's in the Bible."

Fighting back a totally inappropriate bark of laughter, Isaac nodded. "I'm going to go with Mommy on this one. So don't say that one, okay?"

"Oops. My bad." Owen knelt down in front of Belle and held out his hand. "Your uncle and mom are right, and I'm sorry. I'll watch my mouth from now on. I'm Owen, by the way. What's your name?"

"I'm Bella," she said proudly, shaking his hand. "And you're pretty." Then she held up her finger that had a bright pink-and-yellow bandage wrapped around it. "Mommy put a Band-Aid on my ouchie. She could put one on yours, too." She pointed to the scars bisecting Owen's cheek and the corner of his mouth. "You can have my Hello Kitty one." Bella scrunched up her nose, then after a moment, shook her head. "No, you can have Elsa. I want Hello Kitty."

Isaac's heart had stopped when Bella baldly mentioned Owen's facial marks. They were a result of a bad car accident that had almost ended his football career. In her innocence, the little girl had prodded a sensitive area for the other man, and Isaac cupped Bella's shoulder, prepared to draw her back into the shelter of his body and apologize for her guileless remark.

But to his surprise, Owen tilted his head back and laughed.

"Well, I'll take Elsa. She just so happens to be one of my favorite people. Thanks, Bella, and it's really nice to meet you."

Standing, he twisted, waving to a woman behind him, as well as another couple.

"Isaac, I'd like you to meet my fiancée, Leontyne Dennison." He slid his arm around the waist of a lovely slender brunette with blue-gray eyes. "And this is my brother-in-law and Rose Bend's mayor, Cole Dennison, and his wife, Sydney."

Cole Dennison was a tall, lean Latino man with dark curls and Sydney a stunning, petite Black woman with natural, dark brown, shoulder-length hair and a curvaceous form. The Dennison family had a gorgeous and diverse family tree.

"Nice to meet you, Isaac. And you, too, Bella," Leontyne greeted with a smile that echoed in her bright eyes. "Everyone calls me Leo."

"Everyone calls me Belle," his niece piped up. "And my brothers Ed and Jake. But their names are Edward and Jacob."

All four adults gaped at her...then at Isaac.

"Get out," Leo breathed.

Isaac shrugged. "I cannot make this up."

A grin broke out on Cole's face. "Oh you're going to love our family then." He held out his hand and gave Isaac's a firm shake. "I can't lie, I've been pretty eager to meet you. I'm a big fan. Sooner or later, you'll meet my brother Wolf. Big. Viking-looking guy with a ridiculous man bun. Can't miss him. He's probably going to try and convince you that's he's the bigger WFC fan. Ignore him. It's a lie."

"Right. It's our brother Sonny," Leo interjected.

Cole shot her a withering glance. "Stay out of this." Shifting his attention back to Isaac, he grinned again. "Ignore her, too. I'm the biggest fan in the Dennison family. Welcome to Rose Bend."

Isaac laughed, releasing his hand. "Appreciate it."

If *this* was the current mayor, Isaac could definitely see, just from this first impression, why the people in this town threw out the prior one. Cole Dennison seemed infinitely more personable than Jasper Landon.

That man was an ass.

"And hi, now that he's done fawning over you," Sydney said, with a wry smile and a wave. "I'm his wife. Although, we've kind of already met. At Mimi's Café a couple of weeks ago. You might not recognize me because I had my daughter attached to my leg then. We didn't have a chance to speak."

Yes, that's why she seemed familiar.

An echo of the tightness that had clutched his chest in the coffee shop weeks ago pinched his ribs. She'd been the woman with the little girl who'd reminded him of Sam. Who'd triggered his panicked response. Then, he'd been too preoccupied to notice anything beyond the child, but now regret for his rude exit crept through him and he dipped his chin in acknowledgment.

"I remember. And I also need to apologize for my behavior that day. I—" *was in the middle of a panic attack* "—had a lot on my mind and was a little out of it. But it's good to officially meet you now."

"Oh. And here I was thinking it might've been the company that day." Sydney snorted. "Jenna Landon tends to have that effect on people. She was going to be my excuse."

Isaac stiffened. "I'm sorry?"

"I saw you talking to her in the coffee shop. That could have an adverse effect on anyone's indigestion."

"Uh, Syd…" Leo murmured, a small, weird smile curling her lips.

"Oh please, Leo." Sydney rolled her eyes. "If you come to her defense one more time… I don't want to hear it. Not only will a leopard change its spots before she does, but it will sport pinstripes and patterns first."

"Sydney," Leo said again. "Jenna is Isaac's next-door neighbor."

"Oh. *Oh.*" A sheepish expression crossed her face. "Well, I don't need to tell you about her then."

"No," Isaac said, his tone even but firm. "You don't. I've come to know Jenna pretty well."

Sydney silently studied him for a long moment. Then she heaved a loud sigh. "God. She's gotten to you, too. What is this? Some new religion? A cult where she's recruiting converts? I swear, I'm five minutes away from hiring a van for a kidnapping and a mind-wipe." Sydney waved a hand toward the field behind them. "Case in point. This carnival."

"Actually, the carnival is her father's project," Cole said. "And it's not a nefarious plan for world domination, Sydney. It's just a carnival, and it'll be fun for the town. As well as bring in revenue."

"Not world domination," his wife grumbled. "Just Rose Bend domination. Nothing Jasper Landon does has such altruistic motives. If he was being so thoughtful about the town, then he would've scheduled this thing for the week before or after the Spooks 'n' Books Bash at the library. Being on the town council, or just a member of this community, he knew Remi and the other librarians planned a weekend-long event to raise funding they really need. Who's going to visit the library on a Saturday night now when there's a carnival in town? No one, that's who. Nope, Jasper's the same self-serving jerk and he's up to something. And you bet you're a—" she glanced down at Bella "—Adirondack chair that Jenna's at his right hand, all up in it."

"I've recently met her father," Isaac said. "And let me say, based on first impressions alone, I'm glad to have moved here under your regime—" he nodded at Cole "—instead of his. But Jenna is nothing like him. I can't speak for your experience with her, but from mine, she's a good person. More than that, she's been kind and welcoming to me."

The other four people stared at him, wearing varying degrees of surprise in their expressions. Owen and Cole gazed at him, bemused. Sydney appeared as if torn between wanting to hug him and shake him. And Leo... Leo still wore that small, weird smile that carried a hint of satisfaction.

"Ms. Jenna!"

Bella's scream rang out several seconds before she

yanked her hand out of his and darted to the small knot of people gathered several yards way. He hadn't noticed them before, but now, he couldn't drag his gaze away from them.

An electrified jolt streaked through him, crackling across every nerve ending and sizzling down his spine. Until now, he might as well have been sleepwalking, because it only required one glance at *her* and he jerked to abrupt, vivid wakefulness.

It'd been a week since that Saturday motorcycle ride. Since that day spent with her. Since that evening when her parents had shown up and he'd witnessed her shrink right before his eyes.

Part of him had expected her withdrawal. It'd happened after the night on her porch and after the time on the dock. It seemed to be her MO—when she allowed someone too close, she fled. But this was different. He'd been completely iced out. No casual nods if they happened to pass each other while arriving or leaving their houses. No waves. No acknowledgment of any kind.

Because he hadn't glimpsed her at all.

It was almost as if she'd followed through on her confession to him and moved out of Rose Bend. If not for the presence of her car, he might've marched over to her house just to see if she still occupied it. He'd mentally skirted around the irrational panic that had ripped through him.

Now, staring at her—that lovely, tight body elegantly clothed in an emerald sweater dress and heels that made her toned legs look impossibly longer—and that sheet of red-gold hair streaming down her back, he understood that flare of panic.

Feared it, resented it, but understood it.

He couldn't think of this fresh start in Rose Bend without her in it. She'd branded herself on his life. She'd marked him. And something in him rebelled at the prospect.

He didn't want his body humming to exquisitely painful life from just being within feet of her. Didn't want this razor-sharp awareness sliding over his senses like a searing kiss.

Didn't want his heart damn near crashing against his chest like a ten-car pileup at just the sight of her.

How pathetic did it make him that in this moment he envied Bella her complete abandon in running across to Jenna and throwing her arms around her thighs? In showing her affection without fear of rejection or betrayal or abandonment? How sad did it make him that he envied his niece that hand to the top of her head?

Very.

The answer was very.

"You better get your niece," Leo advised. "Jenna might not hurt her feelings for interrupting that little gathering, but her father eats children for lunch. I'm 96.3 percent certain he sleeps under a toll bridge. We just don't have photographic proof yet."

Isaac snorted but didn't need her suggestion. He'd already checked Jasper Landon's pinched expression of distaste as well as the irritated confusion on the other man's face. If he said anything to bruise Bella's heart, Isaac would bring Mr. Right's celebrated finisher out of retirement and lay both of them out cold.

"It's nice to see you again, Belle," Jenna said as he approached the group.

"You, too, Ms. Jenna. When are you coming back

over to ride motorcycles again? You gots to go again now that you're not scared anymore."

"You? On a motorcycle? A lot of things have changed since I was last in Rose Bend," the younger man standing with the group drawled, giving Jenna a smile.

A knowing smile.

A smile that said he possessed intimate, personal knowledge of just how much she disliked motorcycles.

Isaac didn't like him.

Not his dark, stylishly cut hair. Not his custom-made blue suit. Not his face, which would sell a ton of magazines…or a shit ton of used cars.

No, he didn't like him.

"Yep." Bella tilted her head back, arms still wrapped around Jenna's thigh. "She rode with my uncle Isaac! Didn't you, Ms. Jenna?"

"Belle, you know you're not supposed to run off like that," Isaac interrupted, gently scolding his niece—and letting Jenna off the hook from answering Bella's question. He held his hand out toward her, and with a grumbled apology, she took it. "Sorry about that." He dipped his chin at Jenna, meeting her blue gaze. "Hey, neighbor." Shifting his attention to the other men, he said, "Nice to see you again, Mr. Landon."

"Right. My daughter's neighbor. Hunter, isn't it?" Jasper asked, and his supercilious voice grated on Isaac's nerves.

But a man didn't enjoy a long career like Isaac's without employing a game face that had been tried by rabid reporters, angry fans and trash-talking gossip columnists. Jasper Landon definitely couldn't crack it.

"Please, call me Isaac."

"Or Mr. Right." The wattage on the newcomer's

smile ratcheted up to ingratiating. Isaac ground his teeth together. "It's a pleasure to meet you." He extended his hand toward Isaac, and though he didn't trust the other man's manner, his too-wide, too-slick smile or how he spoke and looked at Jenna, Isaac shook it. Then checked to make sure his watch remained on his wrist before he lowered it to his side.

"I'm Chris Rappaport. And a huge fan."

Doubtful. But it sounded good.

For some reason, Isaac suspected that was Chris Rappaport's specialty—making things sound good.

"Jasper, looks like things are coming along with the carnival." Cole appeared beside Isaac and slipped his hands in the front pockets of his pants. "Chris, nice to see you again."

"You, too, Cole. It's good to be back in Rose Bend. I've always liked this town."

His gaze shifted to Jenna and lingered on her. Isaac physically curbed the urge to step in front of her and order Chris to keep his eyes to himself.

Huh. He silently sneered at himself. Who knew he possessed a latent caveman gene?

"If I remember, you left right after the election. I guess there wasn't anything…or anyone to keep you here. A pity," Leo mused, stepping up next to her brother.

Chris's smile froze, as did his green eyes.

Isaac glanced between him and Leo, sensing he'd missed something. Neither Chris nor Leo looked away from each other, until Jenna murmured, "Leo."

The brunette frowned at her, scrunching up her nose. "You're no fun."

"Your kind of fun causes a man shrinkage," Owen said, sliding an arm around his wife's shoulders.

"Owen Strafford," Leo gasped. "Tender ears," she hissed, jerking her head in Bella's direction.

Isaac snorted. "When I return her to her mother, I'm blaming everything on all of you."

"Excuse me," Jasper interjected, his voice dripping with disdain.

Right. Isaac had tried to forget the other man stood there. But Jasper had to go and remind him.

"We are having a private meeting here, if you don't mind," Jasper continued.

"A private meeting about the carnival?" Cole arched an eyebrow. "Since this is a council-approved and financed function, is the information in this meeting something the council needs to hear as well?" he asked. The question, though pleasant enough, carried a vein of steel.

And Jasper didn't appreciate it. At all.

Shit. Small-town politics were a hotbed of intrigue.

Okay, maybe not intrigue. But hell if they weren't messy.

"No, it's nothing like that," Chris assured Cole with a chuckle.

"I believe him, Cole," Leo said, patting her brother's forearm. "After all, Chris is Jasper's *campaign manager*. So he wouldn't have anything to do with the carnival because this doesn't have anything to do with a *campaign* for a position that's already filled."

No, not just messy. Messy as fuck.

Isaac jerked his gaze to Jenna, who remained silent and stoic throughout the entire exchange. She briefly met his eyes, and everything in him...stopped. Just...

stopped. Because he'd spotted nothing in those summer-blue eyes. He'd seen anger, haughtiness, wistfulness, vulnerability and even a glimpse of delight. But he'd never seen—nothing.

Those eyes he found to be one of the most beautiful things about her were dull. Lifeless.

He wanted to stalk across the few feet separating them, sweep her into his arms, carry her away to his truck and shelter her from whatever put that look in her gaze.

Then he wanted to return to this field, get up in Jasper's space and tell him just how much of an asshole he was to not recognize the effect he had on his daughter.

Jasper shut her down as effectively as if someone stole the batteries from one of Bella's toys, rendering them silent.

Isaac didn't have any proof, had never heard the words from Jenna's lips, that her relationship with her father was, at best, dismissive, at worst, toxic. But he'd bet his left nut he wasn't wrong.

Jenna was as vibrant as her hair, and Jasper had snuffed her out. Which made his behavior toward his daughter an unforgivable sin.

Bella slid her hand out of his again and sidled over to Jenna's side, wrapping her fingers around Jenna's.

It was official. His family rocked.

"Since Jasper is taking point on this event, I offered to lend a hand along with Jenna." Chris treated Leo to another one of his politician smiles, which was all teeth, but contained a little bite, too. "Which reminds me, Ms. Dennison. I heard how you recruited Sherrod Forrester to be a judge in the spring festival a few months back. Convincing an all-star and championship-winning wide receiver to participate in your little chili contest was quite an accomplishment. But I'm sure having his best friend as a fiancé helped." The asshole chuckled, and yeah, that shit was mean.

Why couldn't he hit him? Just once? And it didn't have anything to do with how Chris looked at Jenna as if he knew secrets about her that Isaac didn't.

Well, not really.

"Leo didn't need any help from me," Owen calmly said, but his eyes narrowed on the other man. If Chris didn't spot the ominous warning in the quarterback's gaze, then he was willfully blind. "She's pretty damn persuasive on her own."

"Oh I'm counting on it," Chris agreed. "For the carnival, we were considering something fun like a kissing booth. Nothing too offensive, just a buss on the lips or cheek. But, Leo, I was hoping you'd convince Owen to participate. And maybe, Mrs. Dennison—" he turned to Sydney "—you'd lend us your husband, the mayor, here. And Isaac, what about it? I bet having Mr. Right included would bring in a ton of traffic."

"No."

Isaac tried but failed to contain his snort at Sydney's blunt and flat refusal. Cole's mouth twitched, and he shrugged when Chris looked at him.

"I can't go against my wife. What's the saying? Happy wife, happy life."

"Oh I don't know, Sydney," Leo drawled. "Where's your town spirit? I'm willing to donate Owen for the cause."

"Oh really?" Owen arched a dark eyebrow.

"Of course." She nodded. "We should all sacrifice

for the good of the town. You for the kissing booth. If Chris is willing to volunteer for Pin the Tail on the Ass."

"Uncle Isaac," Bella chimed in, helpfully. "She said—"

"I know, honey. Make sure and tell your mommy."

"Sweetheart, I think you mean Pin the Tail on the Donkey," Owen corrected his wife with a smirk.

"Oops." Leo grinned. "My bad."

"If you'll excuse us, we have work to do," Jasper said coldly. "Chris, Jenna, please meet me back at my office."

Without a glance or word to them, Jasper walked away, Chris beside him. Jenna hesitated, still holding Bella's hand.

After a moment, she peered down at her and murmured, "I have to go, Belle. I'll see you later, okay?"

"Okay, Ms. Jenna! You promise?"

"I promise."

Bella grinned, then skipped the few feet back over to Isaac. He held out his hand to Bella, who grasped it, but he couldn't remove his attention from Jenna. And she wouldn't meet his eyes. Instead, she glanced over her shoulder in the direction of her father and Chris Rappaport then looked at Leo. But not before her gaze skipped over Sydney.

He frowned, as did Sydney.

There was something between them. And not just the animosity Cole's wife clearly possessed for Jenna. Another emotion brewed underneath, just beneath the surface. An emotion not as easy as anger.

"Pin the Tail on the Ass? Really?"

Leo sniffed, buffing her nails against her jacket then stretching her splayed fingers out in front of her.

"What? It was one of my best. And he deserved it. I know he was more than Jasper's campaign manager. And when he lost the election, he just hightailed it out of here without a backward glance. Now he's back and what? He's thinking he's just going to pick back up where he left off with your father's campaign *and* with you? F-U-C-K that," Leo spelled it out, a snap in her voice, jabbing a finger at Jenna. "And don't try and convince me that he's not here to do *both* of those things. I have eyes and a brain."

He'd suspected the truth—hell, he'd known it. But still, the confirmation rammed into him like a two-by-four to the rib cage. That asshole knew what her kiss tasted like. Knew what pleasure looked like on her face, how it flushed her body. Knew what how it felt to be lost in her, to be welcomed.

Pain bloomed along his jaw from grinding his teeth together and trapping his growl from rolling out. He'd never considered himself a jealous man before. Never seen the point in it. Even now, he got that Chris was Jenna's past, and standing here envisioning tearing into the man for touching her was senseless. She was his neighbor, for God's sake. That's it.

Didn't stop him from wanting to wrap the douche up in a cradle, though...

"Why do you care?" Jenna asked. But the question lacked belligerence. Instead, it contained a wary curiosity that struck Isaac as guarded, vulnerable, almost childlike.

"Same thing I want to know," Sydney muttered.

Leo crossed her arms and glared first at Sydney then Jenna. "Because, *Ginny Weasley*, reasons."

The undercurrents between the three women could

tow a person under and drown them. Sydney returned Leo's glare and the flash of yearning in Jenna's blue gaze was there and gone so fast, Isaac believed he was the only one to catch it. But a glance to his right had him questioning that assumption. Cole regarded Jenna closely, frowning.

"Jenna," Jasper called, irritation rife in his voice.

A slight flinch jerked her body, but she swiftly controlled it.

"You're a menace, Leo," Jenna snapped.

"And I still owe you a pasta dinner, Jenna," Leo cooed.

With one last flinty stare, Jenna stepped back. But before she turned to follow her father and her ex, their gazes connected. Held. Then slid away. But that brief connection reverberated in his chest, his gut…his cock.

She left, catching up to Jasper and Chris. And from the stiff set of her father's shoulders and the rapid movement of his lips, Isaac could only guess what he said to his daughter. Her ruler-straight posture and the tilt of her chin telegraphed it probably wasn't affectionate.

"Leo, you've got to be kidding me with this Jenna thing," Sydney hissed. "Why are—"

Yeah, he was done with this shit.

"Bella, close your ears," Isaac gently ordered his niece.

The little girl clapped her palms over her ears but tilted her head back and stared up at him as if trying to read his lips. He wouldn't be surprised if she had the ability. He switched his attention to Leo and Sydney.

"I'm new here so I can't speak to who Jenna's been up to now or what happened between the three of you," Isaac interrupted. "But I hope that if you ever need

grace and room to change, that there are people willing to give you that forgiveness."

Sydney recoiled as if his words delivered a verbal
slap, and Cole stroked a hand up his wife's back, wrapping it around the nape of her neck.

"Isaac, that's enough," he said, a warning in his tone.

"You don't know," Sydney breathed.

"And I get that," Isaac softly agreed, glancing at
Cole, then back at her. "I don't know your history. But
I do know what it is to desperately want the chance to
change. To make amends. To prove I'm more than a
name or a reputation or my past. And I also have something you don't. New eyes. I don't see her through the
lens of old hurts or anger. I just see her. That's all I'm
asking you to try and do. Not be her friend. Not even
talk to her. Only try and *see* her." He cleared his throat,
because damn, he'd said entirely too much. Glancing
down, he tapped Bella on the shoulder, "Belle, you can
uncover your ears now."

"Okay, Uncle Isaac." She smiled up at him. "I'm
going to be Ms. Jenna's friend and see her, too, okay?"

For fuck's sake.

"Yeah, honey. You do that. How 'bout we get to the
park before it gets too late?"

"Yeah!" Grabbing his hand, she tugged him in the
direction of the sidewalk.

"Good seeing you again, Owen. And nice meeting
you, Cole, Sydney and Leo." He nodded and allowed
himself to be dragged across the field, feeling their
gazes on him.

They were probably wondering where the hell he
came off lecturing them about Jenna Landon. He
couldn't answer that. The last thing he intended to be

for anyone—the last thing he was equipped to be for anyone—was a knight in shining armor. First, he was no knight and second, his armor sported too many dents and scratches.

Besides, no matter what he'd said to Sydney, he didn't truly know Jenna.

An image of those lovely, shuttered blue eyes flashed across his mind. He doubted anyone truly knew Jenna because that would require her letting someone past the barbed wire barrier wrapped around her. She remained a beautiful enigma. And if there was one thing he'd learned in his marriage, especially toward the end, it was that keeping secrets meant a person didn't believe their partner was strong enough to handle the truth.

He couldn't knowingly be in a relationship with a person who held secrets. Because those secrets would eventually destroy everything. And only a masochist signed up for that kind of pain twice. A masochist and an idiot.

He was neither.

So no, maybe it was better that Jenna had placed distance between them.

Now if he could just get his body to agree with his head, he would be fine.

CHAPTER FOURTEEN

JENNA SIPPED FROM her cup of coffee, then placed it down on the small table next to her chair. Between the warm brew, her bulky cardigan and the flames in the firepit, the bite of the October evening air didn't really touch her. Not enough to send her back inside the house.

This was her favorite time of day—when the moon was high, the night peaceful and the creek a streak of ink past her backyard. Her parents had claimed a lot of her time this past week. As if in punishment for missing dinner with them the previous Saturday, they'd done their best to monopolize all her hours in the days that followed. Breakfast and dinner at the house with Chris. Working lunches in the conference room at her father's investment firm. And most of the time, she just sat there like a decorative ink blotter. Pretty to look at but useless.

That's what she'd been reduced to for the last six days.

Trapped.

And she'd suffered in silence because the alternative meant another scene like the one at her house. She hated herself for caring. Resented herself for still *craving* her parents love and approval…their forgiveness. So much that she would subjugate her desires, her personality, her needs to place them first.

Just how long was she willing to do that? Just how long could she go on living this lie? This half life?

Two more months, a voice whispered.

And then what? Never return to Rose Bend? Avoid her parents for the rest of her life? That didn't make her less of a coward. That was just geography.

Picking up her coffee again, she took another sip and closed her eyes, savoring the warmth as she cradled the cup. At least this evening, she'd found the courage to beg off from another dinner. After rising early in the mornings and grabbing hours late at night, this was *her* evening. To work. To write.

To escape.

Her phone pinged, and a notification popped up.

I. M. Kelly: Time. I got 877 words this round. What're you looking like?

Jenna pulled up her calculator on her phone, entering the number of words she'd started with at the beginning of the hour and the number she'd written by the end. Satisfaction filled her.

Beck: 922.

I. M. Kelly: That's awesome. You're killing it tonight. Welcome back. :-D

Beck: Yes. It feels good.

God, it did. She'd promised herself she wouldn't allow anything or anyone to interfere with her career again after her father's last run—and loss—for mayor.

But the first test of that, and she was failing. Pressing the heel of her palm to her chest, she rubbed, trying to ease the pressure. Tonight had been good so far. The writing challenges with Israel had been amazing, the words were flowing and the story was shaping up solidly. She didn't need to get derailed now.

I. M. Kelly: Hey, I need to call it a night but before I let you go, I have a favor to ask. Please don't feel you have to say yes.

Beck: You know me by now. I won't.

They'd been friends—online friends who didn't know each other's true identities, yes, but still—for years now. She'd just discovered Israel's true name months ago, and he still didn't know who she was, yet she'd "talked" more to him than she had most people in this town. And that was before he'd moved here to play bartender in a dive bar. Yes, she could describe him as a friend. He was only one of two people she could actually call that. The other was Olivia, who had been a friend since high school. The difference, though? She didn't hold anything back from Olivia as she did Israel. Because if he ever suspected Beck Dansing was Jenna Landon, she harbored zero doubts he'd have nothing to do with her.

So she kept her secret. Or rather, another secret.

She had so many, she needed a tally board at this point.

I. M. Kelly: LMAO. I do know.

I. M. Kelly: My local library is having a fundraising event at the end of the month. If I paid for the books, would you mind sending me signed print copies of your latest release to donate?

Jenna tipped her head back and stared at the dark night sky. Every year, the Rose Bend Public Library hosted the Spooks 'n' Books Bash on Halloween. It was a popular event for families, and this year, her father had managed to convince just enough council members that the carnival wouldn't diminish the library event's attendance. It'd been bullshit, of course. But it'd all come down to money. The carnival would bring in more money for the town as a whole, while the library's event would not.

She hadn't agreed with his decision or tactics, and she'd been painted guilty by association. Could she blame most people for thinking that, though?

No.

Not when her ass had been standing by her father's side in The Glen today.

She sighed.

Beck: I'm not allowing you to pay me for anything. Tell me where to send the books and I'll donate the signed copies myself.

She'd have to do some subterfuge with driving to another town or city to mail them off, but she'd figure that out.

I. M. Kelly: Thanks, Beck! I appreciate it.

I. M. Kelly: Fair warning. Expect an email from Remi Howard, the head librarian of Rose Bend Public Library. Last time I was in there, I mentioned I knew you. Apparently, she's a huge fan. :-D

I. M. Kelly: She's going to reach out and ask if you can be a guest at the annual Halloween event. She knows you're a notorious hard no when it comes to public events, but she's desperate to drum up publicity, media attention and attendance. Who better than Beck Dansing?

Should she do it?

Could she do it?

Could she step out of the shadows into the light and reveal herself to the friends she had, the people in town? To Isaac?

To her parents?

Her heart crept up to her throat and lodged there. Her fingers fluttered up to meet it. What was she thinking? No. God, no. How would this unveiling go? Her life wasn't some Disney channel sitcom where everyone would get past their surprise then surround her with congratulations, finally embracing her.

Life didn't work like that. At least hers didn't.

Her mouth twisted into a wry smile. She wasn't a Dennison.

Beck: I'll keep an eye out for the email, but I don't plan on retiring my recluse act anytime soon.

I. M. Kelly: Understood.

I. M. Kelly: Hit me up if you're writing tomorrow.

Beck: I will. Night.

I. M. Kelly: Nite.

Placing her phone down beside her coffee cup, she returned to her laptop, and soon lost herself in the world where the offspring of the Nephilim attended Anakim Academy, a private school where they learned how to harness their special abilities even as the armies of heaven and hell wanted them wiped from existence.

"I feel like I should whistle or something."

"Shit." Jenna's spine hit the back of her chair, and she splayed her fingers over her heart.

The rapid pounding of her pulse thrummed in her ears. But then, the familiar voice penetrated her shock, and the tall frame stepped fully into the circle of light thrown by the flames from the firepit.

"I come in peace," Isaac said, holding up his hands, palms out.

"You scared me." With a huff, she lowered her hand from her chest, but glared at him. "What're you doing here?"

"I was coming home and saw smoke. Didn't smell burning leaves so that left intentional fire or accidental fire. Both required investigation, just in case I needed to call the fire department like a good neighbor."

"Well, you can see my house isn't in danger of burning down." She swept an arm out, indicating her very safe fire contained within its tall, decorative pit of stone. "Thank you for checking on me and potentially saving me from a fire but nearly giving me a heart attack."

A smile tugged at the corner of his sensual mouth, and she tried not to stare at how the flames cast shadows, lending his lips a wicked slant.

"You must've been scared. You said the s-word." His voice dropped to a hushed tone, ending on a dramatic gasp.

"Cursing is for those with small vocabularies and even smaller minds." The words leaped out of her mouth by rote.

His smile eased into a smirk, though something flickered in his eyes. "Why does that sound more like your father talking than you?"

Her mother, actually. She looked away, her gaze locking on her laptop.

"You're still working? Which is it tonight? Secretarial or bookkeeping?"

Jenna's hand hovered over the top of the monitor. What if he caught a glimpse of her screen? His brother read her books, so maybe Isaac would recognize character names or the name of the academy... Then the choice to reveal an essential part of herself would be taken out of her hands. And she could be free of one of these burdens.

She lowered the screen.

Hid the temptation.

"What're you doing here, Isaac?" she asked again.

"I came by to see if you're okay. Earlier, you seemed...off." He strode forward and settled into the chair next to her. "No, actually, fuck that. I'm being too polite."

"Are you?" Jenna murmured.

"My version of it." He leaned forward, propping his elbows on his thick, denim-covered thighs. The dancing flames lent his strong, bold features an orange glow, and in its light, she traced every uncompromising line. "But since we're past that, obviously, what the hell was that today?"

Jenna picked up her cup of coffee. Not because she had a sudden need for caffeine. But to ward off his questions and that stare. That damn unnerving, piercing stare.

"You're going to have to be more specific," she said, peering down into the cup's depths. "The show my father put on today? Christopher's pompous act? The hatred Sydney has for me?"

He nodded. "Let's start there and end with, is that pompous ass really your ex, and why did you disappear in front of me *again* with your father? And if we have time, maybe we can touch on why your father doesn't seem to give a fuck if the current mayor knows he's making a run for his seat."

I don't disappear, sat on her tongue. But she couldn't voice it. Because it would be a lie. But the fact that Isaac had noticed…it hurt. God, it hurt.

Deciding to tackle the less incendiary of those topics, she lifted her gaze to his. "Yes, Chris is actually my ex. I'd call it a momentary lapse in judgment, but it lasted for seven months." She lifted a shoulder. "What can I say? Convenience since he was here leading my father's campaign. Charmed by the facade. Boredom. The why doesn't matter. I stayed in the relationship much longer than I should've and didn't end it when I definitely should've. Instead, when Dad lost the election, Chris packed up and left Rose Bend without a goodbye. Well, I take that back." She lowered her cup to her lap with a small huff of dry laughter. "He sent me an email once he arrived back in New York."

"Well, shit, why didn't he just stick a Post-it note on your door?" The disgust twisting Isaac's lips smoothed a balm over a spot on her soul she hadn't even been aware was still sore from that rejection. "So that's what Leo referred to earlier. Is he trying to pick up where he left off?"

She scoffed. "Men like Chris only do anything if it's beneficial to them. He figured out over a year and a half ago that money, influence and power are the way to my father's heart, not his daughter. That's how he could leave town so easily and show up here again with a smile and no regret. He won't waste his time on me when it doesn't advance him. And I wasn't that good a lay to incur my father's wrath by being a distraction now."

"The fuck?" The quiet demand rippled across the space separating them but it might as well as have been a roar.

Isaac slowly straightened, fury darkening his face before his expression went carefully, *fascinatingly* blank. It sent a trill of sharp-edged excitement tripping through her, and she had no idea how to handle it.

"Are you offended on my behalf?" she murmured. "That's really nice."

"Nice?" he spit as if he'd tasted something foul. "I don't know what to be more pissed off at right now. That asshole for letting you believe that a problem getting you off was on you and not him. Or at you for being surprised that I could be offended for you. Damn, Jenna. Who hasn't fucking failed you?"

"Me," she whispered, the coffee swilling in her

belly though she sat perfectly still. "You've received
a glimpse into my family. Enough to know they aren't
yours. They aren't bright, shiny people given to quick
teasing and quicker laughter. They're freer with criticism than affection. More stingy with praise than harsh
words. You couldn't possibly understand what it is to
have terms and conditions placed on love. When you
live with that kind of uncertainty, you learn to depend
on yourself. To strengthen yourself. To pick your own
self up because no one else will do it."

"Malibu," he murmured.

"No, I've made a mess of how I've protected myself. I've hurt people with my actions, my inaction. My
words, my silence. My compliance, my fear. I've been
a lot of things. A bitch. A princess. A gossip. A darling daughter, a disappointment. And God yes, I have
a lot to apologize for. But failing myself is not one of
those things. I've always been there for myself when
no one else was. I won't allow anyone to take that away
from me."

Only the pop of the flames punctuated the weighty
silence between them. Her too passionate, too *telling*
declaration seemed to ring in the night air, and she tried
not to cringe at all she'd inadvertently revealed with that
deluge of emotion.

"You're wrong."

She stared at him. At the hard slant of his mouth, the
glitter in his narrowed eyes.

"Excuse me?"

"I said, you're wrong. Not about failing yourself. I
stand corrected on that and thank you for setting me
straight. But there's no damn way you could ever be a
disappointment. Not to yourself or even to your par-

ents, who could really benefit from having the sticks
yanked out of their asses. No, I don't know the ins and
outs of your life, your family. But I don't care who or
what you've been in the past—what've you've done.
You, Jenna Landon, are impressive."

"You don't know what you're talking about," she
rasped.

"Then tell me." He inched forward on the wooden
chair, his voice low, insistent. "Dammit, Malibu, let
me in. Take a risk like you did getting on that motorcycle. Trust me not to hurt you, not to fail you. And if
you need it from me, to shield you. I look at you and I
see a woman who's stood on her own for a long time.
Just…" He flipped his hands palms up, splayed his fingers wide. "Just let me be someone you can lean on for
a little while. Take that from me because I'm offering
it. Willingly. I'm begging you to take it."

I'm begging you to take it.

This man…so big, strong, proud…begging her to do
anything, sought out each chink in her defenses. How
did he make her feel as if her thoughts, her opinions
were so important to him?

I want to feel that important to someone.

She wanted to shut down that wistful, saddened
voice.

But…

The very people who were supposed to love her, accept her, forgive her without conditions, had rejected
her when they discovered her truth, her secret. To this
day, they viewed her in the stain of her sins. The sins of
imperfection, of failure, of disloyalty. And the cardinal
one—of failing to remember who she was and whose
name she carried.

If her own parents couldn't forgive her, couldn't look at her without remembering and condemning, then why would Isaac? And to see that same disgust stamped on his face...

Her throat closed up around the truth.

As damaged and deep as their history was, she and Leo still had just that—history. And Leo was... Leo.

Isaac was an unknown variable. A variable she desired with a hunger that mocked her. A variable she feared with all the pain of a girl and woman who bore scars dealt by heartbreak.

"Try me." Isaac didn't demand, didn't plea, even though he'd claimed to be begging. But those two simple words fell into a place somewhere between.

She met his cobalt gaze.

He's not your parents.

The clarity of that truth rang in her head as clear as the bell in the steeple of St. John's Catholic Church. And she trusted that truth, clung to it. Because part of her was so. Damn. Tired.

Of carrying secrets. Of bearing guilt. Of being alone.

He'd begged her to take a risk on him. For a moment, the wind from that motorcycle ride blew across her face, and she leaped again, heart in her throat, praying he'd catch her.

"I had a miscarriage when I was fifteen years old."

The confession burst from her like a ball expelled from a cannon.

She couldn't look away from him. Needed to catalog every emotion that flickered over his expression.

Needed to glimpse that first hint of shocked disappointment so she could fold in on herself, say, *See? I told you so. This is what trusting gets you.* There existed this tiny part of her that wanted to be proved right.

But the harder she peered into that face of dramatic angles and carnal curves, the more she spotted…nothing.

No condemnation. No surprise. No pity. Not even sympathy.

Nothing but a fierce concentration that enabled her to continue in the thick silence.

"His name was Holden Daniels and he was a junior in high school, a drummer in the marching band, so smart and so incredibly *nice.* And for a band nerd—" her lips curled at the title her first love had proudly claimed "—he'd been just as popular as the quarterback. And he liked me.

"I couldn't believe it, but I felt so lucky. Even if he insisted we keep our relationship a secret because he was seventeen and I was a freshman. I understood, but God, I wanted to let everyone know he was my boyfriend. Because I was in love. And when a girl is in love for the first time, she should be able to shout it, wear his jacket, hold his hand walking down the hall, kiss him by his car. But that never happened. Toward the end of the school year, I discovered I was pregnant."

Echoes of the disbelief, the horror and the fear from that long-ago day when she'd stared down at the pregnancy test she'd bought in a drugstore the next town over rippled through her.

The discordant scrape of wood against stone snatched her from the past, and she flinched. Long, warm fingers enfolded hers as they removed her forgotten coffee cup and set it on the table. Isaac's knees bracketed her. It seemed impossible that with just her hands wrapped in his and her legs bordered by his long ones, she felt cradled.

Supported.

"I was terrified. We'd only had sex three times and once without a condom. How could I be pregnant?" Her chuckle, though soft, chafed her throat like rusty wire. "God, I was so naive."

"You were so young," he gruffly corrected.

"Old enough to know better," she said. After a moment, she shook her head and stared down at their clasped hands. So foreign yet…familiar. "I tried to deny what was happening, but after a couple of weeks, I couldn't. My fear followed me into my dreams, and it was a nightmare that betrayed me. I woke up screaming—I don't even remember the details now, just the terror that hunted me down like I was a criminal. And I guess I was in a way. I'd committed a sin and was paying the consequences."

A sound rumbled in Isaac's throat, and it struck her as somewhere between a scoff and a curse. Funny how in that rough sound she finally found the disgust she'd been waiting on. And it didn't scrape her raw. It didn't break her.

It emboldened her.

"At fifteen, raised by conservative parents, afraid and pregnant, that was my mindset. And so when my mom came into my room, when I was fresh out of a nightmare and crying, I told her everything. I expected her to be shocked, of course. And angry, even. But I also expected her, needed her, to comfort me, to tell me everything would be okay. That *I* would be okay. That's not what happened."

Jenna paused, and she dragged in a deep breath. The past crept over her.

"She called my father into the room, told him, and before my eyes, my parents became strangers. Until that day, I'd always been the apple of their eye. They'd been proud of me, bragged about my grades, how I was on the cheerleading team, popular in school, so pretty, the perfect daughter. But in a matter of seconds, I lost that admiration, that affection, that—" she swallowed "—that love.

"They sent me away. All their friends and mine believed I was visiting my aunt in Oregon for the summer, but the truth was they couldn't stand to look at me. And not because I'd had premarital sex. But because I'd been stupid enough to get pregnant and dare to embarrass them in front of their peers, my father's business connections, the town. They worried about how everyone would judge them as parents."

"Sweetheart," Isaac rasped.

"That meant I had to go," she continued, unable to allow that soft endearment to dissuade her from this... purging. "They told people I was away for the summer, but I understood I wouldn't be permitted to return home until after the baby had been born and given up for adoption. There was no choice about that. I wasn't given one. Only if I followed their orders to the letter would I be allowed to come back home to Rose Bend. As much as I loved my aunt, and there was a certain... relief in being with her, I wanted to go home. I hated that I'd hurt them, embarrassed them.

"About three weeks after I arrived in Oregon, I lost the baby. Woke up one morning, cramping, spotting, and within hours, I miscarried. According to the doctor, there was nothing I could have done—it just happened. That didn't stop me from blaming myself, though. But at least, I could go home. Or so I thought. My parents wouldn't let me. I had to learn my lesson. And so I was forbidden to return to Rose Bend until three days before school started."

Isaac's hold on her hands remained gentle, but his features hardened. He reminded her of a tightly coiled spring, so still and tense just before a furious release.

"They punished you," he said, his voice, like his hands, a direct contradiction of his expression. "They blamed you, and they punished you. And if I'm hearing what's said and unsaid, they're still at it. All because you were a kid in love who made a mistake. That's not a life sentence. Forgive me later for saying so, but your parents are self-righteous, hard-hearted dicks."

She blinked. Outrage should be flaring inside her over that insult. But…how many times had she secretly whispered as much to herself before shame had her banishing the thought from her head? Even if they weren't dicks. Their behavior then, and now, was dickish.

"Isaac, I get why—"

"If you defend them in this moment, I promise you I will back my truck up into your driveway tomorrow morning and blast Lynyrd Skynyrd," he snapped, indigo eyes gleaming.

In spite of the conversation, an unexpected spurt of humor bubbled up inside her.

"Are you really threatening me with…country music?" she murmured.

"Lynyrd Skynryd is actually rock but yeah, I did." He gave his head a hard shake. "Jenna, my younger sister Violet became pregnant when she was sixteen. A junior, supersmart, volleyball player, already planning which colleges to apply to. Then that happened. My mother didn't turn on her. Yes, there was disappointment, but even more there was love, understanding, compassion. She *mothered her*. We all supported Violet in whatever decision she would make, and when she turned her baby over to his adoptive parents, we were all there for her at the hospital. That's what family does. They encourage one another, bolster one another. Your parents should've given you that. You *deserved* that. Not this unattainable, ridiculous goal of perfection. And definitely not this eternal sentence. You're human, Jenna. Not a saint."

"I think we all know I'm not a saint." She smiled, but it faded as a heavy pressure shoved against her sternum. "There's more. There's another reason my parents consider me a failure as a daughter." She hesitated, having never said these words aloud. Not even to Leo. "I can't have children. Because of my mistakes, they will never be grandparents."

Even the crackle of the fire seemed to quiet as her admission dropped between them. Once more, she couldn't glance away from Isaac's face, needing to see every flash of emotion in his eyes, every tightening of skin over his chiseled cheekbones.

Unlike earlier, his silence didn't encourage her. It sent trembles stumbling through her and she stiffened against them, needing to purge herself of this part. Release the poison.

"I started having…issues around twenty-two. Pain, irregular, heavy bleeding. At first, I just chalked it up to stress. But after several months, I couldn't ignore it. Again, I told my mother and she took me to a doctor outside of Rose Bend. Her reasoning? Just in case I had to disclose information about 'the incident.'" Jenna huffed out a dry chuckle. "That's what they call it. 'The incident.' As if someone could always be listening. Or maybe they just can't stand to say the word *miscarriage*. I really don't know."

"Neither reason is a good look."

She nodded at his growled indictment of her parents. "After an ultrasound and MRI, they determined I had polyps inside my uterus that extended into the uterine cavity."

"Cancerous?" Isaac's grip on her fingers tightened, almost bruising.

"No," she hurriedly assured him, and only after his gaze swept over her face, as if ascertaining the truth for himself, did his hold relax. "They were benign. But there were a lot of them." The breath shuddered out of her lungs. "I had surgery, but a couple of years later, they grew back. I had the polypectomy again, but the results are that I'm unable to get pregnant. At twenty-five, I found out I'd never give birth to my own children. It was devastating. Motherhood hadn't been in my immediate plans for the future, but I'd always seen it as part of my life. It wasn't until that day in the doctor's office, as he explained why I would never feel a baby's fluttery kick in my belly or experience bringing a child into this world, that I realized just how much I wanted it. *God*, I so wanted it."

"Sweetheart, I'm sorry. I'm…" A big, warm hand cradled her cheek. "I'm so damn sorry."

"I had to grieve that dream like a death. And it was, in a way. But I had to grieve it alone. Mother blamed me, or rather, the miscarriage for the infertility. Even though my doctor explained that wouldn't have caused the polyps, she refused to believe it. In her mind, my mistake stole their opportunity to be grandparents. Stole their legacy."

"Stole their legacy?" he repeated, disgust twisting his mouth. "What the fuck is this—*Game of Thrones*? They have a castle and fiefdom we don't know about? This isn't the damn Middle Ages. You are more than their progeny, and your purpose on this earth isn't to ensure their name perseveres in the land. You have goals, dreams. And one of them died. Instead of comforting you, assuring you that, yes, you're beautiful, you're whole, you're *fucking perfect*, they heap more blame on your shoulders."

He shot to his feet. Cupping her shoulders, he guided her from the chair. His hands shifted from her shoulders, skimming up her neck to cradle her jaw and cheeks and tilt up her head. His thumbs caressed her cheekbones, sweeping back and forth.

Her breath soughed in and out of her lungs, and a whimper crawled up her throat, but she trapped the needy sound before it could escape. Shock and desire raced along her veins, and for a delirious moment, she thought the flames from the firepit had transferred to her body, filling her, licking at her. His hands on her… they branded her skin, and she hovered between jerking away and sinking into that touch.

"You will never hear me say that I know how you feel. It's not fair. Nothing about this shit is fair. And sweetheart, it sounds like you deserve a little bit of fair." He lowered his head so the thick, dark strands of his hair grazed her temple. His breath brushed her lips, and she parted hers to sample it. Peppermint and underneath a hint of beer. "If no one else has told you,

Jenna, then let me be the first... You are blameless. You have nothing to feel guilt or shame over and nothing to apologize for. I'm sorry you experienced too young what even adult women have a hard time dealing with, and then not having a safe place to land. I'm sorry that one of your dreams disappeared before it even fully formed and that you suffered that loss alone. You're beautiful, and I believed you were strong, but now I know exactly what fire you were honed in. And it only makes you lovelier in my eyes."

His words slid through her like warmed oil. Until that moment, she'd clenched her fingers at her thighs, unsure what to do with them, but now she lifted them, curving her hands around his trim waist. Feeling the hard flex of muscle underneath her palms. Savoring the hitch of his breath against her lips. Like that day of the motorcycle ride, he pressed his forehead to hers, his lashes lowering.

But he didn't cover the scant distance separating their mouths, didn't give her what she craved.

"Do you want to kiss me?" she asked.

His eyes opened and the indigo flashed like dark lightning. His hold on her face tightened. But he didn't reply. That was her answer.

"Kiss me."

Her nails dug into his sides. He shifted. Closer. And the hard wall of his chest pressed against her breasts. Lust arced through her, beading her nipples, and before she even acknowledged the movement, she rubbed herself along those strong, firm muscles, teasing herself. The whimper she'd imprisoned earlier made a break now, and she didn't care. Not when an ache bloomed between her legs, and she grew swollen, wet with need.

And he hadn't even put his lips on her yet.

Yet.

She hungered to eliminate that *yet*. Replace it with *now*.

"I'm not broken," she said.

"I know that."

"Then don't treat me like I am by thinking I'm asking for this from a broken place. I want your mouth on me, Monster," she breathed.

For an instant, he stilled.

Then, in an explosion of movement, his fingers thrust into her hair and his mouth covered hers.

Opening wide to him, she welcomed his tongue. On a moan, she engaged him—dueling, advancing, retreating, countering... Their erotic battle started as a skirmish and turned into a full-out carnal war. His fingers held her still for the siege, and as he licked, sucked and took her mouth, she surrendered. Surrendered to this dirty, wild and complete conquering.

How could a man taste so damn *good*? Yes, like that peppermint and hint of beer, but *him*. Rich, hot and, oh God, addictive. Already so addictive. As she fisted his hoodie and pushed up on her toes to give him more, to take more, a tiny kernel of worry burrowed its way deep into her subconscious.

It's too good. Too addictive. You're making a dangerous mistake.

But then he angled her head, slanted his mouth over hers, plunged deeper. Gave her a whole new purpose for her tongue, lips and teeth. Showed her that a kiss could be a revelation.

One hand untangled from her hair and dropped to her hip, tugging her closer, aligning them from chest to thigh. The press of his big body was almost too much. She feared sensory overload. Especially when the thick ridge of his cock nudged her belly, igniting a deeper, hungrier need.

He drew his head back, nipped at her bottom lip, then sucked it into his mouth. When he started to pull away, she chased him, pursuing one last taste. And she took it, licking inside, savoring that bold, rich flavor that surpassed the strongest hit of caffeine.

She dropped back down on the soles of her feet, breaking their kiss. Because she wanted to rise back up and claim that sensual mouth again, she stepped back. And stepped back again. With the flavor of him still on her tongue and the brand of him still burning her lips...

She stepped back again.

"Thank you, Isaac," she rasped.

"You're welcome," he said, his voice as rough as hers.

He didn't ask her, *What for?* And she was grateful. How did she put *Everything* into words?

She refused to glance down his body. If she caught a glimpse of the erection that even now she could feel hot on her skin through her sweater, she might just reclaim the space she'd inserted between them.

"I'm going to put out the fire, then head inside. Good night." She inclined her head toward the small bucket with water near the firepit.

"I'm not going to let you do it, Malibu."

She jerked her head toward him and found herself entrapped by his piercing stare.

Look away. She needed to look away. And any second she would...

"What?" she breathed.

"I'm not going to let you ghost me for another week."

He cocked his head. "I see you. More clearly than I ever have. You make a habit of running and reinforcing those walls so no one can breach them. But you've never had anyone come after you."

Her mouth went dry. Even as another part of her grew wetter.

"I...I don't know what you think this is..." she stammered. "It was just a kiss. Nothing more—

"That you have to tell me what that kiss *wasn't* tells me exactly what it meant. And it wasn't 'nothing.'" He turned fully toward her but didn't move to cross the distance separating them. "And this can be whatever we decide it should be. Nothing but a kiss or...more. But no matter what you choose, Malibu, I'm not letting you disappear."

With those words hanging in the night air, he strode from her backyard, the shadows on the side of the house swallowing him.

She remained standing there, staring at the spot where he'd vanished.

Stared and wondered why his declaration continued to ring in her ears like a warning.

CHAPTER FIFTEEN

JENNA STRODE ACROSS the parking lot, sliding her hands into the pockets of her peacoat. Her boots tapped out her irritation on the sidewalk as she headed toward her mother's store.

An emergency, Helene had said.

Jenna's lips twisted. That could mean anything from her father's election campaign losing a major donor to a piece of gossip about Jenna circulating the Rose Bend grapevine. Her mother would've demanded her immediate presence for both "catastrophes."

For an insane moment, Jenna had considered ignoring the summons. Or telling her mother she was in the middle of work. But that would've begun a line of questioning she'd rather avoid. So here she was. Obeying the summons. As she always had.

A small seed buried itself just under her ribs, sprouting tiny roots of discontent.

Always had didn't seem like a good enough reason to do anything. Not anymore.

Not since that late-night conversation with Isaac.

In the three nights since she'd shared her past and they'd shared a—okay, she'd call it a kiss because a cosmic mating of lips, lust and souls sounded a *wee* bit over the top. But since the kiss, she'd done nothing but go over and over every moment. Isaac had emblazoned himself on her memory, and she couldn't remove him.

Neither could she pretend that she hadn't emerged from that conversation changed. He'd stirred an irritation in her, like a pebble in the shoe, that rattled around, chafing. Whereas before she could effectively snuff out the what ifs, she found it harder to do now.

What if you told your parents the truth?

What if you told them no?

What if you stopped running and were brave enough to discover if people could accept you for you?

What if you finally lived for yourself?

Those rebellious, terrifying, exhilarating thoughts swirled in her head, squeezed her chest. But before the buzzing of those hopes could become too loud, she turned down the volume. Isaac had known her for a matter of weeks. Unlike most people in this town. Memories were long, and as Sydney had proved with each encounter, folks' willingness to believe in change was short.

But then again, Jenna hadn't given anyone a reason to offer her the benefit of the doubt, to extend her grace. Even now she was her father's puppet and dancing to her mother's tune. Unburdening herself in that backyard and receiving the soothing balm of Isaac's compassion and the heated possession of his kiss had indeed shaken something loose in her. But her feet remained too mired in the muck of her reputation to truly be free. And her heart remained too filled with the fear of a girl who desperately yearned for her parents' approval.

God. She slid her hand between the lapels of her coat and rubbed her knuckles over her heart. When would that little girl grow up? And let go?

Dropping her arm, Jenna spotted the awning to her mother's store.

For one brief, glimmering moment she'd believed maybe she could answer those questions.

Then reality and her own cowardice snuffed out that hope.

She thrust her fingers through her hair, so fucking *tired* of herself. Take risks, Isaac had urged. Only people who didn't have anything to lose jumped without a net.

She had a lot to lose. Her relationship with her parents, as dysfunctional as it was. Her plans for leaving and starting over.

Her heart.

Sighing, she grabbed the handle on the front door and entered, schooling her features. When facing Helene Landon, a person couldn't afford to show any weakness.

"Jenna, it's about time you got here." Helene murmured something to the woman behind the front counter, then rounded it and strode toward Jenna. "What took you so long? I've texted you twice to see when you were arriving."

"I was driving and couldn't answer my texts. I came as soon as possible," Jenna said, deliberately keeping her voice even, unemotional. It was an effective defense when dealing with her mother. "What's the emergency?"

"I had an employee call in, and I have to attend a luncheon with your father this afternoon. That's going to leave me shorthanded. Please take over behind the cash register." She'd included a *please*, but in no way did Jenna misunderstand Helene's statement as a request. It was pure demand.

Anger welled up in her, searing and bright, and she battled the urge to snap, *What the hell?*

"You couldn't have told me that over the phone?" she asked, hearing the hint of irritation in her voice.

Helene must have, too. She arched an eyebrow, her gaze going hard, assessing.

"I'm telling you now. And you're here. Is there a problem?" Her lips twisted into a faint smile. "Unlike the rest of us, you don't have a job, so what else could you have been doing that helping me is a hardship?"

I was working. Earning a living. Being my own person.

But loosing those words would be bringing hell down on her head. And the fallout? God, she didn't possess the emotional bandwidth to deal with it.

Yet, that pebble rattled in her shoe...

"Of course helping you out isn't a hardship," she said, voice as composed as Helene had taught her. "But 'Good manners are ageless, priceless and classless.' I believe that's one of your quotes." Actually, it was Diana Mather's but her mother quoted it often.

Helene's shoulders drew back, her lips flattening into a thin, forbidding line. Ice glittered in her eyes. "Excuse me?"

Jenna forced a smile. "I do love your quotes. They're so...instructional."

With a nod, she walked over to the front counter, stowed her jacket and purse underneath and got to work. Her mother's boutique enjoyed a brisk business, and the hours slid by. Thank God. She'd had to rework her synopsis the night before. While writing, the characters had taken a detour from the outline she'd plotted out, and now she had to tweak the last half of the book. But she didn't mind. That kind of magic—when the characters stole the reins of the story and created something unexpected with dialogue and plot—delighted her. In those moments, she could almost feel her imagination take flight. Now just to guide it back to where she needed them to go—

"Hi."

Jenna glanced up. Not seeing anyone standing in front of her, she lowered her gaze. It settled on a young girl who couldn't have been older than seven or eight. Her dark brown hair dangled over her shoulder in a neat side ponytail, and her green eyes peered up at Jenna through the cutest pink-and-purple glasses.

"Hi," Jenna replied. Surveying the store, she noted the rest of the boutique employees were either busy helping customers or placing stock. Satisfied that none of them paid attention to her, Jenna smiled, pouring the warmth filling her at the sight of the adorable child into it. "How're you doing?"

The little girl returned Jenna's smile, though hers was shier. A dimple dented her right cheek.

"Fine. I'm Joy." She blinked up at Jenna, her green eyes appearing big behind the lenses. "You look like Ariel," she announced, a bit of wonder in her high voice.

Jenna smothered her laugh, and another wave of warmth flooded her. That wasn't the first time she'd heard this compliment. Isaac's niece had said the same.

"Thank you. That's really nice of you to say, Joy. I'm Jenna. How cool that both our names start with *J*." Joy nodded, and Jenna squinted down at her with an exaggerated purse of her lips. "Y'know, you remind me of Belle. You wouldn't happen to be hiding Chip and Mrs. Potts in that pretty backpack, would you?" Jenna nodded toward her pink book bag with pink and purple flowers dotting it. Going out on a limb, pink and purple might be her favorite colors.

Joy's shy smile bloomed into a grin, revealing a missing bottom tooth. Just when Jenna had thought it impossible for Joy to get cuter.

"Belle is my favorite. I can read just like her," Joy declared proudly.

"I bet you can. Can I tell you something?" Jenna propped her folded arms on top of the glass counter and lowered her voice to a pseudowhisper. "Belle's my favorite princess, too." Joy giggled, and Jenna smiled wider. "Where's your mom, Joy?"

"She's over there." She twisted her torso and pointed in the direction of the shelves full of hand lotions and matching soaps. Jenna noted the petite, curvy woman with gorgeous, long brown hair the same shade as Joy's. "I want to buy Mommy a present," Joy whisper-shouted up at Jenna. She held out her fist and a couple of dollar bills stuck out either end. "I have money."

"Oh wow. How sweet of you! She's so lucky to have a wonderful daughter like you." Jenna swallowed a laugh as Joy nodded so hard in agreement, her glasses slid back and forward on her nose. "Can I see how much money you have?"

Coming around the counter, Jenna gently took the wrinkled bills from Joy and counted them as well as the slightly damp coins. Three dollars and twenty-three cents. In Helene Landon's high-end shop, that couldn't even buy a sample-sized bottle of bubble bath.

But she'd never tell Joy that.

"Three dollars and twenty-three cents? Wow, Joy! Did you save all of this yourself?"

"I got it from my piggy bank. It's all my birthday

money," Joy bragged, granting her the gap-toothed grin once more.

"You're practically rich." Jenna smiled and held out her hand. The little girl wrapped her fingers around Jenna's, and it might as well as have been her heart the child gripped.

She'd always loved children—their innocence, their brutal honesty, their pure, unfiltered way of looking at the world, their capacity to love without reservation. In high school, after Holden, she used to babysit, although her parents looked on her job with scorn. They hadn't understood why she'd needed to work, but it hadn't been about the money. Instead of children reminding her of the one she'd lost, they'd brought her comfort. And they continued to do so after she discovered she couldn't have any of her own.

Guiding Joy to the far end of the counter, but still within visual distance of her mother, Jenna picked up a small jeweled jar of perfume in the shape of a heart.

"How about this? It smells really good and it's pink. You think your mother would like pink?"

Jenna didn't know about her mother, but Joy would probably love the color.

"Yeah, that. I want that!' Joy practically jumped up and down.

"Awesome! I think she's going to love it."

Moving back behind the counter, Jenna ignored the $16.99 price tag on the small bottle and rang up $2.99. She'd cover the difference later. Quickly, she wrapped the gift in tissue paper and slid it into a store bag.

She returned to Joy and handed her the present. "Here you go. And here's your change. You had just enough money for the perfume.

Grinning, Joy accepted the coins. "Thank you, Jenna!"

"You're welcome. Now let's go find—"

A crash echoed throughout the store and several gasps followed.

"Oh my God!" one of the employees cried out.

"Joy, stay here, okay?" Jenna squeezed the girl's shoulder before hurrying to the area where a shelf of scented soaps had fallen and a small group of employees and clients gathered.

Pushing through them, she spotted the woman lying unnaturally still on the floor, her arms spread wide, her legs bent beneath her.

Joy's mother. *Oh God.*

Without hesitation, Jenna dropped down beside the woman, her heart pounding so hard, she couldn't hear her own thoughts. Her stomach bottomed out and all she tasted was fear.

But her fear didn't compare to what glittered in the other woman's eyes. Ashen and so still, she stared up at Jenna as if she held the answers.

"Lauren, call 911. Immediately," Jenna rapped out, and her tone snapped the woman out of her shock.

The floor clerk closed her parted lips and jerked her head.

"Yes. I got it, Jenna." She disappeared from among the small crowd.

Turning back to Joy's mother, Jenna picked up one of her hands and squeezed it.

"Hey, I know this has to be so scary. But try and stay calm. The ambulance is on its way. Can you tell me your name?"

The woman's throat worked, and her lips moved. But only a slurred, garbled sound emerged. Panic flared in her green eyes—in her daughter's eyes—and she tried to speak again. At the more frantic yet distorted speech, a tear rolled down her cheek, and Jenna enfolded the woman's hand in both of hers.

Oh damn. This couldn't be...

"Ma'am, I'm going to try a couple of things, okay? I know you're scared, but everything will be fine." She had no idea if she was lying or not. "Can you smile?"

Confusion filled the woman's eyes, but her face twitched as if she tried to do as Jenna requested. But her face drooped on the left side.

"Okay, good." Not good. It wasn't good. "Can you lift your arms?"

Slowly, the woman raised shaking arms, but while she could lift the right one, the left sagged. And with a grunt, she lowered both.

A stroke. Jenna wasn't a doctor, but the signs led her to believe Joy's mom might have suffered a stroke.

"Mommy? You okay?" a high-pitched, trembling voice asked from behind Jenna.

She closed her eyes and sorrow wailed inside her head. God, why hadn't Joy listened to her and stayed by the counter? She didn't need to see this.

Still clasping her mother's hand, Jenna turned to look at the little girl over her shoulder.

"Hey, Joy. Your mom's going to be fine. She's not feeling well, but the doctor is on the way. Try not to worry, okay?" Jenna forced a smile for the child's benefit. "Do you know your mom's name?"

"Beth."

"Good, honey. You're doing so good," Jenna praised, and at that moment a siren split the air. Relief rushed through her, and she damn near sagged to the floor beside Beth. Returning her attention to the other woman, she said, "The ambulance is here. They're probably going to take you to the hospital in Haroldstown. I don't know if you're from around this area, but the hospital has a wonderful staff. You'll be in good hands."

In the next minutes, the paramedics rushed in, took Beth into their care. Out on the sidewalk, another, thicker crowd gathered, and Helene pushed through them, grabbing Jenna's arm as she followed the EMTs out of the store.

"What in the world is going on here, Jenna?" she demanded, her tone sharp and accusatory.

"A customer collapsed in the store, Mother. I think she may have had a stroke."

"Oh my God." Helene scanned the crowd, her gaze skipping to the store door. "Well," she said and cleared her throat, face ashen. With a small, hard shake of her head, she quickly recovered. "Don't just stand here, Jenna. Get back in the store. We need to regain order after such…excitement."

"I can't, Mother." Jenna drew Joy in front of her, hands settled on the girl's shoulders. "The ambulance is taking Beth to Haroldstown Medical, and I'm following with her daughter. I'm sorry to leave, but this is more important."

"You can't… But…" Helene stammered, and her gaze dropped to Joy, noticing her for the first time. "Let the child ride in the ambulance with her mother. They'll take care of her and so will the hospital. I need you here. And this isn't our business."

"Mother, she doesn't have anyone." Disgust rose in Jenna, swift and blistering. Why was she even explaining this? "I have to go. Come on, Joy."

Guiding Joy through the crowd, Jenna hurried toward her car with the little girl in tow. She knew all too well how it felt to be alone in this world. No way in hell would she let this child experience the same. Not on her watch.

"MALIBU?"

Jenna jerked, then glanced down at the sleeping girl curled against her side. Assured she still slept undisturbed, she tilted her head up and met a concerned indigo gaze.

"Isaac?" she whispered in deference to Joy. "What're you doing here?"

Here being one of Haroldstown Medical's waiting rooms. Beth Duncan—Jenna had discovered her name from the purse she'd picked up off the store floor—had been admitted for examination hours ago. And they hadn't heard anything from the doctor since.

Isaac hunkered down beside her, his thick thighs straining against dark blue denim. "I heard about what happened from Brian. His girlfriend was at the bookstore across the street from your mother's store when the EMTs brought her out to the ambulance."

Jenna shook her head. "Rose Bend's small-townness strikes again," she said dryly. "But what're you doing *here*?"

"You're here." The answer, simple, blunt, struck her in the chest even as it slid through her like the warmest, sweetest melody. "How's she doing?" He dipped his head toward Joy.

"She's hanging in there." Jenna smoothed a hand down Joy's dark braid. By now, several strands had worked their way loose and clung to the girl's rounded cheeks. "Tired. The doctor still hasn't been out to see her, even though the nurse came by with updates. They're working on her mom, but that's all they can tell us."

"This has to be scary for her," he murmured. Rising, he sank into the chair next to her. Isaac's hand rose, and after a slight hesitation, stroked down Jenna's hair similar to how she'd just touched Joy. "How're you doing?"

"I'm fine." At his raised eyebrow, she sighed, glanced down at the sleeping child. "It's not my mother in the hospital. So compared to Beth Duncan and this little girl, I am fine."

"Tired, too, though." His big palm rubbed a circle over her back, and she bit back a moan of both pleasure and relief.

Pleasure at his caress and relief at the firm massage over her weary muscles.

And yes, relief at his presence. Tears pricked her eyes, and she looked away, staring blindly at the mounted television. She hadn't expected him to show up. With Olivia out of town, she didn't have anyone else. Having him here… God, she didn't know how to lean on someone, but knowing she had the option… She bit her lip to battle back another sting of tears. Yes, she just hadn't expected it.

Or him.

"Thank you," she rasped.

"Careful, Malibu," he said, humor warming his voice. "I could get used to those two words coming from you." His hand settled on the middle of her back, a reassuring weight. "Somehow Leo Dennison found my phone number—that woman scares me—and wanted me to relay a message."

Jenna groaned although another wave of confused delight swept through her. "I'm afraid to ask."

"And I quote, 'Answer your phone so I can check on you, you stubborn...' Well, yeah, I'm not finishing the quote. Anyway, she's worried about you so text her back."

"Damn." Jenna patted the pockets of her jacket, careful not to jar Joy. "I must've left my phone in my purse. Which is in my car."

Leo wouldn't have been the only person trying to contact her. She could just imagine the number of calls and texts from her parents. Suddenly, that weariness bore down on her like a soaked blanket, weighing her down.

"I'll call her back." And she would. Leo seemed intent on forging a friendship—or reforging a broken one—and though it scared the hell out of Jenna, she couldn't deny it any longer. She wanted it.

"Kind of nice to have people worried about you, isn't it?" he murmured. What was he? A mind reader? Not allowing her a chance to reply, he asked, "Do you need coffee or food? I can grab something in the cafeteria."

"No, I'm good. I promise, Isaac. I—"

"Excuse me, are you the family of Beth Duncan?" The blue-scrubs-clad doctor stood in front of them, his hands clasped. Next to him stood an older woman in a plain but pretty navy blue pantsuit. Though more gray than black hair framed her face, few wrinkles lined her lovely dark brown skin.

Didn't that just attest to the intensity of Isaac's presence? She hadn't even heard the pair approach. She eased Joy to the side and stood. The girl curled up in the chair, her head lolling and a soft snore emitting from her parted lips. Beside her, Isaac rose to his feet as well.

"Yes, this is her daughter, Joy." Jenna waved toward the slumbering girl. "I'm Jenna Landon. I was with Beth when she collapsed in my mother's store. As far as I know, Joy is the only family Beth had with her. I've been waiting with her for news on her mother."

The doctor glanced at the older Black woman and then back at Jenna.

"We usually only release information to the family, but this is a…complicated situation." He touched the elbow of the woman next to him. "I'm Dr. Choi and this is Mrs. Angela Ewing. She's with Children's Services here in the hospital."

Mrs. Ewing extended a hand toward Jenna. "It's nice to finally meet you, Ms. Landon. The staff, parents and children here have nothing but wonderful things to say about you."

Feeling Isaac's speculative gaze on her like a hot brand, she accepted the woman's hand, shaking it. "Thank you. That's always good to hear. This is Isaac Hunter. A friend of mine." She waited until they greeted one another before asking, "You said a complicated situation? What's wrong? Will Ms. Duncan be okay?"

Dr. Choi once more glanced at Mrs. Ewing. "Ms. Duncan should be fine eventually. She suffered what we call an ischemic stroke. This is when the arteries supplying blood to the brain become blocked. More specifically she suffered a cerebral embolism. This happens when a blood clot forms in another part of the body, enters the bloodstream and hits an artery that's too narrow for it to pass through. The clot becomes stuck, blood flow stops and this causes a stroke.

"Right now, we're treating it with thrombolytic drugs. They break up the blood clots, stop the stroke and reduce brain damage. Because of the short time between the ambulance response and when we were able to start treating her, we're hoping Ms. Duncan will not have any long-lasting disabilities. If the TPA injection doesn't work then we'll do what's called a mechanical thrombectomy, which is when we'll insert a catheter into a large blood vessel inside her head and pull the clot out. Only thing is, this surgery is most successful if performed within the next twenty-four hours."

"So she's going to be here for the next several days?" Jenna asked.

"At least a week," Dr. Choi confirmed.

"A week?" Jenna glanced down at Joy. "But what about Joy? She can't stay here—"

"In the hospital?" Angela Ewing said. "No. We have been able to get in contact with Ms. Duncan's sister, but while Ms. Duncan and her daughter live in Albany, her sister is in Savannah, Georgia. She said it will take her three or four days to get here. In the meantime, we can place Joy in foster care…"

"I'll take her."

The words exploded from her.

And from the gleam in the other woman's eyes, Jenna had a feeling this outcome had been her intent all along.

"Jenna." Isaac's fingers tangled with hers. "You sure about this?"

At that moment, Joy stirred and when she sat up, rubbing her fists into her eyes, Jenna's heart flipped in her chest like a gymnast.

"I'm sure," she murmured.

But she would be lying to herself if she denied the

anxiety careening through her at the thought of caring for a tiny person on her own.

She glanced down at Joy, who blinked rapidly at the group of adults standing around her, and then she scooted to the edge of the waiting room seat and reached for Jenna's hand, wrapping her small fingers around hers.

Jenna squeezed the child's hand.

The girl was going home with her.

She'd keep her safe and healthy until her aunt arrived.

"Joy can come home with me," Jenna repeated, for not just Angela Ewing's benefit, but for Joy's.

And hers.

Mrs. Ewing nodded, a soft smile curving her mouth. "I was hoping you would say that. Just in case, I started the process for emergency foster placement. Given your ties to the Rose Bend community, history here at the hospital and connection with the child, this temporary placement shouldn't be a problem. I'll be out at your house tomorrow to do a check."

"Of course." For the first time, Jenna appreciated the Landon last name and her father's connections. If it paved an easier path for her here, then this one time, she couldn't complain.

Joy tugged on Jenna's hand, and she glanced down at the girl. "I'm going home with you, Jenna?"

"Just for a little while. Your mom has to stay in the hospital for about a week so the doctors can get her better. Your aunt is on her way, but it's going to take her a few days to get here. So if you're okay with it, you can stay with me until she comes to pick you up. Would you like that?"

Even though everyone had already made the decisions about where she would go, Jenna still asked Joy for her approval. The little girl had just witnessed her mother collapse and had spent the last few hours in the sterile hospital, surrounded by strangers. Her whole world had radically changed back in that boutique. Joy must feel terrified, confused and powerless. Jenna couldn't do anything about the first two, but she could at least make Joy feel as if she had a choice. A voice for her mother. For herself.

"Aunt Ray is coming here?"

"Yes, honey. All the way from Georgia, just for you. But like I said, it's going to take a little while for her to arrive. So do you mind staying with me until she does?"

Joy studied Jenna for several moments then shook her head. "No, I'll spend the night with you."

It would be a few nights, but at least she'd agreed. Jenna blew out a breath then shifted her gaze to Angela Ewing.

"We're all set then. The hospital has my information so you can text me when you have a time for your visitation tomorrow."

Mrs. Ewing nodded. "That's perfect. And thank you, Ms. Landon. I represent the foster care system, but I'll be the first to admit it's not perfect. And it's people like you who step up in emergency situations like this who ease the load on an over-burdened system. And I haven't met Beth Duncan, but I think I can safely speak for her when I say she would be grateful for you caring for her daughter."

Pressure thickened in Jenna's chest and as Joy's grip tightened on her hand, that weight expanded, shoving until even breathing became difficult. This kind of…

praise flustered her. Give her harsh criticism, cold shoulders, even intimidated glances—those she knew how to handle. But compliments? No, she mentally and emotionally scrambled away.

A wide palm settled on the middle of her back, steadying her. Supporting her.

In the midst of being thrust into a temporary-custody situation, she'd almost forgotten Isaac stood behind her, next to her.

Almost.

His presence pulsed too loud, too hot to be dismissed. He was a force, and right now, gratefulness for his quiet yet unshaken strength flowed through her.

Because with Joy's trusting gaze fixed on Jenna's face, she couldn't betray her fear. But dammit, yes, she was scared.

Scared of not being enough for Joy.

Scared of failing her.

Inhaling a deep breath, Jenna called on the acting ability pretending to be the perfect daughter had required of her over the years. And smiled.

"Are you ready, Joy?"

Joy nodded though her small chin wobbled just the tiniest bit. "Ready."

"Let's go do this then."

CHAPTER SIXTEEN

ISAAC JOGGED UP the porch steps of Jenna's house, his fist already raised by the time he reached the storm door. Anticipation crackled in his veins as he knocked and waited.

It'd been eight and a half hours since he'd last seen Jenna, and yeah, he craved another glimpse. Why deny it at this point? Walking away from her the night before, when exhaustion had bruised her eyes but hadn't bowed her shoulders as she'd guided Joy Duncan from her car, had been one of the hardest things he'd ever done. Every protective instinct he possessed had howled that he follow and make sure both of them were safe, fed, cared for. That he meet their needs so they'd want for nothing. And then sleep in the hall just in case either of them needed anything in the middle of the night.

Yeah, who was he kidding?

He'd wanted to sleep curled around Jenna's slender, strong body, in her bed, which undoubtedly smelled like her—gardenias and moon-kissed skin. And that was after she allowed him to lose himself in her fire. The fire that had seared him when they kissed. The fire that had burned so passionately for a little girl she'd just met but protected fiercely.

How could anyone look at this woman and not see the beauty inside and out?

Not see the tender heart she guarded?

He slid his hands in the front pockets of his jeans and bowed his head, staring at the weathered boards of her porch.

What the fuck was he doing?

This wasn't why he'd moved to Rose Bend. Family. Finding his own path—that's why he'd come here. Not to get caught up in a woman, in a relationship, when he'd just untangled himself from both. The wounds had barely scabbed over, and here he stood, poking at them. Courting the pain.

Because Jenna had heartbreak written all over her.

Not just his.

If it was only his, it would be easier to walk away. Fear was a hell of a strong motivator.

But it was *her* heartbreak that kept him crossing her lawn. Climbing the porch. Knocking on her door. Trespassing in her backyard. It was her pain that had him desperate to tear down those barbed wire fences shielding her emotions.

That he couldn't walk away from.

And he'd pay for it. He was as certain of that as Jenna's determination to see the back of Rose Bend in her rearview mirror.

Now would be an excellent time to turn and take his ass back over to his house, locking himself inside.

He didn't move.

Christ.

The front door opened, and Jenna stood in front of him, only a layer of fiberglass separating them. It might as well as have been air.

Without removing his gaze from hers, he twisted the knob and pulled. Her eyes widened slightly, and a puff of breath grazed his palms as he stepped directly into her space and cupped her face.

"Isaac," she murmured.

"Shh," he hushed, acknowledging that he took his life into his own hands by daring to shush her.

Hands that didn't tremble. They *didn't*. Okay, so fuck, they *did*. He just should've eaten breakfast before coming over here. Yeah, that was it. Because then her earth-and-gardenia-and-musk scent wouldn't twist him into knots, stirring an insatiable, grating hunger.

Sweeping his thumbs over her high cheekbones, he shook his head. Almost reverently. Which explained the awe in his voice.

"Freckles," he breathed, gently caressing the scattering of cinnamon marks across her upper cheeks and the bridge of her nose. "I knew it. I fucking knew it." Lowering his head, he brushed his lips over them, hearing and feeling her gasp, savoring it. Goddamn, he wanted to taste it. "Beautiful."

Reluctantly, he lifted his head and met her gaze, not knowing what he would glimpse there. Anger at his audacity. Anxiety at his nearness. Or worse. Nothing. Or... The air caught in his lungs.

Yeah. *That*.

Desire threatened to submerge him right there in her doorway, and he would willingly be a victim. Though the insistent, twisting thing inside him demanded he crush his mouth to hers and take, take, take like he had the other night behind her house, he dropped his hands from her face and stepped back.

God, it was a close call.

"Morning," he rumbled.

"Hey." She cleared her throat, and her hand rose toward her face, but hovered, then fell to her side. "Hey," she repeated, shifting backward and waving him inside. "Come on in. We were just about to have breakfast."

He skimmed over her messy topknot and the thick strands flowing over her shoulders. Took in another of those slouchy sweaters she seemed to favor when in the comfort of her own home, dark blue jeans that molded to her long legs and her slender bare feet. Damn, one woman didn't have the right to be so gorgeous.

"Looks like my timing is impeccable then."

"Funny how that happens."

"It's a gift."

She snorted and strode toward the kitchen. He followed her through the living room and dining room to the medium-sized kitchen, where Joy, clothed in a big T-shirt, sat on her knees at a table squeezed under a large bay window. Jenna walked over to the stove, and he couldn't help but stare at the subtle sensuality in the sway of her hips, the pride in the straightness of her shoulders, the vulnerability of her soft mouth....

"Hi."

Jerking his attention from the woman who subconsciously seduced him by simply breathing, he glanced down at the adorable little girl.

"Hey, Joy." He crossed the small distance between them and extended his hand. "We met last night."

She put her hand in his and peered up at him from behind her pink-and-purple glasses, and he recognized that assessing look tinged with a bit of awe. The kid must be a wrestling fan—

"You're *huge*."

He laughed. "Actually, I'm Isaac, and it's nice to see you again."

"Are you Jenna's boyfriend?"

A hacking cough came from the direction of the stove.

Joy looked in Jenna's direction, her eyebrows drawn down, her lips pursed. "Is she okay?" she stage whispered.

As the uncle of a five-year-old, Isaac knew children her age had no skills in the art of the perfect whisper.

"Oh she's fine." He flicked a hand. "Probably just choked on her bacon." Pulling out the chair across from Joy, he sank down on it. "To answer your question, no, I'm not Jenna's boyfriend. But—" he crooked a finger and when Joy leaned all the way across the top, he met her halfway "—she sure is pretty, isn't she?"

Joy nodded. "She's really pretty. And nice, too. Mommy says that's more important. Maybe if you told Jenna she was nice instead of pretty she'd be your girlfriend."

Isaac blinked. A loud snort echoed from behind him.

Out of the mouths of babes.

Laughter rumbled in his chest, and he fought back a grin.

"You know what, Joy? That's some really great advice."

The little girl nodded solemnly as if saying, *I know, you big dummy*. He swallowed another chuckle.

"Here you go, honey." Jenna set a plate of bacon, scrambled eggs and pancakes in front of Joy. After a brief hesitation, she smoothed a hand down the girl's hair, then catching Isaac's eye, dropped her arm and headed back to the stove. "I'm guessing you're eating, Monster?"

"I mean, since I'm here."

"You said your name was Isaac," Joy piped up, eggs halfway to her mouth.

"It is. Monster is Jenna's nickname for me. I think she likes me," Isaac confided in Joy, biting the inside of his cheek as Jenna dropped a plate piled with food in front of him.

"Michael James calls Maura Thomas a poopyhead because he likes her. Mommy said that's silly. And to-sist."

Isaac frowned, rolling Joy's words over in his head before they clicked, and he grinned, unable to hold it back. "Your mom is right again. Michael calling Maura names 'cause he likes her is silly and toxic. But Jenna's name for me is more like your mom calling you sweet-heart or honey. She's not being mean, and I promise you she's not hurting my feelings. Not like poopyhead Michael."

Joy grinned back at him. "Michael is a poopyhead." Then her eyes narrowed behind her glasses. "But you said you're not her boyfriend."

"Joy, eat," Jenna gently ordered, setting a plate on the table and settling in beside her. And saving him from answering. "Then we can head out and buy clothes for you. You're going to need some until your Aunt Ray gets here."

Joy didn't reply but bowed her head and pushed her eggs around with her fork.

"Hey." Jenna glanced at Isaac and he frowned, concerned at the sudden switch in the little girl's mood. She covered Joy's free hand. "What's going on? You can talk to me."

Joy lifted her head, and tears glistened in her green eyes.

"Is Mommy going to die?"

Isaac's chest constricted so hard his ribs ached. No

child should experience the insecurity of having their whole world shaken to its foundation. The all-too-real possibility of losing the person they loved and depended on most.

He'd wrestled men twice his size before, but this was one fight he couldn't win.

"Oh honey." Jenna cupped Joy's hand in both of hers. "Listen to me. No, your mom's not going to die. I won't to lie to you, though. She's sick and is going to need help getting better, and it might take some time. But the doctor said she's going to be okay. Especially with you there for her, she's going to be more than okay. She's going to be great." Jenna pinched Joy's chin, brushing the backs of her fingers down the child's cheek. "I know it's hard, but try not to worry. Your aunt will be here soon, and in the meantime, I'll take you to visit your mom. I wouldn't lie to you, Joy. Everything's going to be okay. I promise."

Emotion bulldozed its way into his throat, and he clenched his fingers around the fork. Better a death grip on the eating utensil than hauling this beautiful, prickly, compassionate woman into his lap to hold her. Just hold her.

Until that wasn't enough.

Yeah, fantasizing about how he wanted to corrupt Jenna Landon at her kitchen table with a little girl present wasn't his best moment.

"One thing I've learned about Jenna," Isaac said, pointing his fork at Joy. "If she makes you a promise, she keeps it. And everyone's too scared of her to tell her no. So you kind of have the best person ever on your side."

"Eat your eggs, Monster," Jenna drawled.

But he caught the twitch of a smile at the corner of her mouth.

And the shine of awe in Joy's eyes.

Yeah, his job here was done.

The next twenty minutes passed in easier conversation and teasing, and by the time he stood and cleared the dishes—against Jenna's protests—the doorbell rang.

Muttering about "pushy neighbors," she left to answer the door. Moments later, Jenna reappeared and his sister and niece joined her.

"Hi, Uncle Isaac!" Belle yelled.

His niece raced across the kitchen and threw herself against his legs. Quickly setting the breakfast dishes in the sink, he swept her up in his arms and smacked a loud kiss on her cheeks, making her giggle. When he lowered her to the floor, she turned to Joy and waved as if she were across the room instead of inches in front of her. "Hi, I'm Belle!"

"Hi. My name's Joy," the other girl said, a little shier.

But his niece, who had never met a stranger, grinned. "I know. Me and Mommy came over to meet you and bring clothes for you 'cause Mommy said Ms. Jenna prolly can't take care of a plant much less a lil' girl."

Holy shit.

Isaac sighed, pinching the bridge of his nose. And squinted at Jenna, who simply arched an auburn eyebrow at Lena.

"Bella Renae Epps," Lena growled through gritted teeth. "What have I told you about eavesdropping?"

Bella bowed her head, scraping the toe of her sneaker over the floor. "Don't do it," she grumbled. "I'm sorry."

"Well, as you can see, she's breathing," Jenna said dryly. "I watered her this morning and everything."

Lena snorted and held up a plastic bag. "After talking to Isaac last night, I figured you wouldn't have time to do much shopping. So we stopped by the store and picked up a few items to tide you over until you could. I guessed on the size."

"That was nice of you. Thank you." Jenna accepted the bag. "Mercury must be good and stuck in retrograde," she murmured.

Isaac coughed, choking on a laugh as Lena's eyes narrowed. But he knew his sister. And he caught the faint flex in her cheek. She bit back a smile. If he wasn't mistaken—and he wasn't—Jenna might be growing on Lena.

"Joy," Jenna called, waving the girl over. "Ms. Lena brought you clothes. Come on over and meet her and say thank you."

The little girl walked over, Belle, apparently her new shadow, skipping behind.

"Hi, I'm Joy," she said, wrinkling her fingers at his sister. "Thank you for the new clothes. Mine were dirty."

"You're very welcome, sweetie." Lena smiled. "And it's nice to meet you."

"Joy, why don't you go ahead and get dressed? We can still head downtown and pick up some things for you and get ice cream, okay?"

Isaac couldn't see the girl's smile from his position in the room, but he could hear it in her "Okay!"

"Oooh! I want ice cream, too!" Belle jumped up and down. "Can I go with Joy and Jenna, too, Mommy?"

"Inside voice, Belle," Lena reminded her. "And we'll see."

That stopped all the jumping, because even Isaac knew, just like every kid, that *We'll see* meant *No*.

The doorbell echoed again, and he sent up a silent prayer of thanksgiving for the divine intervention preventing a temper tantrum. Belle was adorable and, for the most part, easygoing, but she and ice cream had a loving relationship. And she didn't like the thought of missing out.

"Joy, go ahead and get dressed while I answer the door. We'll leave when you're finished." Jenna cupped the girl's shoulder.

"Okay, Jenna." Lifting the bag, she turned to Lena. "Bye, Ms. Lena."

"I'm coming with you!" Belle announced, her disappointment forgotten for the moment as she latched on to Joy's hand, once again bouncing on her feet. As the two left the kitchen, Belle continued to chatter. "Mommy said your mommy's in the hospital. My grammy was in the hospital. They had nasty pudding but really good juice. Can we go see your mommy and get her juice…"

That was his niece. The little mercenary.

The doorbell rang again, and Jenna glanced in the direction of the front door.

"If you two will excuse me," she said, then disappeared from the room.

"Why am I not surprised to see you here this morning?" Lena arched an eyebrow.

"Funny. I can't say the same," he said, mimicking her gesture. "You, coming to Jenna's house? Did the Four Horsemen decide to go out on an early-morning ride and no one told me?"

Lena waved a hand. "There's a child whose mother is in the hospital and your neighbor took said child in. Any person with a heart would pitch in and help."

"Exactly. But I just walked across the yard. You

drove over from the next town." He cocked his head. "Careful, big sister. I think you're starting to like her."

Lena popped up a finger. "*Like* is a strong word." She squinted. "But on the other hand, I like brussels sprouts even though they're despicable to everyone else."

Isaac snorted. "I swear, it's fucking impossible for you to admit I'm right."

"Isn't that what I just did?"

He snorted. "You—"

"What is this I'm hearing about you taking in some strange girl like a stray, Jenna? We aren't the pound, for God's sake."

Isaac stiffened, rage boiling inside him swift and hot. One glance at his sister's face revealed the same anger. Her features tightened, eyes narrowing.

He recognized that voice. As Lena worked in Rose Bend and knew Jenna, he assumed she did, too.

Jasper Landon. The asshole.

"She isn't a strange girl nor is she a stray," Jenna said, her calm tone in stark contrast to her father's harsh one. "She's also in my guest bedroom, so we're taking this out on the porch."

Seconds later, the door opened and then closed again.

Quiet descended in the kitchen.

"Are we listening in?" he asked Lena.

Her chin jerked back. "Hell yes, we are."

He strode across the room, and together they headed down the hall toward the front door.

"Wasn't it you who, just five minutes ago, lectured your daughter on eavesdropping?"

"Shut it."

In spite of his teasing, Isaac harbored no guilt about prying. He'd had a sample of the older Landons' so-called tender mercies when it came to their daughter. No way in hell he was leaving Jenna by herself with them.

Carefully, he twisted the knob and eased the front door open. Lena wedged in next to him, and they both observed the scene. Jasper and Helene Landon and Christopher Rappaport faced Jenna as if they engaged in a showdown, and she was severely outnumbered.

"Hold on," Lena whispered, her fingers curling around his bicep.

Only then did he realize he gripped the handle of the storm door.

Dragging in a deep breath, he held it, then deliberately exhaled and muscle by muscle relaxed his body. Yeah, that was a lie. No way in hell, he could relax when he witnessed potential dogpile of woman he cared about.

"What in the world are you thinking, Jenna?" Helene demanded, her voice a low hiss.

It struck him as ironic that weeks ago he would've believed these two women were cut from the same cloth. Helene, flawless on a Saturday morning, in a dark green suit and matching heels, understated jewelry and perfectly styled auburn hair, could've been attending a business meeting. That's how Isaac had initially viewed Jenna. Beautiful in the way of a cold, glittering, impersonal diamond. Great to look at and able to cut deep.

Now, though... The two women looked—and were—nothing alike.

The question Helene Landon posed proved that.

That she arrived here demanding to know why her daughter sheltered another woman's child illustrated that.

"I was thinking that a mother who suffered a stroke

didn't need to be worried about where her child would end up."

"A woman who had an incident in *my store*. Not only is everyone talking about it, but if she hires one of those ambulance chasers, she could sue me. And you taking her child into your home could be interpreted as a sign of responsibility."

"So you'd rather have me leave Joy in foster care? When I had a perfectly good home to give her for the next few days?" she asked.

Isaac doubted her mother could detect it, but he caught the note of incredulity and disgust creeping into her voice.

"Yes," her father insisted, glaring. "It's called being sensible."

"I call it not having compassion."

Pride swelled inside him. Goddammit, he wanted to charge out there, pick her up and squeeze her to his chest. He knew her story, understood how difficult standing up to her parents must be for her. And he *needed* to have her back.

"Jenna, who—" Jasper snarled, jabbing a finger at her.

"Jasper." Christopher held up a hand, and Isaac flexed. It was impossible to rip a smile off a person's face, but he was willing to give it the ol' college try. "Let's all take a deep breath. And remember where we are." He paused, casting a meaningful look around the porch. "Jenna," he said, turning that ingratiating smile on her. "You can understand your parents' position, can't you? This whole…unfortunate incident turns the conversation away from the carnival and the start of your father's reelection bid. The longer this—" he waved toward her front door "—goes on, then the longer people continue to talk. It especially blindsided your parents when they weren't aware you'd taken the girl in," he gently reprimanded.

Gently or not, who the fuck was he to scold her as if she were a child instead of a grown woman capable of making her own decisions? Isaac shifted, and Lena's grip on his arm tightened.

"Your girl's got this, Isaac," she murmured. "Let her have it."

"Not that I have to explain myself to you, Chris," Jenna said, and the ice in those words could've given a polar bear hypothermia. *Hell yeah, sweetheart.* "But I did call you, Dad and Mother. I left messages this morning letting you know what happened last night."

"I didn't get a message," her mother snapped. "And that's not the point. That you interjected yourself, my business, in a situation that is none of our concern is the point. I tried to get you to step back yesterday at the store, but you refused to listen. And now here we are. The topic of needless gossip. You don't think, Jenna. But that seems to be a pattern with you."

E-fucking-nough.

That probably wasn't the first low blow her mother had delivered but it was the first she'd thrown while in *his* presence.

"Isaac—dammit!" Lena whispered.

But she didn't stop him when he pulled the front door open wider and pushed through the storm door. Nope, his sister followed him.

Because that's what family did.

"What is *he* doing here?" Jasper thundered, pointing at Isaac. "It isn't enough that you're housing random orphans—now you have a strange man in your home? Do you *want* to embarrass me?"

"I'm strange?" Isaac asked Lena, frowning.

His sister shrugged as she leaned against the wall next to the large front window. "He's only saying what the rest of us have said for years."

"Rude." He sniffed.

"Excuse us," Christopher interrupted, his smile gone. Good. It was the most real thing about him right now. "But this is a discussion between family. If you don't mind…"

"Oh but I do mind." Isaac dropped all pretense of humor and affability. He moved until he stood just behind Jenna and leveled his stare on her parents before returning it to her ex. "When the discussion calls for three against one, I mind very much. So we're just evening the odds. But Jenna's doing a damn fine job defending herself, so we're only here as backup. Carry on."

"Isaac," Jenna murmured.

"What?" he pseudowhispered back. "You are handling your business, sweetheart. And looking gorgeous doing it, I might add."

"Sweetheart," her mother sneered. Was that the only expression she ever wore? "Is this who you're associating with now?"

"Who I am or am not associating with isn't why you're here—Joy Duncan is. And the fact is, she's here. Her aunt is on her way to Rose Bend, but it's going to take a few days. In the meantime, Joy will stay here."

"It never occurred to you to ask us before you so rashly decided to do this, did it?" Jasper asked. "Never once considered your family and how it might affect us?"

Isaac said it once and he'd say it again. What. An. Asshole.

Jenna slowly shook her head. "I'm sorry, Dad, but no. I didn't. There was a scared child who needed a home, and I offered mine. Besides, most people in this town will find the story heartwarming not salacious. And Mom, yes, they might drop by the store to gossip about what happened, but they're also in the store. They will probably shop while there. This isn't an issue."

"She's right," Lena said. "We heard about it and brought clothes over for Joy this morning. I'm sure we won't be the only ones."

Both of the Landons' attention swung to his sister, scowls darkening their expressions. From childhood, he'd learned Lena could take care of herself, but if they offended her...

"Who are you again?" Helene asked, a thin eyebrow arched high.

"Aren't you a teacher over at the high school?" Jasper demanded at the same time.

"Yes, I am." Lena smiled, and it contained a sharp edge that any fool would heed. "A *tenured* teacher."

That had all the subtlety of a two-by-four to the back of the skull. And since Jasper Landon wasn't only the ex-mayor but a current town council member—Isaac had done his homework—he'd get Lena's point. Damn, he loved her.

"Jenna could be correct." Christopher stepped forward, and Jasper and Helene switched their focus to him. "But until we know for certain, let's just go with our statement regarding yesterday's events. 'It was a tragic, unfortunate event for everyone involved and our thoughts and prayers are with Ms. Duncan and her daughter.' We have no comment about her condition or the status of her daughter. Agreed?"

"Yes, of course," Jasper grumbled.

After Helene nodded, Christopher turned to Jenna. "Jenna?"

"I'll amend that statement to say it's not my place to discuss Joy's private business. The rest of it, I'll agree to," she said.

Irritation flashed in the campaign manager's eyes, but his pleasant tone didn't betray it.

"That's fine. Now," he said and clasped his hands in front of him and smiled. Sharks most likely looked just like that before they swam into a school of fish. "It's two weeks before the carnival and we've convinced the owners to open up the Ferris wheel and the carousel for a test run, so to speak. It's only for a select few, but we need you there. It's tonight at six."

A select few?

Who would be in that exclusive group? The people who donated to Jasper's campaign? Those he wanted to court into donating? And what about the kids who saw the rides were open and wanted a chance to get on them? Would Jasper and Christopher turn them away? This was some elitist bullshit.

Isaac caught a small movement out of the corner of his eye, and Lena straightened. His sister didn't even attempt to hide the revulsion on her face.

"Jenna?" Jasper asked, voice sharp. "We'll see you at six."

It wasn't a request. She glanced toward the front door of her house, then back at her parents and Christopher. "Fine. I'll see you then."

With an abrupt jerk of his chin, Jasper turned to his

wife and offered his arm. Together they walked down the porch steps and headed to their Mercedes.

"See you tonight, Jenna," Christopher murmured, at least having the manners his clients lacked. He stiffly nodded at Lena and Isaac.

Silence lingered on the porch. A tiny frown creased the space above Jenna's nose, and the corner of her mouth pulled down. He couldn't glimpse her eyes, but he could imagine what would darken those sky-blue depths. Worry. Hurt. But not confusion. Or surprise.

That was just...sad. And telling.

"I mean no offense when I say this," Lena said into the quiet.

"Aw hell." Isaac pinched the bridge of his nose.

"Your parents are asses. And now I understand why you weren't fazed by my family."

Jenna turned to his sister, that sad expression gone, replaced by her usual cool composure...except for a gleam in her eyes.

"And by *family*, you mean you," Jenna said. "I wasn't fazed by you."

Lenna shrugged. "Well, yes." Her lips curved into a smirk. Then she glanced toward the street and shook her head. "They won't say it, but thank you for taking Joy in. No child should ever have to wonder about where they're going to sleep or where their next meal is coming from. To that little girl in your house, you wear a cape, and it's a damn shame your parents' heads are stuck so far up their asses that they can't take pride in a daughter who would so selflessly be a child's hero. Or heroine." Clearing her throat, Lena half turned and grabbed the storm door handle. "I'll go check on the girls."

She slipped inside the house, leaving them alone on the porch.

"Is it me or did your sister just hint that she might be proud of me?"

"I'm pretty sure that's what just happened, but to be on the safe side, we're not going to mention it."

"I'll go with that." Jenna nodded and her lips twitched in an almost smile.

One day, he would see a full-fledged grin on her face. And it would trump winning any championship belt or hearing thousands of people yell his name.

Shifting closer, he paused with only inches separating his chest from her back. Several wayward strands of dark red fire brushed his chin, and he inhaled her delicate yet earthy scent.

"Don't panic, Malibu," he murmured. "But I'm going to hug you now."

As he expected, tension entered her slender frame, stiffening her shoulders and spine. But she didn't move away. Didn't tell him no.

No, she turned, faced him…and stepped into his body, wrapping her arms around him.

Relief and a joy so strong, so sharp, like sunlight hitting his eyes after years in the dark, tore through him. He couldn't contain his groan—didn't make a real attempt to. He closed his arms around her, lifting a hand to cradle the back of her head and hold her like the precious, beautiful woman she was.

They stood there for several moments, silent, her gripping him tight. Him, wishing he could completely surround her.

Proud.

Yeah, Lena had called it. He was so fucking proud

of her. Especially because he understood what it had cost her. For a woman who hated taking risks, who'd walked the tenuous tightrope of pleasing her parents for most of her life, she'd defied them today for Joy's sake. And she might not admit it, but she had to be as scared as that little girl.

"I meant what I said," he whispered against her hair. "You handled yourself beautifully. I was ready to jump to your defense, and believe me, it would've been my absolute pleasure. But I didn't need to. You not only stood up for Joy, you stood up for yourself. And it was. Bad. Ass."

Her chuckle warmed his skin even through his sweater. And he forced himself to focus on the here and now…not on how that moist, heated breath would feel against his bare skin.

"They're angry with me," she said.

"No, sweetheart. They're pissed off. Worse than angry."

"Monster, if this is your idea of comforting me, it leaves a lot to be desired."

"It is." He lifted his head and pulled back only far enough to slide his hands underneath her chin and tilt it up. "Honesty isn't always easy, but it should be a comfort. Because there's no point in hiding from the truth when it always has a way of finding you. And yeah, Malibu. Your parents are pissed off right now. Because they came here with a purpose and left without it being accomplished. You didn't fall in line as they expected and they're mad as fuck about that. But you know what's also true? That's their problem, not yours. They'll get over it and will probably have something else to bitch about by tomorrow. And again, not your problem. Unless you allow it to be. That's your choice. Will you keep taking on their issues as yours?"

Her fingers curled into the back of his sweater, the grip tight, almost desperate. But her expression remained smooth, her smile cool.

Then there were her eyes…

Yeah, he would have to look there from now on. They revealed what that carefully composed mask she'd perfected could not. And right now, that bright summer gaze clouded over with storm clouds.

"That's easier said than done," she said. "Especially when I'm such an expert at it."

"See, that's what I've come to learn about you, though." He lightly pressed the pad of his thumb to the corner of her mouth. When her breath hitched over his skin, his gut clenched, twisted. And he pressed harder.

"When you put your mind to something—whether it's riding on a motorcycle for the first time or championing a little girl—you do it. So I have faith that you got this, too. Because this mouth isn't just for flaying the skin off people." Her lips curved the barest amount and he skated his thumb across the sensual flesh, caressing the almost smile that he hungered to taste. "This mouth was created to be fierce, to protect and stand up for the underdog. Even if the underdog is herself."

"I don't need saving, Isaac," she whispered. "I'm not weak.

"Weak? Hell no." He lowered his head and just rested his mouth against hers for several seconds. Traded breaths with her. Became reacquainted with the texture of her. "Sweetheart, I think you're the strongest of us all."

Her lips parted on a small gasp, and he inhaled it,

tasted it before plunging deep to sample for himself. Sample, hell. Feast. He gorged himself on her mouth like a starving man and she was the first offering of food in a millennium. That's how it felt. That he could take and take and take and never satiate this hollow ache in his belly, in his damn soul.

But damn if he wouldn't give it a try.

Tilting her head back farther, he licked harder, sucked longer. He should be gentle. But one slide of that wicked tongue against his and he lost reason. Didn't care about anything but her singular flavor.

Goddamn, he needed to be inside her.

In every way possible.

In every way she would let him.

Threading his fingers through her hair, he thrilled at the thick strands sifting over his skin. Fisting that flame-touched hair, he held her head right where he wanted her, needed her, and thrust harder, forcing her lips open wider.

No, not forcing. She parted for him, willingly, sweetly, and his cock throbbed as he imagined her impossibly long legs parting just as willingly, just as sweetly. Letting him in. Inviting him in...

A cough penetrated the lust-thickened haze and he reluctantly lifted his head. But couldn't resist returning to her damp, kiss-swollen lips for one more sip.

She blinked up at him, her breath labored against his chin. The clouds had evaporated from her eyes. Now another glaze replaced them—pleasure. The same pleasure that coursed through him.

Another cough, louder this time.

He glanced toward the front door and Lena stood there, along with Joy and Belle.

"Eew!" Belle scrunched up her nose. "Uncle Isaac, you were kissing Jenna!"

As if he didn't know that. But maybe their neighbors needed the information.

"I thought you said you weren't her boyfriend," Joy accused, eyes narrowed on him behind her glasses.

"Yeah, Isaac," Lena drawled. "What's up with that?"

"Joy, are you dressed and ready to go?" Jenna unwound her arms from around him, and he grudgingly untangled his fingers from her hair, releasing her.

"Yes, that's what I wanted to tell you. But you and Isaac were kissing." She looked from her to him, giving him the stink eye, if he wasn't mistaken.

"Great, you're ahead of me. Let me go change really quick and we can head out," she said, side-stepping the kiss question.

Quite neatly, too. He was impressed.

"Might want to hold up on leaving for a minute." Lena held up her cell phone. "I just got a couple of calls. A few people are headed over here with things for Joy. You may not even need to go shopping, depending on what they bring. That's what I wanted to tell you. But you and Isaac were kissing," she added, echoing Joy with a smirk.

Isaac swallowed a chuckle and waited for Jenna's snarky remark but it didn't come. One glance at her face, and all humor fled.

He stepped forward, settling a hand on the small of her back. "Hey, Jenna. You okay?"

"People are coming here?" she whispered. Her blue eyes widened and the pulse beat like a snare drum. "When? Are you sure? Can you call them back and tell them that's not necessary? Can you—"

"Belle, Joy," Lena said, her gaze fixed on Jenna's pale face, "do me a favor and go watch TV in Joy's room for a few minutes, okay? We'll be right in."

"Is Jenna okay?" Joy asked, her small voice quavering.

"She's fine, sweetie. Just do what I say and we'll be behind you in just a few."

Once the girl obeyed, Lena crossed to Jenna and grasped Jenna's hand.

"Babe, look at me. Really look at me," Lena ordered in a firm tone she probably reserved for her students. "What's wrong? Why do you want me to call your friends and tell them not to come over?"

"Friends?" An ugly chuckle escaped her, and Isaac fought not to gather her in his arms again. "If anyone knows I'm not the kind of person to have friends, you do."

"What has you more upset, Jenna?" Lena murmured. "That you don't have friends…or there's a chance that you could have them?"

Jenna stared at her, and the indecision, the conflict and *pain* that flickered across her face had his own heart constricting.

"Let them in, sweetheart," he urged. He pressed a kiss to her hair. "Give them a chance and they'll give you one. But you have to let them in. Take the risk."

"Look at me." Lena waved a hand back and forth between them. "I don't *not* like you anymore." At Jenna's soft snort, Lena smiled. "They want to be there for that little girl. You know how this town operates. They take care of their own. It's just different being on the receiving end of it. But if you give it a chance, you'll find out it's kind of nice." She studied Jenna for a long moment, then added, voice low, "I think if you'll allow people to see the real you, they won't not like you either."

Jenna's lashes lowered, then she nodded. "Okay." Pause. "Thank you." Another pause. "That hurt, didn't it?"

Lena exhaled a long, loud breath. "God, did it."

Isaac winced even as he curved his hand around the nape of her neck and lightly squeezed. "I was going to ask if I should run into the house and get an ice pack, but I didn't want to ruin the moment."

"Shut it, you," Lena muttered, turning on her heel and striding back in the house.

"Your sister likes me."

"She totally does."

A heartbeat of silence. And then they both snickered.

As their humor ebbed, he stroked his thumb along the column of her neck and took delight in the shiver that shuddered through her.

"You okay?" he asked.

"I'm not weak," she said in lieu of an answer.

"No, Malibu, you're not."

She dragged in a breath, slowly exhaled it. "I'm okay."

He had zero doubts she would be. But he would hang around today and have her back just in case. That's what friends did.

And that rang hollow even in his own head.

Friends. Right.

Then he probably needed to stop picturing her naked, sweaty and coming undone beneath him.

Because "friends" didn't do that.

CHAPTER SEVENTEEN

"IF YOUR GOAL was to avoid pissing off your parents, bringing a plus-one to their exclusive lil' shindig pretty much screws the pooch on that." Isaac smirked, the colored lights strung high around The Glen gliding over his face like a kaleidoscope.

Jenna arched an eyebrow, focusing on the bold slant of his cheekbones, the lush curves of his mouth and the dark scruff that shadowed his jaw and chin. They all proved the perfect distractions to avoid glancing down from the Ferris wheel bucket where she and Isaac sat suspended.

When one possessed a fear of heights, one should really avoid rides higher than two hundred feet.

"I didn't bring a plus-one... I brought a plus-five. Big difference," she corrected.

"Right. My bad." He grinned. "Oh Malibu. When you decide to rebel, you don't do it halfway." He chuckled, and the wicked sound danced over the nape of her neck. Much like his fingers had earlier that day. "Your parents' expressions when you showed up with all of us in tow? Priceless."

By *all of us* he meant himself, Joy, Bella, Edward and Jacob.

And no, her parents had not been pleased to see her show up at The Glen with a whole group when they'd expressly invited only her. If they hadn't been in front of friends, donors and potential donors, then Jasper and Helene would've let her know just how displeased they were. And they wouldn't have been kind about it.

But with them on the ground and her so high her fingertips could graze the sky if she but stretched out her arm, she couldn't bring herself to care.

Not with the images of the children's delight still stamped on her memory.

Not with the anger at her parents' actions tonight simmering in her chest.

Not with the big, beautiful man sitting next to her, his body shielding her from the coolness of the evening.

No, she couldn't bring herself to care right now.

"There's more people here than I expected, though." Isaac peered down over the back of their car. She opted to keep her gaze trained on his face. "I got the impression your father intended to have a smaller, more—" his mouth twisted "—selective event tonight."

"I'm sure he did."

Isaac's gaze snapped to her. He studied her, and her skin tingled from his visual caress.

"Malibu," he murmured. "What did you do?"

She lifted a shoulder. "Nothing much. As a member of Jasper Landon's campaign team, I just placed a call to This Is Home, apologized for the short notice and let the director there know about the soft run of the carnival tonight. I then invited all the children to attend."

"This Is Home?" He frowned.

"It's the foster care youth home here in town." The anger flashed from a simmer to a full-out boil. "I remember when I was a little girl and the carnival would come to town. The excitement of watching every ride be erected and every booth set up. Seeing the lights flashing. The anticipation was nearly as exciting as actually going to it. Yes, adults enjoy carnivals, but there's a reason why. They make us feel like children again. And my parents and Christopher would exclude the very kids who need that carefree joy most. Did they stop to think how they, and the other children in this town who haven't been *blessed enough* to be born to influential or wealthy parents, would feel walking past, seeing some kids able to ride on the Ferris wheel, eat funnel cakes and drink hot chocolate, and they couldn't join in? No, they didn't think. Didn't *care*."

She clenched her fists around the bar across her lap, staring down at them for several long moments before lifting her gaze to the bucket seat above her. She couldn't see them from her current vantage point, but Joy's and Belle's giggles drifted down to her. And the happy sound doused some of her anger.

A big hand curled around the back of her neck, and she barely managed not to arch into it. Barely. The sharp retort of, "No woman likes being held by the scruff of her neck like a naughty puppy," died a quick death on her tongue. Because it would be a lie. And a desperate one at that. And Isaac would probably see right through the protest like a clear pane of freshly washed glass.

She liked it. More. She loved it. The gentle, yet firm grip should've been too dominant, too controlling. Instead, she felt protected, sheltered. As if, as long as he touched her, nothing could harm her.

The illusion was both tempting and dangerous.

"But you did. You thought of them. You cared." Isaac rubbed his thumb up and down her neck, and like earlier, she shivered.

Heat poured into her face because he had to feel it. Had to know his effect on her. She could deny it with her words, her distance, but as soon as he put his hands on her body...

She was undone.

"Well, I just took a chance. That seems to be a theme around you." She huffed a short laugh. "I took a chance that Dad and Chris wouldn't turn away twenty-five foster children and risk being the subject of scathing articles from all the reporters he's invited." She smiled, self-deprecating. "It seems I've picked up a thing or two from my father over the years."

"I wouldn't give him that much credit," Isaac said. "He meant for tonight to be about ambition and exclusion. You turned it around and made it about community. Take the win, Malibu."

A pang echoed just behind her breastbone. She rubbed a fist over it.

"I don't want it to be a win. Because that would mean he has to lose. And as messed up as it makes me, I don't want him to lose anything. Especially if it's at my hands."

Tender fingers pinched her chin. And because old habits died hard, thoughts of who could see them, if it would spark gossip, flashed through her mind. But then he brushed his fingertips along her jaw, leaving a trail of flames licking at her skin.

"Since you refuse to glance down—what? You think I didn't notice that?" She frowned, and his mouth kicked up at the corner. "But since you obviously have a thing about heights, close your eyes." After a brief hesitation, she acquiesced. "Now, listen. Block out everything else—really listen."

She inhaled, held the breath and then deliberately exhaled. Doing as he instructed, she…listened.

The canned carnival music dancing on the air from the carousel.

The high pitch of Bella's and Joy's voices and the slightly lower pitch of Jacob's from above them.

The squeal of children's laughter drifting up from the ground far below.

The deeper drone of adult voices underneath the laughter and excited cries.

"What do you hear?" Isaac asked, turning to face her more fully.

"Happiness. Fun. Life." As soon as the last word passed her lips, she wanted to rescind it, feeling foolish for even saying it.

But Isaac nodded. "This—" he waved a hand behind him "—is why I returned home. What I missed in Florida. Yeah, I had a successful career, fame, wealth, a big home and all the toys to go in it. But after a while—after the glamour wore off—I wasn't happy. At first, I wanted to blame that on the dissolution of my marriage, on the failed pregnancies, on the affair. But the truth is Tampa wasn't *this*. Family. Community."

His long lashes lowered for a moment, hiding his indigo eyes. If she were bolder, she'd demand he look at her, let her see his thoughts. But she didn't. Instead, she remained quiet and did as he requested earlier. Just listened.

"Of course, I had friends, I had Diana. But I grew up in a place where neighbors looked out for one another. Where no one in the neighborhood went hungry because if we ate, they ate. A place where, yes, I had a single parent, but I wasn't raised by one because I had

Mrs. Leonard and Mrs. Arnold, who ensured I got home from school safely or checked my homework because Mom was at work. I had Mr. Anthony, who taught me about cars, and Mr. Griggs, who snatched me up and ripped me a new asshole when he heard me call Melissa Bell a bitch. Mount Holly, Rose Bend—these places are special, the people are special. They're not just made up of DNA, biological family. But chosen family. Found family. And where there's family, there's life. There's laughter. There're tears. Pain. But most of all, there's love. It's what I was missing. It's what I want to give my own kids one day."

She glanced away from him and wished she could somehow shut out the beauty of his words. They carved a path deep inside her, and she bled.

It's what I want to give my own kids one day.

Even though heights made her squeamish, a primal part of her longed to throw back her head and scream to the sky.

That family he described? She'd never experienced that. Didn't know it. And she'd never know it for herself.

But God, did she want it.

And almost resented him for having it.

Shame crawled through her, and she tipped her head back on her shoulders, closing her eyes. Maybe she *was* more like her father than she imagined. Selfish. Petty.

"Mr. Right was a character I played," Isaac murmured. The words, so out of context from their previous conversation, drew her attention, and she jerked her gaze to him. "He was charming, a gentleman, a real knight in shining armor. And until this moment, I've never wanted the persona and the real man to be one. But to erase the pain that caused the look on your face moments ago, I need to ride to the rescue." His gaze roamed her face, and she curled her fingers tighter around the safety bar. "But you're not going to let me slay your dragons, are you, Jenna?"

Dragons. Demons. She had too many to ask him to take them on. It wouldn't be fair to either of them. No, Isaac shouldn't be riding into battle *for* her; he should be racing *away* from her.

"Do they teach you that, too, as soon as you cross the Mason-Dixie Line? To say such perfect, pretty things?" she whispered, trying to dodge his question and dispel the weight behind his words. Or the weight pressing on her chest. Neither worked.

A slow grin spread across his face although his indigo eyes remained shuttered.

"Pretty nothings and genteel manners."

The Ferris wheel slowly descended, and they didn't speak, just stared at one another. Her pulse pounded in her head, and part of her wanted to beg him to, *Please, touch me again. Ground me. Make me burn so nothing else matters.*

Yet the other half recognized the danger of getting lost in this man. Christopher, the other men she'd dated through the years…they hadn't beckoned her to let it all go, to leap. To believe.

Not like Isaac.

The Ferris wheel car jerked to a stop and the safety bar loosened. She lifted it just as a carnival staff member stepped up. Before she could move down the ramp, Isaac cupped her elbow and guided her down. Joy and Bella met them at the bottom, and the two girls nearly tackled her, while Jacob stood next to his uncle, his expression long-suffering. Jenna bit her lip to hold in a laugh, and when Isaac pointed out Edward several feet away at the cotton candy booth, the nine-year-old took off so fast he left smoke behind him.

"What did you two do to poor Jake?" Isaac asked.

"Jake has a girlfriend," Belle tattled.

"Good God," Isaac muttered. "'Nuff said."

"Jenna, can we go on the carousel?" Joy tugged on her hand, her green eyes shining, and Jenna's heart swelled. No traces of sadness there. In this moment, she was only a little girl enjoying the town fair.

"Again?" Jenna teased. "What will this be? The thirteenth time?"

"Only the third," Joy corrected. "Can we go?"

"Of course." Jenna smiled. "But if you don't mind, I'm going to sit this one out. I'll be over by the gate waiting for you."

"Okay!" Joy grabbed Bella's hand, and the two girls ran the few feet to the line for the carousel, their heads bent together.

For only having the two rides available, and a few booths with snacks and drinks, Jenna still called the night a success. Though the event hadn't turned out as…intimate as they'd planned, if the objective had been to stir excitement for the carnival opening, she'd say mission accomplished. And over on the far side of The Glen, holding court like royals, stood her parents with Chris nearby.

Yes, well, she would be spending the rest of the evening as far away as possible from that corner.

"So," Leo began, sliding up beside Jenna, hooking their arms, "I'm going to grill you over how you came to have custody of a little girl because from what I've heard around town, it's a fascinating story. And I'm pretty sure I overheard talk of a Jenna Landon Day 'n' all that, but first…" Her voice dropped, her blue-gray eyes roaming Jenna's face, searching. "Are you okay?"

She didn't need Leo to explain what she meant. They'd both suffered through the same loss of a pregnancy. And while it'd been years since Jenna had experienced anxiety or stress when it came to being around children, Leo didn't know that. And Jenna blinked against the emotion that crowded into her throat at her thoughtfulness.

"Yes, I'm fine," she rasped.

Leo smiled. "Good. Now, I hear you're not only Mary Poppins-ing, but you're also shacking up with Mr. Right? As your bestie, why am I the last to know? And I'd just like to say, with all my heart, I told you so."

Jenna snorted. "I swear, I'm going to card you just to make sure you're actually twenty-nine," she muttered. Side-eyeing the other woman, she added, "And you need to stop listening to gossip. There's no shacking up. And therefore, no 'I told you so.'"

"Woman, please. We both know I'm still right about Mr. Right." Leo arched her eyebrow. "Do I really need to go into all the canoodling on the Ferris wheel?"

"How has your fiancé not smothered you in your sleep yet?"

"Because I sleep with one eye open… And then there's this thing I do—"

"*Oh God*, stop talking. Now," Jenna ordered.

Leo grinned, shrugged. "What? You asked."

"I recognize that particularly tortured expression. On behalf of all the Dennisons, let me apologize for whatever harassment Leo's doling out." Cole Dennison walked up to them, and he smiled first at his sister, who subtly flipped him off by scratching her nose with her middle finger.

Then he turned that pretty smile on Jenna. There'd been a time when she'd convinced herself she wanted Cole. That had been a lie; with time and distance, she could admit she'd wanted what he represented. Safety. Security. Peace.

Family.

Still, there was no denying his pretty smile.

"Hi, Jenna," he greeted.

"Hi, Cole. It's nice to see you."

"You, too." He dipped his chin. "Good to see you again, too, Isaac."

"Mr. Mayor." A warm, wide palm settled on the small of her back.

She could get used to that.

Which was why didn't she dare to.

"Jenna, I hear we have you to thank for inviting the kids from This Is Home tonight. Ms. Marcell really appreciated you thinking of them. And they're having a wonderful time. Thank you."

She lifted a shoulder. "It was nothing."

"Translation, no problem," Leo drawled.

"Take the win," Isaac whispered in her ear, and she almost repeated her mistake from earlier today of holding on to him as if he were the last driftwood in a storm-roughened sea.

"That little girl is adorable. Both of them," Sydney announced, approaching them, smiling. She glanced over her shoulder toward the carousel line, but when her gaze met Jenna's, that smile tightened. "Hey, Jenna. I just met Joy. She's great." Her attention shifted to Isaac, and warmth reentered her expression. "And Belle is still too cute and hilarious." Sydney laughed. "She told me Patience is too small to ride the carousel with her and Joy, but I'm old so I could take her."

Leo snickered and Cole bent down, sweeping Patience up in his arms, smacking a loud kiss on her rounded cheek. The toddler giggled, wrapping her arms tight around her stepfather's neck and returning the kiss.

The hand low on her waist suddenly became a heavier weight, and Isaac's fingertips pressed hard into her flesh, as if trying to clutch her.

She didn't have to glance behind her to know he stared at Patience. Memories of his panicked reaction at Mimi's Café flashed across her mind, and now that she understood why, her heart ached for him. Shifting back a step, she leaned her weight against him, grounding him in the here and now.

For an eternally long moment, he remained stiff and unyielding. And just when she braced herself for him to charge away like he had before, his big body relaxed into her. His chest pressed to her back, his hips to her ass, and in the small of her back... The air evaporated from her lungs at the thick cock wedged against her. Yet, even as desire poured through her, that wasn't the prevalent emotion locking them together. Protectiveness. She wanted to protect him, shield him, as he'd done for her.

"Jenna!" Joy yelled from the line just before she shot through the gate and clambered onto the carousel. "Jenna!" she called again, climbing onto a unicorn. "Over here! Hi!"

Smiling, Jenna lifted her arm and waved back at her.

"She really likes you," Sydney murmured, staring at her.

Jenna couldn't help it; she bristled at the hint of disbelief in Sydney's voice.

"Right. But then, children are notoriously gullible, aren't they?" Jenna drawled. Sliding her arm free of Leo's, she turned to Isaac, giving him a grim smile that undoubtedly didn't fool him. "Would you mind waiting for Joy and Bella by the gate? I'm going to grab a couple of cotton candies for them."

"I got them, Malibu."

She nodded, noting his gaze skimmed over Patience as he said goodbye to Cole, Sydney and Leo. Jenna took a step in the opposite direction, but then halted and pivoted, her attention focusing on Sydney. Her former childhood best friend stiffened, eyes narrowing.

"You consider us mortal enemies, and I get it. And more importantly, I deserve your anger and comments. But what I'm going to ask is that you keep it between us. When we're in front of that little girl, don't air your grievances with me. You think I'm a bitch. But she doesn't. And since she's staying with me in my home, I'd prefer it stays that way. So don't taint that."

Not granting Sydney an opportunity to reply, she stalked toward the cotton candy booth, her heart a wild, battering beast in her chest. Contrary to most people's perception of her, she hated confrontation. She often used a barbed tongue to avoid it. Still, challenging Sydney about her attitude... It left her shaken and, dammit, exhilarated.

Exhilarated because turning over a new leaf had left her feeling too much like a doormat. And true, she deserved Sydney's animosity.

But hell, the woman got on her nerves.

A thrill sparkled through her like one of those blinking lights on the carousel. Damn, if that didn't feel good to admit. And it was *okay* to admit it because she was human.

"Uh-oh, a smile like that usually means trouble for someone."

Jenna handed several dollar bills to the person behind the cotton candy booth and met the playful dark blue eyes of Israel Ford, standing next to her. Or as most people probably knew him, I. M. Kelly, the *New York Times* bestselling romance author. It seemed incongruous that she, the reserved mayor's daughter, wrote apocalyptic paranormal YA, while he, a man straight out of a casting call for *Vikings,* penned the most breathtaking and sensual romance in the business. But there they were. Two authors. One, no longer plagued by writer's block, living his best life and in love. And the other?

The other would be her, living a lie and hiding everything about herself.

For instance.

She considered this man a good friend and he didn't even know it. He didn't know her.

Forcing another smile to conceal the sadness, she collected the girls' treats and faced Israel.

"Hi, Israel. I didn't expect to see you here tonight."

He snorted. "No offense, but your father couldn't afford to exclude the pastor of his church. He needs that direct pipeline. And seeing as how I'm now an unofficial member of Pastor Noel's family…" He spread his arms wide, a wicked grin growing across his face. "Here I am."

"That's the second time today someone has told me 'no offense,' then proceeded to offend me by disparaging my father," she said, though with no heat.

"Are we really, though? Offending you?" A smirk rode his mouth as he looked in the direction of where her father stood, surrounded by his admirers. "I've never mentioned it, but Ryland Ravensmith, the evil councilor on the Anakim Academy's board, bears an uncanny resemblance to your father. Maybe it's subconscious, but I can't believe that's a coincidence."

Shock left her frozen, speechless. Questions, denials crowded into her head, howling so loudly, they momentarily deafened her. But she couldn't push anything past her locked vocal cords.

Israel nodded, and though his smirk remained, his eyes softened. As did his voice.

"Yep, I know. And have known for a couple of years now. One of the publicists let it slip when he expressed what a coincidence it was that two of their authors lived in the same small town. That publicist no longer works for our publisher, by the way," he added with a chuckle. "But yeah, I know that Jenna Landon and Beck Dansing are one and the same."

She frantically scanned their immediate surroundings. *God.* What if—

"No one heard me," he assured her. "I'd never betray you, Jenna. I haven't in all this time, I wouldn't now. You may not realize this but I consider you one of my best friends. So your secret will continue to be safe with me. I just thought it was about time we could be honest with each other. I already have a pen name. That's all the subterfuge I can manage. Walking past you and we're not good? Yeah, I'm through with that. If no one else knows, at least we will."

A smile slowly curved her mouth, and relief bubbled inside her alongside happiness. She crossed her arms over her chest. Either that or throw them around the Viking look-alike in front of her.

"Just this morning I told someone I only had one friend. I was wrong. I have two. I've always had two."

"Damn right." He mimicked her position. "Now, I'd pull you in close for a hug but that might start people wondering. Plus, that professional wrestler of yours keeps sending looks over here, and I value my spleen." He chuckled, then nodded in his direction. "Does he... know?"

"No. Just you." She shook her head. "I take that back. Leo Dennison does, too. I wasn't careful enough and she found out."

"Or maybe you really wanted her to find out." He arched an eyebrow.

Jenna scoffed, waving a hand. "I've never bought into that armchair psychology stuff."

He cocked his head. "We'll argue about that later online. But think about it. Maybe you're a little tired of hiding in plain sight. Your situation isn't the same as mine. A pen name is necessary for me because of the often unfair bias against men writing romance. Fear lies behind your pen name." He glanced toward her parents again, his jaw flexing as if he ground his teeth. "But you also have a town that would fucking celebrate you if they discovered you were Beck Dansing."

"You're talking about the library event."

"Hell yeah, I am."

"Which is also the same night of the carnival," she reminded him. "I can't betray my father like that."

Israel shook his head. "Too bad your father didn't think of that when he scheduled the carnival for the same weekend as the Spooks 'n' Books event. People are going to attend a fair, but with you in attendance at the library, they can get the publicity and attention needed to get people in those doors for at least one good night."

"Israel…"

"No guilt trip." He held up his hands, then smiled. "Okay, maybe a small one. But just something to think about. You've been in the shadows way too long. And anyone who can't be proud of the fact that Jenna Landon is a badass bestselling author needs their head examined. Or their own ego checked at the door," he added pointedly.

Nothing subtle about that.

"Thank you, Israel," she said.

He nodded. "I know when to shut up. Or," he said and shrugged, "I promised Korrie to learn." Grinning, he saluted her with two fingers. "See you tonight?"

"I'll be there."

With another wicked grin, he sauntered off, and she headed over to Isaac just as the carousel ride ended.

"Everything okay?" he asked, concern darkening his eyes.

She huffed out a chuckle. "If you're not careful, asking me that is going to become a habit."

"Compared to biting my nails or not getting enough sleep, it's not my worst."

She hesitated, but then brushed her fingertips over the back of his hand, savoring the power and gentleness in those long fingers.

"You're going to be my next heartbreak," she whispered.

When his eyes darkened even further and his full mouth flattened, it hit her that she'd spoken aloud.

"And here I was worried you were going to be mine," he murmured.

She might be. That's what she did. Broke people's dreams. Disappointed them.

Her lips parted to warn him off but then Joy and Bella burst through the gate, running at full speed.

"Hey, Jenna! Is that for me?" Joy skidded to a halt in front of her, pointing at the cotton candy clutched in her hand.

"And me, too?" Belle made grabby hands at the treat.

"Of course. Who else would they be for?" Jenna smiled, handing them to the girls. And deliberately avoiding Isaac's gaze even though she felt it on her like a handprint.

"We're not done here," Isaac said in her ear as the kids unwrapped the candy and stuffed it in their mouths.

Oh yes, they were. They had to be.

Because she couldn't afford the devastation *not being done* would leave behind.

CHAPTER EIGHTEEN

ISAAC KNOCKED ON the front door of his childhood home. He had a key, but it'd been so long since he'd lived there, it didn't seem proper to use it. Of course, his mother would probably tell him to stop being foolish, he thought as the door opened and the woman herself stood in the doorway.

"Hey, Mom."

A wide smile lit her face.

"Isaac. I didn't know you were dropping by this morning." She opened the door wider and stepped aside. "Come on in. It's Sunday, so everyone's sleeping late, except for Lena. She took Belle over to Rose Bend to play with Joy." She chuckled, closing the door behind him. "She's going to be crushed when Joy leaves to go home, I'm afraid. Belle came home last night and declared her and Joy were 'bestest friends.'"

Isaac laughed. "Yeah, you should've seen them together yesterday. They were inseparable from the second they met. Albany's only about an hour away, so maybe they can keep in touch."

His mother rolled her eyes, beckoning him to follow her down the hall to the kitchen. "If I know my Belle, she'll get her way and those two will see each other again." She waved toward the table. "Now, sit. I'll have coffee going shortly. And in the meantime, you can tell me what's brought you by so early on a week-end morning."

He chuckled again, softly this time as he pulled out a chair and sank into it. "There's no fooling you, is there?"

"I don't care how long you've been gone. You're still one of mine, and I know you. And I also know when something's on your mind. Now, spill." She pulled out a bag of coffee grounds because, no matter that a one-cup brewer sat right next to the older model, his mother insisted on making coffee the old-fashioned way. "And you can start with the truth you've been hiding from your mother. Needlessly, I might add," she said, tucking a filter into the top of the white coffee maker.

"What do you mean?" he asked, frowning.

She propped a fist on her hip and turned to him. "Isaac Bernard Hunter—"

"Not the Bernard." He winced.

"If you believe I bought that line about you and Diana divorcing because you just 'grew apart,' then you must think I've grown senile in my old age. And news flash. I haven't. So the truth, please. And finally."

"Mom." He sighed.

"She cheated."

He blinked. Well…damn.

"What is it with you women? Do you have a sixth sense or something?"

Alice snorted. "I don't know what that means, but it was pretty easy to figure out. The only way you'd break your vows and get a divorce is if she broke hers first. I was just waiting for you to admit it to me." She crossed the room and cupped Isaac's face. "And I'm sorry, baby. I really am. I know that pain, and I would never wish it on you." Leaning down, she pressed a kiss to his forehead, and he closed his eyes, inhaling and taking comfort in her familiar lavender scent.

For the most part, he'd healed from Diana's betrayal, but until this moment, he hadn't realized he'd needed this.

"Why did you feel you couldn't tell me?" she asked, releasing him with one last touch to his cheek.

Crossing the kitchen, she returned to the counter and continued fiddling with the coffee maker. Soon, the aroma of brewing coffee permeated the air, and he nearly sighed.

"I didn't want you to look at Diana differently," he said.

Standing, he retrieved cups and saucers out of the cabinets.

"I could've done that, y'know," she groused. "And I wouldn't have treated her differently. Your marriage is between you two."

"But I'm your son."

"And I don't know the details of what happened between you. Not saying there's a good excuse to cheat. Because there isn't. But nothing is ever black-and-white. And yes, you're my son and I love you, but you're not perfect either." She smiled, taking the sting out of the words.

"What?" He gasped. "I'm not perfect? Since when?"

Slapping him in the stomach, she set the cups on the saucers. "So tell me, Isaac. Are you okay? Are you home to lick your wounds and you plan on returning to Florida? Or is this for good?"

Her voice sounded casual but he caught the tension running underneath. The hope, too.

"I'm home, Mom. For good." He noted the quirk at the corner of her mouth before she tried to hide it. "Yeah, I saw that smile."

"Okay, fine." She looked at him, throwing up her

hands. "Sue me for being happy because almost all of my children are home for once."

"Yeah." He nodded, hesitated, but then admitted, "I haven't told anyone yet, but I'm considering partnering with the WFC and setting up a wresting training center here. It would be similar to the FTR in Tampa, but for middle and high school kids. And maybe college. I'm not sure yet. But the purpose would be to train kids who are serious about wrestling and prepare them for college scholarships or careers in wrestling, if that's their goal."

"Isaac!" his mother gasped, clapping her hands, a huge smile brightening her face. "That's amazing! And perfect for you! When will you start?"

"I'm still working on the details and I don't even know if the WFC is on board yet. I need to broach Diana with the idea, but we'll see. If they say no, I still have my own funds and my own brand name as Mr. Right. I'll find a way to make it happen."

"Of course you will," she said, voice firm. She slapped a hand down on the counter. "You have no idea how happy I am to hear that, Isaac. I was…worried about you," she softly admitted.

He leaned back against the counter, crossing his arms. "You never said. Why?"

She rolled her hands in a helpless gesture. "I don't know. Call it a mother's intuition. You didn't visit often, but when you did, there seemed to be a sadness hanging over you like a storm cloud. I always wished I could sweep it away. But then I'd think of your career, how you were living the dream down there in Florida and thought maybe I imagined those shadows in your eyes. But it wasn't my imagination, was it?"

"Like I said, there's no fooling you." He smiled, and

it felt wistful. With a small bump of his hip, he moved her out of the way and picked up the now-full coffee-pot. "You go sit. I'll get the coffee."

In moments, he had the brew poured, and they sat down across from one another at the table. Quietly, they sipped the coffee, just enjoying their drinks and one an-other's company. And then, he started to talk. And talk. And long after he finished his first cup and his mother rose and poured him another, he still talked. She didn't interrupt, didn't ask questions. And when he finished, she reached across the table and clasped his hand in hers. That familiar touch... Emotion barreled up his chest, filling it so he barely had room for air. Flipping their hands, he clutched hers. And held on.

"I'm thinking of every time I asked you about grand-children. Even joking..." His mother swallowed, and she squeezed her eyes shut. "I'm so sorry, Isaac. I didn't know..."

"How could you? We didn't tell anyone. Diana pre-ferred not to..." He shrugged. "And I had to protect my wife, her privacy. It was her right to grieve in the way she chose."

"Yours, too. You had the same right," Alice insisted fiercely.

"Yeah. Me, too. And if I'm honest, I hid behind Di-ana's choice. It allowed me to bottle it all up and not talk. To ignore the cracks that were forming in my mar-riage that had nothing to do with children and a family. Because I can't help wondering, if there had been more love than resentment and pain, would we have turned to one another after losing Sam rather than to other peo-ple? Maybe. If we were Sam's parents today, we might be happy together. A family." He slid one hand free of his mother's grasp and pressed the heel of his palm to his forehead. "I go round and round in my head in an endless loop with the what-ifs."

She sighed. "I can't begin to understand the pain Diana has suffered. Or you, for that matter. And then the adoption? On one hand, I get why you didn't share that with me, with us. Especially after experiencing so much disappointment. But on the other hand, I wish you would've let us be there for you. As your mother, it was my right to be there for you. For both of you. If I could absorb that hurt for her, for you, God knows I would."

She sat back in her chair, releasing his hand. Staring down into her cup, she fell quiet for several seconds.

"But, son, I know what it is to bring a child into a relationship where there is love and into a relationship that is broken. And one of the most selfish, hurtful things we can do as parents is bring a baby into this world thinking it's their job to heal our relationship. To fix our marriage. To mend the pieces of ourselves and try to make us whole, when that's impossible. That isn't fair to that child, and it's placing a responsibility on them that isn't theirs. A child adds to us. It's not their job to be our happiness. That's a weight even an adult shouldn't bear, much less an innocent baby."

He didn't move. Couldn't move. And yet he absorbed her words like bruising blows. Had he and Diana done that?

Yes.

The answer ricocheted through him loud and clear as a bell. He couldn't deny it. And the truth flayed him. They'd focused on getting pregnant and starting a family so they didn't have to confront the issues rotting their marriage from the inside out. The lack of trust on her part. The poor communication on both their parts. The insecurity on his. But as long as they concentrated on the common goal of a baby, they could avoid the painful subjects that could've torn them apart.

In the end, nothing could save them.

"Son, people say, 'Everything happens for a reason,' and 'God moves in mysterious ways.' I'm sure if you head over to the nearest church the pastor can break down for you the whys and hows of divine intervention and all of that. Me? All I can tell you is this." She lifted her head and met his gaze. "You'll be all right. You just continue to be the man I've raised, the one I'm proud to call my son. The man who would shoulder all the blame rather than let anyone slander his ex's name. The man who refuses to rest on what he was and is always seeking to be a better version of who he can be. For that man, life goes on. For that man, it'll be all right."

"I love you, Mom."

She smiled. "I love you more, baby."

He stared at her for several long moments, and the ticking of the clock above the stove resounded in the kitchen like tiny booms.

"What if I'm scared of life moving on?" he whispered.

Her smile turned wry.

"I'd think you were an idiot if you weren't." She arched an eyebrow. "And I didn't raise no idiots."

His laughter echoed in the kitchen and hers joined in.

And it felt good.

Really good.

SHE FELT NAKED.

Jenna fought the urge to wrap her arms around her laptop, shield it from view. As if anyone passing by her porch would glimpse the manuscript she worked on. Paranoia was not pretty.

But that's what happened when she took a risk.

Another one.

Like deciding to write on her porch in the daytime instead of at night, in the shadows like she usually did. No hiding. She wasn't coming clean about being Beck Dansing. But with Israel's conversation echoing in her head, this seemed like a symbolic compromise. She was coming out in the open.

And she felt exposed as hell.

But she refused to go inside.

This was her little rebellion.

Sighing, she refocused on her screen, and after a little while, she lost herself again in the world of Anakim Academy and the Nephilim students who attended.

"Those numbers must be really absorbing."

She jerked, locking down the scream that jolted up her throat. Lifting her head, she met Isaac's indigo gaze, which reflected the humor in his grin. He nodded toward the laptop.

"Must be completely fascinating bookkeeping, Malibu. Are those numbers multiplying like rabbits or something?" He gasped, and climbing the last step, he leaned forward, his voice lowering to a scandalized whisper. "Or are those numbers *conjugating*?"

"You're coaching fifteen-year-olds, Monster, but when did you become one?" she drawled, discreetly tapping save then closing the laptop.

He shrugged, falling into one of the porch chairs. "Eh. It comes and goes." A lazy smile curled his beautiful mouth, and she stared at it. Too long. Giving her head a mental shake, she met his gaze. "Don't you ever take a break? I don't remember much from the Sunday school classes Mom forced us to go to, but I do recall even God resting on the seventh day."

"It actually says the Sabbath, and that's on Saturday."

He narrowed his eyes on her. "You'd think this nearly pathological need to be right would be off-putting. Yet, it's really hot."

She snorted, swinging her feet down and rising. And she chose to pretend the birds in her belly had not just taken flight.

"Only in your world is calling me a compulsive know-it-all a compliment. You better walk close behind me just in case I swoon."

His chuckle followed her as she opened the storm door and entered the house. There'd been a time when her home had been her private sanctuary and she could count on one hand—with a couple of fingers left over—the number of people who'd walked over the threshold. And now not just him, his family and Joy had occupied her domain, but it seemed half the damn town had invaded it.

This was where she should be upset, feel violated. At least a mild irritation.

But when images of how Leo's mom, Moe Dennison, showed up with Patricia Collins, Sydney's mom, and a battalion of other women armed with bags of clothes, books and toys for Joy flickered in front of her head, she couldn't summon a whisper of annoyance. Not when she couldn't banish a vivid picture of Joy's face, so full of awe and delight.

In the end, Jenna hadn't needed to take Joy shopping for essentials; everything had been brought to them.

Along with a good deal of fussing over. Joy had gained a gang of doting aunts and grandmothers that day.

And Jenna had lost the privacy she'd so zealously guarded.

And the fact that she couldn't bring herself to mourn it unnerved her.

"My mother mentioned Lena was headed over here," Isaac said, his heavy footsteps falling behind her on the hardwood floors as he trailed her to the kitchen.

"Yes, she took Joy and Belle to the park and then for ice cream since we weren't able to yesterday."

"Belle," he murmured. When she stopped in the kitchen entrance and glanced at him over her shoulder, frowning, he smiled, and it softened his sharp, blunt features. Had her fingertips itching to brush the hollows underneath his cheekbones, graze the uncompromising line of his jaw. Sip at the sweet, lush curve of his bottom lip. "This is the first time you've called her by our nickname."

It'd just slipped out. Easily. It represented a crack in her guard, in her carefully constructed defenses.

It revealed she'd let them in.

Part of her groaned, *What have you done? What are you doing?*

And the other half groaned, too. But with relief. The sweet relief of finally, for one moment, not feeling...alone.

At this point, it was difficult to discern which half cried out louder.

Needing to veer away from the *weight* of that for the moment, she moved into the kitchen, setting her laptop on the table.

"You mentioned you were at your mom's? She must've loved a visit from you."

"Seven points on the change of subject, but I'm subtracting three for the clumsy execution." He tsked. "Gots to be smoother than that, Malibu." Wincing as if he were truly disappointed, he rested his shoulders against the wall, crossing his ankles. "And yes, I spent this morning with my mom, and she was happy to spend time with her favorite son."

"Her words? Or yours?"

He shrugged, the corner of his mouth riding up. "They were implied." Pushing off the wall, he strolled toward her in that loose-limbed, confident stride that never failed to set off a heated throb low in her belly. And trigger images of what else those hips could do. "I went over to have coffee and tell her about the training center I'm thinking about opening here in Rose Bend—"

She gasped, her chin jerking up. Shock ricocheted through her.

"A training center?" she whispered. "What do you—what're you talking about?"

"I haven't had a chance to tell you with everything that's been going on," he said. "I'm considering opening a wrestling training center here in Rose Bend. Right now, I've reached out to the WFC about partnering with me. If they do, the center could help kids not just with the sport but with scholarships and career opportunities. This could—what?"

Jenna shook her head, she couldn't stop smiling at him. Couldn't stop being so...happy for him if she tried.

"You've found it," she said, a quiet yet fierce joy for him swelling inside her. "Your purpose for coming here. Family might've been your reason, but we both know coaching high school wrestling, as admirable as it is, and even as much as you may love those kids, isn't your passion. But the sport, the industry and children are. I'm so thrilled that you've found a way to marry them. I'm thrilled you've found your happy."

He stared at her for a long moment. So long, she had the urge to lift a hand to her face and rub to see if any smudges came away.

"Now it's my turn to say 'what'?" She tried to chuckle, but it came out too breathless, too shivery under his unwavering gaze.

"You really are thrilled for me, aren't you?"

"Yes, Monster, I am. Mostly, because you're relieved and a weight has been lifted off your shoulders. And because you now know that retiring, leaving Tampa and coming here wasn't a mistake. I'm happy because you have some peace now about your decision. And that's priceless."

He lifted a hand, running the backs of his fingers across her jaw. As impossible as it was, she burned where his hand touched. Who was she kidding? He didn't need to lay a finger on her—hell, he didn't need to come within feet of her—for those same flames to ignite. All he had to do was breathe.

"What was that for?" she asked.

Another one of those soft smiles curled his lips and he dropped his arm, taking his warmth with him. She curled her fingers, ordering herself to *not dare* reach for his hand and put it back on her.

"Do you mind?"

Say yes. Take the out. Avoid—

"No, I don't."

"Good," he moved closer still, and his leather and cedar scent enveloped her, caressed her even when his hands remained by his sides. "Because I've found I like touching you. More than is probably wise and definitely more than I should. But that doesn't stop me wanting it."

A shiver worked its way through her, and her nails bit into her palms.

"Isaac..."

"Tell me to stop if you don't want to hear anymore." His voice lowered, deepened, and it slipped beneath her sweater, skimmed over her bare skin, leaving pebbled flesh in its wake. How could he not even touch her yet— good God, had she said *yet*?—and she already quivered inside as if just moments from coming apart. "Because if you don't stop me, I'll tell you how I've become something of an addict. My drug of choice is the sound of your voice. And the scent that I can't figure out if it's perfume or a shampoo. Then it doesn't matter because it's you and I just want it all over me. It's the taste of you. Sweet. So fucking sweet and powerful enough to have me hooked, craving more," he continued as if he weren't devastating her. Cracking her right down the middle with his pretty words in that rough silk voice.

Stop, she silently pleaded. Too much of herself poured out of that opening, and she feared by the time he finished talking, she would be empty. Nothing of her left.

And where would that leave her?

Raw. Exposed. Vulnerable.

Weak.

Yes, she had to shut him up.

It was a matter of survival now.

Lunging forward, she clapped her hands on either side of his face and crushed her mouth to his. Desperation had goaded her to take the drastic action—or so she told herself—but when his lips parted under hers and she tasted his breath moments before she sampled *him*, desperation surrendered to desire.

This wasn't their first kiss, not even their second. But the press of his lips to hers, the languid tangle of their tongues, her soft sigh mating with his dark groan—they set off a frantic flutter in her belly as if this were their initial meeting of mouths. Yet, at the same time, each firm thrust, each tender sweep, each wicked suck reflected a familiarity of a long-time lover well-acquainted with her needs, her desires. And he gave them to her with a lick to the roof of her mouth, a nip to the corner of her bottom lip, a long, indulgent suckle of her tongue that echoed deep in her sex.

How could a man kiss her and it resonate in her whole body? Her breasts swelled as if he cupped them, as if his thumbs brushed the beaded nipples. Her thighs trembled as if he parted them and wedged his big body between them. Her sex clenched around an emptiness, begging to be filled.

A kiss. A freaking kiss.

And she wanted more. Needed more.

She shifted closer, eliminating the minute space between them. And she could've wept in relief at the press of chest to chest, of powerful legs to her slender ones... to the hard, thick cock nudging her belly. His arms still hung at his sides—God, why didn't he hold her?— but the insistent push of that long, heavy flesh burned through her clothes like flames, branding her skin.

"Touch me," she whispered.

And not waiting for his acquiescence, she reached for his hands, grasped them and lifted them to her breasts. Inside, she burned with mortification, and a too loud yet tiny voice screamed, *What are you doing?* She'd never been this...bold with a man, and she couldn't really say why. Maybe because she'd never wanted a man as much before. Had never felt like if he didn't put his hands, his mouth on her, she might not live to see the next moment.

That kind of hunger eradicated modesty. Or apathy.

His eyes deepened to a dark blue as he cupped her, molded his fingers to her. She hissed as pleasure coiled around her lower back and squeezed. Tipping her head back on her shoulders, she allowed her eyes to close and gave herself over to the lust. And to the underlying tenderness that she couldn't deny—no matter how much she wanted to.

His mouth scorched a path along her neck as he swept his thumbs over her aching, beaded nipples. One. Twice. Three times. And her knees nearly buckled with the onslaught that slammed into her. Her grip on his wrists tightened, and it was the only thing holding her up as he continued to tease her, torment her. Drive her crazy.

"Is this what you wanted?" he growled into the base of her throat.

And she felt the dangerous, hoarse rumble even as it reached her ears. Felt it vibrate against her skin, in the tight tips he lightly pulled on...over her pulsing clit. With a desperate shake of her head, she twisted, squeezing her thighs together to alleviate the sweet pain between her legs. A fruitless gesture, and his low, wicked chuckle relayed that he understood what she tried to do with her restless movements. And that they didn't help.

"Tell me, sweetheart." He lifted a hand, thrusting it in her hair and, with just enough demand to send tiny pricks scattering along her scalp and a backdraft of lust mushrooming in her body, he tugged her head up so she had no choice but to meet his. "Is this what you wanted?"

"No." She shook her head for added emphasis. Without breaking his gaze, she brushed her fingertips over his bottom lip. "I need this," she applied more pressure, her heart pounding, the primal beat filling her ears, "on me."

Then, dropping her hands to the hem of her sweater, she gripped it and yanked the top over her head. And let it fall to the floor.

Though it cost her to be so exposed, so vulnerable before him in the bright light streaming through her kitchen windows, she didn't try to cover herself. She allowed him to look his fill, and he did. His stare stroked over her, leaving scorch marks in its wake, and she trembled, but still didn't raise her arms. And when he met her eyes again, the same fire that licked at her skin burned in his indigo depths. Yet... Yet, underneath, another emotion lurked. Just as visible, but softer. And maybe more devastating than that passion threatening to incinerate her right where she stood.

Tenderness.

That tenderness would undo her faster than any touch from those large, calloused hands could.

Before she could sink into it, she rose on her toes and took his mouth in another kiss, sliding her fingers over the shorter hair at his sides into the thicker, silken strands on top. She fisted them, drawing his head down so she could deepen the kiss, show him with her mouth what she needed from his hands, that oh-so-talented tongue that tangled with hers, that thick, hard cock that branded her belly.

His groan spilled into her mouth, and she swallowed it seconds before he tore his lips free from hers and trailed it down her throat, over her collar bone and down the middle of her chest. Her breath stuttered in her lungs, then expelled on a long, harsh rush when his mouth closed around her nipple. It didn't matter that her bra still covered her flesh; the lace proved an insubstantial barrier to the hungry demands of his tongue, his teeth.

She shivered, her nails raking across his scalp.

A hard arm slipped around her waist, hauling her tighter against the big body bent over her. Isaac cupped her breast, lifting her to him as if serving her up to himself. And his growl relayed he found her delicious. His greedy mouth telegraphed he wanted more.

And she'd give him everything he asked for.

For a moment, a sharp stab of fear penetrated the thick fog of lust.

Because she just might surrender whatever he asked of her—and what he didn't.

Her fingers fisted in his hair, and his small grunt of pleasure snatched her back into the here, the now. And she willingly allowed herself to be swamped by the exquisite sensations he elicited from her body like a magician with an empty top hat. God knew, until he'd touched her, kissed her—*moved next door*, an irritating, unwelcome voice interjected—she'd been so terribly empty.

He switched breasts, sucking her neglected nipple deep while his fingers played with the one still wet from his mouth and tongue. A whimper crawled up her throat, and she didn't bother locking it down. She'd lost all remnants of modesty the moment her mouth claimed his.

When he released her flesh with one last lick over her sensitive, beaded peak, she loosed another whimper, but of disappointment this time. But Isaac bent, cupping the backs of her thighs and hoisted her in the air.

On reflex, she wound her arms and legs around him, and he crushed a hard, burning kiss to her lips before growling against them, "Your room."

Electric pulses danced down her spine at the gravel-roughened tone. It rubbed over her skin like a calloused caress.

"Down the hall. On the right."

He didn't waste time, but strode from the kitchen and, seconds later, entered her bedroom. Pausing only long enough to kick the door shut, he made for the bed and laid her down on it, following her down. Arms braced on either side of her head, he stared down at her, and what breath she had left snagged in her throat at the lust stamped on his face. It transformed his face of bold angles and rugged planes into something harsher, a little forbidding. Excitement and a whisper of anxiety fluttered beneath her navel. This man she hadn't met yet. This man could conquer her, set her afire and leave nothing but ashes.

Leave nothing for herself.

If she had her head on straight—if pleasure and need didn't throb throughout her body like a second, deafening heartbeat—she'd have stopped this before it went further. But those diamond bright indigo eyes, his heady scent and the hard, thick cock damn near branding her thigh through their clothes incinerated all sense of self-preservation.

She'd take all that she could now. And worry about the consequences later.

"You with me?" he asked in that same churned up voice.

"I'm with you," she said, skimming her fingers along his jaw then tunneling them in the cool, thick strands of his hair. Lifting her head, she lightly pressed her lips to his. "There's no other place I'd rather be."

The words slipped from her, raw and unchecked. And maybe later, she'd regret the too revealing statement. Maybe later, she'd re-armor herself in higher, thicker walls. Maybe later she would call this the biggest mistake she'd foolishly made.

But not right now.

Now, with his taste on her tongue, his big, hard body pressing into hers, sheltering hers. Now when she trembled with want, with an emotion she should be running from like an Olympic track star. She surrendered all thought to the "now" as he deepened the kiss, sinking her back under the spell he weaved on her body so effortlessly.

A whimper of disappointment escaped her when, moments later, he reared back, abandoning her mouth. But that sound turned into a gasp as he stripped her of her remaining clothes with an efficiency that left her a little stunned and breathless. But that surprise melted into something hotter, sharper when he slid off the bed and yanked his sweater over his head, then getting rid of his boots and jeans in short order. He stood before her, only clad in black boxer briefs that molded to his trim hips, his powerful upper thighs...the hard, aggressive bulge of his cock.

Her sex clenched hard around...nothing. And the

emptiness had her swallowing down a needy moan.
But it wasn't just the sight of him that triggered a fine
tremble to ripple through her. That honor also belonged
to the small, square packet he clutched between his
fingers.

Put that on and get inside me. Now.

The demand crashed against her skull, and as impossible as it was, maybe he heard her. Because his
dark purple gaze narrowed, and his jaw shifted as if
he ground his teeth together. He placed the condom
next to the pillow then climbed back on the bed, strad-
dling her body.

"I'm not finished with you yet," he announced.

The faintly ominous warning swept through her on a
delicious shiver. And that shiver erupted into a full out
quake as he covered her and his mouth opened over her
neck. Then trailed down to her breasts, licking, sucking, tugging. She arched and twisted beneath him, attempting to get closer to him. So close, even under his
skin wouldn't be enough.

He trailed down her torso, pausing to dip into her
navel, to nibble on her hip bones, to place a searing, wet
kiss where her torso and thighs met.

And when he opened his mouth over her sex, she
damn near levitated off the bed. Pleasure rocketed
through her like a bolt of lightning, alarm fast on its
heels. Her body wasn't made to contain this heat, this
overwhelming sensation. Surely skin and bones were
too fragile and inadequate a vessel. Especially when
he licked a slow, luxurious path between her folds, and
that wicked tongue lapped at and teased her clit... On
a cry, she curled up, grasping his head, holding him to

her as he destroyed her with that lascivious mouth and passion. Pure passion.

He was ravenous, and sliding his hands under her ass, lifting him to her, he served her up like his favorite meal. And he devoured her—and not politely. He consumed her flesh like a starving man, sucking on her, nibbling on her, drinking her down. Once more, his strength stole what little breath she had left when he kept her raised in the air with one big hand and thrust inside her with the other.

She screamed.

Honest to God screamed.

He'd barely finger-fucked her, and that magical mouth had just latched on to the nerve-rich bundle at the top of her sex when she exploded. Just fragmented.

And when the many parts of her reassembled, her hovered over her, hands pressed to the mattress on either side of her head, cock nudging her swollen and sensitive folds. A sensual lethargy weighted down her limbs, but one glimpse in the black-purple of his eyes and, like a pilot light, lust ignited again. The satiation humming through her started to dissipate and the hunger revived. And only him filling her with that beautiful cock would do.

His fingers entangled hers and, with that intense gaze refusing to let her go, he sank inside her.

Her back arched tight, her eyes squeezing tightly closed. A strangled cry lodged in her throat. In this moment, she became a being of pure sensation. And that sensation was pleasure so acute it bordered on a sweet, razor sharp pain. He thrust forward again, filling her... and filling her...and filling her.

She tried to drag in a breath past her constricted

throat, but it did nothing to alleviate the feeling of being claimed, branded, *possessed*. And she didn't want to ease it. No, she *craved* it.

Shifting restlessly under him, she spread her legs wider, wrapping them around his hips. Their twin groans soaked the air as he pushed deeper, took more of her. A violent shudder ripped through him, and Isaac buried his face in the hollow between her shoulder and throat. He remained still for several long moments, and she bit her lower lip, grateful. His cock throbbed within her in a primal rhythm—no, like another, wild heartbeat. She'd never been so...full before, and her body needed just a few seconds to adjust.

That was a lie.

Not just her body.

Her head, her heart, all of her—they needed time to accept the enormity of what was happening in this bed. Of what she'd allowed. Not just sex. Because this exceeded the physical. He'd invaded the most guarded, vulnerable parts of her and regardless of what she tried to tell herself, it was much too late to go back. To shove him out.

Panic arced through her, and for a moment she stiffened with the bite of it.

"Shh, sweetheart." Gentle hands swept her hair back from her face, and Isaac grazed his lips over her forehead, skimmed them down the bridge of her nose and found her mouth. "Easy. Focus on me. Breathe with me." His nose rubbed against hers, and he brushed a tender kiss over her mouth. "In and out. In. Out."

He slowly inhaled then exhaled. Repeated it. Repeated it again until she found herself following his lead, his pattern. And the panic slowly released its grip, leaving her aware of his weight pressing her down into the mattress, of his musky scent enveloping her, of the solid thud of his heart against her breast...of his thick, heavy cock wedged deep inside her.

Of the crackling fire licking at her veins and making her writhe and grind under him.

"Tell me, Malibu. Tell me when," he murmured against the hollow of her throat and the vibration of it trembled through her.

"Move." She wrapped her arms around his shoulders, held on tight. "Please, move."

Before she finished speaking, he withdrew, the drag of his erection through her spasming flesh eliciting a gasp from her throat, then plunged back inside. Hard. Deep. So damn deep.

"Isaac." Her cry broke on her lips, followed by another as his hips snapped back then forward again. Then again. And again.

She held on to him, but as much as he took, she claimed for herself. He fucked her, but she rode his cock, demanding with every buck of her hips and arch of her back and hoarsely uttered praise that he give her everything. And with her relentless, breath-stealing thrust into her sex, every worshipful kiss, every stroke of his seeking hands, he ordered the same in return.

The pleasure built inside her like a tsunami bent on destruction. It whipped and howled and as Isaac lifted her leg, pressing her thigh to her chest, granting him even more access to her, she surrendered to the storm. The ecstasy screamed in her head—or maybe that was just her.

"Give it to me," he growled, reaching between her legs and stroking her clit. Once, twice, three times.

Firm circles that accompanied the hard, almost punishing thrusts of his cock. "Jenna, give it to me. Now."

The combination of his touch, the thick flesh pounding into her and the command in that rough voice catapulted her over the edge. She splintered. Just fragmented. The oblivion she'd been seeking welcomed her with open arms, swallowing her whole. And as Isaac's big body shuddered above her, she knew they couldn't stay in this place where pleasure ruled.

But right now… Right now, with Isaac pressing her into the mattress, and her sinking into the darkness knowing he would be there to catch her, she decided to stay here.

At least for a little while.

CHAPTER NINETEEN

"Hey, you're awfully quiet back there." Jenna glanced in the rearview mirror at Joy, who sat in the back seat, staring out the window. "You okay?"

"I'm okay."

The little girl didn't turn her head away from the window, but Jenna doubted the scene passing by held her enthralled. They'd just left the hospital from visiting her mother and it'd been…tough. So far the drugs were working and the doctors didn't think surgery would be necessary. But Beth Duncan was paralyzed on the left side of her body and her speech was garbled. When Joy had initially glimpsed her mother, she'd clung to Jenna. But eventually, she'd gotten over her shock and climbed up on the right side of her mother's hospital bed. The reunion between them had been poignant and heartbreaking. The love between mother and daughter had been so obvious, Jenna had almost felt like an intruder. And when the visitation hour had come to an end, tears had pricked her eyes when she'd had to lead Joy away from the room.

She wished Joy had cried her own tears now, let some of that terrible grief and anger go. Anything would be better than this horrible, deafening silence that seemed so wrong for such a vibrant little girl.

"Hey, I know," Jenna said, glancing in the rearview

mirror again. "How about we stop by the café in town for hot chocolate? And I bet there are fresh doughnuts, too. It'd be perfect for a day like this."

Autumn had truly moved in, bringing cooler weather. For the carnival next week, people would definitely need to be bundled up in jackets, maybe coats. Joy wouldn't be here for it. Her aunt had called, and she would arrive tomorrow. An ache bloomed in Jenna's chest. Logically, it didn't make sense that she would miss the little girl. She'd only known her for a few days.

But when it came to the heart, logic often went on a long walk off a short pier.

Swallowing hard, Jenna shoved the thoughts aside. Better to focus on the present. Tomorrow would take care of itself. And in the present, she had a little girl to cheer up.

Herself, too, if she were being honest.

"Joy, you in?" she asked again.

"Okay."

"Great," Jenna continued, hoping to draw her out. "You're going to love Mimi's hot chocolate. And her doughnuts. They're so good, you're probably going to beg your mom to bring you back to Rose Bend just to have some more."

That got a reaction. Joy shifted in her seat and their gazes briefly met in the mirror at the mention of being with her mom again.

"I know it doesn't look like it now, but your mom's going to be fine, Joy. After working with the doctors, people speak again and use their hands and walk again. She's coming home to you."

"You promise?" she whispered, voice shaking.

"I promise."

And since she'd had a conversation with the doctors while Joy visited with Beth, she felt she could make that promise.

"Your aunt will be here tomorrow, too."

"Aunt Ray's coming to get me?" She fully turned away from the window and leaned as far forward as the seat belt would allow. "Is she coming to your house? Is she staying with us?"

"No, honey. I'm taking you to the hospital to meet her. She's going to visit with your mom, talk with the doctors. Then you two are going to leave for your house from there."

"Oh."

Joy fell silent again, and ten minutes later, Jenna located a lucky open space in front of Mimi's Café. She parked, then walked around and let Joy out of the car. Together, they walked into the shop, and after several minutes sat down at one of the tables with steaming cups of hot chocolate, a doughnut for her and a strawberry cupcake for Joy.

"Why can't me and Aunt Ray stay with you?" Joy asked, her gaze fixed on her cupcake as she meticulously peeled off the foil wrapper.

Oh her heart wasn't going to survive this little girl.

Following Joy's lead, Jenna pinched off a piece of the doughnut and popped it into her mouth. Usually, she would savor the magic of Autumn's baking, but today all her focus remained on the child across from her. The child she had become so attached to in such a short amount of time.

"Your aunt has come all the way from Georgia to be with you and your mom. To take care of you while your mom gets better," Jenna softly said. "And you're going to feel so much better when you get back to your house, in your own room. Plus, you need to go back to school and see your teacher and friends. I know they all miss you, too."

"Are you going to miss me?" Joy asked the cupcake.

"So very, very much," Jenna whispered.

Finally, Joy looked up and a tiny smile curved the corner of her mouth.

"Me, too."

The next half hour passed in lighter conversation and laughter as Joy demolished her hot chocolate and cupcake. And even amid it all, Jenna found herself randomly glancing out the window to the sidewalk and street in the hopes of catching sight of an ugly blue-and-tan truck with huge wheels or a tall, big frame with an easy, confident stride. Which, considering it was a Monday at two o'clock in the afternoon, most likely wouldn't be happening.

Still…

Memories of yesterday flickered through her mind's eye. She pinched the bridge of her nose, squeezing her eyes closed. Sighing, she dropped her arm and returned her gaze to the window and Rose Bend's Main Street. Though, she didn't see it. No, she pictured Isaac—she was in danger of falling for him.

Who was she trying to fool? Herself? Well, it wasn't working.

She'd fallen for him. And it terrified her.

More than a motorcycle ride. More than standing up to her parents. More than even outing herself as Beck Dansing.

Falling in love with Isaac scared her because she

feared not being enough for him. Feared not being able to give him what he wanted most—a family of his own.

Feared disappointing him.

A small, cowardly part of her wished she'd remained in her house that chilly morning instead of charging across her front yard and confronting him about his loud music. Because if she had, she wouldn't hover now on this crumbling edge, paralyzed by indecision. Afraid to step over.

Another image of Isaac wavered in front of her. Standing on her porch, cupping her face, smiling down at her.

No. *No.*

No matter how this…situation turned out, she'd never regret him. Never regret a moment knowing him, spent with him. Never regret who she'd become because of him.

"I'm ready, Jenna." Joy plopped back down in the chair across from her after putting their garbage in the trash can, dragging her from her thoughts, and not with a little bit of relief.

"Me, too. Let's get out of here."

As they bundled into their jackets, Joy kept up a steady chatter about plans for the evening when they returned to Jenna's house. For their last night together, Jenna suggested they build a fort in the living room along with movies and popcorn. Joy now listed movies, and though Jenna had no idea what half of them were—and doubted the little girl would make it through the long list—she just nodded and agreed.

"This is going to be so much fun! Thank you, Jenna!" Joy threw her arms around Jenna's waist and hugged her tight.

Jenna embraced Joy in return.

Before Joy had come into her life, she'd given up on...this.

She had her volunteer work at the hospital on the pediatric floors, and that soothed a painful place in her. They reminded her why children and life were precious.

Yet, this time with Joy had offered her hope again. Hope that she didn't have to forfeit her dream of being a mother. No, she might not be able to birth a child, but that didn't mean she couldn't love one, protect one, raise one...foster one.

For so long, she'd obsessed about who and what she'd lost, that she'd neglected to see what she had to give. Love. A home.

No matter where that home might end up being, she would look into being a foster parent.

As if a light sparked to life inside her, she warmed, brightened...quickened.

So that's what hope felt like.

She could get used to that.

"Let's get going." She rubbed a hand down Joy's back, and taking the little girl's hand in her own, they left the café.

Joy continued talking about the evening ahead, and Jenna listened, smiling, walking her to the car when the sound of her name startled her. Turning, she frowned, surprised to see Chris approaching them. What was he doing here? She'd made it clear to her parents and him—to their displeasure—that while she had Joy, her responsibilities as far as the carnival and campaign would need to be put on hold.

"Hey, Jenna," he said again, and glancing down at

Joy, he offered her a smile. "Hello, Joy. We met at the carnival Saturday night. I'm Chris."

"Hi," Joy said, pressing into Jenna's side.

"What's going on, Chris?" Jenna asked, getting straight to the point. Because she knew her ex. His finding her wasn't a coincidence. He had an agenda. "Is there something wrong?"

"No, not at all." He smiled and she ground her teeth together. Had she ever found that grin attractive? "Quite the opposite, actually."

"Okay." She arched an eyebrow. "Can you make this quick? I have to get Joy back to the house."

He probably assumed he did a great job of hiding the irritation that flashed in his eyes by dialing up the wattage of his smile, but she caught it.

"Certainly." He dipped his chin. "So, I'm big enough to admit when I was wrong." He smiled again and spread his hands wide. "You were right. The public's reaction to your taking in Joy was overwhelmingly positive. Your mother's business has not been affected— actually sales are up, just as you predicted. And your father has received nothing but complimentary feedback from reporters and others about his daughter, her heroism and altruism."

Jenna didn't reply, but her stomach curdled. Not only because Chris talked about Joy and her mother's sickness right in front of her as if they were a political windfall for Jenna's father, but also because she sensed where this was headed. Anger swilled in her belly.

At her parents, for being willing to use a mother and child's tragedy to their advantage.

At Chris, for jumping on this opportunistic bandwagon. Hell, for probably cosigning it.

At herself. For not foreseeing this happening and unwittingly placing Joy in its line of fire.

"We've also received an interview request for you," Chris continued when she remained quiet.

"No."

Chris' mouth tightened at the corners, but that damn smile didn't fall. "Before you answer right away, let me explain. It's for a Springfield paper. They're interested in doing a human interest article on your father. This would mean wider coverage and greater exposure. And frankly, Jenna, we can't buy this kind of publicity. You did good," he murmured, lifting a hand toward her.

If he touched her, she would throw up. She shifted backward, her spine bumping against her car door. Bile surged toward her throat. He made it sound as if everything she'd done had been some marketing stunt.

"Jenna," Joy whimpered.

God, she was scaring the little girl.

"It's okay, Joy," she murmured, rubbing a hand over Joy's back. Switching her gaze back to Chris, she repeated, "No."

"Jenna," he cajoled, "be reasonable. This is for your father, and it's important. An opportunity like this doesn't come around often. Especially for a small town mayoral election. Besides…" He paused and glanced down the street in the direction of The Glen and the carnival grounds, and when he looked back at her, he gave a sheepish shrug that contained zero sincerity. "The reporter is already on his way here. It would be rude and embarrassing to your father to back out now. I was just about to call you when I spotted you and Joy walking out of the café. So we can all head over to The Glen and wait on him. That way we can review the proper responses, what topics to stay away from and how—"

"I said no," Jenna said from between gritted teeth.

"Jenna." Chris shifted closer, steel entering his voice.

"Back up, Chris," she ordered, holding up a palm.

He halted, and her anger flared hotter. He wasn't going to let this go, but dammit, she refused to give in. Not on this.

She glanced over his shoulder toward the café. Maybe Mimi would agree to watch Joy. No way in hell she could take the little girl with her—

Relief washed over her. Clasping Joy's hand, she skirted Chris and walked up to Sydney and Patience, who strode up the sidewalk.

"Sydney," Jenna called, and maybe her former friend heard the desperation in her voice, because miracle of all miracles, Sydney stopped, frowning at her. "I know this is an imposition and completely out of left field. But would you mind watching Joy for about ten minutes? I wouldn't ask except that I have to take care of something important over at The Glen. I'll be right back, I promise."

Confusion darkened her eyes, but to her credit, Sydney didn't pepper her with questions. Except for one. "Everything okay?"

"It will be," she lied.

Because she intended to protect Joy, but everything being okay for her at the end of this? She doubted it.

"Go," Sydney said, taking Joy's hand. "I have Joy until you come back. Don't worry about her."

Gratitude flowed through her, temporarily blowing over the flames of her anger like a cool breeze.

"Thank you." Cupping Joy's thin shoulder, Jenna

squeezed it. "I'll be right back. Just hang here with Ms. Sydney, and then we'll leave my house and get that sleepover started."

"Okay," Joy whispered, but her lower lip trembled.

And in that moment, Jenna longed to tear into her parents and Chris for causing this child one second of fear. Pivoting sharply, she cloaked herself in a cape of ice and pinned her ex with a stare that he had the God-given sense to avoid.

"Let's go."

She didn't wait for him to reply but strode down the sidewalk toward The Glen. Minutes later, she spotted her parents standing in front of the newly erected bumper cars, speaking to Henry Kingston, bank president. Her pace didn't falter as she approached them, although her heart rate increased, her pulse buzzing in her head.

"Mother, Dad," she greeted. Nodding at their friend and fellow town councilman, she said, "Mr. Kingston."

"Hello, Jenna," her mother said, her gaze scanning down her jacket, jeans and knee-high boots. Her mouth tightened. Probably around a sharp remark about going out in public looking like a sloppy teenager.

"Hello, Jenna. It's wonderful to see you. I was just telling your parents how you're a great example of the younger generation. Too often people have the *I don't want to get involved* ideology, but not you. And no doubt you saved that woman's life. We're all proud of you," Henry praised.

"We certainly are," her father boasted, and the hypocrisy left a bitter taste in her mouth. Just days ago, he'd been the one ordering her not to get involved. "Henry, if you'll excuse us, we need to get ready for a media spot. But I'll call you this afternoon. We need to have you and the wife over for dinner."

"Absolutely!" The bank president pumped Jasper's hand and, with a wave, walked off.

"He's a great guy, but he will talk your ear off." Jasper shook his head and turned to them, clapping his hands once. But then he frowned as he scanned their small group. "Where's the girl? The reporter will be here very shortly and we have to go over these questions. The last thing we need is for her to go off script. As a matter of fact, the less she talks, the better."

"She's not coming, Dad," Jenna said, meeting her father's gaze.

Watching it turn to flint.

"Excuse me?"

"She's not coming."

"What do you mean, 'she's not coming'?" Helene demanded, then glanced behind Jenna as if not quite believing her. "This is not the time for a joke, Jenna."

"Jenna didn't bring the girl with her," Chris said.

Her parents stared at him, blinking. Then their narrowed gazes swung to Jenna.

"Did Chris explain why we needed both you and the girl here?" Jasper asked, his voice even but hard. It raked over her, and she fought not to shudder. Fought not to reveal any weakness in front of any of them.

But that was a lost cause. She cared too much.

She hurt too much.

"Yes, and that's why I refused to bring her. I'm not going to let you use her or her pain for a sound bite. She's in my custody, and I won't allow it." She inhaled a deep breath. "No."

"That reporter is on his way here. He'll be arriving any minute and I can't just tell him my daughter refused. So you'll go get her and will not embarrass me with this childish rebellion, Jenna Landon." Her father jabbed a finger toward the ground, anger mottling his face.

Her chest seized and she wanted to run, but she held her ground.

"Her name is Joy Duncan. Not 'that child' or 'that girl.' She's seven. Her mother's name is Beth Duncan and she is worried that her mother won't be able to push her on the swing or even say her name again. And you want to use her to score points toward an election. My answer is no. I'm sorry you made arrangements for an interview before consulting with me first. Or that you did so before determining if an interview with Joy about her mother's condition would be damaging to her in any way. But I'm not taking that chance so you can have a news moment." She drew her shoulders back. "You're going to have to tell your reporter he made an unnecessary trip or do the interview without Joy and me."

"I can't believe you." Helene slashed a hand through the air. "She is a child you met days ago, who will be out of your house and life in another few days. We are your *parents*. You owe us. We have stood by you when others would have abandoned you. And this is what you do? Your father asks this one small favor and you can't do it? You are so ungrateful."

"If it were about me, I wou—" She closed her eyes, clenched her teeth around the lie that almost slipped so easily from her lips. "No—" she shook her head "—I still wouldn't do this. It's wrong to exploit someone else's pain to your advantage. I won't be that person. Not anymore. And the fact is, this isn't just about me.

I'm sorry you believe I'm being disloyal. And you have to know I'm thankful for everything you and Dad have done for me—"

"I can't tell," Helene snapped.

"But I can't do this for you. I won't. She's been through enough."

"Jenna," Chris interrupted. "That little girl—Joy," he corrected at her narrowed glare, "Joy adores you. We can all see that. And if you asked her to do the interview, she would. I'm certain of it."

"I am, too," she said, hardening her voice. "Which is why I won't."

"When I need you most, you've failed me," her father said, looking her up and down. His mouth curled at the corner. "You're a disappointment." He paused. "Again."

Ice slicked over her skin.

Her father had never laid a hand on her.

And yet he'd hit her a thousand times in a thousand different ways.

Like right now.

He'd intended to throw that low blow, and it landed and drew blood.

"I'm sorry," she rasped.

It was all she could say, and part of her screamed, *Why are you apologizing? Find your backbone!*

But the other part—the bigger part, which had spent the majority of her life needing to please the two people in front of her—turned and walked away before she did something far more humiliating.

Like beg them to love her.

CHAPTER TWENTY

ISAAC PARKED IN front of Sunnyside Grille, pushing open Baby's door and climbing out. Jenna had planned on taking Joy to see her mother at the hospital today, and no doubt it would be an emotional day for both of them. Picking up chopped steak with onions and mushrooms, mashed potatoes with gravy and broccoli for dinner wasn't a cure-all, but it didn't hurt either. The strawberry milkshakes he planned to throw in from Six Ways to Sundae would go a long way, though. He smiled.

Just as he stepped onto the sidewalk, his phone vibrated in his sweatpants pockets. He removed his cell and glanced at the screen.

Diana.

His pulse raced, and his mouth went dry.

Leaning back against his truck, he pressed the answer button and lifted the phone to his ear.

"Hey, Diana."

"Hi, Isaac. How're you?"

"I'm good. And I think you're enjoying this a little too much," he growled.

Her chuckle echoed in his ear. "A little. It's not often I have Mr. Right against the ropes. No pun intended."

"I'm sure," he muttered. He blew out a hard breath. "Just…give it to me straight, Di. What's the verdict?"

"The verdict is—" she paused, and he held his breath "—yes."

Then he exhaled it.

"You're serious," he rasped.

"I'm serious," she said softly. "It's a fabulous idea. I would've immediately said yes when you proposed it, but I had to run it by everyone here. And I didn't want you to think I was in just because it was you."

"That isn't why?"

She quieted.

"Partly. But not why you think. I always believed you were smart, business savvy. You underestimated how I saw that in you. Or maybe I never told you enough. Now, there was some concern over opening a training center in a place called Rose Bend. It just sounds small and sugary sweet."

He shoved off his truck, and swept his gaze around the downtown area.

"Yeah," he murmured. "Not far off. But you hear sugary sweet. I see safe. Secure. Opportunity."

"I did my research. Looked at pictures. And I did, too," she said. "It's a place people won't mind sending their children if WFC finds host families. Also, geographically, it's under three hours from Boston and New York City, an hour from Albany. You were a brand name for WFC for years. You're not coming back to wrestle for us, I accept that. But to partner with you in this new endeavor, to have you train new wrestlers for us, this is the next-best thing."

"This is happening. It's really happening," he whispered.

"It's happening. Congratulations, Isaac. I'm…I'm glad you found what you were looking for."

He pivoted, surveying Main Street again, but he wasn't seeing the town as much as envisioning every place he'd been with Jenna. This town, when he hadn't been looking, had become home. Not due to time spent there but because of a woman. Because each place held a special memory with her. Yes, he had found what he'd been looking for. And she'd revealed it to him.

Acceptance.

Belonging.

A path home.

A path that led directly to her.

Now if he could just find a way to get her to stay. Because now that he'd found her, no way in hell he could let her go.

"Yes," he murmured, "I did."

Silence hummed down their connection.

"You met someone," she said.

He hesitated, not wanting to hurt her, even though it'd been Diana who'd betrayed him with another man.

She sighed. "You can say it, Isaac."

"Diana…"

"I'm happy for you."

His lips parted but no sound emerged. Shock whipped through him. Finally, he snapped his lips closed and thrust his fingers through his hair.

"I can see I've left you speechless." She chuckled, then sighed again. "I mean it, Isaac. Am I hurt? Am I wishing I'd done things differently? Yes and yes. But if anyone deserves happiness and peace, you do. And I want it for you. Even if it's not with me."

"I want the same for you, too, Diana," he said.

"I really think you mean that."

"I do." He did. "Besides, I can't hate you if you're going to be my partner. Kind of bad form."

Another laugh rippled in his ear. "True. That could make things a little awkward." Her voice softened. "I love you, Isaac. Congratulations. And be happy."

He lowered the phone and slid it back into his pocket. Turning around, he headed back toward the Sunnyside Grille. He had dinner and milkshakes to get.

They had celebrating to do.

ISAAC CROSSED HIS lawn to Jenna's, excitement racing through him. The drive home had seemed to take twice as long because he couldn't wait to share his news with Jenna. Plastic bags filled with cartons of food and a cardboard tray of milkshakes in hand, he climbed her porch steps. Before he knocked on the door, though, it opened and Jenna stepped out, closing it behind her.

"Have I ever told you that I love those sweaters on you?" He skimmed a finger over her bare shoulder. "This is the real you, and I love that you feel comfortable enough allowing me to see you in them."

Her lashes lowered, and she crossed her arms, pulling the sweater over her shoulder, covering it. He frowned, and his chest pulled tight.

"Sweetheart." He set the food and shakes on the chair and stepped toward her, cupping her shoulders. "Hey, what's wrong?" Sparing a glance behind her at the closed front door, he frowned. "Is something wrong with Joy? Did everything go okay at the hospital?"

"Yes, she's fine. Her aunt will be arriving tomorrow to pick her up."

Her answer didn't make him feel any better. If anything, it deepened the unease burrowing in his chest. He lifted one hand to her chin, tilting her head up.

"Malibu, what's going on?" He studied her face, but that damnable polite, reserved mask had slid firmly back in place. "Talk to me."

"Isaac, I have to get back inside to Joy." She gently tugged his hand down and then shifted backward.

Away from him.

"Jenna, what the hell is going on?"

"Thank you for buying dinner, but I wish you would've called. Joy wanted pizza so we already ordered one. But thank you, anyway."

What the fuck? "Goddammit, Jenna, I don't care about the food." He reached for her again, but knowing she didn't want his touch, he thrust his hands through his hair, bowing his head. "Please, sweetheart, tell me what's going on."

She closed her eyes for a long moment, still embracing herself. Or holding herself together.

"Today," she began in a low, slightly trembling voice, "I went against my parents. For a good reason. The best reason. And given the choice, I would do it again. But I've reminded my parents—again—why I'm a disappointment to them. And they weren't shy about letting me know that."

"Hell."

Anger toward Jasper and Helene crashed inside of him and he forced it back. That wasn't what she needed from him right now, but dammit, what he wouldn't give to have the two of them in front of him. If two more selfish, self-centered people existed on the face of this earth, then they were all in trouble.

"Jenna." He stepped after her, but she whirled around, stretching an arm out.

"No. I'm fine."

"Sweetheart, you're not."

"I am. It's not like it was the first time I've heard it. And I needed that to happen today. As hard as it was to hear, I *did* need it. Because it reminded me of something I'd allowed myself to forget. Or wanted to forget."

"Jenna," he whispered, a foreboding settling on his chest.

"For a little while I let myself believe there wouldn't be consequences to taking chances, but there always are. There were when I was a girl. And there are now. Except I'm not that naive teenager anymore." She lowered her arm, her fingers curling into her palm. "I can't pretend, Isaac. I can't be who you need, who you want. And I can't give you what you need. It would be unfair for me to make you think I can."

"And what do I need?" he asked past numb lips. A numb body. A thundering heart. "Do you love me, Jenna?"

"Isaac," she whispered, shaking her head. "I'm leaving Rose Bend."

"That's not an answer," he said, his voice as lacerated as his heart. "Do. You. Love. Me?"

"Yes," she admitted, her blue eyes dark with an emotion he couldn't decipher. "And it's not enough. Love isn't enough. If anyone knows that, we do." She glanced away from him. "You would just end up resenting me."

"Resenting you for what? For not being perfect? For not living up to some unobtainable standard? Since that's bullshit—bullshit that's been drilled into your head for years by people who were supposed to love and accept you unconditionally—why don't you tell me exactly what I'll end up resenting you for?

"Isaac," she whispered, lowering her arms. "You want—you deserve—everything your heart desires. A healthy relationship. A family. And I can't give you that. I'll never be able to give you the latter."

His chin snapped back. "Did I ever ask that of you, Jenna? We didn't even have that conversation."

"It contributed to the breakdown of your marriage. And we may not have had a direct conversation, but yes, you have mentioned it. At the carnival you talked about giving your family the childhood you had. A family *I can't give you*. I won't be a disappointment to another person I…" Her voice trailed off, and her fingers lifted to her lips. "This—" she waved a hand back and forth between them "—isn't going to work."

God, how long had she been holding that in? How long had it been festering on her mind?

Logically, he understood what she was doing. Jenna had been dismissed and emotionally beat down so many times in her life, that her MO was to reject first before she could be rejected. Maybe she believed, if she dealt the first cut, the pain wouldn't hurt as much. That was the Big Lie she told herself.

Yeah, logically, he got that.

But his heart? His heart didn't give a flying fuck about logic. It was torn between lashing out and begging her not to ruin them. Not to break them.

Lashing out won.

"You're a coward."

She flinched, but he continued.

"This isn't about me. It's about you being afraid to try. Being more afraid to climb out of this harmful but comfortable space you've created because it's known rather than risk the chance of love because it's scary and unpredictable and it's hurt you in the past. You're grasping at straws with that 'family' card. But, Jenna, I'm not your past. I'm your present and I want to be your future."

"You can't say that," she argued, shaking her head.

"And how do you get to make that decision for me? For us? I can't even look at a little girl around Sam's age and not freeze. Not panic. The truth is I'm not ready to be anyone's parent yet. But you never asked me that. You just decided I want a baby of my own, and since you can't give me that, we can't be together."

He huffed out a humorless laugh.

"As I've been told very recently, Jenna, I'm not perfect. I have work to do on myself. Have you ever considered that *I* don't see myself as good enough for *you*? Whole enough for *you*? What do I have to offer you? A man who has been so traumatized by loss and betrayal that he's terrified of offering his heart to a woman and a family. But the alternative—the thought of letting you walk away, the thought of losing you forever—is so abhorrent that I'm willing to do the work on myself so I can give you the person you deserve. So I can give you the life you deserve.

"If you want children, fine. We'll foster or adopt. I'll do what I need to do to heal so I will be side by side with you for that. If you decide you'd rather not have children, sweetheart, fine. Contrary to what you've heard over and over in your life, you are more than enough. You. Are. Everything. I have enough family for both of us. And I've seen the kind of wonderful, loving aunt you'll be. It's your decision. Yours. So why do you get to take mine?"

Anger vibrated off him like a tuning fork, but underneath, a deep helplessness threaded through, and he had the inane need to pluck at it. But already, it felt unwieldy.

He couldn't fight this.

He couldn't fight her. Just like he couldn't ride in like that knight in shining armor, this was a battle she had to wage on her own.

And damn her for not letting him be there for her.

"When do you say enough is enough?" he rasped. "When do you stand up for yourself and be your own champion? When do you tell everyone who ever hurt you, who ever *failed you* that, *I'm sorry you're disappointed and your expectations weren't met but deal with it and get off my ass.* When do you live for you, Jenna?"

He turned and jogged down the porch steps, but when his feet hit the bottom one, he stopped. Glancing over his shoulder, he studied her beautiful face, her shattered blue eyes.

"And since you didn't ask this question either, I'll answer it. Yes, I love you, too."

He turned and walked across her yard to his.

For the last time.

CHAPTER TWENTY-ONE

DON'T YOU CRY. Don't you cry. Don't you cry.

"Oh shit, Sydney. Jenna Landon is about to cry. I don't know whether to hug her or get out my camera phone."

"Decisions, decisions."

The tears that stung Jenna's eyes didn't spill over, thanks to the antics of the two women standing outside of Haroldstown Medical. She drew up short, staring at Leo and Sydney Dennison.

"What're you two doing here?" she asked—yes, rudely.

After leaving Joy with her aunt and pretending her heart wasn't a cracked mess in her chest from a man and a child, she didn't have it in her to be polite.

"See." Sydney slid Leo side-eye. "This is the thanks we get for caring."

"Cut her some slack. She looks like she's about to ugly cry any minute. And if my memory serves, she's definitely an ugly crier," Leo said.

Jenna narrowed her eyes on the two women. "Really funny. You should take this act on the road."

Sydney blinked, then squinted at her. "Did you just tell us to go play in traffic?"

"For the love of—" Jenna threw her hands up in the air. "What. Are. You. Doing. Here?"

Leo cackled, elbowing Sydney. "I think we broke

her. But at least she doesn't look like she's about to bawl anymore."

That's it. She was going to commit a felony. At the very least a misdemeanor. Good thing they were outside a hospital.

"We're just teasing. Calm down." Leo grinned, moving forward and hooking her arm through Jenna's. "But in all seriousness, let's head to the parking lot just in case you do decide to cry—not saying we blame you after having to leave Joy. But you won't drown anyone in the doorway."

Sydney fell into step beside them.

"Also so no one can claim they saw the great Jenna Landon being human."

That hurt.

And on a day like today, she couldn't deal with Sydney's passive-aggressiveness. Not when she felt like her skin had been turned inside out. Not when her heart had been shattered last night and the remaining pieces broken again this morning.

No, she couldn't handle Sydney's jabs.

"Look." Jenna jerked to an abrupt halt. "I've been a bitch to you in the past. And I'm sorry. There. I've never said that before. I'm so sorry I mistreated you, hurt you. You'll never know how much. And I'm not trying to excuse my actions, because I can't. I do have a reason, though. I was angry as hell. And I was jealous."

A parade of emotions marched across Sydney's face—disbelief, anger, shock. She didn't move, only gaped at Jenna. As if she couldn't quite comprehend what she'd just said.

"Jealous?" she repeated. "Of me?"

"Of you. Of Leo." She waved a hand at the other

woman, who stood silently at her side. "Leo knows this already, and thank you for keeping my secret," she murmured to her.

"Of course." Leo said, squeezing her arm.

"What secret? What're you talking about?" Sydney asked, glancing back and forth between them. "Is this why you suddenly had an about-face toward her?" she demanded of Leo.

"I shared something with Leo several months ago," Jenna said, and Sydney shifted her attention back to her. "Maybe I should've told you, too, but I..." She trailed off, shrugged. Then briefly closed her eyes. "No, the truth is I was scared to tell you. Scared you would..." *Reject me. Abandon me. Not forgive me. Not see worth in me.* "Scared it would be a case of too little, too late. Sydney, fourteen years ago, our freshman year of high school, I got pregnant and had a miscarriage."

Say something, she silently urged, even as her stomach twisted at what Sydney might utter.

This was Sydney, after all.

"What? Pregnant? By who? And why didn't you tell us? We would've been there for you!"

The questions poured from Sydney in a steady stream, gaining speed with each one. She stalked toward Jenna. Her face darkened in anger. At the person who got her pregnant, at Jenna for not telling her so long ago... She didn't know.

"Pregnant by Holden Daniels, and I didn't tell you—didn't tell anyone—because I was scared. I only told my parents and they shipped me off to my aunt in Oregon, where I miscarried." Her lips twisted into a smile that only a fool would call humorous. "They were afraid I'd humiliate them because I'd done something so stupid as getting pregnant. And they've never forgiven me or let me forget that mistake, and I've been trying to make up for it ever since." She inhaled a shaky breath, crossing her arms. "When I returned to school, I was so angry. At my parents, Holden—even though he didn't even know about the baby or the miscarriage—at myself. And I took it out on everyone, including you and Leo. I saw you two as having these perfect lives—"

"Me?" Sydney interrupted with a sharp, hoarse laugh. "A perfect life? The girl who lost her older sister to cancer? And who might as well as have lost her parents the same day?"

"Yes," Jenna whispered. "Because you didn't. No matter how you acted out, rebelled, they never abandoned you. Rejected you. Yes, they were frustrated as all hell and didn't understand you, but they loved you. And I resented the hell out of you for that. Just as I hated Leo because of her perfect family who loved and accepted her. Seeing you two, being around you, hurt because it reminded me of what I didn't have. Of what I lost. So I punished you for it."

Sydney slowly shook her head, the incredulity in her voice shadowing her eyes. "All these years... Dammit, Jenna, I'm so *fucking* mad at you."

"I understand," she said, wishing she was numb because then she wouldn't hurt so much.

"No, you don't," Sydney snapped, and fury replaced the disbelief. Her petite framed seemed to vibrate with it.

"Sydney," Leo murmured.

"No, Leo." Sydney slammed up a hand, stopping her friend. "I get to be mad. When I had my moments of breaking down about Carlin, you were there for me.

When my parents broke my heart for the first time, I ran to you and Leo. When I had my first crush, I had you. But when you faced the hardest, most tragic event and loss in your life, you freeze us out and then treat us like trash. No explanation. And then you become a stranger. You stole our friend from us. For years. So yeah, I'm *fucking* mad. And a part of me still hates you, Jenna Landon." Her chest rose and fell on her harsh breaths. And then a choked cry broke free. "And a slightly bigger part of me loves you. Loves you so much. Still. And I am so sorry you had to go through all of that alone. And I really, really need a goddamn hug right now."

Jenna's feet unglued from the ground and flew across the lot before her head received the message. But her heart had.

She threw her arms around Sydney, and when slender arms wrapped around her too, the tears she'd locked away since leaving the hospital broke loose.

And she let go.

How long they all stood there crying and hugging—at some point, Leo joined their huddle—Jenna didn't know. Didn't care. It felt too good. And it was long overdue. A hole inside her healed in that parking lot, and she didn't want to let go. But they couldn't remain there all day.

As if overhearing her thoughts, Leo drew back, sniffling and chuckling.

"I think they're going to call security on us before much longer."

"If they do, I'm throwing you to them as a decoy and making a break for it," Jenna warned with a smirk.

"And here I thought we were going to see a softer version of you," Leo drawled.

Jenna shrugged. "Can't expect years of habit to come undone like that."

Sydney snickered. "You mean to tell me Mr. Right wasn't making you come undone?" She waggled her eyebrows. Pain exploded in Jenna's chest and she couldn't control her flinch. "Oh shit. What did I say? Did something happen with Isaac?"

"We…" She swallowed hard, the words difficult to push past her throat. "We ended things. Last night. Well, that's not exactly true. I broke it off with him."

"Why?" Leo took her hand. "What'd he do? Do we need to roll up to your neighbor's house with a carton of eggs?"

"I don't mean to brag, but my husband's the mayor. I have connections. He can't park anywhere in this town without getting a ticket. Just say the word," Sydney offered.

"As much as I appreciate your offer of vandalism and abuse of power," she said with soft snort, "that won't be necessary. He didn't do anything. Well, didn't do anything but ask me not to blow us up. But I couldn't do that."

"Jenna, why? What happened?" Leo pressed. "I thought… You two looked so happy together. Especially you. I've never seen you so comfortable and, hell, radiant with someone. You smiled with him, for God's sake. So why did you end it?"

"Because I'm the coward he called me," she admitted on a rough laugh. "Earlier that day, I had an…incident with my parents, and they reminded me of my past, and how much of a disappointment I'd been to them. It…scared me. But more than that, it drove home what I'd allowed myself to forget. I'm leaving Rose Bend."

"You're what?" Leo interrupted. "You never mentioned that."

"I haven't told anyone except for Isaac. I plan on moving at the end of the year to get a fresh start somewhere else. Our timing is just…off."

Sydney flicked a hand. "Sorry, but I call bullshit."

Leo winced. "Sorry, babe. But I do, too." She slid an arm around Jenna's shoulders. "As two women who almost screwed up their own relationships—"

"Speak for yourself," Sydney scoffed. "Your brother almost let this good thing go."

"As I was saying," Leo continued with a roll of her eyes, "we know denial when we hear it. And okay, so maybe you leaving had something to do with it, but you were scared for another reason. No offense, but your parents—"

"I know, I know."

"And babe, you've let their opinion hold sway over you and your life for way too long. They have you so paralyzed in fear of failure that you're afraid to try. And if you don't try, how will you ever know the possibilities of love, of happiness, of a future with that man who clearly adores you?" Leo asked, voice fervent as she squeezed the hand she still held.

"You get one life, Jenna. And you have to live it for you, not them. You are not one event in your life. And your parents shouldn't batter you with it over and over. One mistake doesn't define you. If they don't know that, you should. Because you can't live under a life sentence. Hell, even murderers get parole." Sydney grasped the hand Leo didn't hold. "Don't throw away your chance at happiness because you're afraid he will one day reject you and abandon you. He's not your parents. He apparently saw you—the real you—when no one else did. That's a man worth keeping."

God, he had.

He'd seen through the cold veneer that put off most people and hadn't let that stop him. Isaac had been her friend, made her laugh, given her a pet name—no one had ever given her a pet name. He'd taken her on a motorcycle ride, pushed her out of her comfort zone. Made her take risks even when she'd been afraid.

And it'd ended up that the biggest risk had been him. She'd fallen in love with him.

And she'd pushed him away as her parents had done to her.

"What have I done?"

"I think in those romance novels you read, this is what they would call the Dark Night of the Soul. Where she realizes she's royally fucked up," Leo said to Sydney while patting Jenna's arm. Her grin ruined the sign of sympathy.

"You read 'em, too. And yep. That's definitely the aw-shit face," Sydney agreed. "Luckily, this is where her two plucky friends come in to guide her out of the hole she's dug herself into. Beginning with some hard questions." Sydney squeezed her hand once to get Jenna's attention. "Are you still leaving Rose Bend? Because it's not fair to even think about going to him if you haven't made that decision."

"I…" She shook her head. The idea of leaving didn't excite her as much as it once did. It actually left her… hollow. "I don't know."

"You need to figure that out. And think about this while you do. As someone who was a bit of an expert on running, are you leaving for something better or are you just running away? Because one is going toward a goal and the other is simply trading one set of demons for another. And spoiler alert? You can't run far or fast enough from them."

Jenna stared straight ahead, and for the first time in longer than she could remember, a peace settled in her chest, her soul. And it came from knowing. Knowing what she wanted. Who she wanted to be. And where she was going.

"Okay," she simply said. "Okay."

"This unexpected reunion calls for drinks," Leo announced, tugging them all forward and walking toward their cars. "Especially since I'm headed to New York. But I'll be back for the carnival and Spooks 'n' Books. Ooh. Since we're in the secret-spilling mood, isn't there one more you want to share, Jenna? And as I've been sworn to keep my lips sealed, and I would never betray your trust…"

"Oh girl, spill whatever it is," Sydney huffed. "She's about to hurt something over there."

Jenna laughed, and wow. It was real. And she was *happy*.

"What Leo is desperately trying not to reveal is I'm Beck Dansing."

Sydney drew to a halt, her mouth popping open.

"Say what now?" She gaped at her. "*You're the* Beck Dansing? That's not possible! You can't possibly be one of my favorite authors."

"It's true. I'm her. She's me."

Sydney slammed her palm to her forehead, screwing her eyes shut.

"Holy hell! Do you know what this means?" She

pried one eye open and squinted at her. "I've fan-girled you all this time and didn't know it. Kill me now."

"Oh yeah," Leo whispered. "So worth the price of admission."

Jenna threw her head back, laughing.

Four. She now had four friends.

And counting.

JENNA KNOCKED ON the front door of her parents' home, her stomach knotting. But she didn't move; instead, she waited for someone to answer. Both of her parents' cars were in the driveway so they were there, and this wasn't a conversation to be had over the phone. She needed to do this face-to-face.

Moments later, the door opened and her mother stood in the doorway. Mouth pinched and eyes a frosty blue, she stepped back, waving an arm and silently inviting Jenna inside.

"I assume you're here to apologize," her mother said, leaving Jenna to close the door as she strode off down the hall.

Helene entered the formal living room, where Jenna's father sat in an armchair. For once, Christopher wasn't in sight, and for that, Jenna was grateful. She couldn't be certain that Jasper and Helene hadn't told him about her past, but she didn't relish sharing her private business with him. And though they hadn't been a true family for a long time, this was a discussion that should be kept among them.

"Jenna." Her father set the tablet he'd been scrolling on his lap. "I didn't expect to see you today. What brings you by?"

"As I told her," her mother said as she settled onto the couch next to his chair, "an apology, I hope."

And the stiffness of her tone implied, it'd better be one.

The twisting in Jenna's stomach didn't abate, but she shoved past that. She wouldn't be derailed now. Not when so much was at stake.

Her future with a man who loved and supported her.

Her happiness.

Her freedom from a past that haunted her.

"I didn't come here to apologize, but I guess I should." The frowns on her parents' faces cleared and they relaxed back into their chairs. "But not for what you're expecting." The frowns made a swift return. "I'm sorry that for years I didn't have the courage to speak up and tell you how I felt about my miscarriage and how your reactions affected me. When you love someone, you should be honest with them. You shouldn't be afraid to give them truth, and I used love as the reason for remaining silent when in reality, fear kept me quiet."

"Why are you talking about this?" Helene flicked a hand. "That's in the past, and there's no point in dredging it up."

"It's never been in the past because you and Dad have held it over my head from the moment I woke up crying about it. You've never let me forget, and you've never forgiven me for making a mistake at fifteen years old."

"A stupid mistake that was totally preventable but could've cost us for eighteen years, if not longer," her mother snapped. "It seemed like overnight you went from the perfect daughter to being a selfish child who thought of no one but herself. And you've never reverted back to that perfect girl. I've seen flashes of her, but even with all the hard work I've put into you, it seems like a hopeless cause. Just look at the last few weeks, for example." She launched herself off the couch and paced over to the window, flicking aside the curtain and staring out. "And you want to come in our house and talk about apologies for not telling us the truth about how *our* reactions to your mistake affected you. Of all the self-centered things you've said so far, that trumps them all."

"I won't let you turn this around on me," Jenna murmured, although, God, her mother's words landed like fists. "I'm your daughter. It's literally in your job description to love me, perfect, imperfect, pretty, ugly, through it all. You can't pick and choose. Can't decide to keep me one day and want to return me to some drop-off window the next. Parenthood doesn't work that way."

And now that she had a clearer head and had ripped off the shame-tinted glasses, she could see that her childhood hadn't been a fairy tale. It'd been good, yes. She'd never gone without; she'd been cared for, doted on. But she also remembered the nights she'd gone to bed with stomachaches because she'd spilled something at dinner. Or suffered headaches in the morning before going to school from a restless night because of a test where she had to earn a perfect grade. Or opting out of trying out for the volleyball team that Leo and Sydney signed up for because not trying out was much safer than trying out and not making it and embarrassing her parents and facing their disapproval. Stressing and crying with anxiety over the smallest thing from leaving her lunch box at school by mistake to getting a B on a test.

Prior to turning fifteen, her life hadn't been as perfect as she'd painted it in her mind.

She'd always been striving for their approval, their acceptance.

The difference between now and then was she'd realized that was a race she could never win.

Instead of trying to gain their approval, she was content with her own.

"I didn't come here to argue with you." She opened her messenger bag and removed hardcover copies of the first three books in her series. Crossing the space separating them, she set the novels on the coffee table. "Those are my books. They're the first three in a very popular paranormal young adult series. I've never been able to confide in you that I'm an author and have been published for the last five years. I'll be reading an excerpt and signing books at the Spooks 'n' Books event this coming Saturday night, when I officially come out as Beck Dansing. And I suspect you'll consider that a betrayal instead of being proud that your daughter is a *New York Times* bestselling author. But I can't take on the guilt of that.

"I hope you'll support me, but if you decide not to, that's your decision. From this point on, I'm living for myself and for the future and no longer letting my past dictate either. I would love if you decided to be a part of my life. But if you decide you can't, then I'll accept that, too. I love you both. And if I have to do so from a distance, then that's okay. Because I'm choosing me."

With that, she turned and walked out, ignoring her parents' strident, angry demands.

And as she closed the door for what could possibly be the last time on her childhood home, well…

She was okay with that, too.

CHAPTER TWENTY-TWO

"I CAN'T BELIEVE Beck Dansing is here in Rose Bend!" Colin practically leaped up the front steps of the library, his eyes shining.

Isaac smirked as he followed his brother at a slower pace. Colin carried the hardcover edition Jenna had given him for Beck Dansing to sign. When his brother had hopped into his truck with the book, Isaac had nearly ordered him to take it back into the house so he didn't have to look at it. But that wouldn't have been fair to his brother, who, when the announcement had gone out that his favorite author would be making their very first public appearance at Rose Bend's library of all places, had begged Isaac to take him. How could Isaac deny him?

Even if his plans for the day had been to do absolutely anything but venture into downtown Rose Bend and avoid the carnival.

It was bad enough Jenna lived right next door.

She must have been ducking him as well because so far he hadn't seen one strand of her flame-red hair or one inch of those impossibly long legs. And hell if he'd admit it to anyone else, but yes, he'd looked. Worse, Monday, even after she'd basically said he—and they—weren't worth fighting for, he'd still almost knocked on her door to check and see if she was all right after dropping Joy off with her aunt.

God, he was a total sucker. For her.

That didn't make it any better.

Neither did loving her. Because he feared this was one malady that might not have a cure. Yeah, he'd get over the symptoms. He wouldn't go through the rest of his life wanting to smash his fist through a wall or run his body ragged around the high school gym until he was too exhausted to do anything but shower and fall into bed… But this crack in his soul? That missing part? That, he suspected, was terminal.

And didn't that just suck balls?

"Come on, Isaac. We can't be late! I don't want to miss when he starts reading the excerpt from his new book!" Colin beckoned from the library double doors.

"All right, all right." Isaac laughed, jogging up the remaining steps. "Damn, kid. Who knew you were such a nerd?" he grumbled, teasing.

"Who are you kidding?" Colin grinned, entering the library lobby. "I saw your library in Florida. It's probably bigger than the fiction section here."

"What's this *probably*?" Isaac scoffed. "It's *definitely* bigger."

Colin laughed, scanning the library, probably to catch a glimpse of Beck Dansing. One half of the library was sectioned off and set up with chairs, a small podium with an armchair and table with a stack of hardcovers, but he didn't see anyone who could be the famously reclusive author. But then again, how would he know?

"Why don't you go get you one of those grab bags before all the kids snatch them up?" Isaac nudged him with an elbow to the ribs.

"I'm too old for that," Colin scoffed.

Isaac arched an eyebrow.

"I should probably get one for Belle, though. Lena isn't bringing the kids over until Mom gets off work, so that could be another half hour or so."

"Riiight," Isaac drawled. "You do that."

Grinning, Colin wound his way through the crowd of children and parents playing games, getting their faces painted and eating snacks. Cute Halloween-themed music played out of the speakers, and kids were dressed up in costumes, as were a lot of adults. Chatter and laughter filled the air. The organizers of the event had really gone all out, and it showed.

"Pretty cool, huh?" Sydney Dennison slid next to him with a cup of what he hoped was just punch in hand. "Giving me straight Diagon Alley vibes."

"The green LED lights cauldron for the punch was my idea," Leo bragged, appearing on his other side.

"Isn't Owen playing the 49ers tomorrow?" Isaac asked her, surprised to see her here. He'd been under the impression she split her time between Rose Bend and New York, but that she traveled with her fiancé to his away games.

"Yep, but he understands when I have to beg off for special occasions."

Isaac arched an eyebrow. "The Spooks 'n' Books is a special event? I mean, I heard the library needs funds but…"

Leo slid him side-eye. "Rose Bend has never met a fundraiser we didn't love. You should remember that for your new training center."

Caught between laughter and a sputter of surprise,

he shook his head. "Do I need to ask how you found out about that?"

She shrugged, a smile curving her mouth. "It's Rose Bend. Nothing stays secret around here for long."

"Oh I beg to differ about that," Sydney murmured.

That enigmatic statement snagged his attention, and he glanced at Sydney, but she stared toward the section set up for the guest author. A statuesque, curvy woman with long auburn hair, dressed in a badass Xena: Warrior Princess costume, stood on the podium with a microphone in hand.

"Hey, everyone. I'm Remi Howard, librarian here at the Rose Bend Public Library. If you could make your way over here, we're ready to begin with our guest speaker." She waited until the chairs filled and the space overflowed with people before continuing. Isaac remained standing toward the back of the room where he had a clear view of the podium. Leo and Sydney remained with him.

"First, let me thank you for coming to our third annual Spooks 'n' Books. We are so delighted to have you here and are grateful for your presence. We're thrilled to have our town residents, patrons, visitors and members of the press. As you know, the library is in need of funds in order to purchase supplies, maintain and hire staff, continue to provide events like this and serve our community. So again, we're not only grateful for you, but also for your financial support."

Isaac clapped along with everyone else. If the turnout was any indication, he bet they'd come pretty close to meeting their goal. The seams of the building were bursting with people.

"We are so fortunate to have a celebrated author with

us tonight. Beck Dansing is the award-winning author of the Anakim Academy series, and she's hit the *New York Times*, *USA TODAY* and *Wall Street Journal* best-seller lists multiple times."

She? Surprise winged through Isaac as he searched the crowd for Colin. And here they'd all believed Beck Dansing was a man.

"Though famously reclusive, Beck Dansing has decided to grace our library with an exclusive reading from her new release *and* with her very first public appearance. Rose Bend, please give a very warm welcome to Beck Dansing."

A door next to a row of books opened and…

Jenna stepped out.

Jenna. Stepped. Out.

"What the hell?" he whispered.

It'd been a little less than a week since he'd seen her last, since he'd touched her, since he'd just heard her voice…and it might as well as have been a month. A year. The impact of her damn near knocked him on his ass, and he had to lock his knees.

God, she was stunning.

The sight of her in a perfectly tailored jacket over a white T-shirt, dark jeans and ankle boots with her beautiful hair flowing over her shoulders almost capsized the fact that she walked out onto that podium and sat in the chair meant for Beck Dansing.

He apparently wasn't the only person shocked. Murmurs and whispers hummed through the room, steadily rising. Because, *what the hell*? Jenna couldn't be Beck Dansing…right?

"So, no, I'm not here to introduce Beck Dansing. For those of you who live here in Rose Bend, you know me as Jenna Landon, and yes, I do write as author Beck Dansing. For those of you who are visiting Rose Bend for the first time and are wondering what all the whispering is about, welcome to small-town life. I've lived here my entire life and everyone here has just discovered the truth along with you. Ta-da." She spread her hands wide and smiled at the laughter that filled the room.

And the air caught in his lungs. Because it was a true, warm, real smile. And she let everyone see it.

His heart constricted, and he pressed his palm over it, rubbing and not caring who saw.

"So I want to thank Remi and the rest of the Rose Bend library staff for giving me a safe space to 'out myself,' so to speak, and share my real self with you. And to share my stories, which are part of me as well.

"I started writing my Anakim Academy series during a period in my life when I felt helpless, powerless. I'd suffered a loss when I was younger and years later, I started volunteering at the hospital on the pediatric ward, visiting with the children there. Reading to them, coloring with them, talking with them, playing with them. Watching them bravely battle illnesses and lose a heartbreaking number of times—that humbled me and, yes, angered me. I wanted to change their world, give them one where their bodies matched their warrior spirits. Since that was impossible, I sat down one night and started writing it. And that's how Anakim Academy was born."

A hush descended on the room. No one spoke. He wasn't even sure they breathed. She held all of them enthralled. This was the Jenna he'd known from the moment he'd met her, charging across her lawn like a

Valkyrie. And it was about time the rest of Rose Bend saw it, too.

"I'd like to read you an excerpt from my new book. If you're familiar with the series…"

She set up the scene, and for the next twenty minutes, she read an emotional but exciting scene that ended on the eve of a battle. She finished to deafening applause, and pink stained her elegant cheekbones while a smile curved her mouth. Camera flashes popped from the attendees and media. Beck Dansing might've been popular before she revealed herself, but Isaac had a feeling she would be even more popular now.

"Thank you," she said. "Thank you so much. I'm so glad you enjoyed it." She closed the book and set it on the table. "If you'd like to read it, there will be copies available in the library, and my publisher has graciously gifted copies that I will be signing and giving away after the reading." More applause broke out, louder and longer than the previous rounds. She grinned. "Free stuff tends to make people happy, right?" She laughed. "Before I step down and stop holding you hostage, I'd just like to thank the people of Rose Bend for making this a safe place to reveal the person behind the pen name. I couldn't have done it any other place but here because this is where I belong. Here, with you. I want to give a special thank you to Leo Dennison and Sydney Dennison for encouraging me, for offering me grace, friendship and second chances."

She inhaled a deep breath and then she looked in his direction. As if she'd always known where he stood, her gaze connected with his.

"And I need to thank someone very special in my life. Without him, without his support, his belief in me, his love, I wouldn't have discovered the courage to get up here tonight. He had faith in me, he saw me when no one else did—including myself—and that has made me a better person, a stronger person. And I love him. I love you, Isaac Hunter."

His heart, which had slowed to a dull thud, raced and tried to run to her, hurl itself at this woman who had owned it almost from the moment she'd insulted his truck. He'd known she loved him; she'd admitted that on her porch. But this…this was different. This Jenna was brave. This Jenna might be willing to take a chance on them.

God, let her be willing. Because he wanted the dream with her. He wanted everything.

He wanted her.

"Some of you might know Isaac Hunter. Y'know. WFC World Wrestling Champion, Mr. Right. Something like that." Laughter, thunderous applause and whistles greeted her words. And she grinned as it eventually ebbed. "Who knew that when Mr. Right moved in next door to me he would change my life and show me the true meaning of love and joy? Isaac, I want you to know that I'm not running scared anymore. I'm staying right here in Rose Bend. And if you'll take one more risk, I hope it will be on me. Loving me."

Before she finished speaking, he strode toward her, winding his way through people and chairs, his sole focus on her.

A soft but beautiful smile lit her face as he approached the podium, and he climbed it, tugging her from the chair and into his arms. Lowering his head, he kissed her. Her taste exploded in his mouth, and he groaned, pulling her closer, sinking into her. This. God, how he'd missed this. The connection, the intimacy. *Her.*

Hoots and whistles penetrated the haze surrounding them, and after one last hard press to her mouth, he lifted his head. Nope, he couldn't resist. He took one more kiss. And she gave it to him.

"Eeew!" a kid near the front yelled, and Jenna snickered against his mouth.

Laughing, Isaac buried his face in her neck. Happiness pressed against his chest, and in this moment, he was home.

She was why he'd returned here.

He'd finally found all that he'd been searching for, and he held it in his arms.

"All right, everyone. That wraps up the guest speaker portion of our evening," Remi announced, laughter in her voice. "Just give Beck Dansing, aka Jenna, a few minutes and the signing will begin by the fiction section."

"I think that's my signal," she said, grinning.

"I think so." He cupped her face. "You're amazing. And brilliant. And dammit, woman, is there anything else I should know about you? Like a superhero alter ego?"

She laughed. "This is it. No more secrets. Except I love you. But since I just told all of Rose Bend, that's not exactly a secret."

He closed his eyes and pressed his forehead to hers.

"No, Malibu, it's not a secret. And I love you, too. I love you so much."

"Good," she whispered. "Because my next move was going to be an offer to ride in that godawful truck."

His head jerked back, and he blinked. "Damn, you're serious about this love thing."

She lifted up on her toes and kissed him. "Absolutely." She smiled. "I have to go sign books. But we have just one more decision to make."

"What's that?" he murmured, brushing his thumb over her bottom lip.

Grinning, she stepped back but grabbed his hand, squeezing it.

"We need to decide which next door we're going to call home."

* * * * *

Flo Dennison meets her match when a single dad and his daughter moves to Rose Bend in the next Rose Bend novel from Naima Simone!

ACKNOWLEDGEMENTS

THANK YOU TO my heavenly Father, who has made all of this possible. Thank You for the strength to persevere even when the odds seem insurmountable. Thank You for giving me strength, love and a sound mind—even when sometimes I felt like I lost all three.

To Gary, my real life hero. Though my heroes may be wrestlers, tattoo artists or billionaires, you are the prototype for all of them. Your generosity of spirit and core of honor have been my soft place to land for twenty-three years. I love you.

To Kevin Bryant, my firstborn and wrestling mentor. Thank you not just for the notes on high school wrestling, but thank you for being an amazing man and son.

To Autumn Bryant, my favorite daughter. Okay, you're my only daughter. LOL! Thank you for being my professional wrestling guru. Mr. Right Next Door and his "finisher" move wouldn't have happened without your insight. You kept me straight in this book, and I love you for your help and your beautiful, beautiful spirit.

To LaQuette. Thank you so much for sharing your time, ideas and heart with me. Your strength inspires me, as does that big ol' brain of yours. LOL! I'm so blessed to count you as friend.

To Dahlia Rose, I need a template because I'm running out of ways to say I love you and thank you for being my friend, confidante and shoulder to whine on. So that's what I'm going to say: I love you and thank you. You're a queen, Dahlia Rose.

To Rachel Brooks. Thank you for taking my dreams, turning them into our vision and giving me the tools to go after them. I'm so grateful for your support, encouragement, guidance, and when I needed it, back bone. You are the best.

To Stacy Boyd, who has never failed to take a manuscript and make it shine like the sun. And I, more than anyone, knows how much elbow grease that takes. LOL! Thank you for your patience, your never failing insight and support in not just my books but me, as an author. A great editor is worth their weight in gold, and you're priceless!

TROUBLE FOR HIRE

CHAPTER ONE

WHEW. SO I'M really doing this.

Camille Dansen stared at her phone, and the digits on her screen glared up at her like a quiet shout.

12:00

That's it. Twelve o'clock.

She released a short, incredulous laugh.

Oh my God, am I really doing this?

She gave her head a good, hard shake, laying her phone down on her thigh to, one, keep from staring at that text as if it would go for her throat. And two, hoping the weight of the phone would stop her leg from jumping like a jackhammer on a construction site.

The tattoo artist that had let her inside Forever Ink glanced at her from behind the shop's front desk. The front desk that, if this interview went well, would be her responsibility. The longer she stared at the piece of furniture, the larger it seemed to grow until it nearly swallowed the tall, tatted and pierced man behind it.

Because that desk represented her uncertain present and her murkier future.

"I just spoke with Erik. He's on his way and should be here in a couple of minutes," he said.

She nodded. "Thank you for letting me know."

"No problem." He jerked his chin up, his voice remaining professional, neutral, but curiosity lurked in his hazel eyes.

She didn't blame him. Compared to all the ink covering his dark brown skin, the silver piercing his eyebrows, nose and full lips, the vintage KRS-One T-shirt, black jeans and boots covering his rangy body, she probably looked like she'd veered in here by mistake on her way to the social at one of the local Baptist churches. And that was fair. Considering the last event she'd attended at the church in Providence, Rhode Island, where she'd been a member with her fiancé had been the Women's Day anniversary brunch.

But that had been months ago. Six to be exact. And like everything else except her car, clothes and the few things she'd had when she began their relationship five years ago, her ex-fiancé, Bradley Luck, had received the church in their breakup. Along with the house, their friends...their life.

Spreading her fingers along her thigh, she dug the tips into the muscle through the knit of her dress. She was here.

Here.

Not in the affluent suburbs of Providence. Not in the two million dollar McMansion with its professionally decorated rooms.

Not in the past.

For all the good it's doing you, a sarcastic voice snarked in her head. A voice that sounded so similar to her former future-sister-in-law, thoughts of an exorcism to expel Raquel Luck from her thoughts might be in order. A breakup had taken care of removing that woman from her life.

Well, a breakup and a move to another state.

Dorothy had a bucket of water, and she had a Nissan Rogue—whatever worked to get rid of the witches in their lives.

Now it was time to move forward. Starting with this job interview. That was if this Erik Mann showed up for it.

Camille glanced down at her phone. Eleven minutes late. Irritation stirred in her chest. Sure, she was applying for this position and needed to make a good first impression, but he wasn't knocking his impression out of the park so far.

A warm tingling sparked to life behind her breastbone. She recognized the sensation, though it'd been a long while—years, to be exact—since she'd last felt its presence. That old recklessness she'd believed had been tamed. Or snuffed out. And not by love and contentment as she would've said only a year ago. But by the pressure to conform, the fear of disappointing.

She inhaled a deep breath, but nope. The stench of her own cowardice still coated her nostrils.

Still, that touch of wildness urged her to jump to her feet, say to hell with it and walk out. An employer who didn't respect her enough to be punctual for an interview didn't bode well for a future here. But maturity and, well, desperation kept her tail planted on the black leather couch.

Funny what things like rent, clothes and food did to your priorities.

"Hey, Erik. Your appointment for the front desk position is out here."

The tattoo artist's voice dragged her focus from thoughts of her precarious situation and back to him.

And the man standing beside him.

She blinked. Blinked again.

This couldn't be right. She blinked one more time.

No. Adonis mapped in ink still stood several feet away from her.

And God. He was *glorious.*

Short dark brown hair cut close to his head emphasized a face of razor-sharp angles, bold planes, and blue eyes so bright they gleamed across the distance that separated them. And a mouth… Heat curled like smoke low in her belly, and she fisted her hand on her thigh. There was nothing pure or right about that mouth. It invited sin and all kinds of wrong acts in the dark.

Wide shoulders and a broad chest filled out a plain gray T-shirt, and tattoos in red, black and blue ink sprawled down his muscled arms, even covering his long fingers and strong neck. The desk hid his bottom half, but she harbored zero doubts it was just as impressive as the top.

Didn't stop her from wanting to lean over the wide piece of furniture and verify that fact for herself.

"Camille?" the Adonis asked, his voice a rolling, deep bass.

Not Adonis.

Erik. Erik Mann.

Her brother's friend. Owner of Forever Ink.

And if all went well, her new employer.

So she really shouldn't be drooling over her potential boss.

Slowly standing, she nodded…and ordered her body to calm the hell down. She'd just gotten out of a relationship. A toxic one she could see now with hindsight being what it was. An entanglement didn't interest her. Especially if it hindered The Plan.

Get a job. Set up her own residence. Decide on a new career. Secure it by any means necessary.

Be happy.

Out of all the items included in The Plan, the last one might be the hardest to achieve.

She approached him, hand outstretched. Inside, she braced herself for that first contact. But when his big, elegant-fingered hand wrapped around hers, she was grown enough to admit there was no way she could've prepared herself for this first touch. A rough, calloused palm with a surprisingly gentle grip. It set off warring sensations in her belly. A man who was obviously no stranger to hard work, a strong man going by the corded tendons in his arms. But one who apparently knew how to be careful. Maybe...tender.

She just stopped herself from shaking her head.

Didn't matter. None of that mattered. Not to her anyway.

She just needed him to give her a biweekly paycheck and a W-2.

That's all.

The Plan. Stay on The Plan.

"Yes, I'm Camille. You're Erik Mann?" Oh look. Her voice didn't shake. Kudos to her!

His full, give-me-ten-acts-of-contrition mouth thinned then he gave a short jerk of his head.

Whoa. What was that reaction about?

Had Jeremy lied to her about the job? Had he pressured his friend into seeing her? She wouldn't put either past her big brother. When it came to her, he was a bit of a bulldozer on steroids.

"Come on back." Erik strode over to a short swing door, popped a lock and pushed it open. "Sorry about being late."

"It's no problem." She rummaged up a smile in the face of his lack of enthusiasm and silently cursed her brother. "I appreciate you taking the time to see me."

"Jeremy's a friend and I need someone on the front desk." He shrugged and turned, leaving her to follow him.

O-kay.

Unease settled in her stomach.

Fine. Everything would be fine. Jeremy wouldn't arrange an interview with someone he didn't trust. Or who was an ass.

Well… That last one was debatable. Considering the company Jeremy kept, very debatable.

But this was Rose Bend, Massachusetts. The *Cheers* of towns. Y'know, the place where everyone knew everyone's name. A place of eternal politeness and community. Erik Mann wouldn't have lasted in business long in this picturesque, southern Berkshires town if he was an asshole.

She clutched hard to that as she trailed him down a hallway, past a huge area with tall, gray cubicles to a fairly large office.

And yes, she'd been correct. The bottom half most definitely was as impressive as the top. Faded black jeans hung off slim hips and clung to thick, powerful thighs and an ass worthy of a religion. Hell, she might build a temple in its honor.

She dragged her gaze away from him, guilt pumping through her. What was she doing? Inappropriate wasn't just a word in the dictionary between… Well, whatever came before and after it. She had no business ogling this man like a slab of beef. A particularly delicious slab of beef...

Babe, get it together. The Plan!

"Have a seat." Erik waved toward the armchair in front of his wide, scratched to Hades and back cedar desk as he shut the door.

Rounding the furniture, he took the battered, black leather chair behind it. Her heart fluttered under his sharp blue gaze. Fluttered. Such an anemic description for the frantic drum solo happening behind her rib cage. Still, she ignored the pounding in her ears as she lowered onto the seat across from him.

"Thank you for agreeing to see me," she said, smoothing her palms down her black pencil skirt. Then, realizing how the gesture probably betrayed the nerves twisting her belly into knots, she clenched her hands together on her lap. "Especially since Jeremy called in a favor to you."

"Yeah, he did," he said bluntly.

Ouch. Obviously, prevarication wasn't one of his faults.

"Well, thank you anyway."

Erik tilted his head, and that bright gaze carried out another pass over her, and she stifled the shiver that tried to work its way through her body. But all of a sudden, the sleeveless, green-and-white polka dot blouse with the voluminous bow tie at the throat, the pencil skirt and green stilettos didn't feel like adequate covering. Maybe sackcloth would.

Maybe.

"I'm going to be honest, Camille." He leaned forward, propping his forearms on the desk and pinning her in her chair with his unwavering stare. "If Jeremy hadn't called me, I probably would've told you at the door this wouldn't work. It's only because he's a good friend that I'm doing this interview."

"I'm glad you're being honest." The dry retort popped out of her mouth before she could corral it, surprising herself and him if the flash in his eyes was anything to go by.

And here she'd believed that sarcastic, impulsive part of herself had been snuffed out over the past five years. Being the future wife of a domineering politician had taught her to be seen not heard. To smile pretty, look pretty and be pretty but don't speak unless she'd been told exactly what to say. Bradley Luck hadn't physically abused her, but she had been controlled, dominated, her personality smothered. In the last few months, she'd started emerging from that emotional fetal position, discovering herself again.

But this? Her reaction to Erik Mann shook her.

"I'm sorry," she said. "What I meant to ask is what are your concerns?"

"Don't apologize for speaking your mind. I don't need pleasantries. I want the truth." He arched an eyebrow. "As for my concerns, it's mostly one. You don't belong here."

You don't belong here.

His words struck her like a wildly swung blow to the chest. That could've been her mantra for the past few years. She hadn't belonged with Brad. Hadn't belonged in his world. And in the end, he'd kicked her to the curb because of it. He'd gifted her with jewelry, clothes, cars and other material things over their time together. But he'd never offered her the one present she'd craved: acceptance.

"Considering we barely met ten minutes ago, I don't see how you can make that assumption."

"Look at you." He did another visual sweep of her and, God, she felt it. Felt it graze her throat, brush her breasts, her stomach. Felt it between her thighs. What did that say about her? She was pretty sure he sat here insulting her, and she was getting wet. Damn. She really might be screwed up.

"You look like you belong at garden parties, not a tattoo shop. We curse, blast rock music, wear jeans and T-shirts, and politically correct is a phrase that hasn't made its way through our door. Any of those things seem like they would hurt your sensibilities."

"I take it my brother told you a little about me," she said, trying very, very hard not to be offended. And failing. Miserably.

He shrugged. "A little. And I have Google just like everyone else. I know who you've been engaged to for the last few years."

"Well then, let me clear up some misconceptions. My ex might've held certain beliefs regarding who should marry who, what autonomy women should have over their bodies and the freedoms certain people enjoyed, but that wasn't and isn't me."

"You stood by him and would've married him. That's pretty much cosigning those beliefs in my book."

Shame churned in her belly.

"I agree," she murmured. "You're right."

And she left it at that. She couldn't tell him that she'd been so in love, so desperate to *be* loved, to have a family, a fucking man, that she'd lost her values, *her-*

self. Her silence had made her complicit, and she hated herself for that.

Hated herself more that she hadn't been the one to break off the relationship and leave. Brad had. And if he hadn't? Would she have married him and continued to support a platform she wholly disagreed with while dying a little inside until nothing of herself remained?

God, she was afraid to examine that question. More specifically, that answer.

"Yes, I made truly questionable decisions in my not so distant past. But I'm back in Rose Bend to put all that behind me and begin with a fresh start. And that includes a job. Cursing doesn't bother me, and I listen to Imagine Dragons as well as Josh Groban. I actually own jeans though I prefer my dresses and skirts and can't see what that has to do with whether or not I can man the front desk. And as long as not being 'politically correct' means you still respect me and everyone who walks through that door and it doesn't cause harm, then I don't care. Speak your truth. That about covers it. Did I forget anything?"

"Yes, work experience. I received your résumé. You have none for the past five years and before that was a retail position here in Rose Bend at a clothing boutique. I need someone who not just greets customers, but also schedules appointments and takes payments. The person I hire would also be responsible for keeping track of and ordering supplies, upselling other products, and anything else that's needed from me or the other artists. Selling skirts doesn't cover that."

"What that résumé doesn't show is that I helped organize and supervise many large events, which included ordering supplies, managing staff and ensuring every event was successful and smooth. I also often acted as my ex's secretary, making sure he didn't forget an appearance, dinner or fundraiser. And as you pointed out, I was phenomenal at selling the image of a partner standing in solidarity beside her man. So while I didn't get paid for those duties or have a title other than fiancée, I acted as manager. And I'm sure if I can oversee a gala for two hundred people, I can oversee your tattoo shop."

By the time she finished speaking, a sting had entered her voice, and she bit off any more words before she totally mucked up her chance of employment. If she hadn't already.

Erik didn't speak for several moments, and she tried not to fidget under that direct, too-perceptive stare. It settled on her like a weight—an all too unsettling and delicious weight. She should feel dissected and dismissed. And a part of her did. But another part... Another part wondered what those piercing blue eyes saw.

Because he did see. She knew he did. And that was both intoxicating and terrifying.

Did he perceive her fear that she would mess up this new start back in her hometown? Her insecurity about whether or not she was capable enough, smart enough to make a success of herself? For too long she'd allowed herself to be dependent on someone else. It was humiliating to admit she'd become one of those women who'd let a man take care of her rather than stand on her own two feet.

Never again.

Never again would she degrade herself like that. Never again would she underestimate her worth like that.

Even now, as much as she loved Jeremy, she refused to be dependent on him. Yes, he'd arranged this job interview, but she'd refused his financial help. Instead, she'd pawned her engagement ring and other pieces of jewelry to get enough money to support herself while she figured things out.

But she couldn't tell Erik Mann that either.

Although an inexplicable part of her wanted to.

And where had that urge come from? Nothing about this man with his face of brutally sharp angles and lush, sensual curves inspired her to confide in him. And yet…

She straightened in her chair, leaning away from him and the sheer animal magnetism he exuded. God, it was like a pheromone.

"Point taken," Erik conceded. After a heavy pause, he leaned back in his chair as well. "You have the job. My friends list is short and your brother is at the top. And since he's never asked me for a favor, I figure this one must be important, and I'm not letting him down. But that loyalty only goes as far as the hiring." His eyes narrowed. "You're on probation for the next ninety days just like any other employee. You fuck up, you're gone. No second chances."

"That's fair."

His prejudgment of her, not so much. But this chance? Yes, it was fair. And she'd take full advantage of it. This job meant the difference between self-sufficiency and being a parasite for the rest of her life.

One she longed for like a starving woman crawling out of a wasteland.

And the other… Well, that wasn't an option. Not anymore.

"When do I start?" she asked, standing.

He rose to his feet, slower, still regarding her as if she were some creature he couldn't quite fathom.

"Tomorrow. We start scheduling clients at twelve noon. But be here at nine so I can get you set up, go over the point of sale system, show you where the supplies are and other things you'll need to know. Some things you'll just have to learn on the job, but if you have any questions or need any help, I or any of the other artists will be here."

She stepped forward and extended her arm toward him. "Thank you."

She braced herself this time, for the impact. But again, it proved pointless. Fire arced from her palm, up her arm and down her breasts, sensitizing them before continuing lower where a dull, insistent ache took up residence in her sex.

Loosing his hand, she shifted backward and forced herself not to rub her tingling palm over her thigh.

He dipped his chin. "See you tomorrow. Early."

Taking that as the dismissal it was, she turned and exited the office. And as she walked back down the hallway, a little bit of the weight that had burdened her for the past few months began to lift. Just a little.

Yes, she had a long road ahead. But today, she'd put another foot on that road.

Maybe, just maybe, she was going to be all right.

Now if she could just keep her dirty mind—and hands—off her new boss.

CHAPTER TWO

"I FUCKING HATE YOU."

Erik gritted his teeth as a long, deep laugh greeted his announcement instead of the apology he deserved. That's the very least a person should receive when they'd so clearly been set up by another.

"Aw, I love you, too," Jeremy Dansen said, and Erik could easily imagine the wide grin on his face. Damn him. "Why do I get the feeling this passionate declaration has to do with my baby sister?"

Baby sister.

The hell he said. There was nothing babyish about Camille Dansen. She was a full-grown woman, and wasn't that his problem in a nutshell? If only he could view her as his best friend's little sister, then his life would be easier.

His dick would definitely have an easier go of it.

Heaving a sigh, he scrubbed a hand over his head and turned around, staring through Forever Ink's storefront window at the woman under discussion.

The woman who had claimed a starring role in his dreams. Dreams that could be contenders for several categories in the Adult Video News Awards.

Yeah, he'd keep that information to himself.

Jeremy probably wouldn't appreciate hearing how Erik fantasized about fucking his sister six ways to

Sunday in so many positions it'd make a porn star reconsider their career choice.

Yeah. He'd *definitely* keep that to himself.

In the shop, Camille pushed through the swing door and strode out to the lobby, heading for the merchandise shelf, a clipboard in hand. He should look away, turn back around, do anything to avoid staring at her one second longer than necessary. Especially when she could catch him in the act.

But he didn't.

Because truth? He enjoyed looking at her. Correction. He *craved* it.

Three weeks. Camille had been manning the front desk in Forever Ink for three weeks, but it seemed longer. It seemed like he'd spent his whole damn life wanting her. And yeah, he got how stupid that sounded considering he'd only met her. But his cock apparently didn't care about semantics.

Not when it came to the thick, dark brown hair that fell in a shiny, sleek mass around her shoulders.

Not when it came to the lovely face that could've graced a painting by Johannes Vermeer that he'd studied in one of his college art appreciation classes. Easily.

Not when it came to the body that reminded him of another artist altogether. Peter Paul Rubens would've begged her to pose for him with all those lush, gorgeous curves.

Especially when those curves were poured into one of her tight skirts. Like today. He narrowed his eyes on her through the window. Today's green skirt molded to generous hips, thick thighs and flared just above the knees. Paired with a white shirt that accentuated breasts he'd caressed and tasted more times than he could count in his dreams, she was a walking cock tease.

To be fair, though, she could be in a burlap sack with a serious halitosis issue and she'd still make him hard.

Something else he'd keep to himself.

"You lied to me, you ugly bastard," Erik growled at Jeremy.

"Lied?" Jeremy parroted, and Erik scowled at the overly offended tone. Next thing, Jeremy would be clutching his pearls. "Tell me one thing I lied about. Just one."

"You told me your sister was a sweet, shy woman who wouldn't cause any trouble."

"No," his friend objected. "I said she was quiet and wouldn't be any trouble. And Camille is sweet."

Erik snorted even as he thought about his new hire's mouth. He had little doubt she would be like sugar on his tongue.

Again. Keeping to himself.

"I hate to break it to you, but she's caused nothing but trouble since she's been here. And quiet? She's only quiet when she doesn't ask me to change something. I swear to God, that woman's motto is 'I'd rather ask forgiveness than permission.'" He scanned the front of his shop. Had she changed the couches and tables around *again*? "It's not funny," he snapped over the loud bark of laughter in his ear.

"I may have forgotten to mention she's kind of particular and territorial."

"You didn't forget shit," Erik muttered. "All I asked your sister to do was get with the other artists so she could add their appointments to the scheduling system. Next thing I know, I have a new system, alarms going off on phones that remind us when those clients are set to arrive and a damn coffee service for them when they're in the chair. I'm not running a fucking tea social, Jeremy. This is a tattoo shop, for Christ's sake."

Whether or not Jeremy tried to contain his snicker, Erik didn't know. But he could say the attempt was an epic fail.

"Let me just say this. Is the new system effective? Are the artists okay with the notifications? Because hell, I'm about to call her and see if I can get that shit for my shop. And three, are your clients happy? Because if you can answer all of these with a 'yes,' I don't see what the problem is."

"The problem is those changes came on the tail end of her deciding the point of sale system was outdated. So she bought a new POS. And then ordered Forever Ink merchandise. I now sell T-shirts and leather cuffs along with tattoos. And right after that, she found a new supplier for our ink—"

"Is that why she called and asked me who I use? Huh." Jeremy hummed. "Seriously though, Erik. You were paying too much for ink if you were still using the same place from back in Vegas. I mean, she's actually saving you money."

"Fuck you. And that's after she switched the furniture in the lobby around so much I feel like I'm goddamn Alice in Wonderland every time I walk into my shop. Now—are you listening to me?—now she wants to sit down with me and talk about updating my logo. Hell. No. She's not touching my logo."

Yes, he was bitching but screw it. When Camille had started talking about changing anything on the logo that had been with him since he bought his first shop—the

only thing he'd walked away with from the shit show
his life had turned into in the four years before moving to Rose Bend—his balls had tried to crawl back
up inside him.

No. He was drawing the line there.

"All right, all right, I get it about the logo. Maybe if
you tried explaining to her the significance of it, you
might not walk in tomorrow with a new design. She,
of all people, would understand. After all the bullshit
you went through, I get it."

Not happening. He didn't discuss those turbulent four
years with anyone. Not with the friends he'd made since
moving to Rose Bend, not with the artists who worked
for him now and definitely not with the few persistent
reporters who still called him. Jeremy only knew about
it because he'd gone through that hell with him.

His friend's sigh echoed in his ear. "I already know
the answer to that. No. And all right, fine. But you do
know keeping all that bottled up doesn't make you the
hot, broody type. That's only in books. It just makes
you a bitter asshole who's afraid to trust. And I say that
with all the love."

"As long as you're saying it with love," Erik drawled.

But damn. Was that how Jeremy saw him? Was that
how most people viewed him?

The truth hurt. He was bitter. He was afraid to trust.
But when you were left with scars from third degree
burns, who could blame a person for avoiding fire at all
costs? His fire just happened to be believing in people.

More specifically, believing in people not to use or
leave him. Sometimes both. Because that seemed to be
a pattern in his life.

"Are you through crying now? I have to go. Got a

back piece coming in. I might be heading up your way though. It's the motorcycle rally this week, right?"

Erik nodded, though his friend couldn't see the gesture. "Yeah, it kicks off tomorrow night, but people have already started riding into town."

Every year, Rose Bend hosted a huge motorcycle ride and rally. For two weeks, musicians, vendors and artists converged on the small town for concerts, to sell their work and goods in booths and to entertain. The Glen, a wide, open field at the end of Main Street, became the site for all the festivities. Riders from all over the country visited to take part in them as well as the daily rides into the mountains. Proceeds from the event went to This Is Home, a local youth home.

Erik had been a little shocked when he'd attended his first rally. He'd visited Sturgis several years back, but this ride couldn't be more different. It possessed an almost festival-like atmosphere. And it didn't just bring out the motorcyclists, but their families, as well.

"Yeah, I might take some time here and visit the last week. Don't let Camille know, just in case I can't make it. Besides, if I told her I was coming, she'd tell me no. Probably think I want to check up on her."

Erik snorted. "That is the reason."

"Only part of it," Jeremy argued. "Do me a favor and take it easy on her, okay? We didn't have it easy growing up. Losing our parents early and me having to take over as her guardian at eighteen. I did the best I could with her, but all she's known is people she loves being taken from her. And now this. She's trying to find a place for herself again. Which likely explains why she's going a little hard on your shop."

"Take it easy on her." Erik shook his head even as

his chest constricted at Jeremy's description of his and Camille's past. Because Erik couldn't help himself, he returned his gaze to the lobby and the sexy as hell pain-in-his-ass in it. As he watched, Camille walked over to the front desk and picked up her cell phone. A frown creased her brow as she answered it. Now, he frowned as her body stiffened and then she closed her eyes, pinching the bridge of her nose. What the hell was going on? "I have to go. Later."

Before his friend could reply, he ended the call and pulled open the entrance door. Without glancing at the clients sitting on the couches, he strode directly to Camille.

"I understand. Well, let me think about it and I'll get back to you." She paused and a spasm of emotion he couldn't quite decipher passed over her face. "Thank you for that. I'll get back to you."

She lowered the cell from her ear and tapped the screen, but instead of setting the phone on the desk, she stared at it. But her shoulders were damn near riding her ears.

"What's wrong?" he asked, no preamble.

"Nothing." She tilted her head back and smiled at him.

And he narrowed his eyes.

"Try again. If you didn't look like you're chewing rocks it might've worked. Now, what's wrong? And don't tell me 'nothing.'"

A gleam sparked in her chocolate brown eyes. *Thank fuck*. Anything was better than the dull sheen that had darkened her gaze.

Her smile widened, damn near showing every tooth

in her mouth. Too bad she looked like she wanted to take a bite out of him.

A bolt of lust ricocheted through him. Not that he'd mind her teeth on him.

"Nothing."

They stared at one another for several moments like prizefighters getting ready to throw down in the ring.

Yeah, screw this.

"Jake," he called out over the sound of buzzing tattoo machines, Megan Thee Stallion and talk.

"Yeah?" Jake yelled from behind the wall that separated the front space from the tattooing area.

"Keep an eye on the desk for a few minutes, yeah?"

"You got it."

Returning his attention to Camille, Erik jerked his chin.

"Let's go to my office. Unless you prefer to have this conversation with an audience."

As if she just remembered where they stood, she noted the three customers perched on the couches. The three customers avidly staring at them.

"After you," she ground out.

With grim satisfaction, he headed for his office, Camille following closely behind him. And if he heard "asshole" mumbled under her breath, well, it wasn't the first time he'd been called that…today.

He opened the door and stepped aside to let her enter first. Big mistake when her scent—something that reminded him of apples and soft rain after a furious storm—assailed him, stirring warring but compatible desires to feast on her and wrap his body around hers, sheltering her, comforting himself.

He shook his head. Hard. The first desire he understood. He hadn't lost his love of fucking along with the life he'd left behind in Vegas. But that just as elemental, pulling need to protect and to be cared for in return? That was new. He hadn't wanted that in years. Three to be exact.

"You know this is unnecessary, right?" Camille spun on the heels of her cherry red stilettos—whoever sold those to her should either be shot or awarded a badge of honor, he wasn't sure which—and faced him as he shut the door. "And overstepping. I work here, but that doesn't give you access to my private life."

He crossed his arms, mimicking her stance. And cocked his head. "If there's one thing I've learned over these past few weeks, it's there's nothing easy about you. But, Camille, I saw your face, your whole damn body change when you answered that phone. And not for the good. Since this happened in my shop and could affect your performance, then it's my business."

"That's a bit of a reach." Her lips twisted.

He shrugged.

After several moments, she sighed and threw her hands up. "Fine." She shook her head then tipped it back, blinking up at the ceiling. "I don't even know why I'm telling you this. I must be desperate."

"Or you really do want to get it off your chest."

She lowered her chin, and his chest constricted at the almost wistful smile that curled her lips.

"Someone to listen to me." She huffed out a laugh. "Isn't that novel?" She gave her head another hard shake. "That was my ex-fiancé's sister. Seeing her name show up on my phone screen is enough to sour my day. We never got along. Not for lack of trying on my part. But from the day we met she took an instant disliking to me, didn't think I was good enough for her brother. And she had no issue with letting me know it. So you can imagine how she probably danced naked under a full moon when he broke up with me." Another caricature of a smile, but this time it was wry. "Which is why she's the last person who should be calling me. But she did. And it's about Brad, my ex. He's in trouble, and they want me to help bail him out."

"They?" Erik asked.

"Her. His mother. Brad. His staff." She lifted a shoulder. "When it comes to Brad, it's never a solo affair." She shifted backward and leaned against the desk. Her fingers curled around the edge, and he had the impression of someone holding on in the midst of chaos. "A month after our relationship ended, Brad became engaged to another woman. A socialite who's the daughter of one of his mother's friends. Now, he could've either had a whirlwind romance as I'm sure he tried to spin it or they were already seeing one another while we were together. Call me cynical, but I'm more inclined to believe the latter."

Yeah, he didn't even know the prick but that would be his guess, too.

"You know the old saying, 'if they do it with you, they'll do it to you'? Well, apparently, a scandal has broken out. He was caught cheating, and his new fiancée broke up with him. Publicly. Which isn't all that great for the image of a man running for office much less state representative."

He snorted. "So the other woman was cool with being the side chick but drew a line at him fucking around on her? Makes sense."

A flicker of amusement flashed in her brown eyes before her lashes lowered.

"At least she got out first. I can't say the same," she murmured.

"What is that supposed to mean?" He uncrossed his arms and frowned, stepping toward her.

She didn't immediately reply. And didn't look at him. Instead, she studied his boots. He liked them, but there was nothing that damn fascinating about them.

"Camille?" he said, pressing her.

And not because he was nosy and harbored this insatiable curiosity about her. True, that comprised some of it. But more, he looked at a woman who needed to let go of a weight. Or lance a wound.

Yeah, that made him a complete hypocrite. But it didn't stop him from urging her to talk.

"It means, she may have been the other woman but at least she had enough pride and self-worth to walk away when she'd been disrespected. She didn't stay and sign up for more. Or allow herself to be tossed to the side like garbage. Say what you want about her, but she valued herself enough not to put up with his bullshit."

"And you didn't?"

"No, I didn't," she said quietly. Her shoulders rolled back, her chin notching up. But that dark brown gaze remained somewhere south of his.

She refused to meet his eyes, and that knotted his stomach.

"I didn't leave until he kicked me out," she added in that same low voice.

"Or maybe, after years with a man you loved, the idea of a future without him scared the shit out of you. Or maybe, after being with this man for five years—

since the age of twenty-one when you still had fucking milk on your breath when it comes to experience and living—the thought of losing the world you'd known terrified you. Sometimes the familiar, as toxic as it is, can become more comfortable than the unknown because it's just that—unknown.

"Or maybe, this asshole so dominated your daily life, that everything you did and thought revolved around him, his needs and desires. Maybe you were schooled to be dependent on him. So do we now punish you for doing what you learned? That's bullshit. Nothing is black-and-white. And the shades of gray are often so murky and filled with shadows, it wouldn't just be hypocritical to judge you but harmful as fuck. I'm not one of those people, Camille. And you're going to have to stop being one, too."

Finally, she looked at him.

And it required every bit of control he possessed not to bum-rush that desk…and her. The pain in those chocolate depths was enough to tear at him. But the uncertainty brimming there? He couldn't stand it. Couldn't bear it.

But she wasn't his to touch, to comfort. He didn't own that privilege. And Jeremy hadn't entrusted his sister to his care for Erik to put his hands on her…

Fuck it.

He crossed the few steps separating them, curled a hand around the nape of her neck and tugged her into his arms. A sweet yet almost painful relief pierced his chest. As if his body recognized she belonged right there…

He squeezed his eyes closed and shut down that treacherous thought. His mother might've been the Irish dreamer in his family who believed in fated soul mates and love, but not him. He knew better.

And yet…

Yet, he didn't let her go.

No, he held her closer, his arms tightening. Even as he brushed his lips over the thick, coarse silk of her hair, he instructed his body to stand down. Willed the need pumping through his veins to back off. Ordered his cock to behave.

Because this—her in his arms, pressed against his body from chest to thighs—wasn't about the greed he'd become an expert at hiding. And he wasn't so much of a bastard that he'd take advantage of the situation. Not many people believed he knew anything about loyalty, but he did. His knowledge of and expectation for loyalty had led him to a heartache he could never forget. A heartache so deep the residue still resonated in his bones.

And for a woman who, he suspected, had experienced precious little of it over the past few years, he'd never betray that.

"Go on and finish it. Why did his sister call you?"

He half expected her to draw away from him, return to not looking him in the eye.

She did pull away from him, and returned to her perch on the desk. But she did meet his gaze, and his hands, which still tingled with the phantom impression of her skin, fisted.

"She wants me—*ordered me*—to return to Providence and clean up his mess. Not her words. Mine. Because that's basically what they want from me. To return and play the dutiful fiancée, spin some wild story of true love conquering all with me being cast in the role of 'the other woman' and how he couldn't stay away from me. So instead of a manwhore who can't keep his dick in his pants, he's just a misguided man who didn't realize he had love all along until he lost it. Apparently, it's the true American fairy tale." Her snort wreaked of sarcasm and the pain reflected in her gaze. "And me. First, I'm cast as the naive and jilted fiancée, then put into the role of desperate cheater and finally, the triumphant but pliant girlfriend again."

"That's crazy as fuck." His mouth curled in disbelief. "And I can't believe they think it will work."

"Spin a story well enough, and I have no doubt people will buy it. No one has seen through his lies, his charade yet," she said with only a fair trace of bitterness lacing her voice. "Oh no, they'll sell this so-called romance to the masses and they'll eat it up."

"And they just expect you to give up a life you're building here and return? Why the hell would you? What do you get out of this?" he snapped.

"Yes, they expect it. Because, according to his sister, I owe them. After all, for five years, they paid for everything from my lifestyle to the food I put in my mouth. And why would I do it? It's the same explanation for what I get out of it," she said, that bitterness now thick in the air. "Because I love him, of course."

He stiffened, a sonorous, hollow pounding in his head. It echoed in his chest, his gut, a deepening gong that threatened to block out every sense. And yet he'd still heard her words in his head.

Because I love him, of course.

"You're still in love with him?"

It seemed everything stood still as he waited for her answer. The world. The goddamn air. Why did he

care? He shouldn't. It was her life, her decision. Yet...
He waited. Because it didn't matter if he couldn't explain why.

The answer was important.

A spasm of emotion passed over her face.

"No. I left Rose Bend for love, and it kept me at his side. But distance and pain have a way of making things vividly clear. What I felt by the time we ended wasn't love. A combination of fear, doubt, uncertainty. Desperation. Maybe that was my problem, too," she whispered, her gaze sliding over his shoulder, and Erik sensed she might be admitting some epiphany to herself. "Instead of being in love, I was just too desperate for it. So desperate I settled." She drew in a long breath, and her gaze refocused on him. "But that was then, and I won't demean myself again to take crumbs. Or let a dream of family, of love that I concoct in my head blind me to reality again." She shook her head, and the shadows in her gaze darkened. "I won't do that to myself again."

"There's nothing wrong with the dream, just the people you build it around. When you find that your foundation is shaky, you tear it down and start over with a stronger, more solid base. One you have zero doubts about even when the world goes to shit."

Stop talking, he silently ordered himself. Because now, he didn't know if he referred to her situation or his past. Or both of them. He'd come in here for answers, and somehow he'd found himself stripping away his own layers.

He and Camille... They had more in common than he'd assumed.

"I'm not going back," she murmured. Then louder, "I'm not going back."

"Did you consider it?"

She studied him. "Yes," she finally said. "For a moment, I felt relieved. That maybe I wouldn't have to carry out The Plan after all. That I could become blissfully ignorant again and convince myself that I'm happy enough. That path would be less difficult." She cocked her head. "Do you think I'm weak?"

"Weak?" He huffed out a breath and slowly shook his head.

Pressure shoved against his chest, and, once more, he battled the urge to go to her. And like before he lost against it. He approached her, cupped her chin and tilted her head up. He pressed his thumb into the soft, vulnerable corner of her mouth, lightly smearing her dark red lipstick. He liked it. Liked the idea of messing her up more.

"You could never be weak, Camille. Not the woman who came into my shop and took charge, storming it like a general in battle. Not the woman who goes toe-to-toe with me and more often than I like to admit, wins. She isn't weak." He leaned forward, his lips grazing the shell of her ear. "She never was."

Her breath shuddered against his skin, and he felt it over his chest, his stomach. His cock.

Her hand slowly lifted, circled his wrist. And as his thumb caressed a corner of her lips, hers swept over the pulse at the base of his palm.

They stood there.

Touching.

Staring.

Asking.

But not daring to answer.

A knock resonated on the closed office door.

"Erik, your 12:30 is here," Jake called out.

Surprise rocked through Erik. Only she could distract him to the point that he'd forgotten they stood in his office with a shop full of people on the other side of the door.

"I'll be right there," he replied without removing his stare from hers. "You good?" he quietly asked.

If she wasn't, they would stay right there in this room until she was better. Loved his clients, thankful for them, but in this moment, fuck 'em.

It's because Jeremy put her in my care. That's why they can all wait.

The words whispered through his head, as if they feverishly worked to convince him of their truth. He clung to them.

She nodded. "I'm good."

He dropped his hand, stepped back. But while rubbing his thumb and finger together, massaging the dark red stain into his skin.

"I messed you up," he murmured, tapping the corner of his mouth.

"You don't sound sorry about it," she said in the same low tone.

A beat of silence passed. And he debated whether to acknowledge that or remain silent.

Screw it.

"I'm not sorry."

He turned, opened the door and exited.

Time to get lost in work.

CHAPTER THREE

SHE'D MISSED THIS.

Camille surveyed The Glen that had been transformed into a festival of lights, vendor booths, colorful tents and picnic tables. Rock music pounded along the night air as a local band played from the stage. Mouthwatering aromas of cooking meat emanated from the huge barrel grills on the far side of the wide field. Shouts and laughter from children, chatter from the adults gathered under the tents and sitting on blankets, crowded around the dance area.

Motorcycles packed the parking area and lined Main Street in all their glory, and even though it'd been years, she could still feel the power and rumble of one of those powerful beasts under her. Could feel the wind pushing against her, howling in her ears.

Could feel the adrenaline and freedom singing through her veins.

That had been the most addictive.

It'd been five years since she'd last tasted that particular drug. Five years since she'd started surrendering her desires for someone else's comfort.

Never again.

"You must be really amusing. Otherwise, why would you be over here smiling to yourself?"

Camille briefly closed her eyes at the sound of that

low rumble in her ears, savored its calloused stroke over her flesh. Her breath stuttered, and *oh God, please don't let him have noticed.* But that was wishful thinking on her part. Those sky blue eyes never missed a thing.

"I find myself to be very entertaining," she said, surprised but grateful for her calm tone. Especially, when inside, she was anything but. Glancing up, she met Erik's gaze. And another quake rippled through her. "I didn't know you planned on coming here tonight."

He shrugged a wide shoulder. "I didn't either until a half hour ago. Usually, I just go on the rides when I can fit them around my schedule. But since everyone else was down here and the shop's closed..." He shrugged again. "Seemed better than eating takeout with some Hulu."

"You don't usually go out with your employees?"

He hesitated. It was a very small pause, but Camille caught it. "Not often, no. They have their lives and I have mine. Besides, I've learned the hard way that there should be a line between an employer and his staff. Not having that boundary can create a shitload of problems later on."

Now that sounded like it contained a story. And from the clenching of his jaw and the slight narrowing of his eyes, that story must be heavy. Curiosity flared inside her. What happened to him? Who had hurt him? For him to betray those physical reactions—which were small on him but on someone else would be equal to a full-on tantrum—she didn't doubt someone had hurt him.

Anger and a strange, unwanted possessiveness spiked in her chest, and she mentally balked. Okay, no. She had no right to demand names so she could tear them a new one. He wasn't hers.

Even if she could still feel the imprint of his body against hers from a couple of days ago. Even if the press of his thumb to her mouth continued to brand her. Even if she'd never felt as safe and protected as she had in his arms.

Even if in her dreams at night, no knock on the door interrupted them and Erik replaced his hand on her lips with his tongue, his teeth.

She jerked her head around, pretending to scan The Glen once more. Better he believe she had a complete fascination with the band and their take on Lynyrd Skynyrd's "Free Bird" than he catch a hint of the thoughts her face might be betraying.

What was she doing? She'd spent five years with a man who hadn't invested as much of himself into their relationship as she had. A man who hadn't loved her the same. And yet here she was, standing on the precipice of going down that road again. Even with his tattoos, ripped jeans and vintage T-shirts, Erik could give her ex-fiancé lessons in being reserved, contained. Besides irritation, he didn't reveal much emotion.

He showed plenty emotion in that office.

She drew in a breath, conceding to the smug, annoying whisper in her head. Yes, Erik had *emoted* all over her.

"Excuse me," a voice that wasn't Erik's said.

Camille started, so lost in her thoughts, she hadn't heard anyone approach. Two young men, both in T-shirts and worn jeans with tattoos covering their arms and necks, stood in front of her and Erik. But their rapt gazes weren't focused on her; Erik captured their attention.

"We thought it was you," the guy with long blond hair and a Def Leppard T-shirt crowed. "Erik Mann. I can't believe it."

"Holy shit," his friend, a tall Black man with a smoothly shaved head, said. Then, with a wince, he glanced at Camille. "Sorry about that."

She waved off his apology, too confused and riveted by what was occurring in front of her to care about a curse.

"Hey." Erik hiked his chin. "You guys here for the ride?"

The greeting was nice, normal. But Camille's antenna popped up, and she studied Erik closer. Only someone who'd become a student of all things Erik Mann would've picked up on the tense set of his shoulders. The shuttered gaze. The faint shift in his stance that placed more distance between him and the young men.

"Yeah, my family's been coming here for a long time, but this is my first time back in about four years. I brought Connor with me." The closely shaven guy pointed to the blonde. "I'm Billy, by the way. I still can't believe we're here talking to you." Billy shook his head, grinning. "You here for the ride, too?"

"No, I have a shop in town. I live here."

Connor's eyes flared wide. "No shit," he breathed. "Do you think it's possible to get some ink while we're here?"

"Call the shop on Monday. I'll get you in," Erik said.

"Seriously?" Billy shook his head, obvious hero worship all over his face. "I got my first tattoo in your place in Vegas It's still the best piece I've ever had done. Having some more ink done in your shop? This is going to be wild."

The two men, so excited and caught up in the idea of having Erik ink them, didn't catch the flattening of his mouth. But she did.

Camille frowned. What was going on?

"Hey, Erik, can we get a selfie real quick? Otherwise no one's ever going to believe we met you," Connor joked, already pulling his phone out of his back pocket.

"Yeah, sure."

"I'll take the picture for you," Camille offered.

Something was really off, and as nice as these two guys seemed, the quicker she got the deed done, maybe the sooner Erik would lose that horrible strain in his face and body. It grated on her, and an urgency to make it disappear swirled in her belly.

Moments later, the young men strode off, bumping fists and amped up. She waited until they disappeared in the crowd before turning to Erik.

"Are you okay?"

Surprise glinted in his eyes, but his long, dense lashes lowered, hiding his gaze from her.

"Yeah. Why wouldn't I be?"

"That's my question." She tilted her head. "But something's definitely wrong. Do you want to talk about it? And before you say no," she said, ignoring the hard shake of his head, "do I need to remind you about me spilling all my dirty secrets to you just a couple of days ago? I'd say you owe me. So my question is really a formality. Dish. And you can start with why those two would want a selfie with you."

He didn't immediately reply, but his sigh swelled on the night air.

"I was on TV for a while. I guess it makes me a celebrity in their eyes."

The admission sounded like it'd been forced through churned up gravel. Again, she frowned even as recognition flickered inside her.

"That's right. I completely forgot Jeremy mentioned you'd won a tattoo competition. What was that show?" She scrunched her nose, sifting through her memory. "*Royalty Ink*, right?"

He nodded, the movement stiff, abrupt. "Yeah, but that's not the one I'm talking about, though it started everything else." Another weighty sigh, and he scrubbed his hand over his head. Muscles flexed in his arm and shoulder, and no, her ovaries did not cry out hallelujah. "Do you want to dance? I need to…move."

"Oh." She blinked. Swaying to music and pressed against his body. Again. Good God, that was a bad idea. "Yes, sure."

A big hand settled on the small of her back, and she bit back a moan at the innocuous but solid touch. Before she had time to assimilate to his hand on her, Erik guided her in front of the stage to the area designated for dancing. His hand applied a small amount of pressure, and she turned into his body. With no coaxing, she looped her arms around his neck. His large palms and long fingers cradled her waist, and that damn near sucked the air from her lungs. She almost glanced down to take in the image of those hands on her, making her feel something she hadn't in so very, very long.

Delicate.

Pretty.

Wanted.

Yes, she almost glanced down. But it seemed her sense of self-preservation burned brighter than she assumed.

With a small tug, Erik pulled her closer, his hands sliding around so one rested just under her shoulder blades and the other at the base of her spine. Her breasts grazed his chest, and her nipples tightened, arrowing a sweet pain down to her sex. Her teeth sank into her bottom lip. Dancing was *not* a great idea. Not when every shift and sway had her brushing up against Erik's big, hard body and sparking need inside hers.

"You know, I get why you want to dance," she murmured, inhaling the warm, musky scent at his throat. Cedar. Soap. And that undefinable hint of *him*. Lust twisted inside her.

"Yeah? You want to enlighten me?" His low rumble vibrated over the beaded tips of her breasts, and she swallowed back a whimper.

"So," she breathed, then cleared her throat. Tried again. "So you can say whatever it is you're going to say without looking at me."

He didn't answer, but his fingertips pressed harder into her back. Maybe it was her imagination, but she could swear his lips moved over her hair.

"Not that I'm judging," she continued. "However you need to do it."

Just, please... Do it.

She didn't just want him to confide in her, to trust her with his truth. For some reason she didn't dare analyze too deeply, she needed it.

"Jeremy ever tell you how we met?" Erik asked.

She barely heard the question above the band's really decent cover of Warrant's "Heaven." But she did catch it. And she shook her head.

"He used to work in my shop in Vegas before I went on *Royalty Ink*. He was one of my best artists and we became friends. After *Royalty Ink*, he decided to move on, open his own place. So he wasn't there when the offer to do my own reality show came in. I'd like to think if he had been, I would've turned it down. But I didn't. I never thought of the people who worked with me as employees, they were family. Most of us grew up together. They were closer to me than people that shared my blood and last name. Nothing should've been able to come between us," he murmured.

That sin and grit voice softened, as if he were lost in a memory. Happy memories. Yet her stomach tightened because she sensed they wouldn't stay that way.

"I said yes to the show for them. The opportunities it could bring us, the doors it could open. They convinced me to give it a try even though I hated being on *Royalty Ink*. The intrusiveness of the cameras, no privacy. Don't even get me started on the social media part. People, didn't matter if they loved or hated you, were relentless. No one prepares you for that. But then I was by myself. This time I would be with my family. I was so fucking naive."

His hands flexed and loosened on her back. She stroked the nape of his neck, her fingertips brushing the shorter strands of hair there. Did he realize he leaned into her touch? Sought it? Heat and greed tangled below her navel. She liked that he wanted it.

"It started fine, maybe even a little fun. But soon, everything changed. Gradual at first. The petty arguments, the grandstanding for the cameras. The social media wars. Things like that supposedly bring in higher ratings. But what do they do to friendships? To trust? It erodes them." His head bent over hers, his lips moving over her hair, brushing the rim of her ear. Those large hands rubbed up and down her back as if soothing her. But maybe it was himself he tried to calm. To comfort. "One day I had a family, and it seemed like the next, I didn't. The petty arguments turned into bigger ones. Resentment toward me festered and then the people I called friends were trying to ruin my shop behind my back to get their own show. Like I gave a fuck about a show."

At some point, they'd stopped moving, and she could just imagine what they looked like. The two of them, standing there, arms wrapped around one another, his lips buried in her hair. Lovers. They looked like lovers. She hadn't had him inside her, but they definitely were intimate. In this moment, he shared part of himself with her, and she'd remain in this one spot all night if he needed to purge himself.

"I walked away. From the shop. From the only family I'd had since my mother died. From the show that started it all. I wanted nothing to do with the cameras, fame or being the day's topic on some tabloid site. I came to Rose Bend to start over, and I have. My place, tattooing and peace. I don't want anything else. I definitely don't need any of what happened back there. That was my past."

Camille leaned back, staring up into his face for the first time since he led her to the dance area. The strain of reciting his past was evident in the taut pull of skin over his honed features and in his hooded gaze.

"You say start over, but it sounds like you came here to disappear," she whispered.

"Maybe you're right," he said in return, just as quietly.

She slowly shook her head. "That's a shame then. You shine too bright to ever disappear."

If possible, his features sharpened even more, and a tension entered his body, transforming him into a flesh and blood statue. Warmth flooded her face, and she swallowed a groan. God, why had she said that? She should've shut up because now he probably thought she was a—hell, she didn't know what ideas lurked behind that beautiful, cold facade.

"Look, I'm—"

"Thank you," he said.

The low, rough timbre of those two words rubbed over her skin, vibrated against her chest, affecting her body as much as her heart.

"You're welcome."

With her pulse pounding in her ears and at her throat, she brushed the backs of her fingers along his strong jaw and stubborn chin. And when a shudder rippled through his big body, she closed her eyes, absorbing it. Part of her wished she hadn't noticed it, hadn't felt it. And the other part... The other part longed to elicit another one from him.

Step back. Walk away. Don't do anything foolish that you can't take back.

The warnings filtered through her head, but the desire pumping through her veins muffled them. Even knowing she didn't return home for this...complication didn't compel her to back out of his embrace and insert much-needed distance between them.

Because as unwise as that decision was, she stood right where she wanted to be. Her gaze dropped to his beautiful, made-for-all-things-dirty mouth...

The loud swell of applause and whistles rose on the night, shattering the cocoon that had wrapped around them. She blinked, glanced around them. People cheered for the band as they ended their set, not noticing she'd been so close to granting them another show.

"I should..." She cleared her throat, finally shifting backward and away from Erik. Dipping her head, she glanced away from him on the pretense of searching the crowds. "I should get back to everyone. They're probably wondering where I've gone."

As far as excuses went, hers was pretty lame. But it would do the job, and dammit, she was desperate. Desperate for distance. Desperate to regain control of her rebelling body. Desperate to remember why putting her mouth on him in front of half the town was a bad idea.

"I'll see you at the shop Monday," she said.

Not waiting for his response, she walked away from him. Relief should've filled her. But it didn't. Instead, a need to turn around, return to Erik and bury her face against his chest rose inside her like a piercing howl.

That dangerous hunger forced her to walk faster.

CHAPTER FOUR

"ARE YOU SURE you won't hang?" Jake wrapped an arm around Patrick's neck, another tattoo artist at Forever Ink.

"Yeah, Camille. It's just eleven. Too early for bedtime." Dara, another artist, slid her arm around Jake's waist and grinned. "Have you been to Road's End yet?"

Camille shook her head. "Not yet, but I've heard about it."

"And everything you've heard is true and probably more," Jake bragged. "A good friend owns it and not only does it have great beer and a greater game room, he pulled in a band for tonight. So live music. You wouldn't think li'l Rose Bend would have one of the best dive bars in the Berkshires."

Laughing, Camille held up her hands, palms out. "You guys are really convincing but I'm going to pass. But next time, I'm in. I promise."

With some grumbling and good-natured teasing, her coworkers strode off toward the parking lot. Giving her head another shake, she headed in the opposite direction. She'd left her car near the tattoo shop, having headed over to The Glen right after work.

The Glen emptied of people, and she joined the exodus. The chatter and laughter, and some whines from children, surrounded her, and she allowed herself to sink into it. This, too, she'd missed. Living in the city had its advantages—nightlife, easy access to malls, restaurants and other entertainment. But she'd let herself forget about the charm and comfort of small town living. Of community events like this, of calling out to people you knew and walking outside at nearly midnight with little fear.

At first she'd resented returning home a failure, in the same position—if not worse—than when she'd left. But now…now it was all as clear as the star-speckled night sky above her. She'd needed to come here to heal, where it was warm, welcoming, safe. Where she belonged. This might not have been the path she'd envisioned for herself, but maybe right here was where she'd been meant to end up all along.

Inhaling a deep breath, she held it, then released it. And another chunk of the burden she'd carried around for so long cracked and tumbled from her chest.

Smiling wider, she slowed her pace and meandered down the sidewalk. That's right. She *meandered*. Because she could.

Laughter bubbled up in her chest as she glanced into the dark windows of Mimi's Café and The Ride, the local shop that catered to a motorcycle enthusiast's every need, and other storefronts lining Rose Bend's quaint Main Street.

Soon enough she approached Forever Ink, and without her permission, her feet slowed to a stop. This place had become her haven in such a short amount of time. She'd found herself here—her confidence, her strength, her talents—and had been unconditionally accepted in spite of her very recent past, her clothes and how she talked.

Well, almost unconditionally accepted.

Her heart thudded against her sternum, dispersing the calm that had settled over her like dandelion seeds on a summer breeze.

Erik.

He'd disappeared after their impromptu dance and confession, and yet it seemed she couldn't escape him tonight. She peered through the display window as he stood behind the front desk, and she could no longer escape one vital question: Did she want to?

No.

The answer ricocheted off the walls of her mind, gaining volume and certainty with each pass.

No, she didn't want to escape him. On the contrary, she longed to be found. And held. And...and taken.

Before she even fully acknowledged that she'd made a decision, Camille rapped on the window. Erik's head jerked up and their gazes caught.

Through the glass and the space of the dark shop, shadows partially hid his face. He remained behind the desk, unmoving. And doubt sank in her belly, pooling wide. She lowered her arm—

In one moment, he strode across the lobby in an explosion of movement. Her breath snagged in her throat, and she barely had time to register that he barreled toward her before Erik unlocked the door and pulled it open. Long fingers encircled her wrist in a gentle but implacable grip and drew her inside.

Her gaze locked on his face, drinking in every stark line, every sharply honed angle, every arrogant slope. The only softness in his face belonged to his mouth, and her fingertips tingled and itched to sketch each gorgeous feature.

A thick, drugging need flowed through her like melted, dark chocolate. Sweet, bold and addictive.

"Last chance," he said, reaching around her. The click of the lock punctuated his offer—or warning.

A shiver quaked through her. But not out of fear from his faintly ominous words. No. She trembled in excitement.

"I don't need it." She shifted forward until her breasts pressed against the solid wall of his chest, until the thick length of his cock branded her belly. "I need you."

As if her words snapped a tether leashing his control, he cupped her face, tilted her head back and took her mouth.

That's the only way she could describe it. Took.

And that's when she stopped thinking at all.

His lips parted over hers, and she opened for him. Willingly but not helplessly. Because as his tongue plunged deep, tangling with hers, their breath and groans mating, power sang through her, its melody strong, clear and emboldening. She'd never been the aggressor in her past relationship, but then desire had never burned as bright inside her as it did now. It never permitted her the freedom to fist a shirt and drag a man closer as she rose to her toes to demand more. More of his touch. More of his fire.

So this was abandonment.

It was glorious.

She tunneled her fingers through his hair, dragging her nails over his scalp.

And she accepted another rough groan as a reward, as her due. But satisfied? Nowhere near.

Sliding a hand up his chest, she curved it around his neck, anchoring herself and keeping him in place as she snatched control of this marauding they unimaginatively called a kiss. Tilting her head, she nipped the full bottom lip that had become her obsession, then soothed any sting she might've caused by sucking on that wicked curve.

His growl vibrated against her breasts and she crushed them to him, seeking to alleviate at least some of the sweet ache.

"Not here."

His low, rumbled words were the only warning she received before he hiked her into his arms, cradling her to his chest. Apparently, the kiss hadn't left her breathless because a gust of air escaped her at being swept off her feet—literally. Though she would've never cast herself in the role of damsel in distress, she curled her arms around his neck and hung on, heart fluttering at his casual display of strength.

He strode down the hallway, not stopping until he reached the room where the artists inked tattoos that required more privacy. Kicking the door closed behind him, he whirled around and pressed her back to it.

That mouth—that gorgeous, diabolical mouth— claimed hers again, and she submitted to the pleasure that submerged her beneath its dark waves. How a man's kiss could be sexier, hotter than any sex she'd had, she couldn't begin to explain. It just was. And she chalked it up to this man. This man and his hungry lips that bruised her own.

This man and his seeking hands that fisted her hair, scattering pinpricks across her scalp. His busy hands that slid under the flowy skirt of her dress and stroked up her bare thighs to cup her ass, squeeze it and then moan as if he'd discovered a long-lost treasure.

This man and his big, hard body that promised all kinds of pleasure even as it held her aloft, granting her security and safety.

This man, this man.

God, she wanted him. Needed him.

"Erik, please," she whispered. Begged. Because, yes, she was begging.

Maybe she didn't have the exact words, but Erik didn't seem to need them. His mouth abandoned hers and trailed a damp, searing path over her jaw, down her throat and collarbone to the valley between her breasts.

Oh God.

A cry ripped free from her as he closed his lips around her nipple, right through her filmy, summer dress. Her clothing and bra might as well have been air for all the defenses they provided her. His tongue lashed the beaded tip then curled around it, sucking hard. Bright, sharp pleasure arrowed from her breast straight to her moist, spasming sex.

"Oh God," she repeated, this time aloud.

How could she survive this heat, this nearly overwhelming lust? And he hadn't even touched her naked skin yet.

As if he could read her mind, a hand lifted to the bodice of her dress and tugged it and her bra down. Her flesh popped out over the top, baring her to him.

"Fuck, sweetheart," he breathed, brushing his lips over her nipple. Once. Twice. Again. "You're so goddamn gorgeous. I knew you would be. I knew it."

She didn't have time to dwell on the knowledge that Erik had thought about her naked. The blast of ecstasy that ripped through her as his mouth closed around her obliterated everything but him and how he played her body like a finely tuned guitar. One he might very well smash to smithereens before this all ended.

She curled over his head, wrapping her arms around him, feverish words dropping from her lips. Words urging him not to stop, harder, more. And he acquiesced. God, did he.

Erik lowered her to the floor but didn't release her. Good thing, too, because she couldn't have said with certainty that her trembling legs could hold her up. One strong arm wrapped around her waist while his other hand trailed over her hip and dipped underneath her panties, cupping her flesh.

A keening wail crawled up her throat but lodged there. It echoed in her head as she arched tight as a bow against him. Her fingernails scrabbled at his shoulders, searching for purchase not just in the here and now, but in this carnal, chaotic storm he'd tossed her in.

"Erik," she gasped, surging up on the balls of her feet. Attempting to escape the electrical currents of pleasure that assailed her or seeking more of it? She didn't know. Both?

"No?" he asked, his voice like brand-new sandpaper. "Or yes?" He rolled the heel of his palm over her clit, and she loosed a strangled whimper at the swell of lust that swamped her, pulsed right where he cradled her. "Is that a yes, sweetheart?"

She groaned. Now he wanted to tease her. When he had her body strung so tight she threatened to snap into pieces.

"Yes, dammit," she hissed. Or tried to. It came out as more of a whine.

His low chuckle brushed the base of her throat seconds before he raked his teeth down her neck…and thrust two long, large fingers inside her.

And she broke. Exploded into all those pieces. Pieces he would have to be responsible for gathering because she couldn't think, couldn't move. Could do nothing but accept the pleasure shattering over and through her in endless, exultant waves.

"Fuck, that was beautiful. I want to see that again. Except with you around my cock this time."

Erik's muttered words barely penetrated the erotic fog that encased her brain. And when he swept her up in his arms again, carrying her to the tattoo chair and positioning her so she straddled his thick thighs, she didn't put up any protest. Not when bliss had replaced blood in her veins and she grieved leaving this place of utter peace.

But then his fingers brushed her inner thighs, and she glanced down in time to see him remove a condom from the small foil package and roll it down over his cock.

And that quick lust reignited as if it'd never been sated.

He. Was. Beautiful.

Long, thick, with a wide, flared cap that glistened with slick, pearly drops that slid from a slit at the top. He could've been cast from marble by an artist's touch, that's how hard and perfect he was. Unable to resist, she reached for him…

A tender but firm grip prevented her from obtaining her goal.

"Just the thought of your hand wrapped around my dick is enough to have this over before I get inside you," he growled, and guided her hands to his shoulders. "When I come—and when you come again—it's going to be buried so deep inside you I can feel you when I breathe."

Holy...

She shut her eyes against the blaze of lust in his bright eyes and the stamp of hunger on his face. No one had ever spoken to her like that before. No one had ever transformed her into this needy creature willing to crawl, to beg for the burn of his possession.

"Do it," she rasped, ordered. "Do it now."

He didn't make her wait. His mouth flattened, and again, his other hand grazed her flesh as he aligned his flesh with hers. The broad tip nudged her folds, and without hesitation, she sank down on him.

The air propelled from her lungs as if with every bit of her he claimed, she expelled breath, needing to make room for him. A long, high whimper swirled in her chest, scrambling for her throat, desperate for release. Each inch of his cock stretched her, branded her. This position didn't allow her to hold back; it opened her wide for his inexorable siege on her sex, her senses, her...

No. She shut that down. Quick. No going there.

"Open your eyes," Erik demanded, and the steel in his command—because it was nothing less than a command—left no room for anything but her obedience. His hands gripped her hips, stilling her. "You good? You with me?"

"Yes," she breathed. Leaning forward, she kissed his throat, licking it and sucking on the golden, damp skin. "Yes," she repeated for added emphasis.

Rolling her hips, she gasped, pleasure rocking through her, sharp and breath stealing. Fingernails digging into the dense muscle of his shoulders, she pushed down, driving the last few thick inches of him inside her.

She shook, full body tremors at the depth and power of his possession. Her feminine muscles quivered and spasmed around his cock, adjusting to this invasion, this taking. He filled her—filled her to the point that she felt nothing but him. Inside her. Under her. Surrounding her. She was a castle laid siege to, wasted and left with nothing but ashes.

Oh yes, ashes. Because by the time he was through with her, that's what he would render her to.

And she'd gladly throw herself as a willing sacrifice to burn.

Cupping his face between her palms, she tilted his head back. Lowering hers, she brushed her lips over his but didn't claim his kiss. Instead, their breath mingled, mated, fucked.

Then she moved.

Up. Down. Roll. Grind.

She repeated the pattern, and that long, weighty dick stroked her in places she hadn't known existed. Hitting spots that scattered stars behind her eyelids.

Up. Down. Roll. Grind.

She took and he gave. He demanded and she surrendered. The slide and slap of their bodies punctuated the room. His rumbled orders and her whispered pleas peppered the air.

Up. Down. Roll. Grind.

Even though she straddled him, rode him, she didn't wield the control. He did. His big palms grasped her hips and guided them in a punishing and erotic rhythm that hurtled her toward a climatic end that would do just that…end her. He held her still while he powered into her sex, imprinting himself on her so she would feel him hours, days later.

He owned her.

Cries tumbled free of her lips, straight into his mouth, and when he lowered a hand, sliding it between them to circle and pinch her clit, he slung her into oblivion.

There was nothing gentle or easy about this orgasm. Its power and intensity ripped her apart, breaking her, and leaving nothing to scrape together afterward. It was raw, rude and wild. The cataclysmic pleasure didn't respect her personal boundaries but consumed her whole.

And as he strained beneath her, pistoning into her sex in hard, abrupt thrusts before stiffening with a low roar, she knew, nothing would be the same for her again.

CHAPTER FIVE

JEREMY WAS GOING to kill him.

And dammit, Erik would have to let him. Because he had zero intentions of keeping his hands off his best friend's sister.

Erik pinched the bridge of his nose, muttering, "Shit."

He'd really screwed up. Jeremy had sent his sister to him to provide a safe place to work and land. And he'd betrayed that trust by fucking her in a tattoo chair.

Not only had he broken the Bro Code, but he'd blown it up and salted the earth beneath the pieces.

Guilt crept through him, but another, hotter emotion wound along his veins, settling in his dick—and his chest. This would all be so much easier if he could chalk it all up to lust and sex. Not that Jeremy would go for that, but it wouldn't have Erik firmly stuck in WTF mode.

He'd had sex before. Good sex. Dirty sex. Even phenomenally good, dirty sex.

But what happened here in that back room with Camille Saturday night… That didn't even have a level or a name. Other than What the Fuck Was That?

Just thinking on it—again—had his body hardening, readying. His fingers curled around the armrests as if that would prevent him from launching himself across the office, down the hall and into the lobby where she worked the front desk. This morning had been the first time they'd seen each other or spoken since Saturday night. And while she'd acted as if nothing had happened between them, he'd barely convinced himself that hauling her back to his office and burying his face between her legs was a bad idea.

Barely.

So he'd hidden here in his office until he could get his thoughts and dick under control.

He'd tagged Camille as trouble from the first moment he'd laid eyes on her. And he hadn't been wrong. But instead of being a threat to his daily routine and business, she threatened every resolve and shred of control he possessed. Every decision and opinion about his life here in Rose Bend.

He'd temporarily hired trouble, and now he wanted to keep her.

Shit.

Propping his elbows on his desk, he thrust his fingers through his hair, tugging on the strands. He wanted the right to slide back inside that tight, perfect body. Desired the freedom to touch her, brush his lips over hers or that elegant slope of shoulder. Longed to see her face light up with a smile that reflected in her chocolate brown eyes.

He craved it all. And he didn't know what the fuck he was going to do about it.

A knock on the office door interrupted his spiral of thoughts, and he glanced up to see Jake standing in the doorway, a troubled frown creasing his brow.

"Hey, Erik, sorry to bother you, man, but I think you should head out front. Camille—"

Before the other man could finish the sentence, Erik

erupted from the chair and rounded the desk. Urgency propelled him past Jake and into the hall. Before he reached the doorway leading to the lobby, he heard Camille.

Ice crackled like a spiderweb over his chest. And underneath, a simmering, red-tinged anger.

"I'm only going to tell you one more time. No," Camille said, her tone flint. "It's the same in several languages. Now, I'll ask you one more time to leave me alone."

"I just have a few more questions, Camille—"

"Ms. Dansen," she corrected in the same flat tone that still conveyed her disgust.

"Sure. Ms. Dansen. If you'll just tell me whether or not you were the woman Bradley Luck met at the downtown Renaissance. And if so, how often did you two meet? Did you plan on stealing him back from his fiancée?"

Even before Erik charged through the door, he knew he'd find a reporter on the other side of the desk. Only one of his kind possessed that particular note of vicious yet gleeful avarice. As if he'd scented blood in churning water and couldn't wait to feed.

The tall, slender man in a white shirt and jeans leaned over the desk, crowding into Camille's personal space. Behind him, another man held a camera, filming the entire exchange. Erik didn't even stand in its glaring, intrusive eye and his skin crawled.

But worse than that creeping sensation over his body was the completely blank expression she wore. He didn't know Camille, with her expressive eyes, could appear so…removed.

The anger kindling inside him flared into a fire, and he strode over to stand beside her.

"You're in my shop, bothering my employees, and

she told you to get out. So why the fuck are you still standing here?"

The reporter's eyes widened. "I was just asking Camille a few questions and then—"

"Ms. Dansen. You don't know her like that. Again, she doesn't want to talk to you. And since this is private property, *my* private property, I'm only going to tell you one more time to get out. Or get thrown out."

Out of his peripheral vision he noted Jake, and Paul, another of his artists, leaning against the doorjamb behind him. Apparently, so did the cameraman, because he swung the camera toward them.

"I know you," the reporter said, snapping his fingers, his eyes narrowed on Erik. Fear punched him in the chest, choking him. "You're Erik Mann from *Royalty Ink* and *Downtown Tattoos*." He laughed, moving toward Erik, and with every step his stomach tightened and tightened. "Where have you been? You just disappeared off the face of the earth." His dark gaze shifted between Erik and Camille. "Wait, wait. Are you two…?" The reporter whipped around to face Camille again, a wide smile spreading across his face. "Does Bradley Luck know about this? Did you break up his engagement and now you're with Erik Mann?"

"Is that what you do?" Camille's lip curled in disgust. "If you don't have a story, you just make one up? I'm going to tell you for the last time. Get. Out."

"Is Erik the reason your relationship with Bradley Luck ended?"

Fear and revulsion seeped into him, but he still shoved through the swing door and stalked toward the reporter and his cameraman. He didn't need to glance over his shoulder to know Jake and Paul followed him.

It was in the flaring of the reporter's eyes and the quick
backward shuffling of the cameraman. But he didn't
drop that lens. No, he would catch every bit of this
confrontation.

"Erik, give me just a couple of minutes. I have just
one question—"

Erik rounded the two men in several long strides
and slapped the door open. With a not-so-gentle tap to
the reporter's shoulder, he shoved him outside the shop,
and Jake ushered his buddy out.

"Assholes," Paul muttered. "My next client isn't set to
arrive for another hour. I think I'll sit out here and wait
for him." He stared out the window, fixing his green
gaze on the pair still standing outside the shop door.

Anger clawed at Erik. Anger and a helplessness he'd
vowed never to feel again. It burned underneath his
skin, eating him alive and he couldn't escape it.

"Erik," Camille murmured, "I'm so sorry. I didn't
know—I *don't* know…" That cold reserve evaporated
from her face, and her soft mouth turned down at the
corners. She spread her hands wide, palms upturned.
"I can only guess that Brad or his sister gave them my
number and information. I never meant for them to
show up here."

"It's not your fault," he said, and she didn't quite hide
her flinch at his abrupt tone.

He wanted to soften it, silently told himself to, but
the hold of the past gripped him too tight.

"Erik—" she whispered.

"Can you let me know when my one o'clock gets
here?" he said, interrupting her.

He didn't wait for her reply but shoved through the

swing door and strode for his office. Trapped. He was both trapped and too exposed out there.

For the first time in three years, he didn't feel…safe.

HAD TIME SLOWED and no one told her?

For the umpteenth time, Camille glanced at her cell phone. Eight twenty-nine. Forever Ink would be closing in another thirty-one minutes. In other cities, a tattoo shop would remain open much later into the night. But this was Rose Bend. And Forever Ink closed at the same time as every store along Main. Usually, it seemed early to her. But now, when she desperately needed time to fly, it crawled.

Her fingers curled into her palms, fingernails biting into the flesh. The last client had left ten minutes ago, and she'd closed out the POS system. The artists cleaned up their areas; the rock music blaring from the speakers couldn't drown out their laughter and loud voices.

She glanced at the doorway that led to the hall—the hall Erik had disappeared down hours earlier. Grief and anger merged in her chest like a grimy, muddled mixture. She couldn't separate one from the other. And it threatened to drown her.

Glancing down at her cell phone, she checked on the time again. Four minutes later.

Oh screw it.

Moments later, she knocked on his office door.

"Yeah? Come in."

She closed her eyes at the sound of Erik's voice. Of course, she'd heard the low rumble today after those reporters left. But it hadn't been directed toward her. He'd been avoiding her. And the time for that to end had arrived. Good or bad, they needed to have this out.

She just feared it would be bad.

There was no way she'd missed his stare before he turned away from her. No way she'd missed the pain and resolve in it.

No. Though she hoped for the good, reality assured her this would be bad.

Lifting her lashes, she grasped the knob, turned it and pushed the door open. Erik looked up from his desk as she entered. And though her heart drummed against her rib cage, she met his sky blue gaze. The drumming sped, grew harder, louder.

"Can I talk to you?" she asked.

"Yeah, come in."

She stepped forward, closing the door behind her. Part of her wanted to lean against it for support. Or open it again and rush out, postponing this conversation…forever. But it was that longing that had her moving forward. She had learned to stop putting her head in the sand and avoiding the truth.

"Erik, we need to talk about earlier. I'm sorry that happened here in the shop. I can only assume since I didn't give my ex and his sister a quick enough answer, they went with the story anyway, maybe trying to force me to go along with it. But I never meant for any of that to touch you here."

"You don't need to apologize. It wasn't your fault." He jerked his chin toward the door. "I heard your cell going off all day. More reporters?"

Reluctantly, she nodded. "I have my suspicions about where they got my number, and now I'm considering changing it."

"Maybe you should make a statement and get it over

with," he suggested, and she locked down the shiver that tried to ripple through her at his cool tone.

Even when they'd first met and he'd been at his best blunt self, he'd never sounded so...formal. Distant. As if he'd already placed an uncrossable space between them.

"I don't know if that would help," she murmured, her gaze roaming over his features. "Give them anything, and they'll twist it into something you don't even recognize."

"You'll probably need to say something." He tapped on his laptop's keyboard and turned it around so she could see the screen. "They're already coming up with their own stories whether you agree to talk to them or not."

Camille barely heard his last words. A dull roar had entered her head, and underneath it, her pulse pounded like a hammer against steel.

On the screen scrolled a bold headline, "Has Brad's Luck Run Out?" And underneath, a subtitle, "Candidate for House Representative Bradley Luck's ex-fiancée and 'other woman' seen cavorting with ex-reality TV star." An article followed and above it was a picture the cameraman must've taken earlier while in Forever Ink. Erik stood shoulder to shoulder with Camille, his expression fierce, protective.

And it was all a lie.

"Have to give them points for the clever twist on his name," she said, disgust and pain a sour swill in her stomach. Closing her eyes, she inhaled a deep breath. When she opened them again, she met Erik's shuttered gaze. "I'm sorry," she said, apologizing again.

"Not your fault, Camille." He lowered the laptop monitor and rose to his feet. "You might want to take a few days off, though. At least until all this dies down and the media stops hovering around this place like vultures. Paul spotted a few more of them hanging around at Sunnyside Grille. They're not going away any time soon."

"You're firing me?" she whispered. Hurt and disbelief crowded in on her, and she could only stare at him.

"No." He shook his head. "I'm not firing you. I'm just saying putting space between you and them, giving them a less visible target, might help this die down quicker. Maybe you should go visit Jeremy—"

"This is convenient, isn't it?"

The hurt flickered, giving way to the flames of anger. Good. She embraced the anger. It energized her while the pain sapped her strength, her pride. And after all she'd been through in the last few months, all she had left was her pride. Cold company, and it'd abandoned her once. But she'd found it again, and she wouldn't be giving it up. Especially not here in this office where a man she'd foolishly started to fall in love with couldn't wait to get rid of her fast enough.

A shame how she seemed to be so easy to walk away from. But damned if she'd ever do that to herself again.

She'd never abandon herself again.

"What're you talking about?" Erik's eyes narrowed on her, but she hiked her chin up.

"Just what I said. This whole thing—" she waved her hand toward the laptop "—is convenient. But if it hadn't been the reporters showing up, I'm sure you would've found another reason to put distance between us. To send me away."

"The fuck?" he rasped. "This isn't about Saturday or an 'us.'"

She just barely managed to control her flinch at that sneered "us."

"I've been down this road, living under the microscopes of cameras and having the public give their unsolicited opinions about my life, about me. I walked away from that. Yet, there I am—" he jabbed a finger toward the laptop "—back in that damn fishbowl with random strangers speculating and commenting about who I fuck. About who I am. Bringing up a past I buried. I didn't ask for this and want no part of it."

"I understand your anger. I do," she softly said. "It's invasive and unfair, and it feels helpless when you can't combat the lies being spread about you. I, more than anyone, understand that. I lived it, too. For five years. And believe me, now I want to just hide in a hole." She clutched the back of the chair in front of his desk, leaning forward. "But I can't disappear. And neither can you. I told you once that you shine too bright, and it's true. You, Erik, are a light that draws people. You're safety, a haven, a calm in a chaotic storm. How do you think you were able to move to a small town as far from Vegas as possible and still find another family loyal to you? Who respects you? Who loves you? And that's what you have here, no matter what you want to call them—employees, artists. They're your family. And you can keep them at arm's length, but you're only depriving yourself of the full measure of the joy they can bring to your life."

She drew in a deep breath, loosed her grip on the chair and stepped back. But she couldn't look away from him. Didn't want to look away from him.

"Camille, you don't know what you're talking about," he ground out.

"If it makes you feel better to tell yourself that, go ahead. But this isn't about my ex or those reporters as much as it's about your fear to trust anyone else, to love them. You'd rather be alone than risk the pain of someone betraying you again. Just look around you." She waved a hand once more, encompassing the office. "This shop, this town, your friends here—they're all a beautiful second chance and you won't open yourself to all that they're offering you. Erik, I know about betrayal. You don't have the market cornered on that. But unlike you, I'm willing to let it go. I'm willing to *try.*" She swallowed hard, pain radiating from her chest like a beacon. "I was willing to try with you. You gave me hope. But I guess it's best I found out now that you'll walk away at the first sign of trouble. I need someone who won't just weather the storm with me, but who will let me be their shelter from it even as they're mine."

"Camille," he said, and she could almost believe her name sounded like a prayer on his lips.

No. More like a benediction.

She held up her hands, palms out in the age-old sign of "stop."

"I feel sorry for you, Erik," she murmured. "You came all the way to Rose Bend to start over, and yet you're still chained to all of the pain and anger from the past. You might as well have stayed in Vegas. Moving here was just geography."

She turned and exited his office, gently closing the door behind her.

And still the soft catch of the lock echoed like a small boom in her ears.

Maybe that's what it was supposed to sound like when you closed a chapter in your life.

CHAPTER SIX

"YOU'RE AN IDIOT."

Erik jerked his head up at the sound of that all too familiar and pissed off voice. Slowly, he stood from behind his desk and met his best friend's dark, angry gaze.

Jeremy.

Shit.

"What the fuck are you doing here?" Erik demanded, noticing the balled fists at his friend's sides.

Erik bit back a snarl. Dammit. He really didn't feel like getting his ass kicked. Not when Camille had already delivered a hell of one.

"I told you I planned on visiting for the motorcycle rally, and my schedule lightened so I made the trip this morning. And a damn good thing, too," he snapped, stalking farther into Erik's office. "During my layover, I received a phone call from a reporter asking my opinion on your affair with my sister behind that bastard Brad's back. Now I know the second part is bullshit—she wouldn't go back to that asshole if he came gift wrapped in hundred-dollar bills. But the first part? I did some googling and saw a picture of you two. Something you want to tell me?"

Erik heaved a sigh, thrusting his fingers through his hair. Should he lie? Would it be a lie? As of an hour ago, nothing existed between them any longer. But as quick as the questions popped in his head, he ditched them. The thought of denying Camille sickened him. He'd just have to take this ass kicking.

"Yeah." He rounded the desk and came to a halt in front of his friend. "Your sister and I became...close. I'm sorry I betrayed the trust you placed in me, but I don't regret her." Erik narrowed his eyes on Jeremy, surprise shimmering through him. "Why aren't you mad?"

"I *am* mad," Jeremy said.

"Okay, let me correct that. Why aren't you fucking up my face?"

Jeremy snorted. "The night is still young. And I want to get my hands on that Bradley Luck first. Hell, Camille got away from him. And he's still not happy until he's interfering with her life again. I never liked that motherfucker. Too entitled. Too spoiled. I doubt that family of his let him wipe his own ass. But you..." Jeremy glared at Erik, and he braced himself. But it wasn't a fist flying at him but a verbal blow. "You're damn right I trusted you with my sister. But I also trusted her with you. There's no one I love more than Camille, and you come in a close second. I sent her here because she didn't just need you, but you needed her. Since all that shit went down in Vegas, you've isolated yourself from the world, closed off to any chance of happiness. And with that huge heart of hers, she has so much love to give. For so long my sister has been searching for someplace to belong, to be accepted for who she is. And you could've been that place, been that person. But when I walked in here and saw you sitting there like your dog just died, I knew you fucked it up. And knowing you, royally."

Erik's surprise bloomed into shock, and he damn

near shook with it. Jeremy had set this whole thing in motion? His friend had…? Maybe he should be mad at Jeremy's meddling but he couldn't be. Not when Jeremy's words reverberated through him, rocking his very foundation.

I sent her here because she didn't just need you, but you needed her.

He had—*did*—need her.

Maybe he hadn't acknowledged it until this moment, but deep inside, he'd known it. With every challenge about the shop, every smile, every shared confidence—every touch and kiss—he'd known. He was falling in love with Camille Dansen.

And that was why he'd grabbed ahold of the opportunity and pushed her away as hard and fast as he could.

He'd been the scared coward she'd called him, running from his past, insulating himself from any further hurt. And for what? The pain of losing her before he ever really had her still throbbed within him like an open wound. As soon as she'd walked out of his office, he'd wanted to charge after her, apologize, beg her not to go.

But again, he'd allowed his fears to rule him. Now, in his refusal to let go of the past, he might've lost his future.

Not yet.

He silently snarled the words, and a quiet, aching determination rose within him. Yes, he'd fucked up, but he could fix it. He *would* fix it.

His happiness depended on it.

"I hope the sudden silent treatment means you're having a much-needed come to Jesus moment with yourself. Either that or I'm seriously rethinking the fist to the face," Jeremy drawled.

Erik arched an eyebrow. "And let all your efforts go to waste? No, I'm not an idiot. Although, I'd advise you to prepare yourself for when Camille discovers you practically pimped her out to your best friend."

"Oh shut the fuck up. I'm still trying to convince myself that getting 'close' to my sister means you just held her hand." He snorted. "Besides, I prefer the term matchmaker. And you're welcome, you ungrateful bastard."

Erik laughed at Jeremy's sour expression and at the lightness that suddenly filled his chest and head. He hadn't won Camille back yet, but for the first time in three years, he had hope. He had peace.

And if he could convince Camille to give him another chance, he just might have love.

CHAPTER SEVEN

CAMILLE STRAIGHTENED A stack of Forever Ink tank tops, and her fingers lingered over the black cotton.

How quickly Forever Ink had changed from just the name of a tattoo shop to meaning family. She cringed to analyze what that said about her. Had she been so hungry for true friendship, to belong, for…love that she'd leaped without bothering to look into this group who'd become so important to her? Friends…family. And the thought of leaving them broke her heart.

Well, broke the pieces of that heart. Erik had already shattered the majority of it.

Shaking her head, she drew in a deep breath and moved on to the rack of jewelry and began refilling the stock. Shrieks from running and playing children, the excited conversation and laughter as well as the rumble of passing motorcycles filled The Glen. Technically, she'd been fired the night before. Oh, Erik had given her that line about taking time off, but she understood what that meant.

But she was damn tired of running. And from the first, something about Erik niggled at her. Poked her. And challenging him had become one of her favorite pastimes. So why should that change now? He'd basically ordered her to leave, but she would decide if and when she did. And with the Forever Ink booth at the motorcycle rally needing manning, today wasn't that day. She'd been scheduled to help Dara, and she refused to let her down.

Even if part of her just wanted to return to her apartment and get lost in Netflix and strawberry shortcake ice cream.

"Oh this shirt is adorable."

Camille turned around, gladly putting aside her morose thoughts to focus on the pretty Black woman holding up one of the Forever Ink tank tops. Pride whispered through her. The shirts had been her idea, and this one was a favorite. Black, a faux rip down the center creating the V-neckline and with roses surrounding the logo, it really was adorable. And she'd almost sold out of them since being in the booth this morning.

"It's one of our bestsellers," Camille told the woman with the lovely natural curls.

"I love it." Smiling, the woman extended a hand toward her. "Hi, you probably don't remember me, but I'm Korrie Noel, Pastor Noel's daughter. It's been a while."

"I'm sorry." Camille winced. "I don't, but in my defense, I avoided church like a BOGO sale on Crocs back in the day."

Korrie laughed, and the happy sound drew a smile from Camille. "I totally get that. Well, it's nice to see you again and welcome back home."

"Thank you." Camille nodded toward the shirt. "What's the verdict? A yes?"

"Definitely." Korrie handed it over to her and reached in the back pocket of her jeans, pulling a wallet free. "And someone said you were scheduling tattoos here, too?"

Camille slid the top into a plastic bag. "I am. One of the artists just stepped away for a moment, but she can offer you a consultation if you'd like." She tilted her head, scanning Korrie's bare arms and chest. "Will this be your first?"

"Yes." Korrie grinned then turned, pointing in the direction of a small group of men a short distance away. "See the Ragnar look-alike with the blond mohawk? He's mine." Such love saturated Korrie's voice on that "He's mine," that Camille's heart twinged in happiness for the woman…and maybe just a tiny bit of envy. Did she know how lucky she was to have that? From the light in Korrie's eyes when she turned back to Camille, she'd have to say, yes, Korrie did know. "And we're both getting tattoos. Although, he's had a bit of a head start," she said with a snicker. "But it's on my bucket list of 'firsts.' Israel, my fiancé, and I are still knocking them off together."

"That sounds wonderful," Camille said, handing Korrie her bag and taking her credit card. "And like fun."

Korrie chuckled. "You have no idea."

Okay. That sounded…interesting.

Moments later, Camille rang up the purchase and offered the other woman her card back.

"Thanks, I'll see you—oh, hey, Erik," she said, turning to smile up at the man who'd monopolized Camille's thoughts all night and day. "I was just getting ready to schedule tattoos for me and Israel. Finally."

Erik nodded, his gaze roaming over Camille in a quick scan before returning his attention to Korrie. But just that glance left her scorched and tingling with awareness. It'd only been hours since she'd seen him, but it might as well as have been days. That's what the sizzle in her veins and the tightening of her stomach denoted anyway.

And the squeezing of her chest.

"Good," he said to Korrie. "I'll do the pieces myself. You just let me know when you're ready to come in."

Korrie beamed. "Thank you. And I love the T-shirts, by the way. All the new merchandise. I'll probably be stopping by later for one of those rose and skull necklaces."

"I can't take credit for it. Everything you see here is because of Camille." He glanced at her again, and her breath evaporated in her lungs at the heat in that bright gaze.

How dare he look at her like that? Like he wanted her. Like he...

He kicked you out, remember?

Yes, if her heart refused to recall, that hole in her chest right next to it definitely had a perfect memory.

"Well...awesome." Korrie chuckled softly. "Don't mind me. I'm just going to go...somewhere."

With another low laugh, she walked away, leaving Camille alone with Erik. She damn near called the other woman back.

"Camille," Erik said.

"I know you told me to take a break," she said, interrupting his imminent demand to know why she was working his booth. "But I couldn't just leave Dara hanging today. If you want, I'll stay over here until the rally is over. That way, any lingering reporters will have to bother me out here instead of at the shop."

"I don't give a fuck about reporters at the shop."

"Since when?" she scoffed. "That wasn't your tune last night."

"I've changed my mind."

"How very nice for you," she snapped, her temper crackling like a match to dry wood. She whipped around and grabbed the last stack of shirts and started folding them. Anything was better than studying his beautiful, maddening face. "How very awesome that you can just flip a switch like that. Although I can't imagine how you can care about guarding your precious privacy and life one moment and don't the next."

"Camille, look at me, please."

The "please." That's what penetrated when nothing else could've. Well, that and the hoarse tone that sounded as if it'd been dragged down an unpaved street.

Slowly, she set down the shirt in her hands and turned around to face him.

"I need to show you something," he said.

She nodded, oddly breathless and speechless. An... expectation settled on her chest, and she stilled, watching him. Waiting for...something.

Without glancing away from her, he shoved up the short sleeve of his dark gray T-shirt, exposing the very top of his shoulder. He paused, and it hit her that he wanted her to look there. Ink covered his entire arm and shoulder, but as she leaned forward, she noted a slightly reddened area. She'd been around Forever Ink long enough to spot the sign of a fresh tattoo. And his...

Oh God.

She jerked her gaze to his face, immediately ensnared by his bright blue eyes. Trapped by the emotion she hadn't wanted to acknowledge moments ago. Feared acknowledging. But if she'd doubted her eyes, she couldn't question that new tattoo. Or its meaning.

The Forever Ink logo.

The *new* Forever Ink logo. One she'd designed and presented to him over a week ago and he'd slapped down with a firm, "hell no." Now, knowing his past, she understood why he'd reacted so strongly to her proposition.

And now, she understood even more what it meant for him to change it.

Slowly, she emerged from behind the booth and didn't stop until she stood right in front of him.

"You changed your logo."

"Yeah, I did."

"For me," she whispered.

"Yeah, I did."

"You love me."

Without hesitation, he said in that rough voice that reached to every hurt, every wound, and healed them.

"Yeah, I do."

Tears stung her eyes, and she threw herself at him, flinging her arms around his neck. Rising on tiptoe, she crushed her mouth to his, delighting in his taste again. In being able to hold him again.

In finally loving him out loud.

Over his shoulder, she caught cell phones aimed in their direction and even caught the click of a camera. Sighing, she sank against him.

"We're creating a spectacle. This will probably end up on some blog or site by this evening."

He squeezed her, then cupped the back of her neck and tilted her head back.

"I don't care. As long as they get my good side— which is all you."

Joy took flight in her and she laughed. And laughed. This was happiness. This was belonging. And she was never giving it up.

"I love you," she said, brushing another kiss along his jaw, his mouth.

Cradling her face in his hands, he pressed his forehead to hers.

"Thank you for being my second chance."

* * * * *

Do you love romance books?

Join the Read Love Repeat Facebook group dedicated to book recommendations, author exclusives, SWOONING and all things romance!

A community made for romance readers by romance readers.

Facebook.com/groups/readloverepeat

HARLEQUIN
PLUS

Try the best multimedia subscription service for romance readers like you!

Read, Watch and Play.

Experience the easiest way to get the romance content you crave.

Start your **FREE TRIAL** at
www.harlequinplus.com/freetrial.